One of the greatest and yet [...]
crime writers, **David Goodis** [...]
1917, and wrote his first novel [...] ~~Suuuon~~, in
1938. His big break came in 1946 with the publication of
Dark Passage, which was made into the film starring
Humphrey Bogart and Lauren Bacall. During his life he
wrote many short stories, film treatments, scripts for radio
serials such as *Superman*, and seventeen novels, including
Shoot the Pianist (later filmed by Truffaut). He died in 1967.
Serpent's Tail also publish *Blonde on the Street Corner*,
Moon in the Gutter and *Of Tender Sin*.

In this edition, edited and introduced by Adrian Wootton,
Goodis's novel *Black Friday* is combined with the best of his
short stories, unavailable since they were first written for
pulp magazines in America over 50 years ago, and never
before published in book form. Originally published in 1954,
Black Friday is one of David Goodis's leanest, meanest
melancholy thrillers. In the character of Hart, it features one
of his classic, tortured romantic heroes, a man who becomes
mired in circumstances from which there is no escape.

Adrian Wootton is the CEO of Film London which facili-
tates the making of films in London.

Praise for David Goodis:

"You must buy [*Blonde on the Street Corner*] – you will read
it in a couple of hours but you will want to read it again and
again and again" *Word*

"America's laureate of the low life . . . No-one does existential loners better" *Herald*

"Surreal, disturbing, frequently brilliant. Nobody like him"
Time Out

"Full of despair and secrets and quite, quite brilliant"
Jockey Slut

Editor's acknowledgements:

I would like to thank writer Robert Polito, Jamie Bischoff and Corey Field of Ballard, Spahr, Andrews and Ingersoll, Thomas Whitehead of Temple University, David Goodis's cousins, Bernard Shapiro and Anita Field, David Goodis's friend, Leonard Cobrin, my partner in crime Maxim Jakubowski, bibliophile Mike Ashley, Pete Ayrton and the team at Serpent's Tail, my assistant, Jane Shaw, my colleagues at Film London, and my wife Karen and daughter Beth.

BLACK FRIDAY

and other stories

David Goodis

Edited and Introduced by
Adrian Wootton

A complete catalogue record for this book can
be obtained from the British Library on request

First published in the UK in 2006 by Serpent's Tail,
4 Blackstock Mews, London N4 2BT

website: www.serpentstail.com

Printed by Mackays of Chatham, plc

ISBN 10: 1–85242–469–9
ISBN 13: 978–1–85242–469–5

10 9 8 7 6 5 4 3 2 1

CONTENTS

Introduction by Adrian Wootton

David Goodis (1917–1967) is one of the great, unsung writers of the classic era of American pulp fiction. His highly distinctive work in the crime genre, particularly during the 1940s and 1950s, in both novel and short story form, has earned plaudits aplenty, been translated into several languages and adapted for stage, television and film. Yet he remains resolutely a cult writer, his work drifting in and out of print, admired by a small group of fans and always on the point of being re-evaluated or re-discovered. Maybe it is the nature of his stories – emotionally intense, melancholy and sometimes violent to the point of being grotesque. Or perhaps it has something to do with the fact that he never created a famous fictional detective and, although movies were drawn from his work, there was never one that really hit commercial paydirt.

There is also the fact that Goodis was quite a solitary man and his life still seems somehow indistinct, without either the public profile that other pulp greats enjoyed (for example, Dashiell Hammett), nor was Goodis a man of letters, reflecting on his art form in the way that, say, Raymond Chandler did. Instead David Goodis lived a life of relative obscurity. He was born and lived most of his life in Philadelphia (the backdrop to nearly all of his books), except for a brief sojourn working in New York and an unsuccessful stint as a screenwriter in Hollywood. Resident in the family home, he churned out stunning pulp prose and kept away from the limelight.

The most salient facts about his life are outlined in a biographical appendix but there are few clues to his creative inspiration. There are autobiographical hints in his novels (his love of boxing and jazz, his relationship with his schizophrenic brother and the impact of his failed marriage), but they are subtle inferences rather than explicit memoir. What is certain is that David Goodis's last years were beset by illness, depression and stress caused by bereavement and the debilitating impact of a law suit. In the end David Goodis died in 1967 at the age of forty-nine with little attention given to his passing in the wider world, and with none of his books in print in English. And so it says a lot for his unique voice that, against all the odds, David Goodis's work has survived neglect and obscurity.

This book, which contains both his great novel, *Black Friday*, and a selection of his short stories (the majority of which have never appeared in book form before), is a significant step at trying to put Goodis back in the limelight.

Short Tales about Killings

During the peak of American pulp fiction's heyday (roughly a twenty-year period, spanning the 1920s to the late 1940s), thousands of short stories were churned out for magazines which published short fiction in every conceivable popular genre. Goodis's output is to be seen as part of this explosion.

From the time he left college in the late 1930s, David Goodis was an astonishingly prolific short story writer and published sports fiction, western adventures, crime fiction, horror tales and war stories.

The majority of his short fiction was written during World War Two, when he would sometimes churn out whole issues of war story magazines under a variety of pseudonyms (see Bibliography). His speciality was aviation adventure and he produced punchy pulp on World War One and World War Two fighter pilot heroes, using technical knowledge that he learned from the *Jane's Aviation Reference Guide*. Nevertheless, in this collection, we have selected stories in the crime genre which is where David Goodis's reputation rests.

In terms of his writing career, it is clear that, unlike many of his contemporaries, he didn't use the short story form to create a series with an identifiable popular character, such as a gumshoe or a tough cop. Also, the short stories of Goodis were not précis of plots that would later be expanded into a novel: a process found in the work of Raymond Chandler. Some of Goodis's novels were serialized but only after they had already been finished and in some instances published in their original novel form. No, for Goodis, the short story format was very much a distinct form of writing that allowed him to experiment with aspects of the crime genre not best suited to full-length novels. Maybe, the difference between Goodis and other crime short story writers is that he actually wrote little in the short story genre and only when he had a particular idea that he judged best suited to the form.

In the story "It's a Wise Cadaver", Goodis gives us a beautifully economical exercise in overt vicious black comedy, written for the *New Detective* in the same year that he published "Dark Passage". Similarly, "Never Too Old to Burn" is a wickedly ironic story of poetic justice. On the other hand, in the much more conventional adventure story "Caravan to Tarim", written for the upmarket *Colliers Magazine*, Goodis indulges in some *Boy's Own* Arabian desert exotica. This contrasts nicely with the sophisticated, romantic thriller "The Blue Sweetheart" from 1951 which is set in Ceylon, the only Goodis crime story apart from the Jamaica-based "The Wounded and the Slain" to be located outside the USA.

There are also orthodox detective stories, well told, about a larger-than-life Irish New York policeman, Sergeant Rico Maguire, who features in both "The Case of the Laughing Queen" and "Man without a Tongue".

This leaves a group of prime cut, brilliantly realized noir stories that compare with the best of anything else in the Goodis canon. "Black Pudding", "The Plunge" and "Professional Man" encapsulate, in a few thousand words, the genetic code of Goodis. "Black Pudding" is a gripping novella of revenge that takes a typical Goodis scenario but, unusually, opts for an upbeat ending. "The Plunge" is the story of a policeman who makes a desperate decision in a final effort to regain his lost honour. Last and by no means least, "Professional Man" is a stunningly executed, cunningly crafted, tragic tale of self-sacrifice by a hired killer. (As an interesting aside, in 1995 "Professional Man" was adapted into a very good episode of the American crime television series *Fallen Angels*, directed by Steven Soderbergh.) Stuffed full of existential angst, featuring tormented anti-heroes, reeking of low rent, urban atmosphere and beautifully modulated in their pace and structuring, all these stories show a writer in complete control of his material.

This collection re-enforces David Goodis's reputation as a very particular and original stylist in the crime genre, whose short stories deserve to be again read and appreciated.

Black Friday

Black Friday is one of the most assured novels written by
David Goodis between 1950 and 1954, in a very prolific
period of his writing life, when he produced no less than
nine novels and a number of short stories of extremely
high quality.

Written in between *The Blonde on the Street Corner*
and *Street of No Return*, *Black Friday* is, on one level, a
lean and economical thriller. Using the convention of
the planning and preparation of a robbery by a professional criminal gang, Goodis depicts their skills and the
dynamic tensions within the group. It is one of the very
few Goodis novels, the other notable example being *The
Burglar*, that is exclusively set amongst a criminal
milieu.

The book's freshness comes from Goodis's introduction
of a wild card character, Hart, into the criminal caper.
Hart is a typically tortured Goodis protagonist; once a
well to do artist, he is now on the run for murder and is
forced to pretend to be a professional heister in order to
hide in the protective secrecy of the gang. His entrance
into the team, however, immediately upsets the fragile
equilibrium of their professional and emotional relation-
ships. Aside from the difficulty of assuming the mantle of
a career criminal, Hart has to contend with the atten-
tions of two very different women who split neatly into
Goodis's pop Freudian division of sexy whore (Frieda)
and saintly sister (Myrna). The fact that Hart is also
running from the mercy killing of his brother adds
further autobiographical spice to this steamy melange.
The result, as with all great Goodis, is tense, touching
and eventually tragic. *Black Friday* is set in Philadelphia, the hometown Goodis celebrates, described with

almost maniacal attention to topographical detail and
re-imagined in almost all of his writing. Many writers
have an affinity with particular cities but Goodis's geo-
graphical obsession with his own city is particularly
striking. If this were not enough to recommend *Black
Friday*, there is Goodis's savage enjoyment of depicting
violence so extreme it becomes absurd (for example, the
scene describing the gory disposal of a dead body could
whet the appetite of Quentin Tarantino) and his pepper-
ing of the novel with his own pop culture interests, like
jazz and sports. All of this is bound together by his
densely textured and evocative descriptive language. As
the critic Geoffrey O'Brien has commented,[1] there is a
kind of hyper realism and hallucinatory quality to his
writing which allows Goodis to take inanimate objects
and the urban landscape surrounding his characters and
turn them into external expressions of the characters'
feelings. For just a small example, you only have to look
at the opening sentence of *Black Friday* which neatly sig-
nals the character's isolation and the fact that he is
being hunted: "January cold came in from two rivers,
formed four walls around Hart and closed in on him."

As other critics have noted, it is possible to bracket
Black Friday as part of a loose trilogy of major Goodis
novels of the 1950s, with *The Moon in the Gutter* and
Down There. Interestingly enough, all three have been
made into movies in France, a country which has almost
single-handedly held up a flame for Goodis. *Black Friday*
was loosely rendered by veteran French director René
Clément into the 1972 US-French co-production *And
Hope to Die*. Although starring Robert Ryan, it was not a
big success and remains a footnote in the canon of Goodis
movies.

Leaving aside the movie connections, there are

definite similarities between this triumvirate of Goodis pulp poetry. All seem to push the existential exploration of Goodis's world to extremes, all feature recurrently recognizable elements of autobiography, including very noticeably characters who were once successful and are now failed artists (Goodis is the novelist of the loser, where he consistently manages to transform potentially tedious self pity into pithy, plausible empathy). It may be trite to suggest this reflects bluntly David Goodis's own perception of his self worth as a creative artist but, in the few interviews we have, he was fond of self deprecation and one of his most familiar quotes was to compare himself with another legendary crime writer and say, "I am no Dashiell Hammett". Perhaps not, but the emotional depth of his work, the rendering of complicated philosophical and psychological ideas into a simplified pulp idiom and the atmospheric readability, with its laconic, edgy prose, all combine to make Goodis one of the great crime novelists. *Black Friday* exemplifies all of these skills and shows Goodis as a writer who mined the deep, rich and magnificently realized landscape of tortured emotion.

In the light of David Goodis's subsequent career and the fluctuations of his reputation in the years since his death, the title of his first novel, *Retreat to Oblivion*, seems more and more like a hollow joke. Let's hope that readers of *Black Friday* and these short stories start to reverse this process.

Note

1 Geoffrey O'Brien: Introduction to *Black Lizard* editions of David Goodis novels (1984).

Black Friday

CHAPTER 1

January cold came in from two rivers, formed four walls around Hart and closed in on him. He told himself an overcoat was imperative. He looked up and down Callohill Street and saw an old guy coming toward him and the old guy featured a big overcoat and big, heavy work shoes. The overcoat came nearer and Hart worked his way into an alley and waited. He was shivering and he could feel the cold eating into his chest and tearing away at his spine. He came out of the alley as the old guy walked past, and he was behind him. The street was empty. He moved up on the old guy and then noticed how the old guy was bent and the overcoat was old and torn. The old guy would have a hard time getting another overcoat.

Hart turned and walked down Callohill Street. He pulled up the collar of his chocolate-brown flannel suit and told himself a lot of good that did. He turned around again and walked toward Broad Street, and he was hating Philadelphia.

The cold was even worse on Broad Street. From the east it brought an icy flavor from the Delaware. From the west it carried a mean grey frost from the Schuylkill. Hart had been brought up in a warm climate and besides that he was a skinny man and he couldn't stand this cold weather.

He looked south on Broad Street and the big clock on City Hall said six-twenty. It was already getting dark and lights were showing in store windows here and there. Hart put his hands in his trousers pockets and continued north on Broad Street. Then he took his hand out of his left pocket and looked at three quarters, a dime, a nickel and three pennies. That was all he had and he needed an overcoat. He needed a meal and a place to stay and he could use a cigarette. He thought maybe it would be a good idea to walk across Broad and keep on walking until he reached the Delaware River and then take a fast dive and put an end to the whole thing.

He grinned. Just thinking about it made him feel better. It made him realize that as long as he was alive he'd get along somehow. He could hope for a break.

The cold hit again from four sides, got inside him and began to freeze there. He walked on fighting the cold. He passed a store window with a mirror border and stood looking at himself. The flannel suit was still in fairly good shape and that helped some. The collar of the white shirt was grey at the edges and that wasn't so good. He had a mania for clean white shirts. That was something else he needed, a few shirts and underwear and socks. It was a pity he had to get off that train in such a hurry. In a few months or so the railroad would be auctioning his suitcase and his things.

He stood there looking in the mirror, and the cold beat into his back. He needed a haircut. His pale blond hair was wisping around his ears. And he needed a shave. His eyes were pale grey and there were dark shadows under his eyes. He was getting older. In another month he'd be thirty-four.

He smiled sadly at the poor thing in the mirror, the poor skinny thing. Once he had owned a yacht.

It was really dark now and he told himself he better get a move on. He walked on another block and then stopped in front of a clothing store. A sign in the window announced a sale. A prematurely bald man was arranging garments in the window. Hart walked into the store.

The salesman smiled eagerly at Hart.

Hart said, "I'd like to see an overcoat."

"Why, certainly," the salesman said. "We've got a lot of fine ones."

"I only want one," Hart said.

"Why, certainly," the salesman said again. He started toward a rack and then turned and stared at Hart. "How come you're stuck without an overcoat in this weather?"

"I'm careless," Hart said. "I don't take care of myself."

The salesman was looking at Hart's turned-up coat collar.

Hart said, "Do you want to sell me an overcoat?"

"Why, certainly," the salesman said. "What kind would you like?"

"The warm kind."

The salesman took a coat from a hanger. "Just feel that fleece. Try it on. You never wore anything like that in all your life. Just feel it."

Hart got into the coat. It was much too large. He took it off and handed it back to the salesman.

"What's the matter?" the salesman said.

"It's too small," Hart said.

The salesman handed Hart another coat, saying, "Try that on and see how it fits."

Hart got into the coat. It was a fair fit.

"There's your coat," the salesman said.

Hart ran his fingers along the bright green fleece. He said, "How much?"

"Thirty-nine seventy-five," the salesman said. "And it's a buy. I'm telling you it's a real buy. You can see for yourself, it's a buy." The salesman whirled, and as if he was summoning help for a drowning man he waved an arm and yelled, "Harry, come over here!"

The prematurely bald man came out of the window and walked across the store.

The salesman said, "Harry, come here and take a look at this coat."

Harry put long fingers into his trousers pockets and looked at the overcoat and began to nod solemnly.

"That's what I call an overcoat," the salesman said.

"It's one of the specials, isn't it?" Harry said.

"Why, certainly," the salesman said. "Why, certainly it's one of the specials."

"How much did you say it was?" Hart asked.

"Thirty-nine seventy-five," the salesman said. "And if you can get another value like that any place in town, you go ahead. You go right ahead and see if you can find another overcoat like that in town. A genuine Lapama fleece for only thirty-nine seventy-five. I'm telling you I don't know how we stay in business."

Hart frowned dubiously and looked down at the front of the coat. Then, as his head was lowered he brought his gaze up and he saw the salesman winking at Harry.

The salesman said, "Harry, if he doesn't buy this coat you put it in the window with one of the big price tags and five will get you fifty we sell it in ten minutes."

"Do you mean what you're saying?" Hart asked.

"Why, certainly," the salesman said. "Do you realize what fine fleece that is? If you don't take that overcoat you'll never forgive yourself."

"All right," Hart said. "I'll take it." He walked toward the door.

"That'll be thirty-nine seventy-five," the salesman said. He was walking behind Hart, and then he got excited as Hart moved faster, and he said, "Hey, listen—"

Hart opened the door and ran out.

There were three customers in the small taproom on Twelfth Street off Race. As Hart came in the three customers turned and looked at him and the man behind the bar kept on wiping a glass. Hart walked into the lavatory and took off the coat and tore off the size slip and the price ticket. With the coat over his shoulder he came out of the lavatory and went up to the bar and ordered a beer. He was two-thirds finished with the beer when a policeman entered the taproom and stood there in the doorway examining the four faces and then walked slowly toward Hart.

Hart looked up, holding the glass close to his mouth.

The policeman gestured toward the bright green coat. "Where did you get that?"

"In a store," Hart said.

"Where?"

"I think it was Atlantic City. Or it might have been Albuquerque."

"Are you trying to be smart?"

"Yes," Hart said.

"You stole that coat, didn't you?"

"Sure," Hart said, and he tossed the beer into the policeman's eyes, going forward as the policeman let out a yell going backward, and he was past the policeman, hearing the excitement behind him as he ran out.

Holding tightly to the coat over his arm he ran down Twelfth Street and turned east on Race. Then he went up Eleventh and ran down an alley. In the middle of the alley he came to a stop and he got into the overcoat and leaned against a wall of splintered wood and breathed heavily. He was trying to decide where he should go. He couldn't take another risk with the railroads or roads going out of town or boats going down the river. It was at a point where odds on all those things were too big. Now that he was here in Philadelphia he had to stay here. It was a big enough place. What he had to do was find a section of the city where they wouldn't be likely to pick him up, where he could take his time and pull himself together.

He knew Philadelphia because very long ago he had put in a couple of years at the University of Pennsylvania and at that time he had been an impressionable boy who liked to roam around alone and pick up things. In those two years he had covered a lot of Philadelphia, and he found out it was a lot of cities inside of a city. Germantown was complete in itself, and so was Frankford. Across the Schuylkill there was West Philadelphia with its University. And because the city was divided so distinctly he was thinking now that what he had to do was get away from the center and cross a few boundaries. He wondered if there was a lot of crime in Germantown. If things hadn't changed there wouldn't be much police activity up there, because long ago when he was at the University he saw Germantown as a collection of dignity, just a bit smug and perhaps unconsciously snobbish against the historical background and the old colonial flavor. It might still be quiet and dignified up there. He wished he had cab fare. The dime for beer left him eighty-three cents, and he knew a cab to Germantown would cost much more.

"God Almighty," he said, because even with the overcoat it was so biting cold, and he smiled remembering that this was why he had left the University, because these Philadelphia winters were just too much for him.

He remembered one day when it was as miserable as a day can possibly be, no rain or snow but a cold grey day with meanness written all over the sky and the streets, and he decided he didn't have to put up with that sort of weather, even though he liked the atmosphere of the University and the things he was learning there. So he packed his things and took a train, feeling the luxury of walking out on something he didn't care for. But now there was no walking out, there was only running away. There was a vast difference between walking out and running away.

He walked down the alley, then went up Tenth to Spring Garden. The Delaware wind came crashing down the wide street, hitting him hard, almost knocking him flat. He needed food and he needed rest, and he went over to a street lamp and leaned against the pole, wondering if he should take the chance of going into a restaurant. Then all at once there was a policeman standing in front of him.

"Plenty cold," the policeman said.

"What?" Hart said. He had his hands away from the pole of the street lamp and he was wondering if he should run north or west or try his luck across the street and down another alley.

The policeman clapped black leather mitts together and said, "I said it's plenty cold."

"This?" Hart said. "This is nothing. You've never been in northern Canada."

"This is cold enough for me," the policeman said.

"This is summer, compared to where I've been," Hart said. He knew he hadn't lost any of it. It was still good, the way it came out, the way it sounded, with just the right balance between conviction and nonchalance. As long as he could hold on to that way of pitching words, he was all right.

He left the policeman standing there, and he walked west on Spring Garden Street, deciding on Germantown.

He walked up Tulpehocken Street, watching the fronts of houses and hoping to see a room-for-rent sign. He went up two blocks without seeing such a sign, and then he was on Morton Street and he decided to turn there and try two or maybe three blocks east on Morton. He was very careful about it as he walked along Morton Street, watching the doors, the porch posts, the brick walls underneath the porch, any place where there would be a sign. He was finished with one block, starting on the second, when from somewhere back in the blackness he heard the crackling sound that had fire in it, and he started to run.

CHAPTER 2

He knew how to run. For one thing he was built for it and for another he had been working at it for a long time. Without extending himself he was covering a lot of ground, and presently he decided to have a look back there. He turned and looked back and all he could see was the street and houses on both sides of the street and the empty pavements.

That was all. That was what had been chasing him. The emptiness.

He made a fist and walked up to a tree. He slammed his fist against the tree and pain shot through his knuckles. Not enough pain. He had to cure himself now, get this ended before it could really get started, because once it got started he would have much difficulty curing it and maybe he wouldn't be able to cure it at all. He had to hurt himself more than this, make himself realize that he couldn't continue this sort of thing. The pain made him close his eyes. He told himself even if he had to break his hand he had to cure himself now. He shaped the hurt hand into an ever harder fist and readied another blow at the tree.

He had the fist in motion but something got into the focus of his eyes aiming at the tree. The fist stopped a few inches away from the tree. Hart turned and looked down the street. It was quiet, it was still. But it was no longer empty, because something dark was on the pavement a block away.

Hart walked toward the dark thing, knowing this was all wrong. He should be going in the other direction. But he couldn't be a machine all the time. He had to follow the emotional impulse once in a while, and now the impulse was pure curiosity and he kept going forward until at last he was there where the dark form of a man was motionless on the pavement.

Bending down, Hart saw the vague sign of life, the battle to breathe. He got his hands on the man's shoulders. He tugged, and rolled the man over and he had a look at the man's face.

He was a young man and he had his eyes open and he looked at Hart and said, "Are you a doctor?"

"No," Hart said.

"All right, then," the man said, "take a walk." He closed his eyes and his throat contracted and then some blood came out of his mouth. He opened his eyes and when he saw Hart still there he seemed surprised. He said, "What are you hanging around for?"

"I'm trying to think of a way to help you."

"Do you have a car?" the man said.

"No."

"Do you live around here?"

"No."

"Jesus Christ," the man said, and some more blood came out of his mouth. He tried to roll over and his face tightened and he started to let out a scream, forced it back just as it began to shoot from his mouth. And instead the blood came again, and again he said, "Jesus Christ." Then he looked at Hart and he said, "Do you know anyone around here?"

"No," Hart said. "But maybe I can help you anyway. Do you want to roll over?"

"All right," the man said, "roll me over."

Hart did it more gently this time. The man was face down and Hart saw the small hole very black against the yellow camel hair. It was halfway down and maybe two inches to the left of the spine. The man was going to die in a minute or so.

"Where is it?" the man said.

Hart told him.

"Jesus Christ," the man said. "I'm done." His shoulders began to quiver. He seemed to be crying. Then he made the sounds of dying and he was trying to get words into it. Hart bent low, trying to catch it. And he heard, "—pocket – wallet – you might as well – they want it – I don't want them to have it – you might as well – oh Jesus Christ oh Lord in Heaven it hurts it hurts – go on, take the wallet and get out of here and if you know what's good for you don't go to the police don't tell anybody just take the wallet and take the money out and throw the wallet away, you better burn it, that's right, burn it – now take it – now – buy your wife a diamond ring – buy your poor old mother a house – buy yourself a car—"

Hart heard something coming down the street. He twisted his head and he saw two figures a little more than a block away, running toward his eyes. He started to go away, then he twisted again and he had his hand underneath the camel hair coat, going into the back pocket of heavy tweed sports slacks, getting a hold on a wallet. As he took the wallet out, the man who owned the wallet shuddered and died, and then Hart was on his feet, sprinting down Morton Street.

Someone yelled, "Stop!"

"Sure," Hart said. "Right away."

The crackling noise came again. Then again and three more times. He felt a bullet rip some fabric from his bright green coat. He knew he had to get off Morton

Street but he couldn't see any alley on this block and he knew a side street wouldn't be any good. He was going to chance it for another block, if he could last that long. If he didn't see any alley by then, he was going to throw the wallet in the air and let them see it, and maybe they would leave him alone.

He crossed the side street, making it in two big jumps, then he was on his way again, going down Morton Street as fast as he could go. He saw an alley sliding toward him and then a bullet went by and it couldn't have been more than an inch under the lobe of his left ear. As he entered the alley he heard a door opening somewhere, a scream, the door shutting, and he could imagine the housewife fainting dead away.

Running down the alley he put the wallet in a coat pocket. He made a few more yards, selected his garden, vaulted a wood fence four feet high, went flat going backwards and finally hiding behind a bush.

He heard them coming down the alley.

If there was a market, he would have sold his chances for one thin dime. There were two lamps in the alley, and one of them was tossing light toward this garden. They were taking their time about it, going over each garden and Hart could hear them talking it over as they went along. They weren't excited. They were very sure about it, just as he was. He wondered what they wanted most, him or the wallet. If it was him, it was because they thought the dying man had said something that they didn't want repeated. If it was the wallet, it was because the wallet contained something they wanted.

Hart estimated that he had about twenty seconds at the outside. He took the wallet out of his pocket, edged it toward where the light from the lamp was thickest. The wallet was goatskin, very soft, and it opened smoothly and Hart took out eleven bills. They were thousand-dollar bills.

A voice said, "He's got to be somewhere around."

Another voice said, "Talk to him. We'll save time that way."

"All right," the first voice said. Then it was louder and it was saying, "Come on out, mister. You won't get hurt."

Hart was digging a hole behind the bush. When he thought it was deep enough he inserted the eleven thousand dollars and then he quickly patted the soil on top. He rubbed his soil-stained hands on his trousers, put the wallet back in his pocket, and heard the first voice saying, "I'm telling you you won't get hurt if you come out now. We just want to talk to you, that's all."

"Okay," Hart said, and as he got up and came out from behind the bush he said, "You got the wrong man. I didn't kill him."

He saw the two men watching him from the other side of the fence. One of them, tall and young and wearing a skater's wool cap and shaker sweater, went over and opened the gate. The other man, silver hair showing under a soft-brim felt, had a revolver pointed at Hart.

"Come on out and let's have a look at you," the silver-haired man said.

Hart went out through the opened gate. The young man in the skater's cap came up to him and threw a fist at his face. He was under it and the skater without skates was wide open for a left hook. Hart thought of the revolver and kept his hands down and knew he was going to get hit on the skater's next try and there was nothing he could do but stand there and take it. The skater pushed him against the fence, setting him up for a right cross. He stood there and the fist came toward his face and he let his head go back as the fist came in. It was a slow punch, but there was a lot of force in it, and it hurt.

The skater smiled. He had a long, thick nose that came to a knob at the end. He had big teeth in a thin face. Both cheeks were mottled with the scars from a bad case of some skin disease. The skater was getting ready to hit Hart again.

Hart looked at the man with silver hair and said, "Revolver or no revolver, if he tags me again he gets a busted pelvis."

The skater smiled very wide and said, "Well, whaddya know – he's a kicker."

The man with silver hair looked at the skater and said, "Choke him – we've made enough noise with bullets."

"Sure," Hart said, "go ahead and choke me." He extended his head and lifted his chin obligingly. The skater put up two large hands and showed the fingers to Hart, then walked in to put the fingers around Hart's throat. Hart stood where he was, stood quietly until the fingers were fastened on his throat, and then he brought up his left leg and his knee caught the skater between the legs and the skater let out a tremendous screech and went backward. Hart went along with him, grabbed him and threw him at the man with silver hair. The skater screeched again, colliding with the man with silver hair, and Hart heard the gun go off. The skater and the man with silver hair were on the ground and the skater was making weird noises and the man with silver hair was trying to aim the gun.

Hart was undecided. If he ran now he would have his back turned to the gun, and he wasn't sure he would be able to run fast enough. And if he stood here he was going to get shot. The only thing he felt right now was a definite regret that he had selected Germantown.

Now the gun was aimed and the man with silver hair was getting to his feet. The skater was on the ground, squirming and moaning. Hart raised his arms and smiled foolishly.

The man with silver hair was saying, "You're too much trouble."

Hart said, "I don't know about you, but I don't like to be choked."

"Do you think I like to shoot people?"

"No," Hart said. "You're a nice guy. You're a swell guy. You wouldn't shoot anybody."

"Unless I had a reason."

"And would it have to be a good reason?"

"Sure," said the man with silver hair. "I don't like to shoot people. I don't get any special kick out of it."

"That's fine," Hart said. "That means you won't shoot me."

"That means I will shoot you."

"You think you've got a reason?"

"A good reason."

"Oh, all right," Hart said. "You want the wallet? I'll give you the wallet."

He took the wallet out of his pocket.

"Toss it," said the man with silver hair. "If it comes toward my eyes I'll shoot you in the stomach."

Hart tossed the wallet. The wallet was caught and pocketed. The man with silver hair was looking at Hart's face and saying, "We don't have too much time, Paul. See if you can stand up."

The skater was sobbing now. The skater said, "I'm ruptured. I'm all smashed down there."

"Take a look at it, Paul," said the man with silver hair.

"I'm afraid to look at it," the skater said.

"Go on, Paul. Look at it," said the man with silver hair.

Paul sobbed loudly. Paul said, "I'm afraid, Charley. I feel bad enough as it is. If I look at it I'll feel worse."

"What are we going to do?" Hart said. "Stand here?"

"I don't know," said the man with silver hair. "There's not much sense just standing here, is there?"

"I guess not," Hart said. He reasoned he could just about put two yardsticks between his chest and the revolver.

"It hurts something fierce," Paul said. "Charley, do something for me. I can't stand it."

Charley twisted his lips and bit at the inside of his mouth. He was thinking. He seemed to be looking past Hart's shoulder as he said, "Let's get him out of here."

They heard a police whistle. It was short, then it was long, then it was short twice. Then it was very long and then there were more whistles.

Charley bit hard at the inside of his mouth. "All right," he said, "let's get out of here fast. You take his legs. I'll have one hand on his wrist and one hand on the revolver. Turn your back to me and pick up his legs."

Hart obeyed. Paul groaned and was bringing it up to a yell when Charley said, "Now you cut that out, Paul."

Paul sobbed again. They were carrying him down the alley. He said, "I can't stand it, Charley. I just can't stand it, that's all."

"Let's hurry it up," Charley said.

Hart moved faster.

"Please, Charley—" Paul was groaning and sobbing. "Give me a break, will you?"

Charley had no reply for that. They were going rather fast down the alley. They heard the whistles again. As they came toward the end of the alley Charley said they ought to turn toward the right so they could get back to Tulpehocken. Paul was begging Charley to get him to a hospital. Hart was wondering if it would be a good idea to let go of Paul's legs and gamble on a sprint. Then they were at the end of the alley and turning into another alley.

"Let's hold it," Charley said. He was breathing heavily, taxed from supporting half of Paul's weight with one arm.

They listened for more whistles. They didn't hear anything.

"At least get me back to the house," Paul said.

"That's what we're trying to do," Charley said. "Do you think you can walk?"

Paul groaned.

"Give it a try," Charley said. "Let go of his legs, mister. Let's see if we can get him to stand."

Paul was groaning and telling them how bad it was as they got his feet on the ground and then lifted him upright. His knees gave way and they tried it again. On the fifth try they had him standing.

Charley said, "You're all right, Paul."

Paul looked at Hart and said, "I'll be talking with you later. You can think about that."

"Should I let it get me?" Hart asked.

Paul didn't answer. Charley gestured with the revolver and said, "You help him. I'll walk in back."

They walked slowly. Paul began to groan again. They went down this second alley, crossed a narrow street and they were in another alley. Then still another and they came out on Morton. They started to walk up Morton and Charley changed his mind and said they better use the alley and the back entrance. They went back into the alley going parallel with Morton Street. As they walked up the alley, Hart was counting the houses. When they came to the seventh house, Charley said that was it. He told Hart to walk up the steps and knock five times on the back door.

Hart went up the steps and saw dim lights coming from the front of the house. He knocked five times. As he waited for a response he wondered if it would be a good idea to leap off the back porch and gamble on the darkness of the alley. He turned and looked at Charley and saw the high polish of the revolver.

The door opened. A fat woman with fluffy platinum blonde hair looked at Hart and was still looking at him when Charley said, "Come on down here, Frieda. I want you to give Paul a hand."

"What's the matter with Paul?" the fat woman wanted to know.

Hart was wondering what the chances were of grabbing the fat woman and getting her in front of him as a shield, then ducking in, closing the door, racing through the house and going out through the front door. He decided it wasn't a good idea. It was too complicated. He decided to hang around for a while. Maybe an easier opening would show itself.

Charley was up the steps now, telling him to enter the house. He heard the footsteps of Frieda and Paul, very careful and slow against the creaking wood. They were in the kitchen. Charley turned on the light. It was a small neat kitchen with an old-fashioned stove and an old-fashioned ice box. Footsteps came from the front of the house and Hart heard voices. He studied two men as they came into the kitchen. They were strongly built tall men and they wore dark worsted suits, well cut and smartly styled. One of them was good-looking.

They looked at Hart.

The good-looking one said, "What do you call this?"

"I call it aggravation," Charley said.

"*You* call it aggravation," Hart said.

"Look, Charley," the good-looking one said, "we don't need this."

"We won't need it later," Charley said. "Right now we need it. We need it here."

"I could use a smoke," Hart said.

Frieda was helping Paul into another room. The black-haired man who was not good-looking took a pack of cigarettes out of a coat pocket, flipped the pack so that two cigarettes jumped out, extended the pack to Hart. The good-looking one struck a match.

Hart took smoke in and let it out. "Much obliged."

Then they ignored Hart. They faced Charley and the good-looking one said, "Well, we're already packed."

"You can unpack," Charley said. "We got Renner."

"Where?" the good-looking one asked.

"In the alley," Charley said. "I knew I hit him, but I didn't see him drop. When we got up there we couldn't see him. We went out on Morton Street and we didn't see him there either. Paul didn't like Morton Street and I was afraid too, so we went back into the alley and talked it over. Finally I said he had to be on Morton Street so we went out of the alley again and we tried the other side of Morton Street. Then we came back to this side and we saw this guy with him. This guy saw us and started to run. We ran after him and when we got up to Renner we stopped just long enough to see if he was finished."

"Was he finished?" the good-looking one said.

"Yes," Charley said. "He was all done, so we kept running after this guy and finally we got him in a back yard. Paul had to go and get tough so this guy gave Paul a knee."

The good-looking one turned and looked at Hart. "Where did you get connected with Renner?"

"I don't think he was connected with Renner," Charley said.

"Maybe he was," the good-looking one said.

"Listen to Charley," Hart said. "He's got the brains."

The good-looking one made a fist and showed it to Hart. "How long since you've been to a dentist?"

"I'm sure he wasn't connected with Renner," Charley said. "He was just curious. But I'll make sure anyway. As long as we got him here we don't need to worry about it."

"Did you get the case from Renner?"

"I got the case," Charley said. "I didn't get it from Renner. I got it from the guy."

"What do you mean you got it from the guy?"

"This guy took Renner's wallet."

The good-looking one turned to the one who wasn't good-looking and said, "Give me one of your cigarettes."

Hart took off his overcoat and arranged it neatly over a chair.

The good-looking one pointed a lighted cigarette at Charley and said, "You've got to face things, Charley. This guy was connected with Renner. The wallet proves it." He turned and placed a clean hand with manicured fingers on the shoulder of the other man. He said, "Maybe Rizzio here has an outside connection. How do we know?"

"That's a nice thing to say," said Rizzio.

"I'm not trying to hurt your feelings, Rizzio," said the one who was good-looking. "But here's a game where we've got to close every opening. Maybe I have an outside connection. Maybe Frieda. Maybe Myrna. Maybe even Charley. You see what I'm getting at? Who would have thought Renner would pull something like that? If we're going to get dividends out of this we can't let any openings stay open."

"There's a lot to that," Charley admitted. "I'll take one of your cigarettes, Rizzio."

Hart walked around them, took one of the chairs, sighed as he relaxed in it. He leaned an elbow on the table and sat there watching them.

Charley showed him the revolver to remind him it was still around. Then Charley turned to Rizzio and said, "Where's the car?"

"Where I parked it," Rizzio said.

"Go upstairs," Charley said.

"What's upstairs?" Rizzio said.

"Take a look at Paul," Charley said. "Then come down and tell me what condition he's in."

Rizzio walked out of the kitchen.

Charley and the good-looking one stood there smoking and looking at each other. After some moments they both turned and looked at Hart. Then they looked at each other again.

"What do we do with this guy?" the good-looking one said.

"We talk to him," Charley said.

"I'll talk to him," the good-looking one said.

"Don't get tough with him, Mattone," Charley said.

"Why not?"

"If you get tough with him he'll hit back."

The good-looking one started to rub a fist, grinning at Hart and saying, "I like that. I like when they hit back."

"If he hits back you'll lose your temper and kill him," Charley said. "I want him alive for a while. Maybe he's got some talent we can use."

"Are you trying to sell me something?" Hart said.

"Let me hit him once," Mattone said. "Just to give him the idea."

Charley worked the cigarette for a lot of smoke, got it

out slowly at first, then steamed it out in a sudden volley. "Look, Mattone, I said I didn't want you to hit him."

Charley started to walk out of the kitchen. Mattone touched his arm and said, "What about cops?"

"There were cops."

"They see you?"

"We heard whistles."

"They'll be dragging the neighborhood," Mattone said. "As long as we're packed already—"

"No," Charley said. "We stay where we are."

"Wait a minute, Charley—"

"I said we're going to stay right where we are," Charley said. He walked out of the kitchen.

Mattone reached into his jacket pocket and took out a revolver. He grinned at Hart and then he walked toward the vacant chair. The grin widened as he saw the bright green coat hanging over the back of the chair. Then he looked at Hart and he looked at the chocolate-brown flannel suit and he came over and rubbed a finger on the fine quality flannel. He walked back to the other chair and put a hand against the bright green Lapama fleece. He looked at Hart again and he said, "It doesn't figure."

"Every man has his ups and downs," Hart said.

Mattone raised the front of the coat and had a look inside the label. He looked at Hart and he said, "You mean to tell me you went into that place and bought a coat?"

"I went into that place and stole a coat," Hart said.

"Oh." Mattone took the cigarette out of his mouth, held it delicately as he sat down at the table across from Hart. "You stole the coat. What else did you steal?"

"Nothing."

"Nothing from that place. How about other places?"

"Nothing."

"You see?" Mattone said. "We're starting all wrong. You stole the wallet, didn't you?"

"No," Hart said. "I didn't steal the wallet. He told me to take it."

Mattone leaned forward. "Take a good look at me."

Hart took the look. He said, "No, you don't look like a moron. And I'm not talking to you as if you were a moron. That's what happened. He told me to take the wallet."

"Why would he want you to have the wallet?"

"Ask him."

Mattone turned and crossed one leg over the other and put cigarette ashes on the floor. He grinned at the ashes. He said, "You're going to be a pleasure. A real pleasure. I've been away from the ring a long time. You know how it is. I get so I want to put my fists on a face. How much do you weigh?"

"One forty."

Mattone let out a brief laugh. He looked at the revolver in his hand. He said, "I guess I won't need this."

He put the revolver in his jacket pocket.

"Do you use rouge?" Hart said.

"What's the matter, are you in a hurry for it?"

"The eyebrows," Hart said. "Do you pluck them every day?"

"Three times a week," Mattone said. "You're going to get it now. You can't take it back."

"Oh, come on," Hart said. "You're not that angry. You're not angry at all. You just want some fun. But remember what Charley said."

"Now that's funny," Mattone said as he stood up. "I can't remember. That's my big weakness. My memory."

"You're a scream," Hart said.

Mattone's eyes were bright with joy. "This is wonderful. He's begging for it."

"Can't live without it."

"All right, stand up and get it."

Hart stood up and sat down quickly to get away from a straight right aimed at the mouth. Mattone leaned over to try the right again and Hart brought up a shoe and kicked Mattone a few inches below the kneecap. Mattone hopped back and lowered a hand toward the knee and Hart stood up and leaned on the right side and then brought up a right hand uppercut and missed. Mattone went hopping back and started to dance. Hart started to go forward, then stepped back quickly, reached down and grabbed a chair leg. As Mattone came in to break up the chair project, Hart already had the chair in both hands and he threw it at Mattone's face. Mattone stopped the chair with his arms, stumbled over it as he rushed at Hart, and Hart's face was all twisted with effort, body and arms working fast, fists hitting Mattone in the nose, in the lips, on the chin. Mattone was bleeding and he wasn't liking it. He hit Hart in the chest, hit him again in the ribs, had him against the wall, showed him a right hand and hit him with the right hand three times on the jaw. Hart started to go down and his head was hanging low and he saw Mattone dropping the right hand and getting it ready for the uppercut. Hart let his head go down still further until it was down against Mattone's stomach. Then Hart brought his head up as fast as he could and the top of his skull caught Mattone under the chin.

"Oh," Mattone said, and then he was unconscious. Hart grabbed him under the armpits as he started to go down. Then Hart lowered him slowly and when he was on the floor Hart bent over him and reached for the shoulder holster.

"No," Charley said. "Don't do that."

Charley was in the doorway and he had his revolver with him.

"I wish I could get a decent break," Hart said. He straightened up with his arms hanging loosely at his sides.

"You got no kick coming," Charley said. "You're getting all the breaks. If you'd made it with his gun you'd be on your way out the back door and I'd be shooting at you from the living room. You're drawing all good cards tonight."

"Sure. I'm so happy I feel like singing. Did you see any of it?"

"I came in when he was ready to give you the uppercut. I had an idea you were going to give him your head under the chin. I was going to warn him about that, but you were handling it pretty and I wanted to see if you'd get away with it."

Hart put a hand to his jaw. His jaw wasn't swollen, but it hurt.

"What started it?" Charley asked.

"I wanted to know if he used rouge."

Charley went over, picked up the overturned chair. He brought up a knee, rested a foot on the chair, leaned his arms on his leg, keeping the revolver aimed at Hart. He said, "You continue this sort of thing and I'm going to tie you up."

"Suppose I don't continue this sort of thing?"

Charley appreciated that. He nodded. He said, "That was all right. That was a peach. You got me there."

"Sure, I got you. Like a monkey in the cage has the keeper outside." And then he said, "What time is it?"

Charley glanced at a wristwatch. "Eight-twenty."

"I had breakfast at seven this morning. Nothing since then."

"What stopped you?"

"Broke."

"All right," Charley said. "We'll fix you up. What's your name?"

"Al."

"All right, Al. I'll have Frieda arrange a meal for you. All you need to do now is start something with Frieda."

Rizzio walked into the kitchen and looked at Mattone and said, "What happened to him?"

"He saw a mouse," Hart said.

Charley looked at Rizzio and said, "Go get Frieda."

Rizzio started out of the kitchen and Charley said, "Hold it. How is Paul?"

Rizzio said, "He's causing a lot of commotion up there, but he's all right,"

"Give me a cigarette," Charley said.

Rizzio took the pack out of his pocket and looked at Hart and said, "That's all I do around here. I run up and down steps and I drive the car and I supply everybody with cigarettes."

Rizzio held a match to Charley's cigarette and said, "I'll get Frieda." He left the kitchen.

Charley went over to the sink and loaded a glass with cold water. He went over to Mattone and threw the water on Mattone's face.

Mattone sat up and looked at Charley. Then he looked at Hart. Then he stood up and rubbed wetness from his face. He took a large white handkerchief from the top pocket of his worsted suit and pressed the handkerchief against his face. Then he walked past Charley and went out of the kitchen.

"A fine boy," Hart said.

"At one time he was a smart light heavy," Charley said. "Then one night he came up against a body puncher and he went to the hospital with kidney trouble. When he came out of the hospital he started to gain weight. He became a heavy and one night a colored boy hit him high up on the jaw and gave him a concussion. When he came out of the hospital he got connected with a mob in South Philly and started to pick up numbers. One night he was in a poolroom and he saw a guy he didn't like making a call in the phone booth. He picked up a billiard ball and slung it clear across the room and it went into the phone booth. The guy came out of the phone booth with a fractured skull. Mattone did a year for that. He was on his way to gasoline station and grocery store jobs and I met him one night and told him he could do better. He told me to leave him alone. One night he was robbing a gasoline station and the attendant hit him in the kidney with a monkey wrench. He got away but he was in the hospital for the better part of a month. When he came out he looked me up. He's been with me ever since."

"How long ago was that?" Hart asked.

"Two years ago."

Frieda came into the kitchen.

Charley said, "Fix him a meal. I'm going into the living room." He looked at Hart. "Frieda could go to Iowa and be a champion hog caller. I'll have the revolver in my lap. Put it together."

"It's together," Hart said.

Charley left the kitchen.

CHAPTER 3

Frieda was a big woman. She was one-sixty if she was an ounce, more solid than soft, packed into five feet five inches and molded majestically. He guessed she didn't wear a girdle and when she turned her back to him and leaned over slightly he was certain of it. She was wearing another dress now, a purple creation that was more than just tight. It looked as if it had grown up with her. He remembered before she had been wearing a plain house dress and he wondered if the purple dress was for his benefit. She bent over even further. Her calves were the same as the rest of her, solid round fat coming down rhythmically to slim ankles giving way to high-heeled shoes that she hadn't been wearing before.

She turned around and looked at him. She said, "You like eggs?"

"Scrambled."

"You like scrapple?"

"Like poison."

"I'll make you something nice. You like coffee?"

"I live on it."

She smiled. She wanted him to examine her and he examined her. The platinum blonde hair fluffed all over her head and rolled on her forehead and came down behind her ears to a big fluff at the back. Her eyes were brown, clear and healthy. Very little mascara. And underneath her smoothly shaped nose her large mouth was deep red with some purple in the red paint. The rouge on her pink round face was deeper pink with a trace of purple in it.

There wasn't a line on her face.

Hart frowned with interest and said, "You keep yourself in good condition."

"I manage." Her voice was full and solid.

"I'm trying to guess your age," Hart said.

"Thirty-four. I've been married four times."

"You married now?"

"I guess so. I don't know what he's doing. I don't know where he is. The last time I heard it was Cincinnati. That was a year ago. Really interesting boy, and generous, too, but he played too rough."

"What did you do to him?"

"I broke his collarbone with a silver hand-mirror he gave me for my birthday."

"Did that do it?"

"No. He wanted more. When he got out of the hospital he traced me to Florida. I had to spit in his face a few times and the last time it was in front of a lot of people. And that was what did it. He hauled off on me but I was with a professional wrestler that night. He really tried with that wrestler. He lasted almost five minutes, then he went flying over a few tables and they had to carry him out. I didn't see him after that until he looked me up in Cincinnati. He wanted money. That tickled me. I got such a kick out of it that I actually gave him money."

Hart shaped a laugh and let her hear it. She laughed with him.

Then she waited on him. She was a good cook, and she knew the finer details, all on the modern side. She sat there watching him enjoying it.

He was slow with the second cup of coffee. He had his eyes on the blackness in the cup, knowing she had her eyes on him. He knew he had started a wedge but he didn't want to widen it too quickly because then it might break.

He said, "Did you hear about Renner?"

"Yes," she said. "Paul told me."

"How is Paul?"

"I gave him a couple pills. I guess he's sleeping now. He'll be all right. If you're still around when he's up on his feet you're in for a terrible lacing."

"I don't think I'll be around. Is that real platinum blonde?"

"No, and you know it isn't. You don't think you'll get away, do you?"

"Yes, Frieda," he said solemnly. "I can't help it, but that's what I think."

"Suppose you get away," she said, as if she didn't hear his last remark. "What would you do then?"

"I'd stay away."

"Would you open your mouth?"

"If I was a fool."

"That sounds like something. Build on it."

He said, "I'm wanted in New Orleans."

"For what?"

"Murder."

She leaned her head to one side and smiled dimly. "Now look," she said, "you're not trying to show me a good time, are you?"

"You wanted me to build. So I'm building."

"All right, build some more. Who was it?"

"My older brother."

"What name you using?"

"Al."

"Look, Al, you mean to sit there and tell me you killed your own brother?"

"Sure."

Frieda stood up. "Charley!"

Footsteps came banging toward the kitchen. Charley appeared in the doorway with the revolver all ready. Charley said, "What's he doing?"

Frieda said, "Charley, I want you to hear something." She looked at Hart. "Go ahead, tell it to Charley."

Hart drained the cup and said, "I'm telling him because you're asking me to. I told you because you asked me. Just remember that." He turned his head toward Charley. "I told her I'm wanted in New Orleans for killing my brother."

Charley rested the revolver flat in one palm and smoothed the other palm over it. Then Charley said, "Why did you skip?"

"I had no alibi," Hart said.

Frieda said, "Why did you pick Philadelphia?"

"I couldn't get a boat across the Gulf," Hart said. "I couldn't go north at first because I couldn't get the right connections. I had to go east. I went to Birmingham and from there I went north. This is as far as I got."

"When did you come in? How?" Charley's voice was quiet.

"The afternoon train from Baltimore," Hart said. "Some men in plain clothes stepped on the train when we pulled in at Thirtieth Street Station. I didn't know what they wanted and I wasn't going to stay there to find out. I got out of my seat and took a walk into the next car. Some more men in plain clothes were watching the doors. I kept walking through the cars. I was about two cars from the end and I had to turn around and look. So I turned around and I saw two of them coming after me. The next door was unguarded and I took that door before any of them could come down there from the outside. I had to leave all my belongings on the train, and that included about seven hundred dollars tucked away in a Gladstone."

"I think you got a weakness there," Charley said. "What's wrong with a wallet?"

"When you're running away you do funny things."

"It's still weak," Charley said.

"All right, it's weak," Hart said. "Tonight I walked into a store on Broad Street and stole the overcoat you see there on the chair."

Charley looked at the overcoat. "Broad and where?"

"Above Callohill."

"All right," Charley said. "What store?"

"I think it said Sam and Harry."

Frieda was looking at the bright green overcoat. She said, "It looks brand new."

Charley turned to Frieda. Charley said, "Get the telephone book and look up Sam and Harry in the classified section under men's clothing. Come in and tell me if there's a Sam and Harry clothing store on Broad Street above Callohill. And bring Mattone in with you."

Frieda walked out.

Charley put a forefinger through the trigger guard and twirled the revolver. "You don't mind a little checking, do you?"

Hart shook his head. He looked at the floor. Charley leaned against the icebox and kept twirling the revolver. They could hear the flipping of telephone-book pages from the living room. Then Frieda came walking into the kitchen and Mattone was behind her.

Frieda said, "There's a Sam and Harry on Callohill Street above Broad."

Charley acted as if he didn't hear. Charley said to Mattone, "Take a look at that overcoat."

Mattone went over and examined the overcoat. He rubbed the bright green fabric between his fingers.

"Would you say that was quality?" Charley said.

Mattone said, "If I know anything about clothing it's a ninety-dollar article and it doesn't come from Sam and Harry."

Charley looked at Hart, and Hart looked at Mattone and said, "You're some brain, you are. Ten minutes ago you were looking at the Sam and Harry label."

Mattone dropped the coat and went over to Hart and took a swing and connected. Hart walked backward to the stove, came away from the stove and put his arms down to break the fall. Then he was on his knees and after that he was face down on the floor.

Charley said, "Stay with him, Frieda."

"Let me stay with him," Mattone said.

Charley looked at Mattone. "You come with me."

They went into the living room. Charley picked up the telephone book, found the number and made the call. When he got his party he said, "Did someone steal an overcoat from your place tonight?"

At the other end a voice said, "Just a minute—"

Charley hung up. He looked at Mattone. He said, "They want to trace the call. Is that good enough for you?"

"Look, Charley, I don't like that guy."

"And I don't like you," Charley said. "But I put up with you because you know your work. I like the way you work, but there's got to be satisfaction on both sides. Do you like the pay?"

"Look, Charley—"

"Do you like the pay?"

"I like the pay."

"All right, then, do as you're told. And don't do things I don't want you to do."

In the kitchen Hart was sitting up and tapping fingers
against his jaw. Frieda was sitting at the table, leaning
her face on a cupped hand and watching Hart and then
turning as Charley came in. She looked at Charley's
eyes.

Hart stood up and said, "Did you make the call?"

"Yes," Charley said. "If you want to go now you can go."

"What would you advise me to do?" Hart asked.

"Go back to New Orleans," Charley said. "You're
already traced here, I mean as far as Philly, because of
that Gladstone – that is, if you bought the Gladstone
down south."

"I bought the Gladstone in Nashville after I threw
away the other bag. But I was traced to Nashville."

"That means you're traced here, so your best move is to
go back and do your hiding in New Orleans. Don't try
little towns. Little towns are bad."

"I'm broke," Hart said.

Charley put a hand in a trousers pocket and took out
some bills. He handed Hart a ten-dollar bill.

"Much obliged," Hart said. He pocketed the bill and put
on his overcoat. He looked at the kitchen doorway. Then
he looked at the back door.

Charley said, "Stay away from Tulpehocken until you
get to Germantown Avenue. Then come back to
Tulpehocken and get your trolley. If I were you I'd go to
Frankford tonight and stay there a few weeks and try to
pick up a little change. Then I'd go straight back to New
Orleans and put it on a speculation basis for at least a
month. Then I'd try the Gulf or I'd try the border from
Texas."

Hart opened the back door and walked out. The cold
air slammed into him like a sheet of stiff iced canvas. He
went down the alley, and every few seconds he would

turn around and look and listen carefully. Finally he decided that Charley probably wasn't following him after all. Hart knew what Charley would do instead. Charley was smart. Charley would know where to wait for Hart – and the eleven thousand. Hart figured Charley would give him another five minutes, at the outside, before he took off to do what he would have to do when Hart didn't show up. It was cold, and Hart was no fool. He'd show, all right.

Some thirty yards down the alley he came to his garden and began digging away at the cold hard soil.

He rolled up the eleven thousand dollars, inserting the bills into an overcoat pocket. Then he walked along the alley and headed back to the house.

The door opened and Charley stood there, showing Hart the revolver.

"All right," Charley said. "Come on in."

Hart entered the kitchen. He saw Frieda sitting at the table and looking up from a movie magazine. He took the rolled bills from the overcoat pocket and extended the money to Charley.

Charley took the bills and counted them.

"All there?" Hart said.

"All there," Charley said.

Frieda frowned. "What goes on here?"

Charley smiled mildly. "Al brought back the money."

Frieda pointed to the bills in Charley's hand. "That's the money Renner took."

Charley widened the smile. He said, "Frieda, you're right in there."

Hart said, "You knew there was nothing in the wallet. So all you did was send me out for the money."

Charley nodded slowly.

Hart said, "You were giving me around five minutes to

get back here with the money, and if I wasn't back by then you were going to go out and wait at Germantown and Tulpehocken and get me there."

"Is that why you came back?"

"Not exactly," Hart said.

"All right," Charley said. "Let's have it complete. Why did you come back?"

"It's too cold out there."

"You mean it's too hot out there."

Hart grinned. "It's both. I don't need this weather. And I don't need all that Law running after me. Only thing I need is a place to hide. Only place I can hide is here."

"I thought you'd see it that way," Charley said.

They stood there grinning at each other. And then Charley said, "You owe me ten dollars."

Hart took out the ten and handed it to him. "That's for a week's room and board."

"You're getting a bargain," Charley said. He went to the doorway and called for Rizzio. He told Rizzio there was a folding-cot somewhere in the cellar and he wanted it brought upstairs. Without looking at Hart, he murmured, "I hope you'll be comfortable."

Frieda got up from the table and moved toward the sink. As she passed Hart, her hand drifted down and she touched him. She said, "I think he'll be comfortable."

CHAPTER 4

They could hear Rizzio banging around in the cellar and then they could hear him battling with the cot up to the second floor. Mattone entered the kitchen and helped himself to a glass of milk and some chocolate cookies. Frieda was with the movie stars again and eating an apple. Hart leaned against the back door and looked at the floor. Charley was standing in the middle of the kitchen and biting the inside of his mouth and looking at nothing. The kitchen was quiet except for the sound of energetic munching as Frieda ate the apple.

Someone was coming down from the second floor, coming through the house. She came into the kitchen, an extremely thin girl about five-two with extremely white skin and very black hair. Hart didn't have time to note the color of her eyes because just then Charley turned toward the door and told Hart to follow him.

They went through the house. It was just another quiet little row house in quiet Germantown. The cleanliness of the kitchen was extended through the rest of the house.

In the room where Rizzio put the cot, Hart saw two water-colors hanging on the wall; both were signed "Rizzio."

"They're very good," Hart said.

"Are you telling me they're good?" Rizzio said.

"Hurry up with that cot and get out of here," Charley said.

"I can't find anything wrong with them," Hart said.

Rizzio took hold of Charley's arm and said, "You hear that?"

"All right," Charley said, "one of these days I'll sponsor an exhibition. If you're finished with that cot, take a walk. Give me two cigarettes before you go," he added.

Rizzio obeyed and faced the wall and stared unhappily at his water-colors. Then he walked out of the room and closed the door. Charley handed a cigarette to Hart and then took a match out of his pocket and struck it on the sole of his shoe.

Charley seated himself on the edge of the wide bed and Hart sat on the edge of the cot.

Charley said, "You'll share this room with me and Rizzio."

Hart gazed contentedly at the window beside the cot. He said, "I'm first in line for the fresh air."

Charley smiled and said, "A crook tried to climb through that window a month ago. Rizzio hit him in the face and threw him out the window. We went down and picked him up out of the back yard, the alley part along this side of the house. He had a broken back and both legs were broken. Mattone ended it for him with a knife and then we put him in the car and rode to a quiet street and threw him in the gutter."

"Where did Renner sleep?" Hart said.

"Don't ask questions about Renner. Don't ask questions about anything. If I feel like telling you, I'll tell you. Renner slept in the back room with Paul and Mattone. There's three beds in the back room but I don't want you in there with Paul and Mattone. You wouldn't last long with them. I want you to stay away from them as much as you can – until they get used to you. And now here's what we do. We take mansions on the Main Line.

Every section where there's wealth. I think there's more wealth concentrated in the Philly Main Line than any city in the country. We don't load ourselves down. We take just enough to make a profitable little haul. Two or three burlap bags, never more than that, and it's mostly silverware and antiques. We got a fence connection in South Philly and he's been working with me for seventeen years, and we have a fairly good arrangement. What brought out that comment about Rizzio's water-colors?"

"They're good," Hart said.

"How do you know they're good?"

"It's just one man's opinion, but I know a little about it. I majored in fine arts at Pennsylvannia."

"Do you do any painting yourself?"

"No, but I've done a lot of collecting. In New Orleans I had a very nice collection."

"What else did you do in New Orleans?"

"I loafed. I could afford to. My old man piled up about three million in beet sugar. He left it to my mother and when she died she left it to my older brother Haskell."

"Is that why you killed him?"

"Yes," Hart said. "I wanted the money."

"How many brothers altogether?"

"Three of us. Haskell, myself and Clement."

"Any sisters?"

"Two of them and they're both dead. They were students at Tulane and one night they were coming home from a dance and the car turned over a few times. I belong to a very happy family."

Charley was looking at Rizzio's water-colors. Charley said, "Was this Haskell married?"

"No."

"Clement?"

"Clement married when he was eighteen. Now they've

got three children and it's one of those unusual marriages, I mean it's really a pleasant arrangement."

Charley leaned back on his elbows, the cigarette tight in his mouth and snapping up and down as he said, "Let's hear something about the killing."

"Well," Hart said, "I did it with a blackjack. I wanted to make it look like burglary. Haskell lived alone in a big home near Audubon Park. I went up there one night and got in through the back door without any of the servants seeing me. And I know they didn't see me get into his room. I hit him over the head with the blackjack and kept on hitting him until he was dead. Then I went through his room and took all his jewelry — he went in for diamond-studded watches and emerald cuff links and that sort of thing. He had fifteen hundred dollars in his wallet. I thought it was going to look like a genuine burglary, because I got away all right, and the room was messed up and so forth. But later I was worried. The police were putting too many things together. Besides, they had a witness who saw me near Audubon Park that night, and it knocked my alibi to bits. When I saw they were really closing in on me I took a walk."

Charley stood up, walked around the bed and placed himself in front of Rizzio's water-colors. Frowning at the paintings, he said, "I'm not sure, Al. Maybe we can use you right in on the jobs or maybe it would be better for you to go with Myrna and Frieda to get the leads. But I don't know about this painting business. I've always found it best to stay away from oils and that sort of thing. And the fence will have something to say about it. So we'll just let it ride for awhile, even though I've got the feeling your knowledge would come in handy."

"What do I do meanwhile?"

"Just stay here. I'll find things for you to do. You don't get bored easily, do you?"

"Not easily."

"You want to go to sleep now or do you want to come down and listen to the radio for awhile?"

"I think I'll go to sleep."

"All right, Al. I'll see you in the morning." Charley glanced again at Rizzio's paintings and then he walked out.

In the middle of an endless plain of soft snow there was a pool of black water. A man's head emerged from the pool and the man opened his mouth and began to shriek.

Hart opened his eyes and sat up. There was movement on the other side of the room, then the lights went on. Charley was there with his hand still near the light switch and Rizzio was getting out of bed. The shrieking came from the back room.

Mattone came rushing into the middle room and said, "Listen, that boy needs a doctor."

Charley followed Mattone out of the room. Rizzio inserted his feet into slippers and went out after them. Then Hart heard Charley saying, "You go back to bed," and a few moments later Rizzio re-entered the room and closed the door.

"Open the door," Hart said. "I want to hear what's going on."

Rizzio opened the door. They could hear the shrieking from the back room. They could hear Frieda's voice and Charley's voice. Rizzio produced an unopened pack of cigarettes out of nowhere, along with a book of matches.

"You want one of these?" Rizzio said.

The shrieking became higher and louder.

"Let's have one," Hart said.

Rizzio came over and gave him a cigarette and a light. They listened to the shrieking from the front room. All at once the shrieking stopped and the talking went down to a murmur and then the murmur stopped. Hart had the cigarette in his mouth as he sat there rigid on the cot, watching the quiet wall beyond the opened door. A shadow hit the wall and Charley followed the shadow and entered the room.

Charley said, "Paul passed away."

"No," Rizzio said.

"All right, no," Charley said. He was looking at Hart. He said, "I didn't think it was that bad, even though I knew it was bad enough. You must have broken him to bits in there. He had internal bleeding and I guess the blood went up and choked his heart, or something. I don't know."

"Why didn't we get a doctor?" Rizzio said.

Charley looked at Rizzio and said, "I'll let you answer that."

"We ought to have our own doctor," Rizzio said.

Charley looked at Hart. "We used to have our own doctor. He died a few months ago. I've been looking around, but there's a shortage of doctors nowadays; especially the kind of doctors we need. It's a problem."

Rizzio was rubbing his chin and saying, "What are we going to do with Paul?"

"That's another problem," Charley said. "Is the furnace hot?"

"Jesus Christ, Charley."

"When I ask you a question," Charley said, "why don't you give me a direct answer?"

"I guess it's hot," Rizzio said. "I put in some coal a couple hours ago."

"Do we have a meat cleaver downstairs?" Charley asked.

"Oh Jesus Christ, Charley, I don't know, I don't know."

Charley turned and looked at Hart and said, "I got some organization here." Then he turned again to Rizzio and said, "Come on, we'll take Paul downstairs."

"Wait just a minute, Charley, please." Rizzio was putting fingers in a bathrobe pocket. "Let me smoke a cigarette first."

"Smoke the cigarette later. It'll taste better then," Charley said.

Rizzio said, "What are you going to do, cut him up?"

"No," Charley said. "I'm going to put him in starch and shrink him. Do you want to help me carry him down or do you want to stand there and smoke cigarettes?"

"Charley, listen—"

"No, I don't have time to listen." Charley went back to the window sill. He was biting the inside of his mouth.

Hart sat very still. He could feel it coming and he was afraid of it but there was nothing he could do about it.

Charley looked at Hart and said, "Mattone's no good for it, either. Mattone's only good for causing a commotion. And I can't carry him down by myself."

"All right," Hart said. He got out of bed. Charley came off the window sill and looked at the pajamas and grinned.

"My best silk pajamas," Charley said.

They were pale green pajamas, and Hart was thinking dizzily of pale green background and dark bright red.

CHAPTER 5

They went into the back room. Paul was naked on the bed and his eyes were half-closed and didn't seem like part of his face.

"Take his legs," Charley said.

They carried Paul downstairs. Hart was shivering. He was telling himself it was because the house was cold. They carried Paul down the cellar steps. They had Paul in the cellar and they put him on the floor near the furnace. Charley told Hart to stay with Paul, then Charley went upstairs and he was up there for a full five minutes, and Hart heard clanking around, as if Charley was looking for something. Then Charley came down the steps and in one hand he had a hack-saw and in the other hand he had a large knife.

Charley said, "Get some newspapers."

The front of the cellar was divided into two sections, one for coal, the other for old things that didn't matter too much. There was a pile of newspapers. Hart lifted half the pile and carried it toward the furnace.

"Get out of the way," Charley said. "I'm going to take his head off."

Hart stepped away, then went walking away as he heard the swish, the crunch, the grinding, the resistance, more grinding, the heavy breathing of Charley. Then the rustle of paper, the sound of paper getting wrapped around something. Then the furnace door opening. The sound of paper around something going into the fire. Then the furnace door closing.

"All right," Charley said. "I'll need you now."

Hart turned and came walking back. The light from a single bulb hanging from a long cord gave the cellar pure white light getting grey as it came toward the furnace. Under the grey light the headless body of Paul was grey-purple. Hart wondered if he could go through with this.

"Hold the legs tight," Charley said. "Hold them tight."

Hart took hold of the legs and closed his eyes. The sounds of the hack-saw and the knife were great big bunches of dreadful gooey stuff hitting him and going into him and he was getting sick and he tried to get his mind on something else, and he came to painting and started to concentrate on the landscapes of Corot, then got away from Corot although remaining in the same period as he thought of Courbet, then knowing Courbet was an exponent of realism and trying to get away from Courbet, unable to get away because he was thinking of the way Gustave Courbet showed Cato tearing out his own entrails and showed "Quarry," in which the stag under the tree was getting torn to bits by yowling hounds, and he tried to come back to Corot, past Corot to the gentle English school of laced garments and graceful posture and the delicacy and all that, and Courbet dragged him back.

And Charley said, "Hold him higher up."

With his eyes shut tightly, Hart said, "Tell me, Charley, did you ever do this before?"

"No," Charley said.

Hart opened his eyes and he saw the blood and he closed his eyes again. Charley was telling him to do things and he had to open his eyes to keep at it, but it was as if his eyes were closed, because he was gazing past the activity, and he was listening past the sounds of steel and flesh and paper. Now the work was going faster, the furnace door was opening and shutting in speedier rhythm, and yet time was bouncing all around the cellar, going so fast and melting as it went, so that finally time was all melted and there was no measuring it, and no measuring the smell of blood.

Then there was nothing on the floor but blood and newspapers. Charley went to the rear of the cellar, came back with a can of household cleanser. He ripped off the top of the can, threw the cleanser on top of the blood. Then he went away and came back with a bucket of hot water and a mop, and went to work. Hart took the unused newspapers back to the front of the cellar. Charley cleaned the tools, drying them as he came back.

They stood before the furnace and listened to the sound of burning.

"We better take these off," Charley said.

Hart looked at Charley, wondering what he meant, and saw that he meant the pajamas. And Hart looked at Charley's pajamas, looked at the blood all over pale blue, then he looked at the pajamas he was wearing, and he saw the pale green background and the gashes of dark bright red.

Charley opened the furnace door, threw in the pale blue pajamas, then Hart stepped over in front of the door and as he threw in the pale green pajamas he caught sight of the paper packages burning in there with a glaring purple and white flame. Then he caught a whiff of the smoke and he shut the door quickly.

"All right," Charley said, "let's go up."

They went upstairs. Coming away from the heat of the furnace area their naked bodies came into a cold living room and a colder stairway, and they moved quickly.

They went into the bathroom and although there was no blood on their hands they washed their hands anyway.

Finally Hart climbed back into the cot, propped the pillows to make himself comfortable, sucked smoke into his mouth, filled himself up with the smoke and let it seep out between his teeth. He wondered why he wasn't sick. He thought maybe he was beginning to get tough. He told himself it didn't really make any difference, because he didn't give a hang, but underneath he knew he did give a hang and it made a lot of difference and no matter what he kept telling himself he was really afraid of what was happening inside him.

Hart settled back against the pillow and brought up his arms, resting flat on his back and folding his hands behind his head. Across the room he saw the glow of a lighted cigarette and he knew it came from Charley and he tried to think of what was in Charley's mind right now. Then he closed his eyes and he tried to sleep.

He worked on it for an hour. He was going toward sleep, trying to dive into it, pulled back by something and then he tried to crawl toward it, pulled back by the same something that was mostly memory and hardly any planning. He was beginning to feel tired and he made one big try, throwing everything out of his mind except one big circle on which he tried to ride as it went around in the blackness under his eyelids. He managed to get on the circle and it took him around a few times and then threw him off with violence. He opened his eyes and sat up and he could hear the steady breathing of Charley and the heavy, distorted breathing of Rizzio. He wondered where Rizzio kept the cigarettes.

He left the cot, moved quietly across the room and pulled on the chocolate flannel trousers over the fresh pajamas. Then as he worked himself into the chocolate flannel jacket he was facing the window and he could see the black out there without any lights in it. He put on socks and started to put on shoes and changed his mind. Then he was going out of the room and closing the door delicately. Then he was going down the dark hall, so dark that at first he had to guide himself by the wall, then getting lighter because of a thin and vague glow that came from downstairs. And it was confusing, because he remembered Charley putting out all lights downstairs before they came upstairs.

He was going down the stairway. The light remained vague, and it wasn't doing much against the darkness, but he was coming closer to it and for a moment he had the unaccountable feeling that the light had drawn him out of the cot and out of the room. Halfway down the stairway he knew that he could see the source of the light if he turned his head, and he didn't know why he didn't want to turn his head. But he had to turn his head when he reached the foot of the stairs, and when he did he saw the light coming from a small lamp with a blue velvety shade, dark blue to give the light that odd vagueness. The lamp was on a small table and next to the table someone was sitting in a high-backed chair. The entire arrangement, lamp and pale blue light and figure in white and the brown top of the chair, topping the white, amounted to a face, and it was the face of his dead brother, Haskell.

Hart wondered if he would cut himself to ribbons if he went headfirst through one of the front windows.

From the chair a feminine voice said, "Who is that?"

Hart took in what felt like a quart of air and let it out with his mouth wide open. He said, "It's Al."

"This is Myrna."

Her voice wasn't a whisper. It was lower than a whisper.

Hart said, "What bothers you?"

She said, "Paul was my brother."

The space between them was a block of quiet freezing with immeasurable speed.

It was that way for more than a minute, then she said, "What brought you downstairs?"

"I don't know. I couldn't sleep."

She said, "Paul was twenty-eight. He had a lot of trouble with his insides. It was a bad condition and he had no business getting in fights. But he was always fighting. He never had any friends, because he was so hard to get along with. He was sick inside all the time, and he was always irritable and always as nasty as he could be. But I guess that isn't the point. The point is, he always took care of me."

Hart said, "How old are you, Myrna?"

"I'm twenty-six. Paul always treated me as if I was much younger and he was much older. I've been sitting here most of the night thinking of all the things he did for me. He did all those things without ever smiling. When he gave me things or when he did things for me he never smiled and he acted as if he didn't really want to do it. I never knew that was put on. My father used to drink anything he could get his hands on, hair tonic and furniture polish and all that. One night he doubled up and dropped dead. My mother packed up her things and walked out and left us there. Charley came and took care of us. Then Charley had to do a five-year stretch and me and Paul, we had to go to a home. Then Charley was out and one night he came to the home and gave somebody some cash and he took Paul and me away. To look at Charley you'd never think he was past fifty, except for the white hair. Did you ever get so you just wanted to sit alone all by yourself and try to think what's going to happen to you?"

"I get that way once in a while," Hart said. "Not often."

"I looked in the back room," Myrna said, "but Paul wasn't there. What did they do with Paul?"

"I don't know," Hart said.

"I'll find out in the morning," Myrna said. She came out of the chair, toward Hart. The pale blue light rolled over her head and showed her face. In a frail sort of way it was an out-of-the-ordinary face. The eyes were pearly violet. The eyes were ninety-nine percent of her.

She went past Hart and up the stairway. Hart turned off the lamp, groped his way to the stairway, groped his way up and down the hall and into the middle room. A few minutes after he hit the cot he was asleep.

Hart was awake at half past nine. He saw Rizzio moving around the room. He saw Charley still asleep in the wide bed. He turned over and went back to sleep, and at half past eleven Charley was talking to him, asking him if he wanted to get up. He got out of bed, sat on the edge of the cot until Charley came out of the bathroom. As Charley took off the bathrobe, Hart took a good look at him.

Charley was about five-nine and on the thin side. The silver hair was thick, coming up from a low, unworried forehead, parted in the middle, combed back obliquely, then brushed smooth without benefit of water or oil. The eyes were light blue, nicely spaced above a short, firm nose. The lips were a puzzle, firm and at the same time relaxed, and the skin of the face was beige remaining from a summer's deep tanning.

Charley said, "Why are you sizing me up?"

"I'm curious to see if I can wear your clothes," Hart said.

"What's wrong with your clothes?"

"The suit will do," Hart said, "but I like to wear fresh linen every day."

"Look in the bureau," Charley said. "The three top drawers are mine. You're welcome to whatever you find that fits. You can throw the dirty clothes in the laundry box in the bathroom. I'm going to make you a gift of something I got in the bureau. My skin's too tender and I never got the knack of it, but maybe you'll like it."

Charley opened the top drawer and took out a tan calf-skin case, opening it to show a foreign-make hollow ground safety razor. There was an intricate stropping arrangement where the blade was, and Hart picked up the gadget and said, "Much obliged."

He walked into the bathroom, carrying the tan calfskin case.

Forty minutes later Frieda knocked on the bathroom door and said, "What are your plans?"

Hart had a towel around his middle and the bathroom was filled with steam from very hot water going out of the tub. He said, "I'll be out in a few minutes."

"There's breakfast for you when you come down," Frieda said.

"I'll be right down," Hart said.

Twenty minutes later he came downstairs wearing the chocolate brown suit and his own shoes. He wore Charley's white two-piece underwear and Charley's black silk hose with a green clock, Charley's white shirt, Charley's white starched collar, Charley's black tie with small green polka dots, Charley's white handkerchief in the breast pocket, and Charley's silver cuff links with jade facing.

Rizzio looked up from the sports section and looked at Hart. Then Rizzio, wearing a bathrobe and slippers, extended a flat palm toward Hart while looking at Charley and Mattone, who were reading other sections of the paper in other sections of the living room. And Rizzio said, "Look at this, look at this."

Mattone raised his head from Ed Sullivan's column, glanced at Hart and went back to Sullivan.

Charley looked up from the fourth page and examined Hart and nodded slowly. "I thought it was about the right fit," he said. "Where did you find the cuff links?"

"In the second drawer, way in the back, under some handkerchiefs."

Charley smiled. "I've been looking for those cuff links more than a year. I got them out of an estate in Chestnut Hill. Frieda's got breakfast for you."

Mattone raised his head again and looked at Charley.

Hart walked into the kitchen. Frieda was wearing the quilted robe of orchid satin. Myrna was at the sink, wearing a plain dress of checkered blue and yellow cotton.

Frieda put a tall glass of orange juice on the table and smiled at Hart and said, "Look, honey, there's got to be some stipulation about that bathroom."

"Was I in there long?" Hart said. He lifted the glass.

"It depends on what you call long," Frieda said. "What do you do in there?"

"Dream," Hart said. "But I'll cut it out. All I want is toast and coffee. Black. I'll be right back." He went out and came back seconds later with a lighted cigarette in his mouth.

Frieda said, "I fix up a banquet for him and all he wants is toast and coffee."

"I never eat more than that," Hart said. "My usual meal in the morning is six or seven cigarettes and three or four cups of black coffee without sugar. But if you've prepared something I'll eat it."

He finished the orange juice. Frieda was putting hot dishes on the table. He smiled at her. She walked back to the stove. When she came back to the table she poured coffee with her right hand and with her left hand she reached over and put a soft fat palm over Hart's mouth and with her soft fat fingers she gave his face a soft squeeze.

Myrna was placing dishes in a wall cabinet.

Hart lowered his head and began to eat his meal. Frieda put an ashtray in front of him. He balanced the cigarette on the ashtray and the smoke went up in front of his face as he ate slowly. Frieda and Myrna were moving around in the kitchen. Outside it was beginning to snow. The snow came down haphazardly at first, the flakes gradually forming a pattern as they came streaming down from a dismal grey sky, then all at once parading in thick white columns, an army of white, with limitless reserves. Hart asked Frieda for another cup of coffee, and he sat there sipping the coffee and watching the snow. All at once he sensed that Frieda was no longer in the kitchen. He turned and looked at Myrna. She was on her knees, reaching for something in the floor opening of the wall cabinet.

Hart said, "Hello, Myrna."

She turned and stood up and took two steps going backward. Her eyes were focused on the wall behind his head. She said, "Look, you. I don't want you to talk to me."

Hart took another gulp of coffee, got up and walked out of the kitchen. When he came into the living room he asked Rizzio for another cigarette.

"Let's have some radio," Mattone said.

Hart reached over and turned on the radio. A woman was weeping and a gentle elderly man was saying, "Now, now, Emily—"

Hart tried another station. A crisp young man was saying, "And Ladies, if you've never tried it you don't know what you've missed. Really, Ladies—"

Hart turned off the radio.

Rizzio peeled some pages from the section he was reading and handed the pages to Hart, and Hart tried to concentrate on the rapid progress of a young colored welterweight from Scranton and the boy from Pittsburgh this Scranton boy was slated to meet next week, and also on the card was a promising lightweight from Detroit; and Hart felt the quiet of the living room, the essence of something heavier than the quiet. He started to put down the paper so that he could get a look at Charley and Mattone and Rizzio, and when the paper was halfway down he saw that Charley and Mattone and Rizzio were watching him.

He started to read about how Temple had played a game of basketball with Penn State and the game went into several overtime periods. He liked basketball and at Penn he had played on one of the intramural teams, and this write-up should have interested him even if he had other things on his mind, but it didn't interest him.

He started to lower the paper again, bringing it to one side so he could get a look.

Then he looked and he saw them watching him, and he gazed back at them, one at a time, and finally brought his gaze to rest on Charley.

He was waiting for some sort of a break or a sign, and Charley wasn't giving him anything. He knew he was getting angry, and he sat there wondering whether it would be wise to get angry, or wise to try and stay calm in the face of a colder calm.

Finally Charley broke it. Charley said, "We were talking it over a little while ago. We thought maybe you were going to change your mind."

"Look," Hart said, and he stood up. "If I was going to change my mind I wouldn't let you know about it. I'd just pick myself up and walk out. Even then you wouldn't have anything to worry about, because I wouldn't gain anything by making speeches to the police or anybody. But that's a side issue. The main issue is your point of view, and it's up to you to decide whether I'm in or I'm out. If I'm in it's got to be all the way in. If I'm out you might as well tell me now and I'll leave the neighborhood."

"Don't get all upset," Charley said.

"I'm not upset. I'm just damned curious, that's all."

"That's understandable," Charley said. "It works both ways, we're curious about you and you're curious about us."

And Hart said, "What was it with Renner?"

Mattone turned to Charley and said, "Now do you see what's happening?"

Charley didn't hear what Mattone said. Charley looked at Hart and said, "We did away with Renner because he became greedy. His share of our last job was twelve hundred. He knew where I had the rest of the money and he did a sneak caper, took the eleven thousand and waited thirty minutes and then told me he wanted to buy something on Germantown Avenue. I already knew he had the money, so I took Paul and we went out and did away with him."

"That makes sense," Hart said.

"Sure it does," Charley murmured. Then he grinned. "What say we stop this talk and play some poker?"

They set up a card table, pulled chairs around it and sat down. Then Rizzio fanned a pack of cards on the table, scooped up the cards, riffled them, fanned them again, caressed them, tossed them up, turned them over, smacked then flat on the table and indicated them for a cut.

Charley cut the cards as he sat down.

"Open," Mattone said. "Quarter, half and seventy-five."

Frieda came in from the kitchen. She sat down at the table.

Rizzio picked up the deck, riffled the cards four times and extended them for another cut.

Charley again cut the cards.

Hart smiled and said, "I'll be a spectator."

"No," Charley said. "You did some work last night in the cellar. You get paid for that work. What do you think it was worth?"

"Around thirty," Hart said.

Charley took out some bills and selected three tens.

"Open," Mattone said. "Quarter, half and—"

"No," Frieda said. "Why should anybody get hurt? Make it closed poker, jacks or better to open the pot, nickel up and dime to open."

Frieda was sitting across from Hart and she smiled at him and he smiled back. Charley asked Rizzio for a cigarette and Rizzio got up from the table, ran upstairs and came down with three packs of cigarettes. He tossed the packs on the table, then eagerly gathered up the cards, riffled them, fanned them in a straight line, riffled them as he watched the others putting their money on the table, fanned the cards in a half-circle, then fanned them in a full circle, a perfect circle, then cut them

swiftly three times, held them in front of Hart and told
him to take one.

Hart took one, shuffled the deck, cut the deck, and
while he was cutting it again Rizzio grinned and said,
"All right, your card was a lady, right?"

"So far."

"A black lady."

"Right"

"A black lady in clubs," Rizzio said as he lit a cigarette.

"Right," Hart said, noticing that the others were busy
lighting cigarettes and arranging change and bills on the
table.

Rizzio riffled the cards, extended the deck to Hart, and
Hart cut the cards.

At the end of an hour Hart was winning ten dollars.

At the end of three hours Hart was down to a dollar
sixty-five.

When the game ended at five fifteen the following
morning, Hart had won three hundred and twenty
dollars. Frieda was ahead about fifty, Charley was even,
and Mattone and Rizzio were having a dull argument.
They were blaming each other for progressively suggest-
ing raising the ante.

CHAPTER 6

Next morning they slept late, started another poker game at three in the afternoon, finished it at four in the morning. This time Hart dropped sixty from his winnings, Frieda was a heavy loser and Charley was even again. On the following day Hart climbed out of bed at two in the afternoon. When he came downstairs he didn't see Charley or Mattone or Rizzio. He didn't see Myrna, either. He went into the kitchen where Frieda was mixing batter for a cake. She had her back turned to him and without looking up from what she was doing she told him to sit down and she'd serve him some breakfast.

He seated himself at the white-topped table. Lighting a cigarette, he said, "Don't fix anything. Just give me black coffee."

She went to the stove and put a fire under the percolator.

The morning paper was on the table and he picked it up and glanced at the front page. An airliner had crashed in the Mediterranean, no survivors. In downtown Philadelphia a stockbroker had tossed himself out of the ninth-floor window of his hotel. In City Hall the District Attorney was blaming the current wave of juvenile delinquency on television and the movies. A local theatre-owner was blaming the current wave of juvenile delinquency on the negligence of the District Attorney. Hart turned the pages and came to the sports section. He looked at a picture of Kid Gavilan in training camp.

Alongside the picture there was an interview with the Kid's manager.

Frieda poured coffee and put the cup in front of Hart. Then she stepped back and looked him over. He sat there and felt the pressure of her eyes. There was heat in the pressure and he started to wonder what her plans were. He told himself to let it ride, he didn't need anything she had, he didn't go for the meaty bulging type, and besides, a situation with Frieda would only complicate a set-up that was already damn well complicated.

"You look good today," Frieda said.

"Thanks."

The chocolate-brown flannel was holding up fairly well, and under it he wore one of Charley's high-priced white shirts and an olive-green tie with yellow diagonal stripes. His face was mowed smooth and his hair, although brushed dry, was a glimmering yellow. He had it brushed flat and smooth and Frieda put her fat hand on it, her palm gliding lightly across his head.

"Maybe I'll muss it up," Frieda said.

"I wish you wouldn't."

"Why not?"

"You might get excited."

"What's wrong with that?" Frieda asked.

"I think it might create a problem."

"Yeah?" Frieda spoke quietly. "That's one kind of problem I can always handle."

He looked at her. "You sure?"

She nodded solemnly.

"I wonder," he murmured.

"Don't let it bother you," Frieda said. "Let me take care of it. When I'm ready for you, I'll let you know."

He smiled slightly. He snapped his fingers. "Just like that?"

"Yeah." She snapped her fingers. "Just like that."

He told himself to change the subject. Turning his attention to the coffee, he said, "Where're the others?"

"Charley went out with Mattone and Rizzio. They're casing some real estate in Wyncote."

"And Myrna?"

"She's out shopping."

He waited a long moment, then said slowly, "You sent her out?"

"That's right," Frieda said. She put a little pause between each word. "I sent her out."

He was still trying to change the subject and he said, "How come Charley went out? I thought he'd stay inside a few more days. This neighborhood's still hot."

"It's cooled off a little," Frieda said. She picked up the newspaper, turned the pages and came to page four. Her finger pointed to a small headline near the bottom of the page.

Hart glanced through the story. It was about Renner. It said the body of the man found shot in Germantown had been identified as that of Frederick Renner, a former convict, wanted for skipping parole and suspected of several recent burglaries. Police said Renner was probably shot by a personal enemy or a business competitor. The tone of the story indicated that Renner's death was no loss to the public and the police wouldn't be knocking themselves out searching for the slayer.

"It looks like an all-clear," Hart said. "But then, the police are funny. You never know what they'll do."

"Charley knows," Frieda said. "They never fool Charley."

"Never?" He had it down near a whisper.

"That's what I said. Never. And that applies to other people, too. There's nobody can fool Charley. Not for long, anyway."

He decided to let it pass. Then he had a feeling he ought to take her up on that. She was getting at something and if it was going to come out, it might as well come out now.

He said, "Could you fool Charley?"

"I'd be crazy to try." She'd gone back to the shelf near the sink and she was busy again with the cake batter.

Hart waited a few moments and then he said, "What about me? You think I could fool him?"

As he said it, he was lifting the coffee cup to his mouth. He sipped the coffee and the only sound he heard was the gooey stirring of the wooden spoon in the batter bowl. The stirring went on and he sipped more coffee. Then he finished the cup and leaned back and lit a cigarette. And the sound of the stirring went on and on. He told himself she wasn't going to answer.

Then he heard her saying, "What do you think?"

"I'm asking you," he said.

She turned very slowly. "I'll tell you," she said. "If you were a mixture of Houdini and Thurston and the world's champion chess player, card shark and con man, your chances of fooling Charley would be one in a million."

"You quoting odds?"

"Sure as hell," Frieda nodded. "If I had a million I'd put it on Charley against your dollar bill."

"Without worrying?"

"Without a moment's thought."

He took a long drag from the cigarette. He let it out slowly. "Well," he murmured. "Well, now. That's very interesting."

"Yeah," Frieda said. She turned back to the cake batter. "It's something for you to think about. But don't let it throw you."

I'll try not to, he said without sound. But a tiny frown

appeared on his brow and began to grow. He took a tighter drag from the cigarette and hauled it down deep. He told his brain to pull away from Charley and think about Kid Gavilan or the British airliner. Or anything at all that would detour the worry. But the thing is, he said to himself, it's definitely something to worry about. It's what every living thing is constantly facing up against, the problem of staying alive. Except with you it's a matter of an inch here, an inch there, one wrong move, like with those German acrobats you saw not long ago in a picture magazine, they were walking a tightrope stretched between two peaks in the Alps, and under them was some six thousand feet of nothing. Well, what the hell, it might just as well have been six hundred feet. Or sixty feet. You fall sixty feet, you'll wind up in a casket just the same. And when they close the lid, it doesn't make any difference how you passed out, whether it was falling off the rope or down a flight of stairs or pneumonia or typhoid or going to sleep with the gas on. There now, that's getting us away from this Charley business. You think so? You mean, you hope so. I'll tell you something, though. It would be much easier if you didn't give a hang whether you lived to be ninety or thirty-five. Fact is, you do give a hang. So maybe the only move to make is get up from this chair and stroll out the door and keep strolling. Sure, that would be a smart move. Extremely brilliant, just like jumping into a vat of boiling hot oil, with some rookie policemen reaching in to pull you out and take you in and get their promotion. So the slogan for today is: Stay put, leave well enough alone. Just keep it in mind that you're sitting in a chair that's not electric but if you walk out you're headed for a piece of furniture that's strictly from high voltage. You might as well have another cup of coffee and another cigarette and more pleasant chatting with Frieda. That's some rear end she has there. Like a Cadillac. If she weighed some fifty pounds less you might be inclined to play around a little, just to kill time. But all that weight, that's not your speed.

"More coffee?" Frieda asked.

He nodded, and she gave him another cup. The batter was in the pan and the pan was in the oven, so now for a while she could sit down and rest. She took a chair at the table facing him, helped herself to one of his cigarettes, picked up his book of matches and lit it. He had his head lowered to get at the coffee in the cup, but in the instant before he sipped it, he ventured a glance at her face, aiming at her eyes, seeing what was in her eyes and knowing in that same instant that she was having trouble.

He knew there was something she wanted to tell him. It was something she wasn't allowed to tell him and she was very anxious to say it and so there she was with her problem. Well, whatever it was, it wouldn't come out of her unless he pulled it out. And the only way to pull it out was slow and easy, very careful.

The coffee cup was half empty before he spoke. He set the cup in the saucer and said, "I've been thinking what you said about Charley."

"Yeah," sort of sadly, regretfully. "I shouldn't of told you that."

"I'm glad you did."

"Why?" She leaned forward just a little. "Why are you glad?"

He shrugged. "It lets me know the score. It always helps to know the score."

"You think you got the complete picture?"

He didn't reply. His face didn't show anything. He was telling himself this was the only way to handle it.

She opened her mouth, closed it, opened it again, bit her lip as though trying to bite on the words to keep them from coming out. She said, "Let me tell you something—"

But then her lips were clamped tightly and she stared past him as though looking at a traffic light flashing red.

He spoke mildly, not too casually, just casual enough. "What is it? You want me for a boy friend? Is that what's bothering you?"

Her tone was matter-of-fact. "It happens I already got a boy friend."

"Mattone?"

"No," she said. "No, for Christ's sake. What made you think of Mattone?"

"He's very good looking."

"I wouldn't know. I've never gandered him that close. Only thing I'd wanna put on him is spit."

"What about Rizzio?"

She laughed dryly. "Rizzio's one for the books. I mean the kind of books you gotta buy in foreign countries, they're outlawed here."

"Well, like they always say, to each his own."

"Yeah, it's a good phrase." She said it as though there was something sour in her mouth. "Only trouble is, for some people it's more wishing than having. The one I got—"

And again she was biting her lip.

He said, "Is it Charley?"

She nodded.

"You don't really want him?"

"Sure I want him." She said it emphatically, sort of angrily. "I really go for him. And it's vice versa, he'd do anything for me. That is, anything he can do. But there's something the matter with his machinery and he can't."

"Never?"

She spoke dully, in the resigned tone of someone burdened with a blind or crippled relative. "Sometimes he drinks himself into a condition where he don't know what he's doing and then, somehow . . ."

"Well, that's something."

"Yeah, it's marvelous. It happens maybe once every three months."

He frowned slightly. "Say, that's no joke."

"You're wrong there," she said. "It's a big joke. It's gotta be a laugh, and Charley and me, we laugh about it all the time. If I didn't laugh—" she almost choked on the words, "—I'd flip my lid sure as hell."

"Would he care if you—?"

"No, he wouldn't care. If he's told me once, he's told me a hundred times to go out when I need it. As if it's a high-colonic, or something like that. He really means it, he ain't pulling my leg or testing my loyalty. He really wants me to have it, he says it's bad for my health to go without it too long."

Hart nodded seriously. "He's got something there."

She didn't say anything. She was staring at the table top.

"Well," Hart said, "it's no problem to get it on the outside. The streets are filled with men who'd be only too willing. You have the face, you have the body—"

"Sure, I know. I used to go for long walks and they'd give me the eye and then we'd get to talking. With a few of them I'd wind up having a drink somewhere. But that's as far as it would go. I'd always start thinking about Charley."

"Feeling guilty?"

She shook her head. "Nothing like that. Just comparing Charley with these four-star jerks, these absolute nothings. I swear, there wasn't one of them could budge me an inch. They had the looks, the clothes, the smooth approach, but underneath it was zero, no ignition."

"That isn't their fault. It's Charley. You're all wrapped up with Charley. He's got you paralyzed."

She sent a smile past him. "You think so?"

He shrugged. "It figures." Then a carefully-timed pause. And then, "Wouldn't you say it figures?"

The smile faded. She went on looking past him. "I don't know," she said. "I'm trying to see it. Get it added up. It's kind of hazy, it won't build. Something's in my head and it's Charley's face, the sound of his voice, the way he moves around, Jesus Christ, that's what's blocking me, I can't get the bastard out of my head—"

Hart told himself to keep his mouth shut.

Frieda lowered her head and pressed her hands to the sides of her face. She began to breathe hard. She started to lift her head, then forced it down. And suddenly she shivered as though a chunk of ice was applied to the back of her neck. Her hands came down hard on the table top and again she lifted her head and her eyes took hold of Hart.

"You," she said. "You've done it."

He sat there passively, waiting.

"You've done what none of the others could do," she said. "You've sent Charley away for awhile."

His lips scarcely moved. "Have I? You sure?"

It seemed there was flame coming out of her face. She stood up and said, "I'll prove it."

He saw her moving toward him. He felt her hand on his wrist, her fingers sliding across his knuckles and entwining with his fingers.

He heard her saying, "Come on, let's go upstairs."

CHAPTER 7

He sat there at the kitchen table and heard her saying it again. He was telling himself to sit there and not move a muscle. Now she was pulling at his arm and he smiled dimly and let his arm go limp. She gave a hard pull but in that instant he stiffened it and she felt the resistance.

She let go and stepped back and said, "What's the matter?"

"Nothing."

"Look at me," she said.

He looked at her. She had her hands on her bulging hips, her big breasts heaved and quivered. She spoke thickly. "Didn't you hear what I said? I said I'm ready."

"I heard you," he murmured.

"Come on," she said. "Come on, come on."

He didn't move. He went on looking at her. There was no expression on his face.

She gave him a side-glance, a frown getting started and deepening. "You want me to put it in writing or something? I'm telling you I'm ready."

"But I'm not."

She took another backward step. She blinked several times. Her lips scarcely moved as she said, "I don't get this."

"Add it up," he said.

"Add what?" She was near shrieking. "What's there to add?"

He didn't reply.

She was trying to calm down. She managed to breathe slower, and her voice quieted as she said, "What is it? Tell me. Let's get this straightened out."

"I wish we could," he said. He made it sound very soft and sincere. "I really wish we could."

She moved toward the table, pulled a chair close to him and sat down. She leaned forward and took hold of his hands. "Tell me," she said. "What's bothering you?"

"The blues," he said. He arranged a sad smile on his face. "I got the blues."

Frieda frowned again. "What do you mean? What kind of blues?"

"The time element," he said. "Let's call it the Calendar Blues."

She waited for him to explain that.

He said, "It goes something like this. You want me to show you a good time. You want us to go upstairs and have ourselves some fun. Well, that's all right. There's nothing wrong with that. Except I'm just not up to it. I'm thinking in terms of the calendar and how many days I'll stay alive."

She winced slightly. She gave him a side-glance and said, "That's a happy thought."

"Can't help it. It's there."

"But why? What makes you think—?"

"It's the situation," he said. "I'm here in this house like merchandise sold on a time-trial. If I meet the requirements, I'm in. If not—" He shrugged.

Frieda's eyes narrowed just a little. "You worried you won't make the grade?"

He didn't answer. He knew it was time to let her do the talking.

She said, "I can't give you no guarantees, only way I can put it is I'm betting you'll be around a long time.

When you first came here I wouldn't of given a dime for your chances. But then I watched your stock going up with Charley. For instance, that overcoat business. You said you stole the coat and Mattone called you a liar, so Charley phoned the store and sure enough the coat was hot. That was something. That put you on first base."

He shrugged again. "It's a long trip to home plate."

"I think you're getting there," she said.

He waited. He wondered if it would come now.

And then he heard her saying, "What really sent your stock way up was that deal with the wallet, when you came back and handed him the money. That made a big hit with Charley. Another thing. The thing with Paul. When you helped Charley to put him in the furnace. You did what Rizzio couldn't do, what Mattone couldn't do. I think that put you safe on third."

Now he could feel it coming and he had to restrain himself to keep from leaning forward expectantly.

"So what it amounts to," she said, "you're gradually proving you can meet the requirements. You're getting it across that you're really a professional."

And there it was. She'd given him the tip-off he'd been waiting for. She told him he would stay alive just as long as Charley had him checked and approved as a true-blue outlaw.

She said, "You get the drift? That's the big thing, that professional angle. Because we're strictly professional and we ain't got room here for no amateurs."

There was the slightest trace of challenge in the way she said it. He could see her eyes getting narrow again. He said to himself, Don't underestimate the brains of this girl; that head of hers is no empty tool box.

Frieda was saying, "You told Charley you're wanted for murder in New Orleans. You told him the set-up, what you did and why you did it and maybe by this time he's bought your story. Unless, of course—"

He waited for her to go on. She was looking at him and her eyes remained narrow.

"Unless what?" he murmured.

"Maybe you're bluffing."

He frowned.

"If you're bluffing," she said, "it's a cinch Charley's gonna find out. Like I told you, it just ain't possible to fool Charley."

He erased the frown. There was nothing special on his face as he said, "I gave him a few facts, that's all. A few straight facts. It happened in New Orleans, it was my brother who died, it was me who did it, and it was murder."

"You said you did it for money," she said. "And that makes it professional. If you'd done it for any other reason, it wouldn't have been professional. Most murders are strictly hate jobs. Or love jobs. Or something you do when you go crazy for a minute and then you're sorry. But when it's done for money it's purely a business transaction, it puts you in a special bracket, it makes you really a professional."

He thought: She's got me, she set the trap very nicely and I'll be damned if she hasn't got me.

"The way it stacks up," she said, "the fact you murdered somebody, that ain't important to Charley. Or who you murdered. Or the way you did it. Only thing Charley wants to know is why you did it. So you tell him you did it for money. And if he buys that, you're safe, you got a membership card, you're really in. But on the other hand, if he finds out you didn't do it for the money—"

"You think I was bluffing about that?"

"I don't think anything," Frieda said. "All I'm saying is,

if you told him the truth you got nothing to worry about. And if there's nothing to worry about, there's no reason to have the blues."

"You're right." He grinned. "They're gone away. No more blues."

She grinned back at him. "You sure?"

He nodded slowly.

She got up from the chair. "Well," she said, "I'm still in that same condition. I'm ready."

He stood up. "So am I."

She moved toward him and put her arm around his middle. His hand settled on the solid fat meat of her hip. The only feeling he had was the feeling of taking a ride he didn't want to take. But the thing to do was take it and like it, or anyway try to make her believe he was liking it. He thought: This is a very hungry woman and she won't settle for anything less than a first-class job. You disappoint her, you'll really be singing the blues. She's found the loophole in your New Orleans news item and all she needs to do is put a little bug in Charley's ear and next on the agenda is he does some checking and discovers you told him just one tiny untruth, you said you murdered your brother for money and Christ knows it wasn't for money, so when Charley finds out you're not a professional it's definitely the wind-up, he'll give you a kindly smile, a gentle goodbye, he'll put the bullet in you very quick and merciful. Well, all right then, we'll try to handle it so it won't wind up that way. We'll try to keep Frieda happy. It's sure taking us a long time to get upstairs. That's your fault, you're walking too slow. Let's negotiate these stairs a little faster. Another thing, let's give her a smile, get it sort of hot and eager, come on, put it across like they do in the movies when it's just pretending but they gotta make it seem real, like the way they do it when they're aiming for an Academy Award, but then if they don't get it they can try again next year, the lucky bastards, but for you it's just this one try and if you don't make good it's all options dropped, everything dropped, everything finished. Well now, here we are upstairs in the hall and there's the bedroom. Let's stop here just a moment or so and hold her a little tighter, let's give it some preliminary action, a blazing kiss deep to her mouth to let her know what's coming later. Well, that wasn't bad. Looks as though she liked that.

Frieda was taking off her clothes as they entered the room.

CHAPTER 8

It was a few hours later and Hart sat on the couch in the living room, reading a comic magazine. There was nothing else to read. Soon Charley came in with Mattone and Rizzio.

Their overcoats were flecked with snow. They took off the coats, doing it slowly, somewhat tiredly. Hart guessed they'd had a busy afternoon. Rizzio said, "I'm gonna take a nap before dinner," and he went upstairs. Mattone waited a few moments, then said, "I'll get some shut-eye, too," and moved toward the couch. Hart got up and took a chair on the other side of the room. Charley stood in the middle of the floor, pulling a folded sheet of paper from the inside pocket of his suit. He unfolded the paper and stood there reading some penciled notations and a roughly drawn diagram. From where Hart was sitting it was possible to see the diagram. It showed the exterior of a large mansion and the surrounding estate, with tennis courts and a stable and a four-car garage.

Some moments passed, and then without saying a word Charley came toward him and handed him the sheet of paper. Hart leaned back in the chair, puffing gently at the cigarette, seeing what was on the paper but not getting anything from it, getting only the soft but steady pressure from Charley's eyes aiming at his face. He knew that Charley was looking for a reaction and he told himself the best reaction was no reaction at all.

For the better part of a minute he continued to focus on

the diagram and the notes. Then, looking up at Charley, making it quiet and technical, "This looks very juicy."

Charley nodded. "The Kenniston estate. Ever hear of the Kennistons?"

Hart made a negative gesture.

"Society people," Charley said. "They really have it. Let's say around thirty, forty million. They got a lot of it invested in art treasures. Mostly oriental stuff, like jade and rose quartz and ivory. You familiar with that material?"

"A little," Hart said. "When'd you pick up on this?"

"Couple months ago. They loaned the collection to the Parkway Museum for a three-week exhibit. I went down and had a look at it. Mostly small items, about the size of your thumb. In terms of antique value it amounts to a big haul. Some of them things go back two, three thousand years."

Hart looked at the sheet of paper. He didn't say anything.

Charley went on, "As it stands now, it's around a million dollars' worth of goods. If we get it, I figure it'll bring around three fifty."

"That's high," Hart said. He wondered if it sounded professional.

"Yeah, I know it sounds high," Charley said. "But there's a hungry market for this kind of merchandise. They lost it ages ago and now they want it back."

"China?"

"Red China."

"Through what channel?"

"They got some people working here," Charley said. "They got other people in South America. And some in the islands. It goes from one place to another until it gets to China."

Hart glanced again at the sheet of paper. He said softly, very softly, "Three hundred and fifty grand."

"At least that," Charley murmured. He gestured toward the paper. "You like the layout?"

"I don't know yet," Hart said carefully, but with the feeling he was saying the wrong thing. And then, to himself, What else could you say?

Charley was saying, "We do it Friday. It's gonna be Friday night."

Without sound Hart said: Today is Wednesday. It's Wednesday and then comes Thursday and then Friday.

His eyes hit the diagram on the paper and stayed there and then it seemed the penciled drawing of the mansion was rising from the paper and moving toward his face. Then it was really the interior of the mansion and they were in there going for the art treasures, he was doing everything wrong and demonstrating his lack of professional acumen. Charley watched him and smiled at him and when they were outside and in the car, Charley showed him the gun and gave him a final smile and then shot him.

Friday, Hart thought. He remembered the dateline on today's *Inquirer*. It was January 11. So Friday would be the 13th. It had a black sound and he was telling himself that Friday would be a black day. But maybe not. Maybe if he could—

"The hell with it," he said aloud.

"What?" Charley murmured. "What's that?"

He grinned at Charley. He said, "I was thinking, some people are superstitious. I mean about Friday the thirteenth."

Charley was quiet for a long moment. He looked down at the carpet. He said, "Are you superstitious?"

"No," Hart said.

"Neither am I." Charley turned and gestured toward the couch where Mattone was sound asleep. "That one is."

"Friday the thirteenth," Hart said. "They call it Black Friday. You think he'll worry about that?"

"Let him worry. He's always worrying, anyway. Not a day passes he don't find something to worry about."

"All right." Hart gave a slight shrug. "It's all right with me."

Charley looked past him. "I wonder."

Hart grinned again. "I told you I wasn't superstitious."

"Yes, you told me." Charley went on looking past him. "You been telling me a lot of things. The more things you tell me, the more I wonder."

Hart held onto the grin, twisted it just a little, and said, "If you don't like it, Charley, you know what you can do."

Charley looked at him. For a very long moment Charley didn't speak. Then softly, "Maybe I don't know what to do. You wanna tell me what to do?"

The grin stayed there. And his voice was just as soft as Charley's. "You can go to hell, that's what."

"You kidding?"

"No, I'm not kidding," Hart said. "You called me a liar and I told you where to go."

"Don't get worked up," Charley said. "I didn't call you a liar."

"Look, Charley." He stood up. "I don't like to be insulted. You can dish it out to Mattone, to Rizzio, to anyone you choose. If they wanna take it, that's their business. But I won't take it. I never take it from anybody and I'm not taking it from you."

Charley inclined his head and gave Hart a slow up-and-down look. "Tell me something—" It was almost a whisper. "What are you trying to get across?"

"You want me to say it again?"

"Just say what you really mean."

"That's another insult." Hart's mouth scarcely moved. "You're piling them up, Charley."

Again Charley gave him the slow up-and-down and then he said, "It's too bad. I didn't think we'd have this. I was getting to like you."

There was a trace of honest sadness in Charley's tone. Hart began to feel a stiffness in his spine, he told himself he'd taken it maybe a little too far. Somewhere between his spine and his brain he could hear Frieda's voice again and she was saying: You can't fool Charley.

He heard Charley saying, "I actually figured we'd get to be chums."

Hart grinned again. "Go fishing together?"

"And skiing. I've always wanted to try skis but I never had anybody to go with. You know, it's lousy when you don't have a chum. Last time I had a real chum, I think I was twelve years old."

"But now, like the Bible says, it's time to put away childish things."

"You're so right," Charley said. "When you grow up it's a cold world and the only thing you can trust is an adding machine."

It was an opening, and Hart plunged into it. "I'm not asking you to trust me, Charley. I don't trust myself, not completely anyway. It all depends on the time and the place. I might pull a caper next month I wouldn't do today. But that's for the future, and what we're dealing with now is now. I have no plans for now except to be on your payroll and do what you say."

"Only for now," Charley mused. "That's putting things on a short-term contract."

"It's the best I can offer," Hart said. It sounded genuine

and as the words came out he knew it wouldn't need more words.

Charley said, "You know something, Al? I think you made a sale there."

Hart shrugged. He pressed his cigarette into an ash-tray. His other hand held the sheet of paper that showed the Kenniston estate in Wyncote. He looked down at the diagram of the mansion and frowned slightly and said, "Is this according to scale?"

"Not hardly," Charley said. "But I think you can esti-mate some fifty yards to each half-inch. From the gate to the front entrance it looks to be some fifteen hundred yards."

"That's a long walk."

"Yeah," Charley murmured dryly. "It might be a long run."

"They got dogs?"

"We saw two," Charley said. "They were big ones. Bad ones. But that won't be no problem, we got ourselves a dog expert, Rizzio. He's really an expert with dogs."

"What are these dogs?"

"Dobermans."

"He'd better be an expert," Hart said.

From the kitchen, Frieda was shouting, "Come on in, dinner's ready."

The six of them were seated at the table in the small din-ing room. They'd had tomato juice and now they were eating T-bone steak and salad with French dressing. It was a fine steak, cooked medium-rare and they were all busy with it.

Hart sat next to Rizzio, the two women sat across from him, and Mattone and Charley faced each other from the opposite ends of the table. Mattone was eating with his head down close to the plate and suddenly he raised his head and glowered at the table. Then he glowered at Frieda.

"What's the matter?" Frieda asked, her mouth crammed with steak and salad and buttered roll.

"Where's the A-1 sauce?" Mattone demanded.

"Look in the kitchen," Frieda said. "On the shelf near the icebox."

Mattone looked at Myrna. "Get it for me."

"Get it yourself," Myrna said.

She said it very quietly. But there was something about the way she said it. They'd all stopped eating and they were looking at her.

"Get me the A-1 sauce," Mattone said. "And I'm not gonna ask you again."

"That's all right with me," Myrna said.

Mattone put down his knife and fork.

"All right," Charley said. "All right."

"No," Mattone said. "No, Charley. It ain't all right."

Charley looked up at the ceiling. "Get him the sauce," he said.

Myrna didn't move. She had the knife going into her steak while she steadied it with the fork. No one else was eating and they were all watching her as she sliced the steak. She wasn't even looking at the steak. It was hard to tell what she was looking at. And Hart began to have the feeling that her refusal to wait on Mattone had nothing to do with Mattone.

Rizzio pushed back his chair. "I'll get it," he said, and he started to rise. But Mattone pushed him back and said, "You sit there. She'll get it," and then Frieda said, "Aw, the hell with this. I'll get it," but Mattone motioned her to stay where she was. Mattone said, "She's gonna get that bottle of sauce for me, you hear? Her job here is house cleaning and helping with the cooking and waiting on the table. She gets paid for it and she's gonna do it."

Mattone's mouth was clamped very tightly and he was looking at Myrna. He had his hands gripping the edge of the table, his knuckles white and getting whiter. Charley was watching him, studying him, and then Charley started to get up, but just then Mattone made his move, leaping up and then sideways with his arm shooting out, his fingers closing on Myrna's wrist and twisting hard so that she dropped the knife. But her other hand held onto the fork and as Mattone went on twisting her wrist it seemed she didn't feel the pain, she made no sound, her face was expressionless while she hauled off with the fork and then jabbed it into his arm just below the shoulder.

"Jesus Christ," Mattone screamed. He staggered back, grabbing at his punctured arm. He bumped against his chair, knocked it over, then stumbled over it and went to the floor.

Rizzio was up, Frieda was up, and they helped Mattone off the floor. Charley was looking at Myrna, and Hart was looking at the bloody prongs of the fork in her hand. Now it was quiet in the room and they were removing Mattone's jacket. His shirtsleeve near the shoulder was getting drenched bright red, the blood was coming out fast. His eyes popped as he watched his shirtsleeve getting redder, the stain widening. The injured arm hung loose and his other arm quivered as he started to unbutton his shirt. His fingers fumbled with the buttons and Frieda grunted impatiently, stepped in close, pulled the shirt free of his trousers, got a firm hold on the white broadcloth, and ripped it up the front.

"My shirt," Mattone wailed. "You're tearing my shirt—"

Frieda went on ripping the shirt. She sliced it all the way up the front, then over the shoulder and down the back.

"You've ruined it," Mattone screeched. He sounded almost hysterical. "Imported broadcloth – twenty-three fifty – it was made to measure—"

"Shut up," Frieda said freeing the sleeve from the torn shirt. "Get something," she said to no one in particular. "We got any peroxide?"

"I'll look," Charley said. He gave a slight sigh as he got up from the table.

Frieda had arranged a folded rag from a piece of the torn shirt and she was wiping the blood from Mattone's arm. Mattone was speaking quietly now and his features were calm. He gazed at Myrna and said, "Look what you did. Take a look at my arm."

Myrna didn't seem to hear. She was in her chair again, looking at the knife on her plate. Her face was pale but placid and there was nothing in her eyes. Hart told himself that maybe she'd really cracked and he wondered if there was a way to test her. Or maybe, he thought, you better stay out of it, you're not involved in this. Oh yeah? The hell you're not. You're planted right in the middle, brother, it's you she's really after and you know it and you know why.

He decided to test Myrna's condition and his hand went into his jacket pocket, came out with his cigarettes. He offered her the pack, saying, "Have a smoke?"

But there was no reaction. She continued to look at the knife resting on the plate. Frieda and Rizzio and Mattone were watching, wondering what Hart was trying to prove.

"No peroxide. All we got is iodine." It was Charley coming into the room with iodine and a wet washrag and some Band-Aids. He saw what Hart was doing with the pack of cigarettes and he frowned slightly and murmured, "What's happening now?"

"I think she's sick," Hart said.

"No." It was Mattone. He was grinning loosely and saying, "She ain't sick. You know she ain't sick. You know what's the matter with her."

Hart didn't reply. Charley handed the washrag and iodine to Frieda and she applied the wet cloth to the holes in Mattone's arm. Rizzio went back to his chair and resumed eating his steak. Frieda was busy now with the iodine. It appeared that Mattone didn't feel the iodine, he was still grinning at Hart. The Band-Aids were resting on the table and there were four of them and Frieda was picking them up one by one and securing them over the holes in Mattone's arm. Now Charley had returned to his chair and he went back to where he'd left off with the T-bone on his plate. Frieda completed her work with the Band-Aids and moved back to her place next to Myrna, while Mattone stood up and walked slowly out of the room. Then it was quiet in the room and they were all eating their steaks and salad, with the exception of Myrna who continued to sit there with the placid look on her face, the nothingness in her eyes, her eyes aiming at the knife. Hart was telling himself to give his undivided attention to the meat on his plate. But while he chewed on the steak his brain stalled on him, then stumbled away from where he was trying to steer it, his thoughts went lurching and tumbling down an actual flight of stairs to the actual cellar to the actual furnace. He was seeing Myrna's brother getting chopped up and tossed into the furnace. Then he went back to the moment when his knee had made contact with Paul, thudding into Paul's groin, doing something to Paul's insides causing things to go wrong, causing hemorrhage and then the finish, causing the girl to lose her brother. So what he'd taken away from her was something that couldn't be replaced, and now he remembered his talk with Myrna in the living room the night Paul died and she was dazed then with the shock of it, the hurt and the hate hadn't yet set in. And so now, not wanting to look at her, he was forced to look at her and he saw the small skinny girl with the black hair and the violet eyes and the pale placid face. Just five-two, and if the scale showed more than ninety-five pounds there was something wrong with the scale. She looked so little sitting there. And yet he knew he was looking at trouble, big trouble, something more threatening than anything else dangling over his head. He wondered if maybe he could somehow talk to her and—

A blast of music came into the dining room. It was hot jazz jumping out of the radio in the living room, followed by footsteps and then Mattone coming in wearing a fresh shirt and a hand-painted necktie and the same grin he'd worn when he'd walked out. Hart saw the grin was aimed at him and he heard Charley saying, "All right now, Mattone. Cut it out."

"What am I doing?" Mattone asked mildly.

"I said cut it out."

Mattone walked past the table, moving behind Hart, and went into the kitchen. Then he came out of the kitchen and in his hand was the bottle of A-1 sauce. He sat down and poured the sauce on his lukewarm steak. He reached for a roll with his uninjured arm, put a thick dab of butter on the roll. He took a generous bite of the roll, then sliced a big chunk of steak. He shoved the steak into his mouth and chewed energetically and while he did this he was grinning again at Hart.

From the living room there was a trumpet blast climbing high while the drummer banged with all his might on the cymbal, and Rizzio whined, "For Christ's sake. We need all that noise?"

"Leave it on," Mattone said. "It's Dizzy Gillespie. I like Dizzy Gillespie."

"It sounds like someone caught under a steamroller," Frieda said.

"Not exactly," Mattone said. "It ain't like what comes out of the mouth." For some moments the grin was gone, he'd stopped chewing on the steak, he was frowning thoughtfully. And then, "I'll tell you what it is. It's—"

"It's bebop," Rizzio said. "Ain't it bebop?"

"Sure it's bop," Mattone nodded. "But that ain't what I mean. What I mean is – well, when Dizzy takes it way up, gets all the way up there higher than high, he's telling you something, he's putting it to you straight, telling you what it sounds like inside."

"Inside what?" Rizzio asked.

"In here," Mattone said, and he indicated his head and his chest. "You get it?"

"No," Rizzio said.

"Because you're an imbecile," Mattone told him amiably. "It takes someone with brains to understand what I mean. Like our friend here," and he pointed his finger at Hart.

"You starting again?" Charley asked quietly. "Ain't we had enough for one night?"

"I'm just making conversation," Mattone answered. "Sure, our friend here knows what I mean. He knows what she sounds like inside."

"Leave him alone." Charley's voice climbed just a little.

"I'm not bothering him," Mattone said. "It's the girl here. She's bothering him. She's got him worried plenty."

"Oh, for God's sake," Frieda protested. "Do something, Charley. Make him stop."

Charley gave Mattone a very thin smile. It was on the order of a final warning.

But Mattone had started it and couldn't stop it, the way certain reptiles are biologically unable to stop a meal once the victim's head is in their mouth. Mattone said, "She stabs me with the fork but it's really him she wants to stab. And not in the arm, either."

Charley started to rise from his chair.

But Hart reached out and put his hand on Charley's shoulder. "Sit there," Hart murmured. "Let him talk. I want to hear the rest of this."

"Sure you do," Mattone grinned. "You wanna see if it checks with what you're thinking. Ain't that correct?"

Hart nodded slowly. And now he was looking at Myrna. She had raised her head slightly and her eyes were focused blankly on his chin, or maybe his throat, he wasn't quite sure.

"You see the way it figures?" Mattone asked the other faces at the table. "She has it in for him and she takes it out on me. That happens sometimes, I guess. When they get so mixed up they don't know what they're trying to hit, they hit what's closest. But sooner or later they straighten their aim. It's just a question of time."

"You louse." Frieda gave Mattone a disgusted look.

"Me?" Mattone pointed to himself innocently. "You got it backwards, Frieda. I'm only trying to lend a hand. I'd hate to see him get hurt."

"Yeah," Frieda said. "Yeah. Sure."

"I'm giving him advice, that's all," Mattone said. "Just telling him to be careful. To keep his eyes on her. Watch every move she makes. Or maybe—" he hesitated a moment, then let it slide out, "—he oughta do the safest thing and take off."

It was heavily quiet for some moments. Frieda was looking at Charley, waiting for Charley to get up again and go for Mattone. But Charley didn't move. Charley was watching Myrna. She ended the quiet with the scraping of her chair. Then she was up from the table, going around it very slowly, moving somewhat like a sleepwalker as she went out of the room.

Rizzio said, "Who wants coffee?"

"We'll all have coffee," Frieda said. "You got any poisoned coffee for Mattone?"

Charley looked at Frieda. Then he looked at Hart. Then he gazed at Frieda again, and his head moved in an almost imperceptible nod. "Any liquor?" he asked.

"We got some bourbon and some gin."

"Bring the gin," Charley said.

"What's the matter now?" Mattone was staring from face to face and getting no answer.

"It don't concern you," Charley said. His gaze moved back and forth quickly between Frieda and Hart.

Rizzio came in with the gin. He was frowning, puzzled, because Charley rarely went for gin, went for it only when something happened to knock him off balance and he urgently needed a bracer.

Charley took the bottle and began pouring the gin into a water glass. He got the glass three-quarters full. He lifted the glass to his mouth and drank the gin as though it was water.

The radio was playing more bebop. It was Dizzy Gillespie again and Dizzy's trumpet went up and up and way up.

CHAPTER 9

"You'll get sick," Frieda said. She watched the gin flowing from the bottle to the water glass. Charley was on his fourth glass and Hart estimated that Charley had already consumed more than a pint of gin. Mattone had finished his coffee and left the table, and now Rizzio was getting up.

"You're burning up your liver," Frieda said. She was trying to keep her voice down. "It'll be like the last time, you'll hafta have your stomach pumped out."

Charley smiled at Hart. "Want some gin?"

"No thanks," Hart said.

"Don't you like gin?"

"Not especially."

"It's a thin drink," Charley said. His smile was sort of loose. "Not much body to it."

Hart didn't say anything.

"Maybe that's the reason you don't like it," Charley said. "Maybe you like something with more body."

"What's that mean?" Hart asked. He said to himself: You know what it means, all right.

"He means me," Frieda said. She was starting to breathe hard. "Ain't that it, Charley?"

Charley put the smile on Frieda. "You want a drink?"

"No," Frieda said. Now suddenly she was breathing very hard. She looked at Hart. "Go in the other room. You don't figure in this—"

"Not much he don't," Charley said softly. Then he

chuckled, but only with his mouth. His eyes were fixed icily on a path going straight ahead at the wall and through the wall. "Way this stacks up, it's a three-sided discussion."

"It don't hafta be," Frieda said. "You're just making it that way."

"No, lady," Charley said. "It's already made. It was made this afternoon, while I was out." And then, after a long pause, "Tell me, lady. How was it?"

"You're not funny, Charley."

"Oh, but you're wrong, lady. You're so wrong. I'm very funny. You wanna know something? I'm the funniest man I've ever met."

"All right," Frieda said. "Drink your gin. Drink it up and get yourself unconscious and I'll put you to bed."

Charley chuckled again. "Don't get excited, Frieda. What's there to get excited about? After all, it's a perfectly natural state of affairs. You can't get it from me, so you get it from someone else—"

"So?" Frieda shouted it. "Ain't that what you told me to do? You said it was all right if I—"

"Yes," Charley cut in softly.

"Then why the complaint? What are you complaining about?"

Charley didn't reply. He was chuckling again.

"Answer me," Frieda demanded. "Damn you, Charley—"

Charley stopped chuckling. He looked at Hart. He said, "You get the picture? You see what's happening here?"

"I don't see anything," Hart said.

"She really goes for you," Charley said. "You musta showed her a very nice time this afternoon. Musta given her something special."

Hart shrugged.

Charley said, "That's why she got burned up at Mattone when he advised you to take off. She'd be very upset if you took off."

Frieda stood up. She had her eyes aiming at empty air just about midway between Charley and Hart. She didn't say anything.

Charley went on talking as though Frieda was not in the room. "Maybe she's told you about me. About me and her, I mean. Like how it amounts to a problem because I'm jammed up somewhere inside and I can't do anything for her except on rare occasions. So there's no sense being a dog in the manger and I told her to get it from someone else. I think that was a nice gesture on my part. Don't you think so?"

Hart nodded.

"What I think," Charley went on, "it was a very nice gesture but the trouble is, every time I make these nice gestures I get taken for a ride. It never fails. It reminds me, one time I had a pet canary, really a dandy of a bird, I paid plenty for it. But the cage, it looks so stingy, not hardly big enough for the bird to fly around and get the proper exercise. So one day I open the cage and I figure she'll fly around the room and then come back and perch on my shoulder. And that's how I come to lose her. The window is open and out she goes."

It was quiet for some moments.

Then Charley looked at Frieda. And he said, "It ain't your fault, lady. I'm not blaming you."

Frieda remained standing. She went on staring at the empty space between Charley and Hart. She said, "He says it ain't my fault. He says—"

"I'm saying it's nobody's fault," Charley smiled. "If we gotta blame something, let's blame it on the climate. We got a weird climate here in Philadelphia."

Frieda closed her eyes. She put her hands to the sides of her head and her eyes stayed closed and she groaned.

"Yes," Charley murmured. "It hurts me, too. You got no idea how it hurts me."

Frieda opened her eyes. She looked at Charley. Her arms were lifted just a little, somewhat pleadingly. "Can't we—?"

"No," Charley said. "I wish we could, lady. But we can't. We just can't. If you wanted him just for a playmate I guess the three of us could manage it somehow, we could have an understanding. But it's more than having bedroom parties, you want him all the way, you got him so deep in your system you can feel him without touching him. So that chops it off between you and me."

"Complete?" Frieda's head was down.

"Clean break," Charley nodded. "We drop it, we forget about it, and you have my guarantee there won't be any grief."

"Charley—" She spoke thickly. "I wasn't looking for this to happen. I swear to you, Charley, it was—"

"The climate," Charley said. "We're always getting weather we don't expect."

In spades, Hart thought. He saw Charley getting up from the table, reaching for the bottle of gin, the bottle nestled gently in Charley's arm, pressed affectionately to Charley's chest. Then Charley was walking out of the room. For several moments nothing happened, and Hart sat there listening to Charley's footsteps moving off through the house and climbing up the stairs. When the sound of the footsteps was up there on the second floor, he heard other footsteps moving toward him. He looked up and saw Frieda approaching. She came in close and put her big beefy arms around him, sliding her fat rump onto his lap. She put her thick lips against his mouth.

Damn it, he said to himself. Damn it to hell.

CHAPTER 10

Later that night Hart sat with Mattone and Rizzio, they were in the living room playing poker. Charley was upstairs in his room, out cold on the bed with the empty gin bottle clutched in both hands. They'd tried to free the bottle from his grip when he'd passed out, but it was as though his fingers were bolted to the glass and finally they gave it up. That was a couple hours ago, and now it was past eleven and the poker game had been in progress some ninety minutes. At this point the big winner was Mattone, with Rizzio a few dollars ahead and Hart's finances going down and down and getting close to nothing. Every now and then he'd get good cards but he couldn't do anything with them, he was distracted by sounds from upstairs where Frieda was hauling her belongings from one room to another. The sounds told him that Frieda was moving out of the room she shared with Myrna, taking her things into the room she would now share with him.

At half past eleven Hart was down to three dollars and Mattone looked at the two bills and the silver and said, "You're nearly bankrupt."

"You want it?" Hart asked, pointing to the three dollars.

"Sure," Mattone grinned. "It's U.S. currency, ain't it?"

"Come on," Rizzio said to Mattone. "Deal the cards—"

"Wait," Hart murmured. He looked down at the three dollars. "Take it, Mattone. I'm giving it to you."

"No," Mattone said.

"Go on." He smiled at Mattone. "Take it."

"What is this?" Rizzio asked the two of them. "What goes on here?"

"He's offering me a gift," Mattone said.

Rizzio grimaced puzzledly. "I don't get it."

"I do," Mattone said.

"The hell you do," Hart told him. "You couldn't figure it if you had twice the brains you have."

"Listen, buddy." Mattone leaned forward just a little. "Do yourself a favor. Don't underestimate my brains."

"We gonna play poker?" Rizzio spoke impatiently.

"We're playing it now." Mattone was handling the deck, his fingers smooth on the cards, lightly shifting the cards from one hand to the other while he gazed intently at Hart's face. "I think this is bigger stakes than just cash."

"What in Christ's name goes on here?" Rizzio demanded.

"It's what they call bait," Mattone said to Rizzio. "He's tossing me a chunk of bait, that's all. If I nibble, he'll make it more. He'll wind up offering me a lot more than three dollars if I sign up with his team."

"What team?" Rizzio frowned.

"That team sitting there," Mattone said, pointing to Hart. "It's him and him and him. That's all he's got on his side. Just himself. He's looking for a team-mate."

"But—" Rizzio scratched the top of his head. "But that don't fit the picture. It ain't as if he's working alone. He's in with us, ain't he?"

Mattone pushed his eyebrows up. "Really?" he murmured, trying to be suave about it. "Where'd you get that flash?"

Rizzio shrugged stupidly. "Well, I just took it for granted—"

"The thing is," Mattone said, his voice like light oil, "never take anything for granted, Rizzio. Not in this house. Not when you're working for Charley."

"I thought—"

"That's another mistake you make," Mattone schooled him. "You always forget that Charley does all the thinking here."

Rizzio considered it for a moment, then nodded slowly and mumbled, "Maybe you're right."

"Of course I'm right," Mattone said. He leaned back comfortably and continued to pass the deck from one hand to the other. He'd reduced the grin to a thin smile and had it floating toward Hart, using it like a feather to tickle Hart's chin.

There was another noise from upstairs. It was a tiny noise, just a slight scraping of something against the floor and Mattone didn't hear it, Rizzio didn't hear it, but Hart heard it distinctly and acutely and he thought: She's moving things around in that room, putting this chair here and that chair there, and it's a cinch you'll soon be hearing the sound of the bedsprings when she tries the mattress. You're in for some heavy work with that Frieda and this afternoon was just a light session compared to what it's going to be from here on in. You're really in for it now, you'll be doing it and hating it. All right, let's walk away from that; it isn't bedtime yet. You're sitting here facing Mattone, not Frieda, and he's under the impression the only thing you got on your chest is him and his oily smile, his smooth talk that tries so hard to slide under your skin. He'd jump for joy if you'd start sweating and cracking up. I think if you let him take it far enough he could really get on your nerves. He's certainly a skunk and although the only way to deal with skunks is keep far away from them it stands to reason you can't put distance between yourself and this one here, so what's to do except get up there on the mound and pitch a few at his head. We'll see if we can get that smile off his face.

He heard Mattone saying, "You look lonesome, mister. I never seen anyone look so lonesome."

"It isn't that," he said. He looked down at the three dollars. "I was wondering about this," indicating the money. "Just trying to remember why I offered it to you."

"But I told you why," with the light oil dripping again, the smile ever so soft and thin. "You want me on your team."

Hart pretended a thoughtful frown. He spoke absently. "No, I don't think so. It couldn't be for that reason."

"Wanna bet?" And Mattone flicked a wink at Rizzio.

"What I think is—" Hart held onto the thoughtful frown, his voice vague as he imitated someone talking aloud to himself, "—maybe there was no reason at all."

"You can't fool me," Mattone sneered. "I ain't no imbecile like this one here," pointing to Rizzio. The pointing finger moved so that it aimed at the three dollars. "Three worms on the hook, that's what it is. You're lonesome and you want company. You're scared and you want help."

"That would make sense," Hart said, still frowning thoughtfully, "except for a list of items we maybe ought to look at."

"All right," Mattone said. He tried to put a sneer in it. "Let's take a look."

"First thing," Hart said, "the girl. What's her name again?"

"Myrna. Her name is Myrna." And Mattone glanced sideways at his injured arm.

"Well, what I'm saying is," Hart said, "that's item one and we can cross it off; the girl doesn't scare me."

"You sure?" Mattone prodded.

Hart shrugged. He tossed it away with, "She tries anything, I'll clip her in the teeth."

Mattone was trying to be suave again, the oil coming back to his voice as he said, "That's a privilege reserved side. This ain't no social club where all you gotta do is pay a fee to join up. This is what they call a very tight outfit, and as far as you're concerned I'm willing to bet—"

"Save your money," Hart spoke softly. And then he pitched it, "I get the wire from Charley I'm working Friday night."

"Friday—" Mattone blinked a few times. "Charley told you about Friday night?"

This is fun, Hart said to himself. He was nodding slowly, saying, "The Kenniston place."

Mattone looked at Rizzio and said, "You hear this?"

"So?" Rizzio made a meaningless gesture. "So I hear it. So what?"

Mattone had his mouth open but he couldn't talk.

Hart said, "That crosses off item two. I think it sorta louses up your theory that I'm scared. Don't you think so?"

There was no answer, not in words, anyway. Mattone made a straining effort to say something, but all that came out was a twisted grunt.

"Another thing you said," Hart went on, "you made the claim I'm lonesome and I want company. And that brings up item three. It's a little favor Charley did for me tonight, the kind of favor he wouldn't do if I was on the outside or even halfway in, or let's say ninety-nine percent in. He did something an Eskimo husband does when you're his guest, except the Eskimo gives her to you for only one night, and Charley's letting me have her on a permanent basis. He's—"

It didn't need more than that. Mattone had leaped up and the deck of cards was out of his hand, the cards flying off the table.

"You're—" Mattone wrestled with it, choked on it. "You've done it, haven't you? You've really moved in."

Hart didn't reply. He sat there looking at the dismay and defeat in Mattone's eyes. He wondered what showed in his own eyes. Whatever it was, it had nothing to do with contentment. He told himself he mustn't let it show, and he tried to get it out of his eyes but before he could do that he heard a squeak from the mattress upstairs.

And he heard Mattone saying, "You don't seem happy about it."

He shrugged. So here it is, he said to himself. It shows and you know it shows, there comes a time when you just can't pretend.

The truth of it sent a slight quiver along his spine. Mattone was correct after all, you're scared and you're lonesome, there's no one on your team but you and you and you. It's a kind of starvation, and it isn't easy to take, that's for sure. Damn sure.

CHAPTER 11

But later of course it was pretending again when in the bed with Frieda. Somehow it was easier than it had been in the afternoon, but that was due to the darkness of the room, in the afternoon the daylight factor had handicapped him because every now and then she wanted him to look at her. Now in the dark she couldn't ask him to do that, except at one point she murmured maybe they ought to switch on the lamp. He didn't say anything, but kept her too busy to execute the idea.

The sighs that came from his lips were sheer pleasure. But if she'd switched on the lamp and seen the look on his face it would have gone bad, because the look on his face was the tight-wrinkled grimace of doing something extremely unpleasant. There was no way to rub off the grimace; it would stay there just as long as the ordeal went on, the hammering ordeal of feeling the insistency of her fat arms around him, her gasping and moaning that was inexhaustible. From time to time he'd wonder what the clock showed. Its illuminated face was on the table across the room but he couldn't even turn his head to look, she was holding him too tightly.

Yet all at once she loosened her hold and mumbled, "Cigarette," and he rolled away from her, an almost frenzied motion like a fish rolling out of a loosened net. The cigarettes and matches were on the floor and as he reached down blindly he almost fell off the bed.

He heard her saying, "Whatsa matter? You tired."

"Me?" He held back a crazy laugh. "I haven't even started yet."

She took him seriously. She said, "I knew it the first time I put eyes on you."

He handed her a lit cigarette, took a long puff from his own. He was resting flat on his back and gazing across the room at the clock whose green numbers showed twenty minutes past three.

"Tell me something," she said.

"Like what?"

"Anything," she said. "Just talk to me."

"All right." He thought for a moment. And then, not too sure of where it would go, "Ever hear of Indianapolis?"

"Where they teach the sailors?"

"No," he said. "Not Annapolis. Indianapolis."

"So?"

"It's where they have the big race. The auto race."

"On the fourth of July?"

"Memorial Day."

"That's what I said. The fourth of July?" She sounded rather sleepy. Or maybe it was because she had no interest in the topic.

He said, "It's May thirtieth. You're getting your holidays mixed up."

"What?" And then, more distinctly, "What the hell are we talking about?"

"Indianapolis," he said. "The five-hundred-mile race on Memorial Day."

"You were in it?" Sleepily again. "You a racing car driver?"

"No," he said, "just a spectator. I guess you'd call me a fan. This thing at Indianapolis is something to see and every chance I had I'd go there. I remember one year I was lucky and made friends with some mechanics, and they let me hang around the pits. The pits are where the cars come in for fuel and repairs. It's all very interesting, the way they change a tire in thirty seconds, and when it's the engine they jump right into it and it's fixed in no time at all. And they—"

"All right, all right. What's the point?"

As though she hadn't spoken, he went on, "—they cater to that car as though it's something alive. It's a very expensive piece of engineering, and when you look at the motor, you know it's something out of the ordinary. You know that's stamina there, that's real stamina, it'll never wear out."

She blew some smoke out of her mouth. She didn't say anything.

Hart said, "What happens, though, some drivers are too anxious and they forget the race is for five hundred miles, they force it too much, and after a hundred laps or so it can't take the strain and there's a breakdown. Sometimes it's a serious breakdown, the kind they can't fix in the pits. So then the car is out of the race, and it's a pity, really. You see the driver biting his lip to keep from crying like a baby. But of course he has no one to blame but himself."

She remained quiet for some moments. And then, her voice low but not at all sleepy, "You making stipulations?"

"Not exactly."

"Come on, come on." She sat up, looking down at him in the darkness. "Let's not play party games. You wanna tell me something, come on and tell me."

"Well—" and he paused for a timing effect, "I don't want to spoil anything—"

"Be careful, mister." It was a definite warning, as

though she had a can of lye in her hand. "Be very careful."

"I'll try my best," he said.

"Is that for a laugh? If it is, I'm not laughing."

"Look—" and again he timed it, used the tiny interval of quiet to drag at his cigarette. "Whaddya say we drop it?"

"No." She sat up straighter. "This deal is for keeps and we're gonna settle all issues right at the beginning."

"For keeps," he murmured thoughtfully. "That's a lot longer than five hundred miles."

"You'll last it out," she said. "I'm not worried about that."

"It's more than just that," he said. "On my side everything checks, I know exactly where I stand. But you sound as though you're not sure—"

"Me?" Her voice was harsh with a sort of fishwife intimacy. "Did I bring up this thing about Annapolis?"

"I'll tell you, Frieda," he said conversationally. "It's your driving technique I'm getting at. It started me to thinking about that racing car. About the way it breaks down when you push it too fast. Or maybe – you're doing it deliberately."

"Doing what?"

"Getting all you can while the getting is good."

"Whadda ya mean? You mean I'm worried you'll change your mind?"

"No, that isn't what I mean."

"Then what the hell do you mean?"

"I mean, maybe you're worried about yourself. That maybe you'll change your own mind."

"And toss you overboard?"

"That's one way of putting it."

"But why would I do that?" Her voice lowered just a

trifle, there was a trace of uncertainty in her tone. "Why would I give you up when I know you fill the bill completely, when I got what I been looking for, all them months and months of waiting, and then it comes along and I get it, so now I have it and why should I give it up?"

"I can't tell you. I'm waiting for you to tell me."

"Now look," she said, "this talk is getting on my nerves."

"All right. Let's go to sleep."

There was an ashtray on the floor and he took the stubs of their cigarettes and mashed them in the tray. Then, settling himself on his side, he worked his head comfortably into the pillow. Frieda remained sitting up, staring into the dark. After a while, she was reaching over the side of the bed, going for the cigarettes and the matches and the ashtray.

Hart was drifting into sleep and going down and getting the good cloudy feeling that comes just before the slumber takes hold, and then he heard the noise of a match against a matchbook. He smiled dimly and thought, There's nothing like tobacco to steady the nerves.

And a little while later he heard it again, match against matchbook. His eyes were open now because he wanted to stay awake, he liked this noise she was making striking matches. Now there was a lot of smoke around the head of the bed and he inhaled it, sensed the thickness of it and knew she was taking long, thirsty drags.

He was counting it off each time she struck a match, and now she was on the fifth cigarette. He said to himself: Let's figure seven or eight minutes for each cigarette; that makes it around forty minutes she's been sitting there with her problem, the way she's eating up that smoke she's nowhere near getting it solved, or maybe she has it solved already and she doesn't like what came out in the answer. One thing for sure, it's no fun for her. I'll tell you something here, it begins to look as though Charley was right when he said she really went for you, went a long ways deeper than just wanting you for this horizontal business, I'm ready to think she's got what they call the real feeling, and that's bad no that's good no that's bad, oh make up your mind, for Christ's sake, get your strategy straight, will you? This is a fine time to take your hands off the wheel, like on the north turn at Indianapolis – and what got you started with Indianapolis, anyway? You fell right into trouble with that one. And tried to climb out and fell in deeper when you put the problem in her lap, putting a smile on your face when you thought you had her backed up in a corner, when all the time it's you who's pressed against the wall, it oughta be you sitting up and chewing on cigarettes, and there she goes lighting up number six—

A few moments later her hand was on his shoulder.

"You sleeping?" she asked.

He didn't answer.

"Wake up," she said. She shook him.

He imitated a yawn. "What time is it?"

"Come on, wake up. We're getting dressed."

"What?" He frowned, his eyes aiming across to the clock that stated ten minutes past four. He said, "Are you kidding? It's still dark outside."

"That's good," she said. "That's perfect."

He sat up slowly. He stared at her. She was dragging at the cigarette and the glow of the burning end was intensified, he could see the expression on her face and it was somewhere between calm and frantic purpose.

She said, "Let's hurry and get dressed. We're checking out of here."

CHAPTER 12

She switched on the lamp and started to climb out of bed but he took hold of her wrist and said quietly, "Wait, now. Let's talk this over—"

"We'll talk later." She made an impatient grimace and tried to pull her wrist free.

But he held on. "I'd rather talk about it now. Before I do a thing, I like to know why I'm doing it?"

She closed her eyes. She took a deep breath. "Please," she murmured, "don't make it tougher on me. It's tough enough as it is."

He let go of her wrist. "It needs discussion, Frieda." He gave her a smile to let her know she wasn't alone with her trouble. And then, edging closer to her, placing his hand on her shoulder, "What is it? What's this talk about checking out?"

"We gotta do it, that's all."

"But why?"

"Because," she said, "I'm afraid."

"Charley?"

"No," she said. "Not Charley." She sat there gazing straight ahead. "I'm afraid of myself. Of what I'm liable to do—"

"To me?"

"To both of us." And now she looked at him. "It's something I was trying not to think about. I almost managed to get it out of my head. But then you started with that talk about the racing cars. With me the driver and you the engine. Like telling me I'm covering all the ground I can right now because I'm not sure about later. Not sure of myself, I mean."

He didn't say anything.

Frieda said, "What I'm saying is, I just don't trust myself. I'm afraid I might open my mouth."

He stiffened slightly.

And then he heard her saying, "It's this New Orleans business. The story you told Charley. You said the reason you killed your brother was money. But the point is, you didn't do it for money."

The stiffness increased and it was like the cold steel of a forceps taking hold and tightening.

"I know you didn't do it for money," she said. "I don't know why you did it, but I'm sure of one thing, it wasn't financial. I found that out today when we were in the kitchen and the talk got around to New Orleans and your brother—" she took a deep breath, "—I was watching the look on your face."

His hand reached for the cigarettes. His other hand went for the matches. He had to do something with his hands.

"And there it is, there's our trouble," she said. "You didn't do it for cash and so you're not a professional. And you know what happens if Charley finds out you're not a professional."

He was trying to light the cigarette but for some reason the smoke wouldn't pull.

"We gotta get out of this house," Frieda said. "We gotta get out before I spill it to Charley."

The match went out. He lit another and got the cigarette lit. He said, "I don't believe you'd do that."

"Wouldn't I? You forget something. I'm on Charley's payroll."

He frowned. "Let's try it again. That one went over my head."

"All right, we'll put it this way – I've been in this game a long time. I've developed certain habits, certain things I do without thinking – like a machine goes into action when the man pulls the lever. So maybe Charley asks a question and I answer it—"

He was shaking his head, giving her a smile of kindly contradiction. "I can't go along with that. You're stretching the point."

"There's another point." Her voice lowered and thickened. "I'm a woman."

And she paused to let it sink in.

And then she said, "It adds up something like this – when a woman really goes for a man, there's a thing happens inside her, I can't explain exactly what it is, it's sort of on the crazy side, a woman gets in that condition she ain't really responsible for what she's prone to do."

"Now look," he tried a little laugh, "it can't be that bad."

"It can't?" She returned the laugh, giving it a tight twist that made it almost a groan. "If only I could make it plain to you, what happens to us females when we get that one-man feeling. You look at me close enough, you'll see it's a kind of sickness."

"Like what?"

"I don't know. All I know is, you got me dizzy. You got me delirious. I'm so goddam hungry for you—" It was too thick for her throat and she choked on it. And then, catching her breath, trying to get in stride again, "The thing we need the most, it's got to be there all the time, and if I get to thinking it ain't there, I'll flip my lid, I really will."

He said aloud to himself, "This lady ain't kidding."

"I'm so glad you know it." And she gazed at him with a mixture of petal-soft tenderness and rock-hard warning, the warning saying: Just watch your step, mister, you make the slightest move to pull away from me and I'll whisper something in Charley's ear. But in the next instant the warning melted away and there was only the tenderness. Again she took hold of his arms. She said, "Let's play it safe so it won't ever happen. We'll get away from here, away from Charley, away from all of them. It'll be just you and me, we'll get on a train going somewhere—"

"No," he said.

"Why not?" Her fingers tightened on his arm. "What's to stop us?"

"Law." And he shrugged. "You know the way it is. I can't do any traveling right now. There's too many eyes looking for me."

"We'll get past them. We'll figure some way."

He shook his head. "It can't be done, Frieda. They got me traced here to Philly. Stands to reason they have men at every train station and bus depot."

"The waterfront," as she snapped her fingers. "I got some friends along the waterfront."

"That sounds convenient. Only trouble is, in a case like this the Law is very waterfront-conscious. They'll be watching each and every pier."

She laughed sourly. "I oughta be highly pleased. I'm in bed with a celebrity."

"Yes, I'm in great demand these days."

"Tell me about New Orleans. Why did you kill your brother?"

He shrugged.

"Come on," she said. "Tell me."

He shrugged again.

"Why won't you tell me?"

He spoke aloud to himself. "We're past that part of the program."

"In other words, you just can't talk about it and you wish I'd lay off?"

"Something like that." He wasn't looking at her.

He heard her saying, "Hey, mister, I'm still here. Don't hang up on me."

"I'm listening."

"Come closer, you'll hear better."

He moved closer to her so that their thighs touched but he didn't feel the contact, he didn't feel anything at all or see anything in this room. He was thinking about New Orleans.

Frieda put her arm around his middle. Her fingers played along his ribs. She said, "Well anyway, I guess you're right about the Law. It adds up we can't leave this house, we're stuck here."

He made an acute straining effort and managed to pull himself away from New Orleans. He looked at Frieda and made a fatalistic gesture, saying, "Gotta take things as they come."

"Yeah," she admitted. "No use losing sleep about it."

He grinned at her. "That's the way to talk."

"Sure," she said. "Nobody knows what's gonna happen. So what's the use of worrying? Only thing to do is have our fun while we're here."

"Correct," he said. "Keep it up. You're doing fine."

"Yeah, I'm really in form?" But then her eyes were shut tightly and her hand fell away from his side and she said aloud to herself, "If only I was able to convince myself, to get myself to believe it's just for fun – if only I didn't go for him so much, this bastard here—"

"Now look," he cut in gently. "Don't start that again."

"Listen – that noise – downstairs."

"I don't hear anything."

"Listen," she said. "Listen to it."

And then he heard it, a muffled cry, then a chair getting knocked over? And now another cry.

He was out of bed and reaching for his trousers.

"No," Frieda said. "You stay out of it."

From downstairs there was Mattone's voice cursing and saying, "You want more? I'll give you more—" And then a thud and a crash and Myrna shrieking again.

"I tell you no," Frieda said loudly. "Come back here."

Hart ran out of the room.

CHAPTER 13

He was halfway down the stairs when he saw them in the living room, Myrna sitting on the floor with her face in her hands, Mattone in his pajamas standing over her, his mouth tight and vindictive, a suggestion of enjoyment in his eyes. There were two chairs knocked over, and a lamp. And on the sofa, also wearing pajamas, Rizzio sat holding his hand to the side of his face.

Hart took in all of that, wondered about it for a moment, then saw the opened suitcase near the vestibule. Some of the contents had spilled out and he saw a skirt and a brassiere and a high-heeled shoe. He was moving slowly now as he descended the rest of the stairs.

Mattone looked up and saw him. Mattone said, "Go back to bed. We don't need you."

"What happened?" Hart asked mildly.

Rizzio took his hand away from his face that showed some fingernail scratches. "She's crazy, this girl," Rizzio said. "She's gotta be loony to think she can pull a caper like this."

Myrna was trying to get to her feet. She almost made it, then fell on her side and stayed there for some moments. Then she tried again and this time she made it. Hart saw a thin stream of red going down from the corner of her mouth. She stood motionless, gazing at the opened suitcase. She stook a step toward the suitcase and Mattone took hold of her arm.

"You want some more?" Mattone asked.

"Let go," she said dully. "I'm getting outta here."

"She's really gone crazy," Rizzio said. "We better wake up Charley."

"This don't require Charley," Mattone said. "I know just how to handle it."

Myrna tried to squirm away from Mattone's grip. He twisted her arm behind her back and she went to her knees. Her face was very white but there was no expression on it. And Hart wondered why she wasn't weeping. Mattone was really hurting her. She looked awfully frail and helpless kneeling there at Mattone's feet.

"What we oughta do," Rizzio said, "is get a rope and tie her up."

"No," Mattone said. "We won't hafta do that."

"Well, we gotta do something," Rizzio whined. "I wanna get this over with and go back to sleep."

Myrna squirmed again and Mattone put more pressure on her arm. Now he had her arm pulled up high between her shoulder blades and her head was down very low.

"I think she's coming around," Mattone murmured. "She knows she made a mistake and she won't try it again."

"You sure of that?" Hart asked.

"Positive." Mattone looked at Hart. "She's finished for the night. She won't gimme any more trouble."

"Then why don't you let go of her arm?"

"Who's asking you?"

Hart shrugged. "No use breaking her arm."

"Suppose I wanna break it?"

Hart shrugged again. "No use talking that way, either."

"That's only your opinion," Mattone said. "If I feel like doing it, I'll break her neck."

"No you won't," Hart said. He was beginning to realize why he'd come running downstairs.

Mattone said, "Do yourself a favor, jimmy-boy. Don't agitate me. I been agitated enough tonight and I can take only so much."

"All right," Hart said. "That sounds reasonable. But you're hurting her and I think you oughta let go of her arm."

"The hell with what you think." Mattone looked away from Hart and looked down at Myrna who'd stopped squirming and was altogether passive under the pressure of his grip. He did nothing for a moment, and then he took in a hissing breath between his teeth and yanked viciously at her arm. She let out a screech of animal pain and Hart heard it going into him like a hook, the hook in there deep and pulling him forward toward Mattone. His right hand was a fist going up and over and down and hitting Mattone on the temple. Mattone let go of Myrna and staggered sideways, then straightened and grinned. Mattone said, "Know something? I was hoping you'd do that."

Hart grinned back at the tall good-looking light-heavyweight who now raised his arms very slowly, getting set with the right held high, the left easing out tentatively to either feint or lead, the legs arranged in a purely professional stance. Then Mattone began to move in.

Rizzio jumped up from the sofa, saying, "Aw, no, for Christ's sake. No—" and he snatched at the fabric of Mattone's pajama-shirt. But then he took Mattone's backward-jabbing elbow in his chest that sent him back to the sofa and he sat down, looking very worried.

Mattone resumed moving in, coming in slowly.

Hart backed away, then shifted off to one side, looking for a vase or a heavy ashtray or anything at all that might come in handy. He heard Mattone saying, "I could do it with one punch but I ain't gonna do it that way." And there was no vase or ashtray in the immediate vicinity, there was nothing except Mattone's left hand shooting out and almost getting him. He'd moved his head to pull away from it and now his hands were up defensively, the grin was off his face and his eyes became technical, not blinking as he heard Mattone murmuring, "What we're gonna do first, jimmy-boy, is some dental work. You got too many front teeth." So then the left jabbed again, jabbed very fast and neatly but he was ready for it and wiped it off with his right hand coming down as he moved in low and hooked his left to Mattone's middle. "Oh," Mattone said, but it wasn't a grunt, just a slight show of surprise, "that was sorta cute. This looks to be a cutey here. I always like it with these cuties, it's a lotta fun."

So then Mattone moved in again and Hart was cute once more, starting to the left, then to the right, then to the left again to avoid a series of jabs and a chopping right aimed at his jaw. But then Mattone found him with a short left hook to the middle and he took the full force of it, started to bend double, took a right to the side of his head, then another hook to the ribs, and knew he didn't have a chance and was due to get badly hurt. He managed to slip away from a whizzing left coming toward his eyes, ducked very low under another hook trying for his head, stabbed his own left into Mattone's stomach, then received a swinging right that crashed against the side of his skull and put some flashing vari-colored lights in there. He thought: The difficulty is, there's not enough room to move around, it's so much smaller than a regulation ring. He was grinning again, sending the grin past Mattone and giving it to Rizzio who sat there on the sofa shaking his head sadly, then giving it to Myrna who remained kneeling on the floor, rubbing her arm. Then he heard footsteps on the stairs and Frieda's voice yelling they should stop it, while the bright green and orange and lavender lights in his head began to spin rapidly, impelled by Mattone's right hand getting him on the forehead. He told himself he might as well fall down, but as he went down he knew that wouldn't stop Mattone from continuing with him while he was on the floor, and he tried to get up, grabbing at Mattone's middle for support. Mattone pushed him away, set him up with a light jab to the chest, and hauled off with the right, not aiming it for the jaw, but preparing it for damage to the eyes. And Hart saw it coming, and thought in that instant: He'll close both of my eyes, then work on my nose, then my mouth and he won't put across that finishing touch until he's got my face completely ruined. But for some reason the blow didn't land. He was only semi-conscious now, and he wondered vaguely why Mattone had stopped the punch when it was more than halfway home. He blinked hard several times and saw Mattone moving away, Mattone's face in profile. So of course he knew what it had to be, and he looked toward the stairway and saw Charley standing there on the steps above Frieda. Some yellow light came down from the hall upstairs and fell softly on the shiny fabric of Charley's bathrobe. Charley had one hand in a pocket of the robe and in the other hand he held a gun.

The gun wasn't aimed at anything in particular. Somehow it didn't seem like a weapon in Charley's hand, more on the order of a briar-pipe he was holding just to hold onto something. Under his eyes there was the purple of hangover. But aside from that, he didn't seem sick or sloppy or weary. He looked completely awake and quietly capable.

Mattone said, "Now look, Charley—"

"Hold it," Charley said, not looking at Mattone. He came down the stairs past Frieda, then across the carpet past Mattone. He seated himself on the sofa beside Rizzio and then, his head turning slowly, he examined the room with its overturned chairs, its wrinkled carpet, the girl kneeling on the floor near the opened suitcase, and Mattone who stood facing him, breathing hard through the nose. He didn't look at Hart.

Mattone said, "I'll tell it, Charley. Let me tell it—"

"You be quiet," Charley said. "I've had enough from you, Mattone. You open your mouth again and I'll shoot you in the kneecap."

On the stairs, Frieda said quickly, "He means it, Mattone. For God's sake, keep your mouth shut."

Charley looked at Rizzio and murmured, "Give it to me."

"Well," Rizzio said, "I'm sound asleep and Mattone wakes me up and says he hears something downstairs. So then he runs downstairs and I follow him and I see him going after Myrna. She's got that suitcase in her hand and so I know it ain't for no stroll around the block. He grabs her and she pulls away and then I grab her and she does this to my face. So he grabs her again and she won't behave, he's gotta mess her up a little to quiet her down. Then Al tells him to leave her alone and it gets to be an argument and—" Rizzio shrugged.

Charley put the gun in the pocket of his bathrobe. He ran a forefinger slowly across his underlip. His head turned very slowly toward Myrna and he said, "Get up from the floor."

Myrna didn't move.

"It's in the head," Rizzio said. "This girl here is sick in the head."

"Get her a drink," Charley said.

"No," Myrna said. "I don't need a drink."

"What's the matter with you?" Charley asked.

"Nothing," she answered. "I just wanna leave, that's all."

"You can't do that," Charley said very softly. "You know we can't let you do that."

"Yes," she said. There was nothing in her voice, nothing at all. "I know how it is, Charley. I shouldn't of done it. I won't try it again."

"I hope you won't," Charley had it down to a whisper.

"The hell she won't," Mattone said.

Charley's eyes were closed. "I'm begging you, Mattone. I'm actually begging you to keep quiet. You don't know how close you came to getting shot."

Mattone's mouth slackened, then tightened, and slackened again. His eyes became wet. He tried to hold back the wetness but it came out and rolled down his cheeks. He said, "Always blaming me. Why is it me all the time?"

"You're a louse-up artist, that's why," Charley told him. "You're always lousing up a situation. I've tried to tell you how things should be handled, but you never listen."

"I did what I thought was—"

"Not what you thought was practical, don't tell me that. You got no idea what it is to be practical. With you it's muscle, always muscle. The mistake you made, you never should have quit the ring. That's all you're good for, demonstrating your muscle."

Mattone stood there making no sound as the tears came out of his eyes.

"I'll let you demonstrate it now," Charley said. "Come on, use some muscle and pick up the chairs. Straighten up this room."

"Charley, you can't treat me like a—"

"Yes I can," Charley said. He gestured toward the over-turned chairs. "Pick them up."

Mattone wouldn't or couldn't move, and Frieda came quickly down the stairs, saying, "I'll do it—"

"No," Charley said. "He'll do it."

"Will I?" Mattone's voice broke.

"Yes, you will," Charley said, then looked away from Mattone as though to say the subject was dropped. Mattone moved toward the overturned chairs. For some moments it was quiet in the room except for the sound of Mattone setting the chairs on their legs, then straightening the carpet. Rizzio stretched and yawned and said sleepily, "You want me for anything, Charley?" And Charley shook his head. Rizzio yawned again and got up from the sofa, crossed the room and went upstairs. Frieda said to Hart, "All right, it's all over. Let's go back to bed." Charley said, "No, Frieda. I want him down here. I wanna talk to him." Frieda said, "Me too?" And Charley murmured, "No, you go up and get some sleep. He'll be up soon." And then, to Mattone, "All right, that's enough with the carpet." Mattone, not looking at him, spoke with bitter sarcasm. "You want me to wash the floor?"

"No," Charley said. "Just wash your face. Go up and wash your face and go to bed."

Mattone followed Frieda upstairs. Myrna had lifted herself from the floor and now she was slowly re-filling her suitcase. When she had it filled, she carried it toward the stairway but Charley stopped her with, "Not yet, Myrna. Sit down for a while."

She lowered the suitcase to the stairway landing. She came over to the sofa and sat down beside Charley.

Hart took one of the armchairs. He felt chilly wearing only his trousers. He told himself it was awfully cold down here. He wished he had something to cover his chest and shoulders, and trying to concentrate on that, he heard himself saying, "I can tell you what it is, Charley. She did it on account of me."

"Let her tell it," Charley said.

Myrna didn't say anything.

Charley looked at her. "I'm trying to help you, kid. I wanna do everything I can to help you."

She sat there looking at the carpet. She was like a lost child sitting in some station-house, no hope in her eyes.

Charley put his hand on her shoulder. "I can't help you if you don't talk. You gotta talk. You gotta get it out."

"I can't," she said.

"Give it a try," Charley urged gently.

She sighed heavily. Then she tried to speak and she couldn't speak.

Charley said, "You got me plenty worried, kid."

"I know." Her head was down. "I'm sorry, Charley. I'm so sorry—"

"This walking-out business. I'm worried you'll try it again. And maybe next time you'll make it. So then they pick you up—"

"For what? I'm not on the wanted list."

"You think you're not. You forget all them times they hauled you in on suspicion. So all right, the way it was then you knew just what to say and how to say it. But now it's different, you got yourself all knotted up inside, you're in no shape to handle their questions. And before you know it you're breaking down and spilling everything."

"I wouldn't do that, Charley. I'd never do a thing like that to you."

"Not in your right mind you wouldn't. But the way it is now, you got no grip on yourself. You're a long way off from anywhere."

She gazed across the room at the packed suitcase.

For some moments it was quiet. Then Charley said very softly, "You see the way it is, kid? I can't take any chances. If you don't snap out of it, I'll hafta get rid of you."

"You mean – I'm gonna die?"

Charley took his hand off her shoulder. He didn't say anything.

"Yes," she said, "you're telling me I'm gonna die. And then you hafta do away with the body. So it goes where my brother went. It goes down the cellar and into the furnace."

And Hart thought: This is actually happening, look at Charley's face, look at him there getting up from the sofa and taking the gun out of his pocket. And look at her, Jesus Christ, look at her, she isn't even blinking.

"Well, kid?" Charley's voice was purely technical. "What's it gonna be?"

She smiled at Charley. "All I can say is, thanks for everything. You did a lot for me, Charley. You were awfully good to me and Paul."

Charley stood a few feet away from her. He had the gun aimed at her head. She went on smiling, sitting there not moving. Hart could feel the coldness of the room and now it had nothing to do with the weather outside. The coldness came from the ice in Charley's brain. Because Charley was completely a professional and therefore functioning according to the rigid doctrine of the outlaw code. So the only thing the gun was pointed at was an obstacle that had to be removed.

Hart heard himself saying, "Hold it, Charley."

"No," Charley said. "I tried to pull her out of it and I couldn't. So she's done. Can't you see she's done?"

"Not yet," Hart said. He got up from the chair. He did it slowly but with enough noise to delay the action of Charley's finger on the trigger.

"What's the matter?" Charley asked him, not looking at him. "What are you doing?"

"Nothing special," Hart said. "I'm just thinking there's another way to do it."

"How you mean?" Charley spoke to him as one professional to another. "You mean with a knife or something?"

"I meant there's another way to bring her around," Hart said.

Charley looked at him.

And Hart said, "Put the gun in her hand."

Charley winced slightly. Then he frowned.

Hart looked at Myrna. "Tell him you want the gun. Tell him you want to shoot me."

Myrna closed her eyes. She shivered.

"You get it?" Hart said to Charley. "She tries to walk out of this house to get away from me. This man here who killed Paul. She says to herself, if she stays here she'll find some way to murder me. She doesn't want to murder me. And yet she does. She's on a see-saw. Only way to get her off it is hand her the gun, let her make up her mind here and now."

Charley went on frowning at him. "Maybe you think this gun ain't loaded?"

"I know it's loaded."

"And you're really willing to take the chance?"

Hart nodded.

"You're quite a gambler," Charley said.

"Not a smart one. Just curious. I'm very curious now."

Charley grinned stiffly. "What's that they say about the cat?"

"Yes, it got the cat, all right."

"Well," Charley said, and he wasn't grinning now, "there's one nice thing about this. It lets me out."

Hart saw the gun twirling on Charley's finger in the trigger guard, the barrel coming into Charley's grasp, the butt extended toward Myrna. She shivered again, then reached out and took the gun from Charley. She looked at it, got a trembling grip on it, and aimed it at Hart.

CHAPTER 14

He stood there waiting for it to hit him. I would be a .38 slug going into him high in the chest or possibly the throat. Her eyes were focused on that area and he told himself the look on her face was entirely clinical, as though the only thought in her brain was to put the bullet where it would finish him. Then he tried to tell himself he was mistaken about that, maybe she wasn't seeing him at all, maybe she was seeing inside herself and trying to get things cleared up in there. Well, whichever way it was going, he wished she'd hurry up and settle it. He hadn't expected the waiting would be this difficult. But he wasn't sorry he'd told Charley to hand her the gun.

It isn't exactly suicide, he thought. It's more on the order of sacrifice. Some of us are sacrifice-prone instead of accident-prone, we see something and it grows on us, we come to adore it, and all at once we hear the mandolins and get the picture of that moonlight pouring through the trees. It has no connection with logic or anything you can put your finger on, it's just got to be classified as mystical. You're making this sacrifice for purely mystical reasons. If she wants you dead you're willing to be dead. And another thing you know, this waiting is difficult only because you feel the pain she's having, like a current going through a wire from her to you. Look at her eyes, oh Jesus Christ look what's in her eyes.

She lowered the gun.

"No deal?" Charley murmured.

She didn't answer. The gun rested in her lap. Charley reached out and took it. For a few moments he stood close to her, studying her face. Then he put the gun in his bathrobe pocket and looked at Hart and said, "I think she's all right now."

"Of course she's all right."

She was smiling at Hart. It was a dim smile. She said, "You know what I'm thinking?"

"Yes," Hart said. "I know."

"She's thanking you," Charley said. "She feels a lot better now and she's saying thanks."

Without sound Hart said to Charley: You don't know the half of it, not even a small part of it.

"She's gonna like you now," Charley said. "You and her are gonna be friends. Ain't that right, Myrna?"

She nodded slowly, but it wasn't a reply to Charley's query. It was in agreement with something she was saying to herself.

Charley said, "Well, I guess what we oughta do now is get some sleep."

"I'm not sleepy," Hart said.

"Me neither," Myrna murmured. "I'd like to sit here for a while and talk."

"To him?" Charley asked.

"Yes," she said. "That is, if it's all right with you, Charley."

"I think it's a swell idea," Charley smiled. "You and him'll have a nice talk and get to be good friends."

"Would you do me a favor, Charley?"

"Sure, Myrna. Anything."

"Would you carry my suitcase upstairs?"

"It'll be a pleasure," Charley said. He turned and went

to the stairway and picked up the suitcase. He started up the stairs, then stopped and looked at Hart. "You better put something on. There's no heat in this house, I don't want you catching cold."

"I'm all right," Hart said.

"I want you to stay in shape. You're a valuable piece of property."

"Mattone doesn't think so."

"Mattone don't think, period." Charley smiled. "Don't you worry about Mattone. Don't you worry about anything now. You're doing fine in this league."

"Thanks, Charley. But you didn't need to say it. I wasn't worrying."

"Not much you weren't," Charley chuckled. "You were jam-packed with worry." He patted his hand against the gun in his pocket. "This tool here had you scared sick. But you covered it up. I sure like the way you covered it up."

And Hart thought, So maybe Frieda was wrong, after all. This man is only a human being and he can be fooled. Aloud he said, "Tell Frieda I'll be up soon."

"All right," Charley said. "But don't keep her waiting too long."

"I won't."

Charley smiled complacently at both of them. Then he continued up the stairs and they heard his footsteps on the second floor, the bedroom door opening and closing. Hart listened for more sounds from upstairs but there were none and he could feel the quiet cold and dead up there and sweet-cool down here, really a fine climate down here in the living room so very far away from upstairs.

He went to the sofa and sat beside her, not touching her but feeling something so much deeper than touching.

He looked at her, his eyes telling her, and he said, "You see how it is?"

"Yes," she said. "But how did it happen?"

"It just happened."

"I could feel it happening. I knew and you knew, we both knew."

"It's sorta funny," he said.

"But not to laugh about."

"Certainly not. It isn't that kind of comedy."

"What you mean is, it's funny the way it happened, but now that it's happened it's serious."

"That's exactly what I mean," he said. "It's very serious."

"What are we gonna do?"

"I don't know. You got any ideas?"

She shook her head.

"Well," he murmured, "let's try to think."

"I can't," she said. "I can't get any thoughts now."

"Neither can I. And that's the hell of it."

"Tell me something," she said. "Has this ever happened to you before?"

"No."

"Same here," she said.

"It's like—"

"Like—"

"We just can't say what it's like," he told her. "There's no way to say it."

"Maybe it's like when you're walking along and all at once you get hit by lightning."

"No," he said. "That would be negative. There's nothing negative about this."

"You mean this is nice?"

"It's so nice it's painful." And he smiled at her. "Don't you feel the pain?"

"Yes," she said. "It's a terrible pain. But it's wonderful."

"Where's it got you?"

"All over. Every part of me."

"It's the real thing, all right. No two ways about that. It was bound to happen, it just had to happen. And now it's a permanent state of affairs. We got something here that we'll never lose, not even when we die."

"Don't talk about dying."

"It can be talked about. It isn't important now. It's just a thing that happens to the skin and bones. And what's happened to you and me is way beyond that."

"Yes," she said. "That's right. But please, let's not talk about dying."

"All right," he said. "We'll switch to something else. Let's talk about music. You like the sound of mandolins?"

"If you do."

"So that takes care of that. And from there we go to the moonlight. You like to see the moonlight pouring through the trees?"

"Yes, I like that very much. I'm seeing it now."

"Sure, we're both seeing it. We're getting awfully artistic, aren't we? Let's see what happens if we try another direction. Some topic that has to do with science, like airplanes."

"We're flying now."

"Yes, we sure are."

"We're way up, way way up."

"You hear the motor?"

"No," she said. "Just the mandolins."

Then it was quiet but he heard the mandolins and he looked at her and phrases from sonnets floated through his mind. What he actually saw was a small skinny girl with a face that was fairly pleasant but not especially pretty, although the grey-violet eyes were something unique, and the black hair had a soft lustre that they try to get on canvas and sometimes almost get it but not quite.

But he wasn't seeing her with his eyes. It wasn't her face and body he was seeing. It was something she sent to him, something he'd been waiting for through all the years of listless nights and meaningless days.

He started to say something. He was stopped by the voice from upstairs. It was Frieda, yelling to him, "I'm waiting, Al. I'm waiting for you."

CHAPTER 15

There was a long moment of nothing at all. It was on the order of falling off a cliff.

Then he heard Frieda again. "Come on, Al. Come upstairs."

He closed his eyes and put his hand to his forehead.

"You coming?" Frieda yelled.

Good Christ, he said to himself.

"You better answer her," Myrna said.

"All right," he murmured. And he called to Frieda, "I'll be right up."

"How soon?" Frieda yelled.

"Couple minutes."

"Don't make it longer," with some affection in it, and some warning.

He sat there looking at the stairway and hearing Frieda's footsteps returning to the bedroom. Then he heard the door closing up there, and he blinked hard several times and waited for Myrna to say something.

But she didn't say anything and he knew she was waiting for him to speak.

He said, "I'll hafta go back to that room."

And of course that wasn't enough – it needed more telling, so much more.

"It's a ticklish situation," he said. "She has something on me. If I don't do what she says, she'll talk to Charley and then it's the end."

"All right," Myrna said.

"You know it isn't all right."

"It's all right with me," she said. "Anything you do is all right with me."

"But not that."

"Yes," she said. "Even that."

He lowered his head. He said, very slowly, "God damn it."

"Now look," she said. "I can take it. I'm telling you I can take it."

He looked at her. "Thanks," he said, really meaning it. "It's awfully nice of you to say so."

She smiled. "It ain't no trouble at all. It's so easy to say nice things to you."

"Oh, thank you. Thank you very much."

"Don't mention it," she said.

"All right." And he was walking slowly toward the stairway. "We'll cater to society and call it unmentionable. From here on in it's classified tabu."

She didn't say anything.

He was on the stairs and he wanted to look at her, but he knew there was no point in that. And besides, she wouldn't want him to look at her right now. It would only make things tougher for her.

So the only thing to do was continue up the stairs, and then walk along the hall toward the door of the bedroom where Frieda was waiting.

He opened the door and saw the lamp was lit. Frieda was sitting up in the bed and smoking a cigarette. She shifted slightly to make room for him, then gestured for him to get into the bed.

But he walked on past the bed, going slowly toward the window overlooking the backyard. He looked out the window and saw the blackness of Germantown at half past four in the morning. He thought with an inward shrug: Well, the picture can't be any blacker than it is in here.

He heard Frieda saying, "You gonna get in bed?"

"All right." But he didn't move.

"Whatcha doing?" she asked.

"I'm just standing here thinking."

"About what?"

"You'd be surprised."

"Would I? That's nice. I like to be surprised."

"I'm thinking how convenient it would be if I had a bottle of knockout drops."

"For who?"

"You."

"That ain't no surprise," she said. "I figured you were thinking something like that."

He turned slowly and looked at her. He didn't say anything.

She said, "I knew it when I heard you walking up them stairs. The way you came up, so slow and heavy, like an old junkman when he carries too much weight on his back."

"I could make a pun on that," he murmured. "Except that it wouldn't be funny."

"You're damn right it wouldn't be funny." She sat up straighter. "I weigh exactly one-fifty-seven. That's too much weight for you, isn't it?"

"Let's not get statistical."

"Another thing," she said. "You're one of them educated people. I never made it past the ninth grade."

"That doesn't prove anything."

"The hell it doesn't," she told him. "It proves I didn't need schoolbooks to get the brains I got." She tapped a fat finger against the side of her head. "I got plenty in here."

"Really?" he murmured. "Then let's discuss Schopenhauer."

Her eyes narrowed. "You getting fancy with me?"

"I'm getting philosophical," he said. "I think we could use some philosophy at this point."

"You know what? You better come outta the trees."

"But it's nice up here. It's very pleasant."

"That ain't what you mean." Her eyes were narrowed almost to slits, giving her fat face a piggish cast. "You mean it's clean up there. That is, it's clean compared to this bed."

"So now we're on hygiene?"

"Don't," she said. "Don't stretch it too far." Her voice was a mixture of menace and pleading. "You keep stretching it, it's gonna break."

He shrugged. "I didn't start this."

"Not much you didn't."

There was a chair near the window and he sat down in it and looked at the floor.

He heard Frieda saying, "You started it when you heard her screaming downstairs and you jumped out of bed. I told you to stay in this room but you didn't hear me. You hadda go down there to see what was happening to her. And then it's Prince Valiant riding to the rescue."

"Make it Moon Mullins. It was more along that line."

"You wish it was." She said it very slowly.

He looked at her. He opened his mouth to build some sort of a denial, but nothing came out.

Frieda said, "I was watching you. I saw the way you were looking at her."

He murmured, "You're very quick to draw conclusions."

"Not when I'm seeing something right there in front of my eyes."

His mouth remained stiff and tight but the corners

went up just a little. It wasn't really a smile, it was more of a calculating look, nothing personal in it, the emphasis on mathematics as he tried to figure the odds. But the odds were awfully high, like a very high mountain telling the climber he might as well give up.

But then he saw Frieda's eyes widening, and she was biting the side of her lip. And he thought: She's reading me wrong, she thinks I'm sitting here making plans for a drastic anti-Frieda campaign; could be she's got me listed as one of the one-track-mind lads who move very slowly toward a decision and then can't be swayed from it. So now it's very interesting the way the table turns and she's scared silly I'm scheming to do her in.

He concentrated on keeping that look pasted to his face. He managed to keep it there and saw the slight shiver that passed across Frieda's shoulders. Now the fear in her eyes was definite and acute. Her voice tried to hide it, making the synthetic command, "Don't get any clever ideas."

The thing to do, he told himself, is keep quiet and let her go on guessing and worrying.

"Because you're really not clever," she went on with the camouflage that didn't get across. "If you were, you wouldn't have given Charley that phony story that I saw through. Me with no high school diploma, I'm a hell of a lot smarter than you and I got you in the palm of my hand and don't you forget it."

He made no reply, not even with his eyes. The smile that wasn't really a smile went floating across the room to Frieda and caused her to shiver again.

"Well?" she demanded. "What's it gonna be?"

He looked away from her. Then he made a vague, indecisive gesture, as though to say: There's no rush, I got plenty of time to make up my mind.

"Now look, I'm getting tired," she said. "I wanna go to sleep."

"That sounds practical," he murmured.

She beckoned. "Come on get in bed," saying it quickly and matter-of-factly as though the other matter was shelved.

He shook his head.

"Whatcha gonna do?" She spoke a trifle louder. "You gonna sleep in that chair?"

"I won't be sleeping," he said. "I'll just sit here and think for a while."

She tried a light laugh and missed with, "Well, I guess you got plenty to think about."

"True." And he nodded solemnly.

"But don't let it throw you," she advised with a forced grin.

He watched her as she pressed her cigarette into the ashtray and put the ashtray on the floor. Then she reached toward the lamp to cut off the light. Her fingers took hold of the cord and she started to pull it, then let go and said, "I think I'll sleep with the light on."

Then she looked at him and he knew she was waiting for a comment. He made no comment.

She said, "Some nights I like to sleep with the light on."

He shrugged. "Suit yourself."

"Another thing about me," she said, "I'm a very light sleeper. The slightest noise wakes me up."

"They sell pills for that."

"I don't need them kind of pills. It ain't like not being able to sleep." She said it slowly and sort of arranging the words to make it a defensive weapon that covered all territory of possible assault. "It's just that I'm a restless sleeper, and if I get waked up all of a sudden I start to yell."

"That's a bad habit."

"Not all the time. Sometimes it comes in very handy."

Golly, he thought, she's really scared, she looks like she's freezing with it.

She lowered her head to the pillow and pulled the sheet and blankets up to her shoulders. Then very slowly she turned over on her side. Her hand came up to her face, and made a careful maneuver that brushed the platinum blonde hair away from her closed eye. Or maybe that eye wasn't closed all the way. He told himself to quit looking at her, and maybe she'd fall asleep and he could begin to think with no one watching him. It needed some proper thinking now, and the important thing was solitude. Or solitaire, he thought. It'll have to be solitaire, and that's one game you can't cheat or bluff, it's got to be played straight, so straight that it hurts. So it isn't a happy game and you're in for a bad time playing it. There's no getting away from it, it's going to be you dealing the cards to you, and naturally that includes Myrna. This one life you got has two people in it now. That makes it a load you're carrying. And that feminine half is precious material, it's a package marked fragile and please be careful, mister. I'm begging you, mister, please be very careful the way you deal these cards.

CHAPTER 16

He sat there in the chair near the window and waited for
Frieda to fall asleep. Some minutes passed and her
breathing became heavy with the slumber rhythm. It
occurred to him she might be pretending, and he shifted
the chair so that its legs scraped the floor. But the noise
did not reach her and he knew she was really asleep.
Another thing he knew, it wasn't true she was a light
sleeper, like she'd claimed. What he saw there in the bed
was a fat blonde sound asleep, a chunk of sleeping animal that had no connection with him. So now he felt the
solitude and he told himself to start thinking.

And where do we begin? he asked himself. What's the
jumping-off place? Or let's forget that for the moment
and try to figure where we're headed. Referring to the
two of us, the girl named Myrna and the man named
Hart. If we try to leave this house, it's a sure bet we'll be
stopped. But just for the sake of argument, let's assume
that Myrna and Hart can negotiate a getaway. Then
what happens? The Law happens, that's what. The Law
moves in and we're finished. That makes two patterns
that offer no exit. Is there another pattern? There better
be. And make it more definite than that, say to yourself
there's got to be a way out of this, keep saying it and for
Christ's sake try to believe it.

But what you're doing here is looking for a short cut,
or giving yourself a head start. And that's a privilege you
don't get in this game. According to the rules you got to

start from scratch, and that means New Orleans. You'll have to start with your brother Haskell and the way you killed him and your reason for killing him. The method was simple enough, it was a bullet going into his brain. And the reason? That wasn't so simple. It was euthanasia and that's never simple.

In plain words, it was a mercy killing and whether Heaven has it listed as right or wrong, you'd do it again under the same conditions. Because the conditions were unbearable for Haskell and every day he was allowed to live was a hideous session that had him weeping and begging it to stop. But of course it wouldn't stop.

It was a family of snakes crawling through the nerves of his body and eating him up.

It was multiple sclerosis.

And even though the medics are agreed it can't be cured, even though they come right out and admit it's a horrible sickness, they gotta go along with the First Commandment. But you did what he wanted you to do, what he pleaded for with the groans that you can hear yet.

Because you knew he would do it to himself if he could. He told you so. And wept it from eyes that could barely make me out, it's a sickness that hits the eyes as well as other parts of the framework. So he couldn't see where to search for a vial of poison, or a breadknife to use on his wrists. And even if he could see, he couldn't move in that direction, his legs were dead.

And his arms were dead. And his hands, and his fingers.

God yes, it sure had him. All his boyhood and young manhood he'd been the athletic type; at Tulane he won three letters. He was five-eleven and weighed two-twenty and it was packed solid. And a brain, too. And looks. With the kind of personality you don't come across very often. The genuine kindliness, carrying it so far sometimes that people took him for a sucker.

He had an awful lot of money, an approximate estimate would be around three million. And you were next in line to inherit it. So according to the District Attorney the motivation is cash. And in court you stand no chance at all of getting off, and even if some fluke took place and they erased the cash motivation, the law they got against euthanasia is a rigid law and at the very least you'd get seven years.

Seven years for what? All right, don't get sour. It isn't their fault. But God damn it, there ought to be some way to see a thing for what it is, not what Law says it is.

Law calls me a heel and a louse and a murderer. Law says here's a party who did away with his own brother. And the newspapers jump on the wagon and call me worse names, like fiend and demon and dig up stories about how generous Haskell was to me – how he gave me a car and a yacht, and look how I repaid him.

Truth is, he gave me the gifts because he enjoyed giving. I didn't want that automobile and sure as hell I didn't need that yacht. But I drove the car and I sailed the boat and made out I was overjoyed. And that made Haskell happy. It always gave him happiness when he could bring joy to people, whether it was his younger brother or some panhandler on Ransome Street.

You see a man like that, a big fine healthy man with a wholesome yen for living and giving, a man whose only enemies were the envious, a man who was Grade-A clear through, and Mother Nature plays this trick on him. One morning he wakes up with a funny heavy feeling in his left leg.

That's the way it starts, and from there on there's nothing can be done, it gets the leg and later it's both legs out of commission, both arms, the snakes in there multiplying to strangle this and strangle that. He sits there in the wheelchair and you wheel him to the bathroom. And then it gets to the point where the wheelchair is too much for him, he can't sit up. So now he's in the bed and he's getting the weeping spells. You never saw him weep before. In the hall you talk to the doctor, the twentieth or thirtieth in a long line of doctors. You remember this one flew in all the way from Seattle. He sighs and shakes his head and says, "It's hopeless. This multiple sclerosis thing, it's a hellish proposition—" And then, before he can pull it back it comes slipping out, "He'd be better off dead."

It was a statement coming from the mouth of a specialist in the science of keeping people alive. He didn't want to say it, he didn't mean to say it, but he said it.

So you hear it and it's the seed of an idea going into you and staying, and growing. You try to smother it but that same day you hear Haskell saying, "I don't want to live—"

And some days later he says, "You want to know something? Whenever I go to sleep I pray I won't wake up."

"That's no way to talk," you say. "You got to fight this thing."

"With what?"

"Now look, Haskell. You're going to get well. They'll discover something. They got people working on it. They're bound to—"

"I'm tired, Hart. I'm so tired."

You look at him there in the bed. He weighs exactly one-twenty-seven. You think of the three-letter man from Tulane who weighed two-twenty, the discus thrower who came in third in the Southern Conference championships.

One night a week or so later he puts it to you straight. He says, "I want you to do me a favor."

"Yes?"

"I want you to kill me."

You don't say anything. You can't look at him.

"Please do it," he says. "Please—"

But then the nurse comes into the room with the tray and while she starts feeding him like an infant gets fed you walk out quietly. You go out of the mansion and while you walk around the grounds, past the tennis courts and toward the dock that overlooks a moonlit Mississippi, you're thinking. It would be merciful—

But no, you say to yourself. You can't do that. That's unthinkable.

Except that you can't let Haskell suffer like this, you can't stand by and watch him wasting away.

But listen now, they might really discover a cure. Let's hope and pray. Let's picture them working with the microscopes and the test tubes—

But you don't get that picture. It fades out and all you see is Haskell in that bed, not able to move.

You went through night after night of sitting alone and drinking and really swilling it down but not getting plastered, the alcohol washing all non-essentials out of your brain, all the average-man rules and regulations that state it's a crime, it's the worst sin of all, you mustn't do it, friend, you'll be sorry later. Your reply was: The hell with what society thinks, he's my brother and he needs relief and there's only one way to bring him relief.

Now then, here's a creepy angle. During all this time of coming to that decision but somehow unable to go through with it, the same decision had been reached by your other brother Clement. And that was a surprise, that really knocked you flat. For Clement was never much of a participant in family matters. Fact is, Clement never participated in anything requiring a plus of effort.

He was strictly for the hammock and staying home nights with his wife and three children, getting fat and getting bald and the only thing that ever seemed to worry him was his golf score. But Clement was making many visits to the mansion, and for hours he'd sit at the bedside and read to Haskell from *Town and Country*, and *Fortune*, and *Holiday*, and the sports pages of the local newspapers. Then one night you're out on the grounds looking at the tennis courts and thinking of the tennis that Haskell liked to play and would never play again, and Clement comes up and gives it to you blunt and fast, no preliminaries.

Clement says, "I'm going to put a stop to this."

You look at him. You don't say anything.

"The way it's going, it's ridiculous," he says. "It's absolutely ridiculous he should have all that agony."

He says it quietly and sort of tonelessly, and you know he's been giving this a lot of thought.

You hear him say, "I've made up my mind. I'm going to get him out of it."

You wince. This can't be Clement talking.

"I'm telling you and only you," Clement says. "Tomorrow I'm buying a gun."

"Don't talk like an idiot."

"I'm buying a gun and I'm going to shoot him."

"You realize what you're saying?"

You see him nodding slowly and solemnly. And he says, "I'm going to shoot him and then I'll turn myself in. I don't care what they do to me."

"Oh look, you're just talking. Why don't you go home and get a good night's sleep?"

"I haven't had a good night's sleep in three months."

"Why don't you go on a trip? Now there's an idea. You need it, Clement, you need a change."

He smiles. You've never seen him smile like that before. It's the kind of smile they wear when they volunteer for a rescue mission that gives them very little chance of coming back.

He shakes his head. "You can't sell it, Hart. You might as well quit trying."

He stands there, slowly shaking his head, his eyes telling you he's bound to this, it's a sacred vow he's made to himself and there's no way to pull him away from it.

That is, unless—

Unless you move in first and beat him to the punch.

Your brain spins with the thought and you scarcely pay attention as he walks away. You think of this sacrifice he's decided to make, the loss of his status as solid citizen, the ruination of his home, the doom he's bringing upon himself and his wife and children.

But of course you won't let him do it.

From that moment on it's all mechanical, your legs are like wheels on tracks headed straight ahead. You go to the four-car garage and climb into your pale blue Bugatti and some twenty minutes later you're in that particular section of New Orleans where the late-night action is fast and frantic yet somehow on the quiet side because it's mostly illegal trade. In less than a half-hour you've made a connection and the man sells you the gun.

As you drive back to the mansion your hands are steady on the wheel.

You do it very quickly, and there's no strategy, no caution. You go into Haskell's room and he's sleeping. You take out the loaded gun and shoot him twice in the head. As you leave the room you see the nurse coming down the hall and she comes faster and asks you what that noise was. You look at her as though she's asked a foolish question, and you answer, "I shot him."

Then it occurs to you that now you're a fugitive and you'd better start to run.

Jesus, it's been a long run. It's really been no rest for the weary. And the thing that's kept you going and allowed you to live with yourself was the jury inside you, which says, "Not guilty" because what you did was not for cash, not for any personal gain, oh certainly not for that. But even so, it paid off rather nicely for your brothers. It took Haskell out of his misery and it took Clement away from catastrophe. That makes it all right.

Yeah, that makes it just dandy. You better stop rationalizing and come back to these cards on the table, these solitaire numbers and pictures that you can't argue with, can't re-arrange. All you can do is look at the set-up and see it for what it is.

And what you see most clearly now is the time element that announces today is Thursday and tomorrow is the black day when you step over the line from amateur to professional. It's gonna be strictly professional up there in Wyncote at the Kenniston mansion. And you damn well better do everything correctly. All right, stop worrying, it isn't Friday yet, you've still got Thursday to brace yourself and develop a purely pro viewpoint.

So let's say that now the only factor is cold cash, that is, the cash is important because travel takes currency and maybe with some luck it'll soon be travel for you and her, to a place where they'll never find you. That kind of travel needs an awful lot of money but I think your share of the Kenniston haul will more than cover it. You're only doing what you gotta do to stay alive and hold onto this girl.

The thought of her was very soothing and relaxing. He closed his eyes and his head went down. He was falling asleep.

CHAPTER 17

Thursday was like the final day for a fighter in training camp, where it's mostly a matter of resting the muscles and the nerves. They sat around in the living room, listened to recorded music from the radio and played cards. There was very little talk and the atmosphere was calm and soft and almost amiable. None of them made mention of what had happened last night.

Supper was a noisy meal but the noise came mostly from the radio. They had it turned on loud and the disc jockey played a lot of Dizzy Gillespie. They sat there and devoured the tender-tasty veal cutlets while Dizzy's trumpet went up and up, going up so fast and hard that you wanted to look up to see if it was puncturing holes in the ceiling.

After supper there was more poker and then they were all in the living room listening to the radio and there was no talk at all. At eleven-thirty Myrna said goodnight and went upstairs. Some twenty minutes later Rizzio went up, and Mattone followed soon after. Now the radio had switched to classical music. It was a program devoted to the works of Debussy. Charley commented it was very nice music. Frieda said, "It sure is." They looked at Hart and waited for his opinion. He was very far away from the Debussy but when he saw them looking at him, he managed to nod in agreement.

It was one-ten when Charley went upstairs. The Debussy music stayed on for another fifteen minutes.

Then it was a news program and Frieda went to the radio and switched it off. She stood there at the radio, looking at Hart who sat on the sofa gazing at the floor.

Some moments passed, and then she said, "Come on, let's go up and go to bed."

He didn't respond.

"Come on," she said. She moved toward the stairway. She ascended a few steps and stopped and stood there waiting.

He told himself he mustn't move and he mustn't say anything.

She put her hands on her hips. "Now look," she said, "you got a big day tomorrow and you need sleep."

It gave him a chance to reply and he said, "Yes, I know. That's why I'm going to sleep here."

"There? On the sofa?"

He nodded. "I want to be sure I get some sleep."

She was quiet for a long moment. Her hands fell away from her hips and hung limply at her sides. When she spoke, her voice sounded tight and sort of twisted. "Aw, please," she said. "Please—"

He looked at her. He wondered if she was crying. It seemed the mascara was wet and yet it wasn't dripping, he knew she was trying hard to hold it back. "No," he said.

Then it started to drip, a thick mixture of mascara and tear drops. She lifted her hands to wipe it away but couldn't quite manage the effort. A heavy sigh started from deep inside her and became a sob. She tried to stifle it, choked on it, and then ran very fast up the stairs.

Hart took off his shoes. Then he removed his jacket, arranged himself prone on the sofa resting sideways, placed his jacket over his shoulders, and closed his eyes.

The sofa was fairly soft and he was quite comfortable. In a few minutes he was sound asleep.

In the morning it began to snow around ten-thirty and then it came faster, the flakes swirling wildly, caught in the cross-current of cold wind coming from two rivers. It looked as though it would build and become a blizzard. But gradually it died down and by noontime it had stopped altogether. Then later there was a spell of that unaccountable Philadelphia weather, an acute change that brought warm air from somewhere, melting the snow in the streets and the icicles on the tree-branches. The warm air lasted until late in the afternoon. Around four-thirty it became very cold again, and Charley told Rizzio to put some coal in the furnace.

When Rizzio came up from the cellar, Charley had the card table set up in the middle of the living room. Mattone was lighting a cigarette and Hart was shuffling the cards. They played poker until suppertime, and after supper they resumed the game. At a little after eight Charley said they could play for another hour or so and then it would be time to put aside the cards and get started with the plans.

"What time is it now?" Mattone asked.

Charley glanced at his wristwatch. "It's twelve minutes past eight." Then he added, "Twelve minutes and forty seconds."

Rizzio looked at his own wristwatch and said, "I got eight-fifteen."

"Set it back," Mattone said. "Set it back two minutes and twenty seconds."

"I can't set the second hand," Rizzio said. He was turning the winder of his watch.

"Take it off your wrist," Mattone murmured. "Throw it away."

Rizzio frowned. "Throw what away?"

"Go on, get rid of it," Mattone spoke a trifle louder. "It's a cheap watch and you shouldn't have bought it in the first place."

"All it needs is regulating," Rizzio said.

"Your head needs regulating," Mattone told him. "Look now, you gonna get rid of that watch?"

Rizzio looked at Charley. "Tell him to cut it out."

"No, I won't tell him," Charley said. "I've told him too many times already. I'm tired of telling him."

"The watches gotta be checked exactly," Mattone said. "If it ain't split-second it means mistakes."

"You're the mistake," Charley said.

Mattone opened his mouth, almost said something, then measured the look on Charley's face and inhaled deeply to hold back whatever he wanted to say.

Charley looked at Hart. "Deal the cards."

They played for about two hours with Hart winning over four hundred dollars and most of it was Mattone's money. Mattone was betting clumsily and his lower lip looked raw where he was biting it. On the next play, he called Hart on what appeared to be an obvious bluff and Hart showed him a third ace that beat his three kings. Mattone gripped the edge of the table and stared up at the ceiling.

"Stop that," Charley said.

Mattone continued to stare at the ceiling. He said aloud to himself, "There's gotta be a reason—"

"For what?" Charley leaned forward, studying the look on Mattone's face.

"For such rotten luck," Mattone said. And then very slowly he got up from the table. For some moments he walked in aimless circles. Then he moved toward the sofa where the newspaper was scattered. He picked up a section of the newspaper and Hart looked at Charley and knew what Charley was thinking. They both knew that Mattone was looking at the dateline.

Then Mattone let go of the newspaper. It went down past the edge of the sofa and drifted onto the carpet. He was looking at it and talking to it without sound.

"Come over here and sit down," Charley said.

Mattone didn't move. But his head turned very slowly and he looked at Charley and said, "You know what day this is?"

"I said sit down." Charley's voice was a whisper that whistled. "We're playing poker."

"It's Friday the thirteenth," Mattone said.

"So?" It was Rizzio.

"Bad luck." Mattone stared past the faces at the card-table. "Very bad luck."

"Only for idiots," Charley said.

"Charley—"

"No."

"Charley, please—"

"I said no."

And then Mattone cried out, "I'm begging you, Charley. You gotta call it off. We can't do the job tonight. We go there tonight, we'll run into grief—"

Mattone's voice was very loud and it brought Frieda in from the dining room where she'd been sitting with Myrna, the two of them reading movie magazines. Frieda had her magazine in her hand and she was frowning and saying, "What's the matter? What's the matter here?"

"It's Friday the thirteenth," Mattone shouted.

"He wants we should postpone it," Charley said.

Frieda looked Mattone up and down. She said to Charley, "He looks like he's flipping."

"He'll be all right," Charley said, smiling.

Frieda walked out of the room. Charley went on smiling at her back as she returned to the dining room. Then he gave the smile to Mattone, and he said, "I'm ready to talk plans."

"Look, Charley—"

"You gonna join this conference or you wanna be out of it?"

Mattone took a very deep breath. He shut his eyes tightly, his body rigid for a long moment. Then he shook his head spasmodically. He took another deep breath and said, "I'm all right now."

"Sure you're all right," Charley said. "I knew you'd be all right."

Mattone came back to the table and sat down. Charley reached into the inner pocket of his jacket and took out the folded paper that showed a diagram of the Kenniston mansion in Wyncote.

"Now here's what we do—" Charley began.

Then he spoke for close to two hours. He outlined the plan in a general way, then went over it again. And then again and again, so each time he got it more detailed, with every move verbally blueprinted. And when he was finished he sat back and waited for questions but there were no questions because everything was clear and it was really a brilliant plan.

"All right, then," Charley said. "So I've told you and now you'll tell me. You first, Rizzio."

Rizzio repeated the plan. And then Mattone. When it was Hart's turn, he heard himself saying it almost word for word the way Charley had said it. The words came out automatically, like a recorded recitation.

"Very nice," Charley said. He glanced at his wristwatch. "Well, it's time to get ready."

The four of them got up from the table.

It was ten minutes to one.

CHAPTER 18

They were putting on their overcoats. Mattone and Rizzio wore dark brown camel-hair and Charley's coat was a midnight blue chesterfield. Hart was buttoning the bright green fleece and he could feel the heaviness of the cheap fabric on his shoulders.

He turned and faced the door of the vestibule so he wouldn't see the light in the dining room where she sat with Frieda and read the movie magazines. He wanted very much to see her and talk to her and tell her she mustn't worry, that everything would be all right. But seeing her now would be bad for both of them, awfully bad. And he thought: She knows it, too. That's why she's staying there in the dining room.

Then he wondered why Frieda also remained in the dining room. It didn't take much guessing and his brain said: Well, it's certainly no picnic for Frieda. She's torn between her need for you and her hate for you. Her need says she wants you to stay alive, and the hate wants her to come in here and hit back at you for what you're doing to her. Or what you're not doing. You sure did some damage to her last night.

Yes, all she needs to do now is come in here and tell Charley you're not fitted for this job, you're not a professional. But there's nothing you can do about that. All you can do is hope for Charley to open the door so we'll be out and away before she makes up her mind.

He saw Charley moving past him and opening the

vestibule door. Then the front door was open and the four of them filed out and went down cold steps onto a cold pavement. The January wind came at them and it was terribly cold.

"It's freezing out here," Rizzio said.

"All right," Mattone said. "So it's freezing. So shut up, will you?"

They were walking now at medium stride, Charley and Hart walking in front, with Charley setting the pace. At the corner they turned and went south on Tulpehocken. There were cars parked on both sides of the street, packed in close, almost bumper-to-bumper. Toward the middle of the block they arrived at their car and it was a 1951 two-door Plymouth sedan. It was painted black and looked older than it was, it hadn't been washed for some time.

They climbed in and Mattone sat at the wheel, Rizzio beside him. Charley and Hart settled themselves in back.

Mattone hit the starter. There was the sound of the starter but no engine. Mattone hit it again and the same thing happened.

"What's wrong?" Charley asked.

"It's cold," Mattone said.

"Got anti-freeze?"

Mattone didn't answer. He was trying the starter again. The engine turned over and made an effort and then died.

Charley sat up a little straighter. He said very slowly, "I'm asking you something, Mattone. Does it have anti-freeze?"

Mattone turned and looked at Charley. "Yes, Charley," he said, his mouth stretched wide with the words jetting out through his teeth. "You told me to put in more anti-freeze and I put it in."

"All right," Charley said. "Try it again."

Mattone pressed the starter and this time the engine caught and stayed alive. Mattone gunned it and it became very much alive. Hart heard the extra power and he knew it was a souped-up engine.

Now the car was sufficiently warmed and Mattone nosed it out from the row of parked cars and took it north on Tulpehocken to Morton, then west to Washington Lane, then north again to Stenton. At Stenton there was a red light and a red police car parked at the corner. There were two policemen in the front seat and one of them was reading a newspaper under the glow of the streetlamp. The other policeman was looking at the Plymouth.

"What's he looking at?" Rizzio wanted to know.

"Shut up," Mattone said. And then, hissing it, "Quit looking at him. For Christ's sake, will you stop looking at him?"

The policeman leaned his head out the car window and said, "Hey, you."

"Me?" Mattone called back.

"Yeah, you," the policeman said.

"What's the matter?" Mattone asked.

"Dim your lights," the policeman said.

"Sure, officer." Mattone dimmed the headlights. "Sorry, officer."

"Remember, you're still in the city," the policeman said now more politely. "Keep them headlights dim until you're on the highway."

"Yes, sir," Mattone said. "Thanks, officer."

The signal light turned green and they turned left on Stenton, stayed on Stenton and passed the wide road

going north toward Wyncote. There was some teen-age
Friday night traffic on that road and Mattone was looking for a narrower road. He found it about a mile further
up. It was bumpy and in sections it was unpaved but the
Plymouth had good tires and they held their grip nicely.

They came onto another road that was new and
smooth, going past blocks of brand new road houses.
Then they turned onto a curving road, going north past
large homes. As they continued north, the houses
kept getting larger and larger with wider lawns, then
fenced-in properties with private roads leading to the
mansions set far back from the highway. The car went up
a steep hill and on the down-grade it moved slowly past
an iron gate that glimmered like black teeth in the glow
of the headlights. The iron gate went on and on and now
the road was level again and the car moved very slowly.
They kept going past the gate for another quarter of a
mile and then Charley said, "Stop here."

"Here?" Mattone asked.

"Right here," Charley said. "Stop the car."

The car came to a stop at the side of the road. Charley
told Rizzio to get out and switch the license plates. Rizzio
opened the glove compartment and took out a screw
driver and a license plate and got out of the car. Rizzio
did it very quickly and when he came back with the plate
he'd replaced, he flipped the screw driver into the glove
compartment, then slid the plate into a groove behind
the wall of the compartment where it would not be
visible to anyone who might be obliged to see what was
in the compartment.

The engine was idling and Mattone put the car in gear
and they went along the road at around fifteen miles per
hour. There was another hundred or so yards of iron gate
and then some fifty yards of high stone fence belonging

to the same estate and then the wide entrance of the private road.

Mattone turned the car onto the private road. It was a winding road bordered with high trees. They went along the road for the better part of a mile, and then there was the small house of the caretaker coming up in front of the headlights. One of the windows was dimly lit and as they approached the house, a side door opened and a man with white hair stepped out and walked toward the slowly moving car.

Mattone stopped the car and the old man stopped also. He stood about twenty feet away from the car. His old man's voice sounded sleepy. "What do you want?"

"We're going to Doylestown," Mattone said.

"Not on this road," the old man told him.

"Why not?" Mattone asked. "Ain't this the way to Doylestown?"

"This is private property," the old man said.

"Oh," Mattone said. "I guess we made a wrong turn."

"You sure did." The old man stood there with his hands at his sides.

"Say, how do we get out of here?" Mattone asked.

"Just turn around and follow the road."

"I mean, how do we hit the main highway going north?"

"Well, what you do is—" The old man walked toward the car. He was ten feet away from the car and then five and Mattone opened the door and got out. The old man said, "You gotta get onto Old York Road. That's the shortest way to Doylestown. And what you do is—"

Mattone hit him with a short right to the jaw and caught him before he went down. Then Rizzio was out of the car and they put the caretaker in the back seat. He was unconscious and he was sprawled between Charley and Hart, his head resting on Hart's shoulder. Hart glanced at the face and saw it was a very old man with an opened sagging mouth that showed false teeth.

The car was moving again and they went along the winding road going past a greenhouse and a Japanese garden and the two-story structure that was the servants' quarters. Then up ahead in the moonlight there was the white marble of the Kenniston mansion. Now the headlights were off but the mansion was distinct in the moonlight.

It looks more like a college library, Hart thought. Then he heard the groan and he glanced at the face of the old man. The old man's eyes were open and the lips quivered with consternation and outrage and fright.

Charley was talking to Mattone, leaning forward and pointing to some shrubbery about forty feet away from the side-entrance, saying, "Park it over there near them bushes." Then he turned to the old man and said, "What's your name?"

The old man was very frightened now and he couldn't talk.

"Come on, Grandad," Charley urged softly. "It ain't that bad. Just tell me your name."

"Thomas—"

"How old are you, Thomas?"

"Seventy-three."

"Aw, shucks," Charley said. "That ain't old."

The old man closed his eyes and said quietly, "It's too old for this kind of business."

"Don't worry, Thomas. You'll make out all right. All you gotta do is pay attention and do what I tell you."

Then Charley took the the gun from his pocket. The old man opened his eyes and saw the gun.

"Now listen to me very careful," Charley said, holding

the gun loosely but with the muzzle pointing toward the old man's abdomen. "You're coming in with us. If anyone comes downstairs and wants to know what's happening, you'll tell them we're from City Hall, we're detectives."

The old man blinked several times. "Detectives?"

"Yes, we're detectives and someone tipped us off there'd be some action here tonight, a couple ex-cons coming to break in and grab them oriental treasures."

"That's what you want me to say?"

"No, I'll say it. What you do is make out you're in Hollywood, you're a high-paid actor. You nod your head in agreement, you tell them we showed you our credentials and we're really detectives."

"But I'm not an actor," the old man said. "They'll see I'm scared clean out of my wits and—"

"You won't be scared," Charley told him. "You'll be thinking how nice it is to be alive and stay alive."

"All right," the old man said. "I'll do my best."

Now the car was parked near the shrubbery. Mattone and Rizzio climbed out and walked toward the mansion, and Charley said to the old man, "You see how we play this game? Them gentlemen are the two ex-cons. They're the bad guys and we're the good guys. When they break in we'll be staked out, we'll be there to get them."

Hart watched Mattone and Rizzio walking slowly along the side of the mansion. He saw Rizzio moving ahead and crouching in dog-trainer fashion as two large Doberman pinschers came loping across the lawn. The dogs slowed down and Rizzio didn't move as the dogs walked up to him. Hart couldn't hear anything but he knew Rizzio was talking to the dogs. Then Rizzio was patting the dogs and they didn't seem to mind.

"I wonder how he does it," Charley said.

"He better be careful," the old man said, momentarily

forgetting his own fright and feeling afraid for Rizzio. "Them dogs are awfully vicious."

"Not now they ain't. Look at them."

The dogs seemed very friendly. They were rubbing their noses against Rizzio's legs. He went on patting them and talking to them.

"It's remarkable," Charley said. "He never misses. I think he has some dog in him."

Rizzio was walking the dogs, holding their collars, and Mattone followed at a distance of about thirty feet. Then Rizzio turned and beckoned, and Mattone came in closer. Hart watched the merging of the four figures now silhouetted against the whiteness of the Kenniston mansion. He saw the two men and the two dogs moving past the rear-side entrance, and then at the rear of the mansion they turned the corner and went out of sight.

Charley glanced at his wristwatch. He said, "We wait two minutes."

"There's a light on upstairs," Hart said.

"I see it," Charley said.

"It just went on."

"No," Charley said. "That's an optical illusion you get when you first see a lit window. I saw that light about a minute ago."

"It wasn't lit when we got here," Hart said. "None of the windows were lit."

"All right, don't worry about it."

"I'm not worrying," Hart said.

"You sound like you're worried," Charley said.

"You want me to tell you what I think about all this?" the old man suddenly asked.

"Sure," Charley said, "tell me."

"Well, mister, I got the feeling you won't get what you're after."

"Thanks for telling me," Charley said. "Now I'll tell you something, Thomas. I want you to get rid of that feeling. I want you to feel you're working with this crew and we're gonna do this job and do it right. You understand what I'm saying?"

The old man nodded.

Charley brought his wristwatch toward his eyes and murmured, "Fifty-eight, fifty-nine – two minutes." He opened the car door and climbed out facing the old man. Then the old man climbed out, and then Hart. The three of them walked toward the side entrance. On the door-panel there was a large mother-of-pearl button and Charley pressed it. A few moments later he pressed it again. He was pressing it a third time when the door opened and a middle-aged man wearing a bathrobe stood there and stared at them.

"We're the police," Charley said.

So then it was up to the old caretaker, and he nodded and said to the middle-aged man, "It's all right, Mr Kenniston. These men are detectives from City Hall, and—"

"Come in, please." The middle-aged man moved aside to let them enter. In the hallway he switched on a light, and they followed him into a large room that had a Chinese motif. It was all ebony furniture and rose-quartz lamps and vases of delicately carved jade.

The middle-aged man was facing Charley and saying "Will you kindly tell me—"

"I'll hafta tell it fast," Charley said. "We're here to prevent a robbery. We got a tip. It might be happening at this very minute. I mean, they might be on the grounds right now, trying to break in. Or maybe they've broken in already. So you see we gotta move fast. There ain't time to do much explaining."

"But—"

"Look, mister. You got something very valuable in this house. You got a collection of oriental antiques worth maybe a million. We got it listed in our records, it's our job to protect that kind of property. But if you wanna lose it, that's up to you."

"But I don't understand why – I mean, you could have phoned—"

"We can get them with the goods this way."

The middle-aged man was frowning at the floor. The frown was more thoughtful than worried. For a long moment there was no sound in the room, and then all at once some sound came in from somewhere in the rear of the mansion. It was a mingling of footsteps and the scraping of chairs, and the middle-aged man gasped, "What's that?"

"It ain't mice, that's for sure," Charley said.

The middle-aged man became pale. "Why don't you do something? What are you waiting for?"

"I'm waiting for you," Charley said. "I can't protect your merchandise unless you tell me where it's stashed."

Then it was quiet again and the middle-aged man was biting his thumbnail. And Hart thought: It's gonna be yes or no, and what's it gonna be?

The middle-aged man said, "Please come with me."

Charley looked at Hart. "Wait here." And then he was following the middle-aged man across the room. There was a large ebony-paneled door at the far end and they were half-way to the door when something went wrong.

It started with the dogs. Hart heard the growls and then a scream from the rear of the house, the sound of glass crashing, a table overturning, and now the screaming was terrible and the growls were noises from very bad dreams.

The middle-aged man said happily, "The dogs got them."

Charley looked at Hart and didn't say anything.

Hart heard the sounds coming nearer and then a shoulder hitting a door. He turned and saw the door giving way, and Rizzio running in very fast with a Doberman pinscher flying after him and landing on his back. Rizzo went to his knees and the dog had its mouth opened wide to bite into his neck. The look on Rizzio's face was acute puzzlement, his eyes seemed to be saying: How could this happen? I know how to handle dogs.

Charley reached into his overcoat pocket and took out the gun. He shot from his waist and the bullet went along a path maybe two inches away from Rizzio's face, hitting the face of the dog, hitting it between the eyes.

The dog rolled over dead and the middle-aged man shouted at Charley, "Why'd you do that?"

Charley didn't answer. He was looking at Rizzio. And Rizzio looked back at him and said, "I'm sorry, Charley. I—"

"Charley?" the middle-aged man said it slowly and quietly. "Oh, so that's it. You're working together."

Charley shrugged. He moved the gun so that it covered the middle-aged man and the old caretaker. But now there were more sounds, a mixture of footsteps and voices from upstairs, and a feminine voice calling anxiously, "What is it, Merton? Are you all right?"

"Yes," the middle-aged man called back. "I'm quite all right, my dear."

"I'm coming down," she shouted.

"No, don't do that." The middle-aged man said it loudly but calmly. "Just lift the phone and call the police."

Charley smiled wearily at the middle-aged man and said, "Now why'd you hafta tell her that?" He moved the gun just a little so that it was pointed at the chest of the middle-aged man. "You see what you've done? Now it gets sloppy. I hate when it gets sloppy."

Without sound Hart said: Don't, Charley. Don't do that. And then he saw the old caretaker running in to shield his employer, lunging at Charley with both arms raised high. As Charley pulled the trigger, Hart moved in very fast and hit his arm. The bullet went into the carpet. The old man made a grab for Charley's hand holding the gun, and Hart gave the old man a shove and sent him to the floor.

Charley looked at Rizzio. "Where's the other dog?"

"I don't know – I guess—"

"You guess," Charley said. "I thought you knew all about dogs. You're an expert with dogs."

Rizzio sighed. He shook his head slowly.

"Come on," Charley said. "Let's get out of here."

The three of them backed out of the room, Charley's gun covering the middle-aged man and the old caretaker until they were in the hallway. Then they walked to the side-door and out of the mansion. As they crossed the lawn, headed toward the parked Plymouth, Rizzio was pointing and saying, "There's the other dog. Over there, Charley. You looking?"

"No," Charley said. "You look."

"Aw, don't, Charley. Don't be that way."

"What way?" Charley asked mildly. "I'm just telling you to look, that's all. I want you to have a good look."

"Jesus," Rizzio said. And then he sobbed it. "Oh Jesus—"

And Hart was looking and seeing the broken window, with the Doberman standing under the window at the side of his prey. In the moonlight the body of Mattone was very white where his flesh shoved through his ripped clothes. His clothes were almost entirely ripped from his torso. He was resting on his back, his shin tilted up at an acute angle, showing all that had been done to his throat. Much had been done and there was little of his throat remaining.

They were getting into the Plymouth. Rizzio slid in behind the wheel and Charley said, "Get a move on. There's gonna be red cars here in a few minutes."

Hart leaned back against the rear-seat upholstery. He heard the engine starting, he felt the car moving. It moved fast going across the lawn onto the private road. On the road and headed toward the highway bordering the estate, it was hitting fifty on the curves. Then later, on the highway, it was hitting eighty and eighty-five and ninety.

They were on a narrow street in the West Oak Lane area when Charley told Rizzio to stop the car and get out and change the license plates. A few minutes later they were in Germantown and the car moved slowly past red cars. There were a lot of red cars around and the policemen were looking at all small black sedans that drove past, and checking the plates with the written numbers they had in their books.

The car came onto Tulpehocken, going very slowly into its parking place in the row of closely parked cars. They got out and walked north on Tulpehocken toward Morton. On Morton the wind came screeching at them and it was like the blast of a trumpet going up very high.

CHAPTER 19

"Want some coffee?" Frieda asked.

"No," Charley said.

"It'll do you good," she said. "You could all use some coffee."

"All right." Charley was sitting on the sofa. He was still wearing his overcoat and muffler and hat. Rizzio and Hart had taken off their coats and they were sitting in armchairs on the other side of the room.

"I'll make it good and strong and you'll drink it real hot," Frieda said. "It'll do you the world of good."

Then she walked out, going toward the kitchen. The three of them sat there and Charley began to unbutton his overcoat. He freed one button, then the next one, and then forgot about the third. He began to fumble with his muffler, got it halfway off, and let go of it and pressed his hands flat and hard against the sofa pillows.

Rizzio said, "I'm trying to put it together and see how it happened. I just can't understand how it happened."

"It's all right," Charley said. "Forget about it."

Rizzio was quiet for some moments. Then he said, "You know what I think? I think there was something wrong with them dogs."

"Do you hafta talk about it?" Charley asked softly. "Can't you let it drop?"

"I had them dogs under perfect control," Rizzio said. "And then, for no reason at all they get agitated and start all that hell. Or maybe—"

"Maybe what?"

"Maybe there was a reason," Rizzio said.

Charley leaned back against the sofa cushions. He folded his arms. He looked a question at Rizzio.

And Rizzio said, "The date, Charley. Friday the thirteenth."

Then it was quiet.

Finally Rizzio said, "What about it, Charley? You think I got a point there?"

"I'm playing with it," Charley said. He looked at Hart. It was the first time he'd looked directly at Hart since they'd come back to the house. He spoke very softly to Hart, saying, "What's your opinion?"

Hart shrugged. "It wasn't Friday when we made the try. It was after midnight, so that makes it Saturday morning. This is Saturday the fourteenth."

"He's right," Rizzio said.

"No, he's wrong," Charley said. "It's still Friday the thirteenth." And he went on looking at Hart.

Rizzio frowned and scratched the back of his head.

Charley said, "It's Black Friday and for certain people it's a day that never ends. They carry it with them all the time. Like typhoid carriers. So no matter where they go or what they do, they bring bad luck."

"Meaning me?" Hart murmured.

Charley nodded slowly. Then very slowly he reached into his overcoat pocket and took out the gun.

"What's all this?" Rizzio said. "What's the matter, Charley? What are you doing?"

"He's getting superstitious," Hart said.

"That's part of it," Charley said. There was no tone or color or anything in his voice. "The other part is, you're not in our bracket, you can't work the way we work."

Hart shrugged again. He was looking at the wall behind Charley's head.

He heard Charley saying, "What it amounts to, you're not a professional. I found it out when the old man jumped at me and you hit my arm to ruin my aim."

Hart smiled. He knew there was no use arguing the issue. He said, "I guess that did it."

"It sure did," Charley said. "With that one move you gave yourself away."

And Hart thought: So this is the way it usually happens. It doesn't need a Frieda to spill the beans. Sooner or later we do it ourselves, we give ourselves away.

Then he heard himself saying, "Can I ask a favor?"

"Sure," Charley said. "You can ask."

"I'd like to see Myrna."

"Myrna?" Charley's eyebrows went up slightly. "Why Myrna?"

Hart didn't answer.

Charley went on looking at him for some moments, then looked at Rizzio and said, "Go upstairs and wake up Myrna. Bring her down here."

Rizzio got up and headed for the stairway. From the kitchen Frieda was calling, "Coffee's ready," then calling it again some moments later, and finally coming in to see why they didn't answer. She saw the gun and she said, "What's this?" And Charley said, "He's going."

"What?" She whispered it. "What?"

"I said he's going. He's gotta go. We can't use him."

"Oh," Frieda said. She looked at Hart. She saw he wasn't looking at her. His eyes were focused on the stairway. There were footsteps in the hall upstairs, then Rizzio was coming down, and then Myrna.

Charley was looking at Frieda and saying, "He asked me to do him a favor. He said he wanted to see Myrna."

Frieda took a step toward Hart. "Damn you," she said. "God damn you."

He didn't hear that. He lifted himself from the armchair, smiling at Myrna as she came down the stairs. She wore a white satin quilted robe. Her hair fell loosely onto her shoulders, the black strands lustrous against the white fabric. Her eyes were bright, fully awake, so he knew she hadn't been sleeping. He knew somehow that she couldn't sleep because she'd been thinking about him.

And now for a very long moment there was no Charley, no Frieda, no Rizzio. It was just the girl and himself, looking at each other, their eyes saying things that couldn't be said with the spoken word. They stood a few feet apart but he felt her presence very deep inside himself. It was a fine feeling.

He heard Charley saying, "You wanna talk to her?"

"We're talking," he said. But then he knew the talk was ended because Myrna had turned her head and she was looking at Charley and the gun.

Hart thought: Well, maybe I can tell her a lie and maybe Charley will back me up. He said to her, "It's all right, there's nothing to worry about. It's just that Charley is sending me away for a while—"

"That's right," Charley nodded.

But it was no good, it didn't fool her. She went on looking at the gun.

And then there was a laugh. It came from Frieda. It was the closed-lip laughter of negative thinking, negative enjoyment. Frieda let it out and breathed it in, savoring it. She said to Charley, "Do it now, while she's here. I want her to see this."

"No," Charley said. "There's no point in that."

"The hell there ain't," Frieda told him. "Go on, do it now."

"You keep quiet," Charley said. He sounded tired and gloomy.

Frieda made a gesture of frantic impatience. "I'm telling you to—"

"You're not telling me anything," Charley said. "I told you to keep quiet."

Hart wasn't listening to that. He was measuring the distance to the vestibule door. The door was halfway open and he estimated it was less than five feet away. He told himself it was near enough and there was nothing to lose, he might as well try it. He looked at Myrna and her eyes said: Of course you'll try it, you gotta try it.

Frieda was saying, "Shoot him, Charley, shoot him. What are you waiting for?"

"Can't you keep quiet?" Charley said it slowly.

Hart lunged for the vestibule door. In the same instant Myrna threw herself across the path of the bullet coming from Charley's gun. Hart had not yet reached the door and as he saw her going down he lost all interest in getting past the vestibule.

She rested face down on the floor. There was a hole in her temple and a thin stream of red came out and formed a pool on the carpet.

For some moments none of them did anything or said anything. Then Rizzio walked toward the body and knelt beside it and felt the wrist.

"She's gone," Rizzio said.

Hart looked at the corpse. But then his eyes were closed and he was seeing inside himself and she was there.

"Pick it up," Charley said to Rizzio. "Take it down the cellar."

Rizzio lifted the small skinny corpse and carried it out of the room.

Charley was looking at the bloodstains on the carpet. He said to Frieda, "I don't want that there. Get some cleaning fluid—"

"I'll do it in the morning," Frieda said.

"You'll do it now."

"Why can't I do it in the morning?" Frieda whined. "Jesus Christ, I'm all played out."

"So am I," Charley said. And then he sighed. "I think it's caught up with me."

It was quiet for some moments and then Frieda gestured toward Hart and said, "What about him? Whatcha gonna do with him?"

"Does it matter?" Charley murmured. The gun was loose in his hand and it wasn't aimed at anything. "Does it really matter?"

Frieda frowned. "What is it, Charley? What's happening to you?"

Charley didn't answer. His shoulders drooped and his head went down low. The gun fell out of his hand and dropped over the side of the sofa onto the floor.

"Charley—" Frieda went to the sofa and sat down beside him. She put her arms around him and pulled his head down to her bosom.

"I'm so tired," Charley mumbled. "I'd like to fall asleep on a train going away – away—"

"Poor Charley."

"Yeah, you're right. That's what it all comes down to. Poor old Charley."

Frieda looked at Hart. Her voice was lifeless. "Put on

your overcoat," she said. "Get out of here and don't come back."

"Oh, let him stay," Charley murmured. "What the hell's the difference?"

"No," she said. "I don't want him here."

The bright green coat was draped over the stairway railing. Hart took it and put it on and walked out of the house. As he came down off the front steps onto the pavement he remembered the money he'd won in the poker game, telling himself there was more than four hundred dollars rolled up in his trousers pocket.

And maybe that'll help, he thought.

But somehow it wasn't an important thought, and after some moments he let it fade. He was walking very slowly, not feeling the bite of the cold wind, not feeling anything. And later, turning the street corners, he didn't bother to look at the street signs. He had no idea where he was going and he didn't care.

The Dead
Laugh Last

The Beer Joint was deserted except for a solitary drinker hunched over a glass at a corner table. I said, "Hello, Rube," and pulled a chair up to the table and sat down.

Rube Hansen lifted his head. "I don't drink with coppers."

He said it as if he was too tired to really care one way or the other. The old sneer in his voice was gone and so was the ice in his eyes.

I hadn't really seen him since he had pulled out of the rackets nearly a year ago, but I had heard the whispers. It was said that the soul of Rube Hansen had died and that only his ghost remained to haunt some of the less expensive of his former hangouts.

"Thanks, I'm not drinking," I said dryly. "I want to talk to you about some people who were found murdered last year."

I was expecting that disdainful yawn for which he had been famous, but that, too, was in the past. He brooded into his rye. "So you're still plugging away, copper?" he muttered.

"You know the homicide bureau," I said. "You're clever, Rube – or were. But with guys like you, it's the police who write the last chapter."

He lifted the glass to his mouth, but he didn't drink. And when he spoke, it was plain that he hadn't listened to me, because his words had nothing to do with the subject.

"The only thing that lasts is the love of a good woman," he said.

I burst out laughing in his face. I couldn't help it. Coming from anybody, that corny sentiment would have been funny, but the Rube, the ruthless mobster, the merciless killer, made it downright hilarious.

He looked at me. My laughter cracked and then ceased. I had never thought that I would see anything as sad as those brown eyes of his. You just can't laugh at a guy like that.

"You don't believe this about a good woman," he said in sorrow. "You're a guy like I was, copper. You think all women have got to be two-faced."

I started to protest that I had a wife and two daughters that I cherished, but again he ignored me. "In a little while I have a date," he said. "Maybe there's time to show you I know what I'm talking about."

Tensely I leaned against the table. He was drunk, but not very drunk. Still, maybe he had enough liquor in him to say the things I had been working for months to find out.

He rolled the glass between his palms and did not look at me, speaking as if to himself. This was his story:

It was just a year ago tonight that I was in Barney's. I'd dropped a grand on the crap table and had an idea that the dice were phonies. Barney came running over to me from a back room, all his chins shaking in terror, and shoved the grand back at me, saying it was all right if only I didn't make trouble.

That's the kind of lad I was. Six years before, the brightest company I'd known were the cows on my old man's farm, and now here I was sitting on top of the town, with a tough boy like Barney shaking in his socks because I didn't like the way he did business.

Not that the grand meant anything to me, though until I was twenty I'd never seen more that ten bucks all in one piece. There was plenty more where that had come from. I took the money from Barney and passed it over to Mimi who stood on the other side of me. "Buy yourself another trinket, baby," I said breezily.

You remember Mimi Cook, copper? Sure, everybody knew her. She made me think of a diamond – as hard and as beautiful. Guys with oil wells and gold mines wanted to marry her, but it was no soap. She was my woman.

That was something, wasn't it? Mimi Cook, who drove men crazy just looking at her, was the woman of the Rube, the hick who had hit the city with nothing to his name but the hayseed in his hair! I was feeling fine.

With Mimi hanging onto my arm, we walked into the night club part of Barney's. It was still early. The band was tuning up and only a handful of people were scattered about. And this girl was sitting by herself at a table.

She happened to turn her head and our eyes met. I stopped dead.

I don't know if I can make you understand what she did to me, copper. She was the dream I used to dream as a kid in the fields at twilight. Her hair was ripe wheat and her eyes were cornflowers.

I glanced at Mimi standing beside me in an evening gown with little in back and not much more in front and at the brittle beauty of her face, much of which had come out of jars, and I pulled away from her.

White anger flashed across Mimi's face, but I wasn't

interested in how she felt. I walked across the floor to the strange girl's table.

She didn't give me a come-on smile, but she was watching me with her eyes strangely alight, like she knew what was happening to both of us.

Before I could reach her, Al Slavin and Ripper Moore jumped up in front of me. "A word of caution, Rube," Al said in that smooth tone of his. "If you're going after what I think you are, she belongs to Billie Flail."

"I'm terrified," I said. "I took the numbers game away from Billie and he didn't have the guts to say boo."

"He's nuts about that girl," Al warned. "Because he didn't fight back before doesn't mean he can't make trouble."

I poked a finger into Al Salvin's skinny chest. "You're my mouthpiece, Al. Your job is to keep the law off my neck. I'll handle my private life myself."

Al said, "No broad is worth—" I yawned in his face and he didn't finish. He shrugged. "You're the boss, Rube."

"Glad you know it," I said, and went on towards the girl.

She was sitting with her arms extended on the table, watching my approach. Billie Flail came out of the washroom and sat down next to her.

Ripper Moore was tagging after me. He whispered, "Let me stick my shiv in Billie, boss."

"You're a good pal, Ripper," I said. "But run along. All Billie will need is a slap on the wrist."

I took the third seat at the table. Billie Flail's big body was tense and his handsome face twisted like he'd tasted something nasty.

As if he weren't there at all, I turned to the girl and

said, "One will get you ten that you were raised on a farm."

"Why, yes," she said, flushing prettily at the way my eyes ate her up. "How do you know?"

"A big city doesn't turn them out as fresh and blooming as you," I told her, meaning every word. "I'm a farm boy myself. That's why they call me the Rube."

"Rube Hansen!" she exclaimed. But she didn't act scared the way lots of people did when they heard my name. In fact, she smiled. "My name is Lydia Gilmor. And this is—"

"Spare the formalities, kid," Billie Flail cut in sourly. "I regret to say that the Rube and I have met before."

I said, "Tell me, Lydia, how come a nice girl like you is with a heel like Billie?"

She frowned. "I don't understand what you mean. Mr. Flail is going to introduce me to all the big show producers. I came to New York to get on the stage."

"Does he mean the guy who puts on the shows at Sing Sing?" I said. "That's the only producer he would know." I turned to Billie Flail with a pleasant smile. "So long, Billie."

The color drained from his lips. His right hand crept to his bow tie, and I could see the slight bulge of a holster under the left shoulder.

"Damn it, you're not going to do this to me!" he said, trying hard to keep his voice steady.

I leaned back in my chair and yawned, delicately covering my mouth with two fingers.

You've heard the saying in town, copper, that when the Rube yawns, watch out. Billie Flail took a deep breath and put his hands on the table, palms down, showing me he was no tougher than when I'd taken the policy game away from him.

"Are you sick, Billie?" Lydia asked him.

Without a word he rose and moved away from us, weaving between the tables as if he were drunk. I felt a little sorry for him. I could understand how he hated to lose her.

Somebody in the place laughed. It was Ripper Moore, sitting at a nearby table with Al Slavin. Al, though, looked glum, the way lawyers always do when anything happens.

And behind them Mimi Cook leaned against the bar with a tall glass in her hand. Her dark eyes were on Lydia and myself, smoldering, and her scarlet lips were very tight.

Mimi hates me now, I thought. *Well, She's not the first woman or man who hated me, and what did it get them? So long, Mimi. You were fun, but I guess I'm just a Rube at heart. I like the simple things in my girlfriends – the peaches and cream instead of the hardness and beauty of diamonds.*

"Now why did Billie act like that?" Lydia was saying. "Why, he walked out on me without even saying good-night."

I covered her hand with mine. "Forget him, baby. I'll see you home tonight and every night thereafter."

Well, copper, we hit it off right from the start. It was like the hooey in torch songs, only this wasn't hooey. It wasn't like playing around with the tough-skinned glamour girls like Mimi Cook. Lydia was only a sweet-face kid with big blue eyes and maybe not so smart because she hadn't been around much. She knew I wasn't quite legitimate, but she didn't believe the stories about what a big, bad man I was. She was so innocent herself she couldn't imagine that a guy she was nuts about wasn't good, too.

That's right, copper, I had it bad and so did she. The whole town was joking about the Rube and the girl from the sticks. I didn't mind. In fact, I liked it.

But there were two who didn't care one bit for what was going on.

I figured that Mimi Cook would drift on to somebody else, because there were plenty of rich guys who were interested in her. But she didn't. I'd see here around here and there, always alone. She was the only person I couldn't look straight in the eye. I don't know why. I think, maybe, I was a little bit scared of her.

Yeah, copper, that's a laugh. The Rube scared of a woman!

Then there was the other, Billie Flail. Since that night in Barney's, he kept out of my way. I told Al Slavin that Billie was yellow through and through, like I'd always figured him.

But Al shook his head in that solemn way of his. "He cared a lot for that girl, Rube."

"So what?" I said. "He cared a lot for the numbers racket, and when I moved in he moved out."

"Lydia Gilmor is very lovely," Al said.

"You're telling me," I said.

Next day it happened.

Lydia was seeing a producer. That lass had a lot on the ball, but if she was an actress, I was J. Edgar Hoover. But she had the bug and so I got a couple of favors returned from somebody by getting her an introduction to Jasper Weems who puts on all those musical shows. She was being given a tryout that night, and at around eleven I strolled over to the theatre to pick her up.

She was half way up the block, having come out

already, and she called to me. I started toward her when I saw her.

I didn't have any idea that the sedan was crawling along the curb behind me. I wouldn't have had a chance, with me only two feet from the curb and not knowing what was coming. But I got a break.

Some woman in the street saw something suspicious about that sedan. She screamed.

I swung and saw the car about ten feet behind me. Through the windshield I caught a flash of the driver behind the wheel, and he was leaning to his right, poking a gun toward the right car window.

I guess I broke a world's record getting into a doorway and falling flat on my face. The gun chattered seven times – all the slugs in a heavy automatic – and glass tinkled above me. Then the car swept on.

By the time I was on my feet and had my roscoe out, the sedan was out of sight around the corner. There was a lot of commotion in the street and people were running every which way. Only one of them was coming toward me, and that of course was Lydia.

She fell into my arms. "Darling, are you all right?"

"Not a nick."

"You might have been killed. Why should anybody want to harm you?"

That was a question for the books. "Baby," I asked, "did you see who was in that sedan?"

"It was too dark. But there was only one man. I'm sure of that."

"You didn't get a look at his face?"

"No."

Well, neither did I, but I had more than a good idea who it was.

Then I wasn't so sure, because over Lydia's head I saw

a tall, smooth-looking girl step out of the shadows across the street and into a cab.

I dropped my arms from about Lydia. I put my hand on my gun. But I just stood there, watching the cab move away. You can't burn down a woman the way you would a man. Anyway, I wouldn't want Lydia to see me kill anybody. She wouldn't like it.

Lydia's hand was contracting on my arm. "Darling, what's the matter now?"

I said, "I'm taking you home, baby."

As a matter of fact, I didn't – not for a couple of hours, anyway. The street was suddenly filled with cops, and a couple of minutes later we were on our way to headquarters. I raised hell when they took Lydia along. The idea of having that sweet, innocent kid worked on by a bunch of rough-necked cops made me sick.

You remember, copper, that you were one of the reception committee at headquarters. Our story was good, and the funny thing, it was all true. It's still no crime to be shot at, and when Al Slavin, my mouthpiece, came charging in, you coppers had to let us go.

Ripper Moore was waiting outside behind the wheel of Al's car. We didn't do any real talking until after I had taken Lydia up to her place and kissed her good night.

When I returned to the car and got in the back seat with Al, Al said, "Next time Billie Flail mightn't miss."

"It wasn't Billie," I said. "It was Mimi Cook."

Al stopped a lit match half way to his cigar. Ripper, who was about to start the car, twisted around in the front seat.

"You and Lydia and the other witnesses all agreed that it was a man in the car and that he was alone," Al pointed out.

"I didn't say that Mimi handled the gun. She was across the street, fingering me."

"Who did the shooting?" Al asked.

I shrugged. "What's the difference? Killers can be hired for a dime a dozen."

Ripper leaned over the seat. "Listen to this, boss. I know for a fact Billie Flail gave Joe Riker a century to go swipe him a heap for tonight. Why'd he want a hot car except for a job? And Billie's been drinking heavy and shooting his mouth off about tearing your heart out."

"Mimi was across the street all the time," I muttered.

"Say!" Al put a hand on my knee. "Why couldn't Mimi and Billie have teamed up?"

It could be. They both hated my guts.

"Mimi finds out that Lydia has a try-out and knows that I'll call for her," I said slowly. "She waits across the street. When I come along, she flashes a sign to Billie Flail who's down the street in the stolen car. She waits around to see how it turns out and then steps into a cab."

"Exactly!" Al agreed.

Ripper's ugly face lit up. "You want I should carve 'em both up, boss?"

"No," I said.

Ripper sighed. "I guess you're right. It's only bad luck killing dames. So I'll give only Billie the business."

"No," I said.

"Don't be a fool, Ripper," Al snapped. "Don't you realize that this is one job that Rube has to do himself."

"There's not going to be a job done," I said.

Ripper handed me a sharp look of bewilderment and dropped down in the seat and started the car. For a couple of blocks we drove in silence.

Then Al said softly, "It's that girl, Rube, isn't it? Lydia

has been working on you to reform. You are afraid she would not approve."

"Shut up!" I growled.

"Don't tell me that the Rube is getting soft?"

I turned my head a little and looked at Al. "They tell me that the only good lawyers are dead lawyers."

He shrivelled up before my eyes. He wasn't sure how soft I had really gone, if at all. For the rest of the trip he kept his mouth shut.

Days passed and I did nothing. Wherever I went, people gave me puzzled looks. The whole town knew that Billie Flail had emptied a heater at me and missed, and that, strangely enough, Billie was still alive.

Don't get the idea, copper, that I had a yen to make a clay pigeon of myself for Billie Flail. With Lydia around, I was fonder of life than I'd ever been. The thing was, if he made the first move and then I killed him, it would be strictly self-defence, so that Lydia wouldn't think I was a guy who went around liquidating people.

I never claimed Billie Flail was a dope, only yellow, and he pulled a typical yellow stunt.

I was getting ready for bed when the phone rang. It was Lydia, and her voice was hardly more than a choked whisper.

"Darling, I'm at Billie Flail's country place," she gasped.

My fingers almost broke the handset in two. "What are you doing there?"

"I did a foolish thing," she said. "I heard rumours that Billie Flail was trying to kill you because I preferred you to him. Early this evening I drove over to his house in the country where I'd been once or twice before. I went to plead with him not to hurt you."

"Hurt me!" I roared.

"He laughed at me," she said. "And now he won't let me leave. He's drinking a lot and becoming vile. I'm locked in the living room and can't get out. The windows are bolted. But he forgot that there's a phone here. He'll be back any minute and then—"

She uttered a little shriek. I heard a moan and the sounds of a tussle. I yelled into the phone, going half crazy. Then there was a little click and the wire was dead.

Stoop Curio, one of my boys, burned the tires of his hack going out to Billie Flail's place. I kept checking my .45 every few minutes. A few hundred feet from the bungalow, Stoop dropped me off.

All the lights in the bungalow were blazing. I ran on my toes, noiselessly, the gun tight against my side.

At the edge of the lawn a shadow stepped in front of me. I jerked up my heater, but didn't use it. The shadow was tall and slender and feminine. It was Mimi Cook.

She grabbed my arm, hugging it in a kind of desperation.

"Get out of my way!" I said savagely. "You can't save Billie."

"Rube, there's—"

I shoved Mimi hard and she gasped, but she clung to my arm.

"Damn you!" I said. "I think I'll kill you too when I'm through with that other rat."

"Please, Rube! You don't—"

In the bungalow a girl cried out. For a split second Lydia appeared outlined in a window, her hair streaming wildly and her dress torn. Then she was out of sight, but her voice remained.

That was when I hit Mimi. I used only the flat of my

hand, but it nearly tore her head off and broke her hold on my arm. I spun toward the house.

"No, Rube," Mimi sobbed and lurched forward.

Not at me, but a little to my side, so that when the gun roared, she was between me and the killer. She straightened up a little and she smiled and fell forward at my feet.

Well, copper, Billie Flail had had his one shot at the Rube, which is the most any man could hope for. He was behind a rock at the side of the house, close, to make sure of his aim. The flash of his gun gave him away. I saw the white blob of his face rise over the rock for a look at how he'd done.

I killed him.

On my way to the bungalow I heard a car start up and go in the opposite direction. I went into the bungalow and Lydia was no longer there. Then I returned to where Mimi Cook lay on the edge of the lawn.

The slug that had had my name on it was in her head. A thin scarlet line of blood ran across the corner of her mouth. I had done that when I had slapped her.

I knew then that it wasn't the first time she had saved my life. It was Mimi who had screamed that night a few days before when Billie Flail's stolen heap had been crawling along the curb behind me. It wasn't Mimi who had fingered me for Billie.

I walked down the road to where Stoop Curio's hack was waiting. He drove me to Al Slavin's apartment. On the way I reloaded my gun.

Lydia was in the apartment with Al and Ripper Moore. Through the door I head her telling them that she had beat it as soon as she heard the shots without waiting to see how it had turned out. She wanted to be as far away from there when the coppers came.

"What a couple of prize saps!" Lydia laughed. "I tell Billie that I'm nuts about him, but I can't go back to him because I'm scared of the Rube. I finger the Rube for him outside the theatre, but the goof misses. He's so panicky he wants to leave town, but I talk him into waiting outside his place with a gun while I get the Rube to hot-foot it out with a thriller-diller yarn. And does the Rube fall all over himself getting there!"

"You're worth every cent I'm paying you, sweetheart," Al Slavin said. "Somebody else would hire a gun. I hire somebody more deadly – a woman. Brains always pays off. Billie kills the Rube and then stands the rap for it, and I take over Rube's rackets and sit on top of the heap – and I never had to stick my neck out doing it."

I pushed the door in and stepped through a foyer and into a living room. They gawked at me like I was a ghost.

"I was wrong about you, Lydia," I said. "You're a swell actress."

Then the lead started flying. When the air cleared, Al Slavin lay dead and Ripper Moore and Lydia had dived down the fire escape. I couldn't follow because I'd been nicked in the leg by a slug.

I hobbled down the stairs and went home.

Rube Hansen finished speaking and raised his glass to his lips. It was empty, but he didn't seem to notice it.

"Ripper Moore and Lydia Gilmor left town that night," I said. "They were scared to death of you. We knew you killed Billie Flail and Al Slavin, but we couldn't pin it on you. Now I'm taking you in for murder on your own confession."

The Rube shook his head. "Sorry, copper. I've got a date."

"Sure. With a judge and a jury."

He half-rose from his chair and a gentle faraway light came into his eyes. "Here she is now," he murmured. "Hello, Mimi."

The skin on the back of my head crawled. There was nobody there, of course. The only people who'd come in since me were a heavy-set guy and an over-dressed girl with plenty of paint on her face. Both of them were leaning over the bar. Anyway, Mimi Cook had been dead for nearly a year.

The Rube had had more to drink than I'd thought.

The heavy-set guy at the bar turned his head. He was as much surprised to see Rube Hansen as I was surprised to see that he was Ripper Moore and that the girl with him was Lydia Gilmor!

Ripper Moore's face turned the color of dirty chalk. His hand dove for his gun. Lydia backed away, whimpering. Even now they were terrified of the Rube.

And Rube Hansen never even saw them. He was saying, "I've been waiting, Mimi," when Ripper's slug tore into his body.

I dropped Ripper Moore with a bullet through the heart, but it was too late to save the Rube. He was on the floor, coughing his life away, but there was no agony in his face. The Rube smiled and lay still.

I looked down at him. "Give my regards to Mimi," I said.

Come to My Dying!

At the beginning the fog tested its strength with nebulous patches which swirled at the windshield and then scurried away for a fresh try. Then it became sure of itself and sank down in full possession of the road. The radiator cap disappeared; the fog blunted the headlights and pushed the beams in upon themselves.

Dr John Peacock braked his car, trying to get his bearings in a strange and distorted world. He moved on again, cautiously, not sure of anything except that eight miles away a man lay along and in frightful pain, with a broken leg, and that he was getting there too slowly.

The phone call had come in the midst of supper, and Dr Peacock had answered it to the usual complaints of his wife that a doctor's life was never his own.

Over the wire there had been a gasp, then a whisper, then thin, forced words: "Dr Peacock? I've broken my leg. I'm home – alone – on the floor. Managed to crawl to the phone."

"Who are you?"

"Edward Barton, on Pine Hill Road. It's the third mailbox on the left after the blinker. Private road next to the box. Mine's the only house on the road."

"Are you badly hurt? Can't you phone a neighbor till I get there?"

"Damn neighbors! What good will they do? I'm on the

floor; they couldn't move me anyway till you come. But, doctor – hurry!"

Automatically Dr Peacock's toe pressed a little harder on the gas pedal. The front wheel clipped the shoulder of the road and slewed back. That one lesson was enough. He compelled himself to push through the gray-black soup at fifteen an hour.

He had never met Edward Barton, although, after twenty years as a country doctor, he knew at least something about everybody within a radius of thirty miles. Patients enjoyed gossiping about their neighbors. He would have heard of Barton anyway, for his name was signed to the covers of many magazines. It was a lucky thing for the artist that he had been able to get to his phone. In that sparsely settled Pine Hill section, Barton might have lain in the fog all night, or even days. More than one man had died of a broken leg because he had lived alone.

Familiarity with the roads rather than sight brought him at last to Pine Hill Road. A dull star twinkled sluggishly in a sea of muck – the blinker.

Anxiously he peered to his left. The edge of the left headlight scraped the ghostly outline of a whitewashed pole and the jutting, white R.F.D. box. One! And almost at once there was the second. Then a small eternity passed before the third mailbox was barely glimpsed. He cut his wheel sharply and a narrow dirt road leaped up before him.

The car hardly crawled now. Where was the house? He had a weird sense of time and space being obliterated along with sight. There was nothing tangible left except that splotch of hard dirt road falling away abruptly into emptiness a bare ten feet past his car. No trees, no sounds of insects; nothing to denote that there was anything at all beyond the blunted range of the headlights. He felt hemmed in and unutterably alone.

Suddenly, there was the house, springing out of nowhere – or rather, three or four flattened hazes of light indicating windows. The house itself was part of the fog.

Dr Peacock pulled his car up and snapped out the lights. Immediately the car and even his hands vanished. All that remained visible of the known world was a single smudge of light in an upper story window – a back window, for he had passed the front of the house.

He had to point the flashlight at his feet to pick out the flagstone walk. It led to the back door, immediately under the single lighted window. As it was easier than going around to the front, he headed that way.

His hand was on the doorknob when he heard a scraping overhead. He glanced up. Somebody was raising the window – not Barton, certainly, who had a broken leg. A neighbor or visitor must have arrived here first.

A face appeared in the window – anybody's face, male or female, or possibly not even human – just a face. The fog would let him know that much and no more.

Dr Peacock said, "Hello. I—"

Something solidified up there at the window and dropped toward him. For a startled instant he thought that it was the face. He jumped. Whatever it was swished past his shoulder and crashed on the flagstone at his feet.

"Hey!" Dr Peacock called. "What—"

The window slammed down. The face was gone.

Dr Peacock dipped his flashlight. The pieces of a shattered flowerpot were scattered on the flagstone. The long blades of a snakeplant, the dirt shaken from its roots by the fall, lay near his feet.

"The careless fool!" he muttered aloud. "My head could have been split open."

He turned the beam away, then thought of something and swung it back and crouched low. Most of the base of the flowerpot was still intact; it had been a big pot, at least ten inches in diameter. If he hadn't jumped in time, it might have killed him on the spot.

His knees were shaking as he straightened up. One didn't keep that size flowerpot on a windowsill. Whoever had opened and then closed the window had heard his voice. Why hadn't the person leaned out to investigate possible damage? And why was the house so silent? His car had been heard and now the crash, yet the only sign of life had been that momentary hint of a face at the window.

Good Lord! Had somebody deliberately tried to murder him?

The fog entered his bones as he stood there with his lank frame huddled in his topcoat, shivering and at the same time sweating.

Then he laughed, a dry, alien sound in the heavy moist stillness. The fog was distorting his imagination as it had everything else. It had to be an accident.

He turned back to the door, and the instant he reached for the bell the door flew inward. A woman stood in the sudden gush of light.

"Ah, you're here," she said.

This was the familiar world again – the anxious woman relieved at the sight of the doctor for whom she had been waiting.

Then he found himself staring at her. She was, he thought, the most beautiful woman he had ever seen. Her body was tall and slender, yet full-curved; her hair was warm golden-brown and her eyes violet. She was probably a model who had come to pose for Barton and had walked in on the artist lying on the floor with his leg broken. Or perhaps she was closer to Barton than that, for she seemed to be quite agitated.

"How is he?" Dr Peacock asked.

"Scared, but he tries not to show it. Come in."

He followed her up a hallway, wondering why she hadn't mentioned the fallen flowerpot, or if it had been her face in the window.

He entered a living room and looked around. Barton wasn't here, but she didn't move on. She swung toward him and dug red-lacquered fingernails into his arm.

"Mr Corbett, there's one thing—"

"I'm Dr Peacock," he broke in politely. "Evidently you've mistaken me for somebody else."

A wan smile crossed her red lips. "Yes, I guess that's the best way. He objects to you, you know. Dr Peacock then. Try not to use your gun, Mr Corbett."

"Gun?" He blinked at her. "I said I'm Doc—"

A voice from a doorway said, "A friend of yours, Virginia?"

The girl uttered a little cry and whirled away from Dr Peacock. A man stepped into the room, and a double-barreled shotgun rested loosely on the crook of his elbow. His body was as slim as a boy's and his dark, brooding eyes as old as time. As if by accident, the shotgun swung in Dr Peacock's direction and stayed there.

Virginia made a quick recovery. "Henry, I want you to meet an old friend of Father's. He's known me since I was in diapers. Dr Peacock – my husband."

The man named Henry nodded once, grudgingly. He did not shift his gun.

Dr Peacock looked sharply at the girl for an

explanation of her lie. His eyes were checked at her right arm. She wore a short-sleeved dress, and the satiny skin of her upper arm was marred by three distinct bruises. He would have staked his professional reputation that the bruises were caused by a man's fingers closing over her arm with the definite intention of inflicting pain.

Then he remembered that as a doctor his prime concern was with a seriously injured man. "Where's the patient?" he asked crisply.

Instead of answering, Virginia frowned at him in bewilderment.

Henry said bitterly, "So that's it? You brought the doctor here because you think I'm crazy. If he hangs around, he'll get a patient, all right, but it won't be me."

Virginia emitted a light laugh, which wasn't very successful, and intimately hugged Dr Peacock's arm. "That's just one of Dr Peacock's jokes. He says that people on whom he calls socially are always trying to pry free medical advice out of him. That's why he asks right off for the patient."

Clever! But why? It was becoming obvious to Dr Peacock that this was the wrong house. He had passed the third mailbox in the fog and had turned up at the fourth or fifth. And this lovely girl had mistaken him for somebody she had never seen and whose identity she desperately did not want her husband to learn.

It was none of his business. Even if it were, his patient came first.

"I'm afraid you—" he started to say and then closed his mouth.

He was looking down into the girl's violet eyes and he saw that she was afraid. What he had assumed to be worry over an injured man was in reality naked fear. He realized with a kind of shock that she was depending on him. For what?

Yet his duty was to his patient.

"Well, I'll be pushing on," he said, trying to sound casual. "I only stopped off to say hello."

Her pressure on his arm tightened. "But you promised to stay for dinner!"

Henry didn't budge a muscle or say a word. He kept eyes and shotgun fixed unwaveringly on Dr Peacock and Virginia standing together. The cold was again in Dr Peacock's bones, as if the fog had followed him in here.

An idea struck him how to escape without fuss and without exposing the girl.

He said, "I suppose I can stay a little while. Mind if I wash up?"

She gave him a faint, grateful smile.

"George," she called, and a man came in. He had the build and face of a gorilla and the frozen mask of a trained servant. "George, take Dr Peacock's hat and coat and show him to the downstairs bath."

"Yes, Mrs Falk," George said.

Dr Peacock followed the servant into the hall. Virginia Falk was her name, then. It stirred something deep in his memory which would not come to the surface. That he had heard the name before this was not surprising; he had heard at one time or another practically every name in the community. Henry and Virginia Falk— He felt somehow that there was something about those names he should remember.

George had stopped in front of a door in the hall.

He turned to Dr Peacock and said quietly, "How would you like to pick up another five hundred dollars?"

Dr Peacock had no idea what the man he was supposed

to be would have to say to that. So he only looked at the servant, waiting.

"All you have to do is kill Duncan Riker when he comes here," George said.

This isn't happening to me, Dr Peacock thought. *People don't speak like this. It's part of the distortion of the fog.*

George's little eyes in his heavy, ugly face were flat, and so was his precise voice. "I know you're really Chris Corbett, a private detective. All your kind are out for money."

"So I'm supposed to be a private detective!"

"I overheard Mrs Falk hiring you over the phone," the servant went on blandly. "A couple of days ago she suggested to Mr Falk that he hire you to protect him when Duncan Riker gets out of jail. Mr Falk didn't care for the idea. He said that he could take care of himself. He said that if Mr Riker shows up he'll kill him with his own hands. That's why he's carrying the shotgun. Mr Riker got out of jail this afternoon. He should be here any minute."

Dr Peacock was thinking again of his patient alone in agony. A kind of frenzy possessed him. He had to get out of this madhouse.

"But you know all that," George said. "Here's the way I fit into it. I've been with Mr Falk twelve years, years before he was married, and I'll be with him after he's married. It's a good job; I like working for him. But if trouble starts tonight, I'll be out in the cold. Either Mr Falk will kill Mr Riker or the other way around, which means that Mr Falk will be dead or in jail. In either case, I'll be out of a job. If it doesn't happen tonight, it will soon. That's why it's worth five hundred dollars to me."

"And you want him shot down, just like that?"

George shrugged. "It wouldn't be exactly murder. You

might have to shoot anyway, to protect Mr Falk. I want you to shoot, before anything starts, and be sure of your aim. It will be in the line of duty."

Dr Peacock leaned against the wall. "Was it you or Mrs Falk who threw the flowerpot down at my head?"

"I'm sorry, Mr Corbett," George said, without sounding sorry. "I thought you were Mr Riker. You're built somewhat like him and I couldn't see your face from the window. I considered that a good chance to get rid of him. I'd shoot Mr Riker myself, when he comes, but you're police, even though not official, so there'll be no kickback. It will be easy to prove you did it to protect Mr Falk. Five hundred dollars is money."

The squat, powerful servant, with his dead-pan face and cultured accent, sent prickles down Dr Peacock's spine.

He said, "Don't be a fool!" He opened the bathroom door and stepped inside and slammed the door. He put his ear against the door, listening.

There was a brief silence before footsteps receded up the hall. When they ceased entirely, Dr Peacock opened the door. Soundlessly, he moved to the back door and slipped outside.

Immediately the fog enveloped him. And as he huddled against the chill, there was a click in his brain and he remembered the newspaper stories two months ago and the gossip of Mrs Hutch.

It had been quite a local scandal when Duncan Riker had attacked Henry Falk with a golf club. According to the caddies, it had started off as a friendly enough threesome, Mr and Mrs Falk and Duncan Riker, until at the fifteenth tee Henry Falk had slapped his wife across the face. The caddies were on the fairway and had no idea why he did it; all they saw was the slap and then Riker's driver lashing out. They managed to pull Riker off just about in time.

Henry Falk, half-dead from the beating, had pressed charges, and Duncan Riker was given sixty days for assault. The term was severe because all Riker would say in his own defense was that when he got out he would kill Falk, and that was, of course, no defense. Falk said that he was looking forward to the meeting. Virginia Falk did not say a word.

Mrs Hutch, however, had considerable to say, as always, when Dr Peacock came to treat her husband for arthritis. She was a part-time housemaid for the Falks, and, she proclaimed, she had eyes and ears.

"One of them will kill the other sure, depending on which gets the chance first," Mrs Hutch had assured Dr Peacock. "It ain't poor Mrs Falk's fault. She's so sad and gentle. You never saw her? Well, beautiful is no word for her. She's the kind of woman men will kill for and say they're glad they did it. This Mr Riker, he was one of a lot of men who wanted to marry her before Mr Falk got her. He was Mr Falk's friend too, so he still came to visit, and he'd hang around just staring at her by the hour."

"And her husband was jealous?"

"Jealous! You don't know how crazy jealous a man can be till you've been in that house. Mr Falk's a little crazy anyway, one of those brooding kind, never smiling, and when he slapped her before Mr Riker, it wasn't the first time he'd done it."

"Why does she stand for it?"

"Money, I guess. She's got a father and mother that's sick and poor. Mr Falk makes it easy for them. But it's something else too. She's scared sick of him. I've heard him tell her that if she ever tries to leave him, he'll follow her to the ends of the earth and strangle her with his bare hands. And he'd do it, too. Do you blame Mr Riker?"

"I can't say I do."

Now, two months later, Dr Peacock stood outside the back door, remembering. A jagged object slid under his shoe – a fragment of the shattered flowerpot. The night touched him with clammy fingers.

I must get to Barton, he thought fiercely. *I'm a doctor and an injured patient needs me.*

A car was coming this way, laboring up the dirt road. Duncan Riker! George had said that his sixty days were up today.

Dr Peacock stood rigid, shivering. The car sounded too far away, too far on the right. There must be another private road nearby, probably Barton's.

Feeling a wave of relief sweep over him, he started toward his parked car. At the other side of the house something exploded. An instant later Virginia Falk screamed.

She was in the living room when Dr Peacock plunged in. She was gripping the back of the chair and trembling, no sound passing her lips now. The servant George was leaning out of the open window. Between them Henry Falk lay face down on the floor.

Dr Peacock dropped to Falk's side. He could see a neat, round, slightly bleeding hole punched in the back of the skull, and when he lifted the head, he saw that Falk had developed a third eye over the bridge of his nose. That was where the bullet had exited.

Falk had died instantly.

George turned from the window, his face still frozen. "Can't see a thing," he said.

Without glancing at his dead master, he picked up the shotgun Falk had dropped in falling. He looked at Dr Peacock and nodded at Virginia. "Mrs Falk says the shot came from the window."

"Duncan Riker," Dr Peacock mumbled. "I heard his car coming."

"I heard it too," George said. "I was listening to the car from the kitchen, and I was still listening to it when the shot rang out. So it couldn't have been whoever was in that car. Anyway, it wasn't coming up this road." He paused and then added with sudden bitterness in his tone, "Mrs Falk was alone in the room with Mr Falk."

Virginia said dully, "I was sitting in this chair and Henry was standing with his back to the window, facing me. Then there was the shot and he pitched forward on his face."

George moved stiffly over to the front of her chair and faced her. His eyes came alive through the mask and they glowed with pale fury. "You hated him. You hated him from the day you married him. But you stayed with him because you needed his money. Now you'll get his insurance."

Virginia straightened up behind the chair. "Are you accusing me, George?"

"Yes!"

"Just a second," Dr Peacock broke in. "It took you only a second or two to come in here after the shot was fired. Where's the gun?"

"She could have tossed the gun away somewhere," George said. "Perhaps she's got it in her clothes."

"It seems to me that's the business of the police," Dr Peacock said. And he thought: *Lord, won't I ever get to poor Barton?*

"It's my business to see evidence isn't destroyed,"

George declared grimly. "You go phone the police. I'll watch this room – and her."

Dr Peacock went into the library and phoned the state police barracks. He was stepping back into the living room when the commotion started outside. It sounded like a dog fight at first. Then he heard human voices, cursing wildly.

George was staring out of the open window.

"Blast the fog!" he said and raced across the room.

Dr Peacock and Virginia were at his heels. The three went out through the front door and stood on the open porch.

In the fog a voice snapped, "Now get up on your feet!"

"Hello?" Dr Peacock said. "What's going on?"

"That's what I want to know," the voice replied.

Dr Peacock tried to stab through the fog with his flashlight, but it was like directing a beam against a solid wall. A blurred spat of light appeared around the corner of the house. The three on the porch waited, peering.

Two men walked up the porch steps, one behind the other. The first was young and tall and there was a sullen twist to his mouth. His hair was disheveled and necktie askew. The other was stolid, heavy-set. He had an automatic in his right hand and a flashlight in his left and he was holding a rifle against the side of his body with his left elbow.

"Duncan!" Virginia exclaimed.

"Duncan Riker, eh?" the man with the two guns said. "I figured that's who he was. I came across him snooping outside a window after I'd heard a shot. We had a tussle, but he wasn't much trouble."

"I didn't do it," Riker said. "I came here to kill him, sure, but not in the back. I planned it to be face to face, so that he could see me do it."

"So Falk's dead and the shot I heard killed him!" the armed man grunted. "Too bad I didn't get here sooner. You'll have to blame the fog, Mrs Falk. You are Mrs Falk, aren't you?"

"I am," she said stiffly. "You haven't explained who you are and what you're doing here."

"I'm Chris Corbett."

Dr Peacock felt rather than saw Virginia and George swing toward him, and he felt their eyes on him.

"You're an imposter!" she cried. "And you were outside when Henry was shot. You could have—"

Dr Peacock didn't much feel like smiling, but he did then, wryly. "I'm Dr John Peacock, as I told you. It wasn't my fault that nobody in the house would believe me."

Corbett growled, "There's a lot screwy going on. Let's go inside where there's light and a guy can get a chance to use his eyes again."

"Look here," Dr Peacock protested. "There's a man near here with a broken leg. I've got to get to him."

"There's a man who's dead and somebody murdered him," Corbett said dryly. "Start moving."

They trailed into the living room, Corbett bringing up the rear. He glanced at the dead man on the floor, then carefully placed the rifle on the table.

"The fog tangled me up in these roads," Corbett said apologetically to Virginia. "Then I took the wrong road up. Anyway, I guess it's the wrong road because when I heard the shot I had to cut across a field and climb a stone fence to get here."

"That's Mr Barton's road," George told him. "He's our neighbor." His voice dropped. "We thought it was Mr Riker's car we heard."

Then Duncan Riker was the murderer after all, Dr Peacock thought. The patterns was completed. Riker had said that he would kill Falk and he had killed him. Murder was as simple as that.

"Doc, you looked at the wound," Corbett said. "Any idea what kind of gun the slug came from?"

"Off-hand, I would say a steel-jacketed bullet from a rifle. The bullet penetrated cleanly, although it appears to have been of small caliber."

Corbett nodded. "That's the rifle then. A .22, but at close range they pack plenty of wallop. I found it under the window where Riker dropped it when he started to battle me."

Riker's sullen mouth twisted. "I tell you I wouldn't shoot even a rat like Falk in the back."

"Then what were you doing snooping at the window?"

"I wasn't snooping. I walked here from the station. I had almost reached the house when I heard a shot. I passed a window and looked in, and the next thing I knew, you attacked me."

"Couldn't you think up a better one?" Corbett sneered.

"I believe Mr Riker is right," George said softly. He was at the table, looking down at the rifle. "This is – or rather was – Mr Falk's gun. I saw it in Mr Falk's den upstairs this morning."

"You see!" Riker said triumphantly. "I didn't get out of jail until noon. I can prove I left the station forty minutes ago. So how could I get my hands on the rifle and—"

He choked on the last word. Everybody in the room was staring at Virginia Falk.

George's frozen features cracked in a vindictive grimace. "Mrs Falk shot him and threw the rifle out of the window before I could get in here from the kitchen. That's the way it had to be."

She stood very still, her lovely face immobile, as if she had not heard the accusation. Dr Peacock could see the marks of cruel fingers on her bare arm. *Anybody can be driven to murder*, he thought – *a man because a woman is too beautiful; a woman because she has reached the end of endurance.*

"Wait!" Dr Peacock said aloud. "Would she hire a detective if she planned to murder her husband?"

"It's an old gag," Corbett scoffed. "Divert suspicion from yourself by being the one to bring in a detective."

Virginia found her voice then. "Don't you see how it was? I couldn't let them murder each other over me. I had to stop them. That's why I hired you, Mr Corbett."

"And that's why you killed your husband," George said, flatly.

"No, no! That would have been even more horrible!"

Duncan Riker tore his eyes away from her and faced Corbett, his jaw firm, his shoulders square.

"All right, I'll confess," he announced. "I killed him."

Corbett snorted with disgust. "Whenever there's a beautiful woman, you'll find a man trying to pull a noble act. You're a lousy actor, Riker."

Dr Peacock felt suddenly a little sick. It had to be Virginia Falk, and that was the depth of tragedy.

But not this tragedy, not his business. His business was Barton. He started for the door.

"Where do you think you're going, Doc?" Corbett demanded.

"I told you I had a patient nearby."

Corbett chewed over that. "Well, I guess I can't stop you."

"That's right, you can't," Dr Peacock said. "All the hate and killing in the world won't stop me now."

Because he had delayed so long, every second was now infinitely precious. He did not take the roundabout way with his car; he plunged on foot through the fog in the direction he reasoned Barton's house would be.

Dr Peacock's flashlight picked out the stone fence Corbett said he had climbed. He was in a field then, moving warily over stubble. After an eternity of wandering like a lost soul in an empty world, he glimpsed a vague, ghostlike blob which might be a lighted window.

He broke into an urgent trot, and only the sudden swinging of his flashlight kept him from crashing into a fieldstone retaining wall. It was a good ten feet high. He walked along it until he came to stone steps. He ascended them and was on a terrace, and there in front of him was a rambling fieldstone house.

The front door was wide open. Inside a man was moaning.

The man lay on the floor beside an overturned table. Barton had had to pull it down to get at the telephone.

Weakly he turned an agony-twisted face to Dr Peacock. "Damn you! I called ages ago."

"Sorry, but I was unavoidably detained," Dr Peacock muttered as he deftly cut away the trouser leg. There was blood on the cloth and a ragged edge of bone protruded sickeningly through broken skin. "How did you get into this mess?"

"The damn fog!" Barton said. "I fell off the terrace wall."

"I saw it. That's a nasty drop."

"I should have had a rail or something put around it," Barton said, his lips tight against the pain. "God knows how I managed to drag myself into the house. But I had to get to a phone somehow or die out there."

Dr Peacock stood up. His eyes swept the room.

"Looking for something, Doctor?"

"Yes."

Dr Peacock walked over to the couch beside the fireplace and reached under it and pulled out a heavy monkey wrench. Then he returned to where Barton lay and scooped up the telephone from the floor and quickly stepped as far as the length of the cord would let him.

From the floor Barton stared up at him with something more than pain in his eyes.

"Barton was in love with Virginia Falk," Dr Peacock told his wife. "I can't say I blame him; the trick is for a man not to fall in love with her. I'm not sure she returned his affection, but she was starved for kindness living in that house with those two men, Falk and the servant, and Barton was kind to her. Anyway, he thought she loved him and that she would marry him if she was free of her husband. And he hated Falk for the way he treated her. There was also the matter of the fortune she would come into if her husband died. So there you have the most powerful motives there are for murder."

It was after midnight. The police had at last let him go home, and now his wife was preparing a late snack for him in the kitchen.

"But if Barton knew that Duncan Riker was coming to kill Falk that night, why didn't he wait?" his wife asked.

"He wanted to be sure. The chance was that it would merely end in a fist fight, or that Falk would be the one to kill Riker. He wanted Falk thoroughly dead, and dead in a hurry. Being a neighbor, it was easy for him to slip into the Falk house and steal the rifle. He did that in the afternoon when nobody was in the house. His alibi seemed perfect. Even if Riker wasn't blamed for the murder, Barton certainly wouldn't be suspected, because he had me to testify that he had broken his leg some time before Falk was killed."

His wife frowned. "How could he get over there and back to his own house with a broken leg?"

"That's the point – he couldn't. Then, when I looked at his leg, I saw that he could. I remembered how, when I stood outside the Falk house, I clearly heard Corbett's car going up Barton's private road and a moment later there was the shot. Barton had been crouching on the other side of the house with Falk's gun, waiting for the sound of the car. He thought it was mine. He shot Falk and cut across to his own house. The fog made it easier for him to be completely out of sight from the beginning. Knowing the way, it took him only a minute to get back to his house. He figured on getting there before I parked my car and groped my way to the door."

"Oh," his wife said. "*And then he broke his own leg.*"

"That's it. Except that in his hurry and anxiety to do a good job of it, he did too good a job. As soon as I saw that he had a compound fracture, I knew he couldn't possibly have dragged himself along the bottom of the terrace wall and up the steps and into the house. He would have passed out a dozen times and then not made it. Anyway, it was obvious from the wound that he hadn't moved around much. So I looked for something heavy and found the monkey wrench where he had tossed it, under the couch. After an hour with the state police, he broke down and confessed."

Dr Peacock bit into the sandwich his wife had set down before him. He found that he was shivering. The fog was still in his bones.

And he knew that it would be a long time before it left.

The Case of the Laughing Queen

Death was swimming beside him. You could see it in the set of his jawbone, white against the black water, sense it in the vacuous, fixed unhaste with which he fought the bludgeoning waves, fighting terribly forward.

Yet this dot of living stuff which flailed in the ebb tide off the Narrows at dawn had no fear of death as such. It had passed him and touched him in passing – he knew it intimately, and too well. Already, in fact, it was a part of him.

It had not yet seized his brain, this dying man off Sheepshead. Later, very soon now, it would claim him in full. But first he had to deliver a message and a warning, sharper than his pain, more urgent than the suck of the undertow.

The queer little sobbing noises he made were dwarfed by the howl of the wind. The man threshed on.

And then, suddenly, he stopped and clutched wildly at the thing that rasped his face. It had been hitting him at intervals for several seconds, but his numbed senses had failed to complete the nerve signal to his brain. It was far less his strength than the vagrant tide that clapped him hard against its blessed solidity, so that at last he had both hands taloned into it, and perceived that it was a low-hanging hawser.

The man from the sea clung to the hawser for a long time, searching the darkness ahead. The hawser was pulling him along the water rapidly. He could feel the drag of it, stronger than his strength. And the rope, he could tell from the feel, was sloping down into the sea.

Slowly he reasoned it out. The hawser connected two boats. The boat in front, from the slope of the rope, must be a good distance off. But the boat which was being towed – it must be just behind him. Was it close enough to—

The man let the backwash take him, coveting the rope with his heart and the tag-end of his life, fighting for it against the sea. Slowly, foot by agonizing foot, he crawled up it, helped by the wind and the slap of the water.

Up, up, until he didn't feel the tear of the hemp any more, and the drag at his shoulder was one with the numb of the wind. Inch by inch now, and then the pain, sweeter than joy, of the solid bulkhead when it pushed against his fingers.

The man whose body had died fell forward blindly, hitting a solid deck. For a moment he lay there, waiting, hoarding the minutes that were left. Then he crawled to his feet, shouting as he ran forward.

The wind and the waves answered, mocking. The man from the sea opened his eyes, and saw for the first time that he was alone. Alone on a barge – with living people two hundred yards away, and the world between!

For the first time, then, he realized that it was over. The mast light on the other ship was an eternity ahead, dipping and receding, but for a last hopeless second he ran toward it, shouting and clawing at the night, as though to draw it back to him.

And then, as the forward rail checked his rush, he stopped and groped at his coat. There was a pencil inside; he could feel the edge of it against his forearm. But his fingers could feel nothing, and the pull of the buttons was a terrible, iron-barred thing, greater than his strength, tougher than his will.

The message! If he didn't tell them now, who would stop that murdering—

The man from the sea flagged himself to one last surge of physical effort. Stiffly. Bludgeoning one hand through the half frozen muck at his feet, he started to trace wavering letters. But after a moment he stopped. His hands were one with the night, and as cold.

Then, as a certain breed of men can, he shrugged and set his jaw, and crouched in the bow, staring hungrily at the lights of Manhattan which beckoned, mockingly close. They rose and fell with the waves and were waiting for him, two hours away . . .

The tugboat *Elsie D* scuttled briskly under Brooklyn Bridge and docked at dawn at the Arbuckle wharf.

But the man on the barge behind her was past knowing or caring – ever.

Detective Sergeant Ricco Pasquale Maguire swung briskly into headquarters and Patrolman Gannon, languishing at desk duty, woke up with a start.

"Hey!" he yelled. "Not in there!"

Ricco Maguire stopped, fingers taloned on a doorknob, and lifted his eyebrows.

"Beg pardon, sir," Gannon made haste to explain, "Captain Bellamy's in there an' he's mad as hell. He told me not to let St Nick himself in there, not till he rang."

Ricco Maguire swore in a surprisingly cultivated voice and sat down on Gannon's chair, nodding.

"St Nick – the devil," he said. "Copper, it's not far off he is this day, which is just beginning!"

Gannon sat down hastily on the desk and the sergeant smiled.

"Tabloids are funny," he said. "You never can hide 'em, by sittin' on 'em, no matter how big you are down there. Better stick it in a drawer before Bellamy rings. The captain's hell for regulations."

Then the smile went out of Ricco Maguire's black eyes and he prodded the deskman's shoulder.

"What would you do," he said soberly, "if you found a dead king – in Brooklyn?"

Gannon looked ruefully at his book of regulations and nodded his head sagely.

"It beats hell the things that happen in that daffy town," he said. "The sarge himself remembers—"

The bell from the other room barked angrily and Gannon got up, but it was Ricco Maguire who pushed open the door.

Which, all things considered, was just as well.

Captain Bellamy was fat, but even the sagging jowls couldn't hide the jut of a fighting jaw.

When he saw Ricco he hit the desk and the ink bottle jumped.

He said, "What the hell! Just when I need you you go moseying out of the precinct, and—"

Ricco pulled the ink bottle out of range and sat down.

"Morning," he said. "We have a bit of a mess on our hands, Captain. We'll have to work fast to beat the tabloids. You see—"

Bellamy looked appealingly at the ceiling and his face got red.

"Trouble – tabs," he barked. "Kid I got the commissioner on my tail and photographers gettin' me outa bed at four, an' the damnedest, craziest mess in front of me a guy could find in three administrations, an' by God you talk to me about—"

Then, catching for the first time the strange, somber look in the younger man's eye, he sat down, very quietly, and let his big shoulders sag.

"What is it, Rick?" he said grimly.

Ricco Maguire lit a monogrammed cigarette and stared at the fly-specked ceiling.

"It is – or was – a king, sir," he murmured. "A king who sat on a scow in Brooklyn Harbor, till I dragged him off to lie on a slab at the morgue."

Captain Bellamy hit his head and made little groaning noises.

"Dressed in the finest silks, he was, and blue with the cold, but he had a strange, foreign look in his eyes. And sitting, dead and sheathed in ice, on a garbage scow in from the sea!"

Bellamy got up and walked around the room, puffing out his cheeks.

"Last night," he said, "I had a headache, an' the wife said I was workin' too hard an' ought to relax. Relax!" Bellamy spat wildly at the cuspidor, and Ricco pulled in his foot.

"He was a fine, brave-looking lad," Ricco said. "And the evening clothes he wore looked class, even on a garbage scow, which ought to be a good test. No marks of identity. No external violence, as far as I could see."

Gannon poked his head in the door, and seeing Bellamy's face, shut it again hastily and disappeared.

Ricco stared out the window.

"Take it easy, sir," he soothed. "I'm just beginning. You see, this dead man, he had a silly-looking goldish crown on his head!"

Bellamy muttered, "Relax!" and his face got purple.

"That would make a bit of an enigma," Ricco said, "but this crowned man, he saw fit to add to it, best he could. Frozen in the muck at his feet, he'd tried to write a message, but death came to him first. But I could read some of it – and here it is, for the captain to figure out, afore the tabs start asking questions.

"'The queen was smiling.'" That was the message he wrote in the ice."

Bellamy hugged his head.

"Rick," he said, "the world's gone daffy or I have. If he's a king, he's a dead one now, an' he picked Brooklyn to die in which is out of my district. He can wait for the noon shift. I got something really big!"

Ricco Maguire whistled softly.

"Franzen, up at Eighteen, found it – while he was stealin' milk bottles in a doorway, I'll bet. The damn fool must of had three reporters in his back pocket they got there so fast. That lug, I'll see him shifted to a night beat up in Harlem—"

"You said," Ricco murmured, "it was urgently important?"

Captain Bellamy waved his fists.

"I kept a squad car waitin' for you," he said. "Let's go!"

Ricco Pasquale Maguire was none of your ten-cent stogie, hit-'em-and-talk-later shamuses.

He looked like an old man, but when you got past the gray hair and the somber sadness in his dark eyes, you were looking at a man of thirty.

It was said that Ricco Maguire had never returned to his playboy haunts – not since the night they called him from a party at the Plaza to identify his mother, murdered in an alley under the arch of Brooklyn Bridge.

Ricco's father had been Terry Maguire, who came from Dublin to swing a pick and stayed to collect more millions than was good for his roistering soul.

But that was before he met Rosa DeLisa, who lived in the Bowery, just off Chinatown.

Ricco Maguire had been the only child of that strange-omened marriage. A curious child, with his mother's dark eyes and the squarest Hibernian chin you'd see south of Kilkenny.

Ricco Maguire had a large slice of the old roistering Terry in the cut of his jib. His mother, quiet, reserved — and wiser than all of the rest put together — was a lesser figure in his mind. Until that day she made her usual weekly charitable visit to the narrow, dark streets of her youth — and met trackless death instead, for the money which she had been carrying.

You could call it a holy mission, or you could tag it a search for vengeance. Just what it was, Ricco couldn't have told you, even if he talked about it, which he didn't. But the week that Terry Maguire shot himself, which was a month after Rosa's death, he took police examinations. He reached the Homicide Squad in less than four years.

Ricco had the spare ranginess of an Irish fighting man and the Italian guile to make sure of winning. Ricco called the commissioner by his first name and stored his rare books in the Waldorf. He had a million dollars in his own name and would rather eat ravioli than *filet mignon*. He paid his dues to the Royal Order of Hibernians, and his mother's genealogy went back, by a murder and three scandals, to a rake-hell prince of the Borgias. He could write a limerick in Sanskrit — or talk East Side Brooklyn with Captain Bellamy, who rated him a thin step higher than his hero, Richard the Lion-hearted.

So, being what he was, Ricco had neither shouted to the skies nor questioned Bellamy's sanity when that worthy had taken him away from the hot scent of murder to a squad car, speeding up Riverside Drive.

And when at last they ground to a stop, and a patrolman had pulled a tarpaulin away from a crimson blotch that profaned the dawn, he knew why Bellamy had been worried. For if the other had been fantastic death by night – this was sheer horror in the morning!

He sat on the steps of Grant's Tomb, staring out over the city. He was thin and austere, and he wore the cloth of a priest. He was middle-aged, fairish, and moderately tall. And he was quite definitely dead.

But it was not these things that made Ricco Maguire catch his breath, and clutch Bellamy's fat arm. It was the spear which, transfixing the dead man's back, held him immobile on the terraced stone.

"You see," Bellamy was saying, "this is the kind of case you think about when you're dozing off after supper, and call it a nightmare. You can talk away big shots, and stall 'em off on politicians. But when it's a man of the cloth, you got to produce results!"

Ricco Maguire was humming, a song which had something to do with a certain ill-born king, and Bellamy, who had his hat off, sighed and put it on again.

"Maybe I'm old-fashioned," he growled. "But a holy man and them words don't exactly mix with me."

Ricco turned the dead man over.

"The coroner's through?" he asked. And when the other nodded, he rifled the dead man's pockets and sang a verse about the queen of Spain.

"Captain," he said, "our friend here won't keep any congregation waiting at mass, I'm thinking. In fact, I'm afraid for his soul, which is more than I can say for the captain."

Bellamy waved his arms. Ricco held three squares of cardboard in front of his eyes, and he subsided abruptly.

The papers had been taken from the dead man's billfold. Two of them were tickets for Broadway's most popular striptease palace. The other was an advertisement for a wholesale liquor firm.

"Surprised you didn't see it before," he said chidingly. "Besides, our deceased friend here sports a pair of the finest cauliflowered ears south of St Nicholas Arena. Sir, I'm thinking the fingerprint bureau will have a report on yonder boy, an' when you get it, you won't have to worry much about his high estate."

Then Ricco turned the corpse over so that the spear, which had been driven with terrific violence through his upper torso, propped him balanced on his side. He whistled and his eyes narrowed.

"Hello," he said. "Fifteenth Century! A conquistador's seal – that's the thing that looks like a scratch on the shaft. Toledo steel too, I'll warrant. Captain, this spear may have hewn down Inca temples!"

"Maybe," Bellamy grunted, "but that's not in my district and I don't give a damn. They can't do this to me, not on the steps of Grant's Tomb!"

Ricco Maguire was staring at the sun coming up over the still quiescent city. There was something like baffled hunger in his eyes.

"Royalty in Brooklyn," he was saying. "Medieval spears and holy cloth in Manhattan. And death out of a story book riveting them together. I wonder!"

Captain Bellamy was not to relax this morning. When they got back to headquarters, they found the coroner, Dr Jamison, waiting for them.

Dr Jamison was plump and affected Windsor ties. He had a Phi Beta Kappa key on his watch chain, and he looked slightly down his nose at Captain Bellamy, who used to sit home nights and dream about the feel of a rubber hose against Dr Jamison's padded rear.

The coroner smiled brightly.

"I have a real mystery for you, Captain," he chirped. "Shall we have a spot of coffee while I elucidate?"

Bellamy reached in his drawer and poured some bicarbonate into a dirty tumbler, stirring it with his finger.

"My belly's full – plenty," he rasped. "Spill it, an' make it snappy!"

Ricco gnawed his lip.

"We're really in a bit of a hurry," he said mildly. "What did you turn up on that Brooklyn baby? Say it fast, because the captain's on the prod and there's four reporters waiting outside."

Dr Jamison crossed his plump little legs and beamed pontifically.

"We may make history today," he said. "We may trace a murder, by the odor of the corpus. The sinister aura of homicide, you might say."

Bellamy said two curt words.

"It may be an aura to you," Ricco said, "but Bellamy calls it by a different handle. Remember, it's from a garbage scow we found him."

The coroner uncrossed his legs and looked hurt.

"Singular," he remarked to the telephone, "how man distrusts man and that sort of thing." He took a bit of blotting paper out of an envelope and waved it.

"Very well, then," he said. "I will begin at the beginning, and speak in words of one syllable. There were no marks of violence on the dead man. I did find, however, an inflamed surface in the chest cavity. There was some minor hemorrhage, and a layman might have assumed that death had been caused by this means."

Bellamy was leaning forward, and the coroner gave him a friendly smile.

"But," Jamison nodded significantly, "such was not the case."

Bellamy clicked his teeth together and the coroner jumped.

"Maybe," Ricco said, "you'd better come to the point."

Dr Jamison stuck the blotting paper under Bellamy's nose and that worthy rolled his eyes.

"Smells like Madame Flo's place, back when I used to – when it was on a raid," he said.

"That," Dr Jamison said chillingly, "was blotted from the dead man's lungs. From a lower lobe, in the point the greatest distance from the bronchi."

"You might say then," Ricco murmured, "that the man was literally smothered by this substance? So that the alcohol in it eventually would stupefy and cause anesthesia or death?"

The coroner nodded, glaring at Bellamy.

Ricco closed his eyes.

"Smothered in incense and tossed into the harbor," he mused. "It's a funny way to die. Especially when they stick a toy crown on your noggin and send you off to write, 'The queen was smiling,' in the snow. Because—" he pushed the blotting paper away and shuddered slightly – "the perfume is *Fleur de la Jeunesse*, which Pondeur first distilled to royal command for a lady at Vincennes some hundred and sixty years ago. That lady was Marie Antoinette, and before she lost her head, she used to be a queen!"

Patrolman Gannon stuck his head in the door and smiled blithely.

"The fellow from the *Clarion* says if you got the answers he'd like to have 'em now," he said. "He's got to meet his wife at ten-thirty to pick out some new bridgework."

Nobody laughed.

Ricco Maguire was sitting on the extreme edge of his battered desk when Bellamy came in the following morning. Ricco had his feet on the window ledge, and his eyes were closed. Bellamy stood in the doorway for a minute, looking at him. Then he strode across the room and shook him.

Ricco yawned and opened his eyes.

"It's early you are," he said. "Me, I like to sleep. It keeps you thin. You ought to try it, Captain."

Then the light swung around so that he could see Bellamy's face, and the easy languor whipped out of his eyes.

"What is it?" he demanded.

Captain Bellamy didn't look like a hardbitten fighter this day. Not like the fighter that had been battling politics and gangdom for a score of years, and glorying in it. The fire had gone from his eyes and his hard jowls sagged. He looked like a beaten, suddenly old man.

"It's all right," he said slowly. "You done your best, Rick. You work different from me, I know. Only if you coulda got off your tail faster on this affair, maybe I wouldn't of got—"

Ricco took the yellow paper from his superior's

suddenly flaccid fingers and spread it to the light, and whistled softly.

It was a departmental order signed by the commissioner, and it relieved Bellamy from duty, effective the first of the following week.

"I called him this morning, but he wouldn't talk to me," Bellamy said dully. "Well, it's all right. Any time I can't deliver, I don't want no job."

Ricco frowned.

"After all, sir," he said thoughtfully, "people have died violent deaths before in this town. Two murders in a day is only par for this city. I don't see why they're making a fall guy out of you on this."

The choleric Bellamy's eyes were hard.

"If you'd had your eyes open," he said, "you'd maybe looked at the teletype in my office. It ain't two murders, boy. It's six. Six that I know of. They picked Joe Rodney outa the Harlem River this morning."

Ricco sat up.

"Hey!" he exclaimed. "Joe Rodney – the black numbers king, they called him. Scarcely a useful citizen, but he would swing a lot of votes, come primaries."

Captain Bellamy sighed, picked up the teletype tape on his desk and showed it to him:

Calling all cars. Roland France, colored, age about sixty-five, found beaten over head in front Clement Mission, 209 East 125th Street. Died Bellevue Hospital without regaining consciousness.

Bellamy said, "That old guy never had an enemy in the world, Rick. Joe Rodney was in the rackets, but this France was almost a saint to his people. He wasn't ordained in any church I know, but he conducted vespers up there in the Clement Mission for twenty years, and he did more good for Harlem than all the police rules ever made. I tell you, Rick—"

Ricco Pasquale Maguire stared out over the city. His face was a little gray under the tan.

"You said there were six, sir," he said

The big captain crushed an unlit cigar in his fingers.

"The others were more or less routine," he said. "A girl, name of Barnett, jumped or was thrown from a car on Sunrise Highway. No gang killing. The kid was a stenographer, good family, no record. The other one was a colored girl who jumped or fell from the top of the Trans-State building. They found her on an annex roof this morning. Thirty floors is a long drop. Nobody's identified her."

The phone rang and Bellamy snatched the receiver.

He listened and his face grew red.

"No, boy!" he said. "I got my own troubles! You better forget that foolishness and tend to business. G'bye."

He hung up and glared at the little coroner, Dr Jamison, who had just entered.

"Oh, it's you," he said. "Always bargin' in when you're needed somewhere else. You're such a smart guy, Jamison – where would you go to find a horse's head?"

The coroner's eyebrows lifted.

"I'm sure I wouldn't know, sir," he said.

Bellamy growled. "That kid of mine. Got a good job at the D.A.'s office, and he ought to be workin' nights on that vice probe. Instead he calls up an' wants me to find a mask for him shaped like a horse's head. Some masquerade dance he's goin' to tonight. Dancing he is, when his old man's head is ready for the basket!"

Dr Jamison pursed his thin lips.

"A great loss it would be, I'm sure," he murmured primly.

Bellamy glared at him suspiciously, and finding no malice apparent in the other's eyes, sank wearily into a groaning chair. And then he sat up straight again, staring at Ricco. The big's man's eyes were slitted ice, and he was clenching the arms of his chair.

"What is it, Rick? You smell something out on this? If we can only—"

Ricco Maguire was indeed thinking fiercely, trying to assemble and pin together the vagrant, deadly pieces of a pattern that ebbed and faded madly in his swirling brain. A picture-puzzle murder parade – which had yet to strike its most deadly blows. And then suddenly his eyes opened and the color was whipped completely out of his face.

He said, in a voice that he tried to keep steady, "That boy of yours, Captain. Call him up – now. Tell him not to go out of the house until we get down there. Don't ask me why. Just hurry, damn you!"

Bellamy dialed the phone, listened for the connection, barked quick words, and hung up grimly.

"He – he's gone, Rick. Left word he wouldn't be back the rest of the day. In God's name, what is it?"

Ricco said slowly, "I'm not sure. I may never know. But if I'm right – and I hope I'm not – your kid is—"

He shook himself, trying to keep hysteria out of his veins.

"Get out of here, both of you," he said. "Locate that boy of yours and keep him with you until I call for you. I'm locking this door and trying to remember something. Something that had to do with a horse's head and a man with a crown. Because when one dies – the other must follow! I'm not crazy, Captain. Find your kid. And be ready when I call you – with a squad car."

That was at ten o'clock. At seven o'clock Ricco got up from his chair for the second time that day. The stubble on his face was black against the white of his cheeks.

On the floor, spread in crumpled disorder, was a large-scale map of metropolitan New York.

Ricco opened the door and Bellamy was waiting outside. The older man's face was haggard.

"They – they couldn't find Johnny," he said dully. "He hasn't been to the office all day. He's never done that before, Rick. I don't like it."

Ricco Maguire waved the captain to a seat and crouched down again over the map. His eyes were feverish.

"Did you ever play chess, Captain?" he asked.

Bellamy looked soulfully at the ceiling.

"My son is vanished from the earth an' he talks about chess!" he groaned.

Ricco's fingers were talons, digging into his shoulder.

"Damn you, we haven't too much time. I've got to have— Wait a minute. I remember seeing a chessboard in Jamison's desk. Bring it in here, with all the pieces."

A minute later the small traveling chessboard was set up on the floor, in front of the map.

Ricco said, "I couldn't get it at first. Remember, six people killed without a trace. Three black and three white."

He set up some of the pieces on the board.

"Here—" pointing to Brooklyn Bridge on the map – "we find a white king. Remember the crown? And here—" he made a dot opposite the Harlem River – "we find the black king. We find a white bishop at Grant's Tomb, the corresponding black bishop sacrificed at the opposite end of the board, which is this city. The other two, unimportant people, pawns – don't you get it, Bellamy? The black and white pawns, the opening of the game!"

Under his fingers, superimposed over the map of New York, he was outlining black and white squares. Eight deep, eight to a column, covering roughly the entire borough of Manhattan, from Brooklyn Bridge to the Bronx line.

"Chess came from Persia, over a thousand years ago," Ricco said. "During all that time the rules were never changed – save one. You see, Captain, in chess as we know it the king is always sacred. The knights, the castles, the bishops, the pawns – all of them lay down their lives to protect the king. Or, if the king is checkmated, all other pieces cease to be. He is conquered, but he never dies. He can't be taken."

Bellamy said dully, "You said we didn't have much time, Rick. I'm tryin' to be patient."

"Only once did they change that pattern of play," Ricco said. "During the Restoration, when Cromwell and his bloody iron hats cut off a good king's head. They played a sinful game then, those pious killers. A perversion of chess it was, and it lasted only eight years. In that game the queen was the protected one, the king but a weak, feeble pawn, for all his fine crown. First to be sacrificed, he was least to be valued. The piece to be most feared, the enemy of the queen—"

He stopped and his hands made little feverish motions across the macabre map of the city.

"Your boy was on a big case in the D.A.'s office," he said. "You told me it was secret stuff. I'm asking you to violate that secret now, sir. It may mean a lot."

Bellamy said dully, "It's that Greene dame. The boss of the girl shows they're tryin' to close."

Ricco sighed. "The queen of the strippers," he said irrelevantly. "The queen's play!"

Something in his voice brought Bellamy's head up taut.

"I got a squad car waitin'," he said. "For God's sake, boy, we're—"

Ricco said, very quietly, "The Cromwell chess game, Bellamy. Check me carefully. I don't think I'm crazy. Your son wanted a mask of a black horse's head. A horse's head – the symbol of the black knight. In the Cromwell variation of chess, the black knight dies that the white queen may live to attack again!"

Bellamy's face was red no longer. It was gray and sagging.

"That Greene woman has been in hiding for months," he groaned. "We got no place to look. Six million people an' no place to—"

Ricco's finger was on the map of the city, the chess-board-marked murder game that had already cost six lives.

"We've been talking about a game, Captain," he said. "So far we haven't mentioned one important thing – the player who is moving the pieces. A very fine player he is. Fine enough to keep to the Cromwell opening to the letter. Contemptuous of lesser people – so contemptuous that he draws a clear diagram of his plays. Now—" Ricco's fingers were trembling a little, adjusting a ruler to the map – "if he makes the next move correctly, the knight's fatal sally against the cruel queen, it would occur in the middle of square number—"

He made a swift point on the map, and Bellamy copied

down the key numbers, turning it upside down to look at the chart.

And then Ricco swore hollowly.

The key read: *Euclid Ave. & Dayer St Excavation for subway under construction. No house on property*.

The sun was down. The shadows were gray on the skyline. Bellamy sat down heavily and buried his head in his hands.

And then suddenly Ricco had the map, shaking it in front of his eyes.

"Euclid and Dayer!" he said. "There's been no subway work done around there since the Independent—" He looked at the map again and the sound of his gun holster slapping as it buckled around his hips brought Bellamy up at his side.

"That fine map of yours," he said, "is right as far as it goes. But it happens to be ten years old. Get your shooting irons, my friend. We may be needing them this night!"

Two hours later, even Captain Bellamy had given up hope. The junction of Euclid Avenue and Dayer Street contained a fine imposing mass of limestone and chromium called the Underwood Arms. Two squad cars went through it from vegetable cellar to penthouse. Net result, several score alarmed burghers, a dozen threatened suits – and not a trace of a clue.

Wearier than he had ever been in his life, Ricco dismissed the cars. To Bellamy, he said, "I'm sorry, sir. I wish I could—"

The big captain was strangely white under the arc light. He said, "I'm goin' back to the office, Rick. Something may break there. You hang around and call me if you get any ideas. I don't want you to stick your neck out alone. That's an order."

He got into the squad car and it vanished around the corner.

Ricco sat down on the entrance steps. A fatigue that was akin to sheer nausea had gripped him.

The district was shabby-genteel, a corner of Manhattan where the slums and the upper crust rub elbows lightly in passing. Far down the street some dead-end kids were playing ball, oblivious to passing traffic. A few blocks above him, fine old town houses kept disdainful vigil against the world that was trying to reach into their sheltered domain.

A newsboy shuffled by, stopped and stood under the light.

"That's a bad place to park, buddy," the kid said. "They got a doorman in there that don't like bums."

Half dead, Ricco said wearily, "Beat it, kid. I'm busy."

The newsboy stared at him. Half consciously Ricco noted that the figure before him was considerably older than he looked at first glance. Older, with the wisdom of the slums whipping the youth out of his hard little eyes. He stood at the corner, directly under the ray of the lamp light and the single newspaper he held was black against the glare.

The newsboy whined, "All the news while it's hot, mister," held the paper up plainly against the light, and vanished into the darkness.

And suddenly, out of the black despair that gripped him, Ricco came to his feet, taut as a cat.

For this was no ordinary tabloid. It had black, uneven headlines pasted raggedly over the original text. And the headline said, *The Queen Is Smiling – for the Last Time*.

The Police Positive was in his hand as he ran down to the corner. The street was empty. But somewhere he could hear shuffling footsteps – in the darkened alley, behind the apartment house. Too late Ricco remembered that that narrow space also fell within the fatal dot on the murder map. The shuffling figure disappeared, melting into a formless dark shadow in the distance.

His heart hammering, Ricco inched along the sheltering wall. Death was waiting in this place, he knew. But there was no time to call Bellamy now.

The shapeless mass materialized into a rickety shed-like structure, evidently used as a workhouse. The door was open.

Ricco's flashlight pierced the gloom. Some rusted garden tools, a box of rubber hose, the worse for wear. And another box, still more moldy. The newsboy was sitting nonchalantly upon it, his eyes mocking. He said, "Fancy meeting you here, copper!"

Ricco said, "Keep your hands in sight, pal. I'm coming—"

There was a muffled cough behind him. Too late his drugged senses whipped his body into action. Offstride, whirling, he had a nightmare kaleidoscope of a spread-eagled shadow, deeper than the night, more swift than his lunging dive.

There was a blinding shock of pain that swept out of the night and he knew no more.

It was cold, and the back of his head was torturing fire. Groaning, he tried to sit up, and tight cords bit into his wrists.

Behind him, a voice said, "Our friend is coming to his senses."

The voice was hauntingly familiar, an urgent summons under his eyelids, which would not seem to open. The voice said, "Let us face it, Ricco. Death is not as unpleasant as – many things I could name."

Something like a sob of sheer amazement struggled for utterance in Ricco's throat, and then he opened his eyes.

The voice said, "You would find us, you alone of the stupid mob. I knew you would come to me."

It was Dr Jamison. The smiling mask was gone from his face, and what was left was not pretty. There was cunning behind his eyes, cunning and a long-leashed madness free at last.

Behind Ricco a woman's voice husked, "We must watch him, my dear. This man is more dangerous than the rest."

A hideous, mottled figure came out of the gloom. Once, Ricco remembered, Laura Greene had been beautiful. This night she was an obscene travesty of a woman, shapeless, shuffling, evidently prey to some obese illness. And on those shapeless shoulders, yet more horrible by its incongruity, was the face of a young, smiling girl.

"She is beautiful, is she not?" the coroner whispered.

Ricco said dumbly, "That – that boy of Bellamy's, Jamison. I – you can't—"

The tight smile vanished from the older man's round face. He said, unhearing, "She is indeed beautiful, my enemy. Picture us, a mere decade ago – the greatest dancer on Broadway and I the young doctor who was her lover. Until the day a young policeman saw a chance to add to his honor list by chasing a murderer down the Great White Way just when the shows were letting out on a summer night. He was a fine, brave lad, this young policeman. His name was Bellamy. But he was not as good a shot as he later became. The bullet Ralph Bellamy meant for one Hal Mayer is in my Laura's spine. She never danced again."

Ricco said, "I never knew. I know Bellamy has been looking for Mayer ever since—"

"Mayer?" the little man laughed harshly. "I strangled him with my bare hands. It was my sickbed present to my dear. Since then – men and women have died, from time to time. It's been a merry game we've played. But I weary of it. It is time to bring it to an end. And a fitting end it will be. The son of the man who has spoiled my life, and you, his proudest boast."

He forced Ricco's head down across what seemed to be a bottomless pit. After a minute his eyes grew accustomed to the blackness and he could see. A dusty, unused space of subway track. Young Bellamy was spread across the rail.

"A spur of the new subway," Jamison explained. "An error in the original building plan. Eight hundred feet long, yet removed from the world by a switch. A switch that has never been thrown, yet will be this night. I fear a goodly crowd will never see their homes this fine night. Two bodies on the rails, plus a three-foot bright wall barrier, should be enough to mess up an express train."

Ricco felt himself falling through space, to land cruelly against the outside track.

The smiling beldame was ageless, pale beauty in the dim light. And out of that same light Ricco saw what he had prayed for. The steel underside of the rusted rail spur, crumbling, yet razor-sharp against the cords at his wrist. He sank back against the sharpness and felt the blessed pain of the cut as the cords gave.

She who had been Laura Greene said nervously, "I think we should hurry, my dear. Tomorrow will be a busy day. You must—"

She screamed then, shrilly, as Ricco's hands taloned around her ankles. Whirling, Jamison shot from the hip and fire hammered into Ricco's good shoulder. But the smiling lady was falling, falling horribly through the air.

The little coroner plunged directly after that falling shape, so close to young Bellamy that the blinding blue flash lit up all three faces before Ricco's fading eyes.

The poor, mad lovers who had plotted to slay a city – but died together on that city's third rail . . .

Young Bellamy was all right. He stamped the circulation back into his arms, keeping his face averted from the blackened things in the pit, barely three feet away from him. He said, "We've got to warn them, Rick. I don't know—"

Ricco was hardly conscious of his own voice saying, "The power – shut off automatically – by them. The laughing queen saved them, boy. But she – she sacrificed her pawn and lost the game. You don't play the Cromwell – that way—"

It was many an anxious week before the kid knew what the bleeding man's whispered words meant . . .

And he still can't look at chessmen without shuddering!

Caravan to Tarim

Eleven miles out of Maglaf, the caravan ran into a mob of Bedouins. It started out as a pleasant negotiation with rifles.

Kelney cursed the Arabian sand and the Arabian sun and said, "Who gave them rifles?"

A bullet ran past Tiggs' cheek and he muttered, "Anyway, it's better than knives." Tiggs had three knife scars from the Bedouin blades. He had been working back and forth across the desert for nine years. He was used to this sort of thing.

The Bedouins were moving in now. They knew all about Kelney's caravan, the spices and perfume and rugs that were being taken to the market in Tarim.

Kelney cursed and started up, wielding his pistol. He tried to leap over the parapet formed by the spine of his camel. Tiggs pulled him down. And the next bullet came sailing across his crouching body and went on going and hit one of the Arabian guides in the forehead.

Kelney was not used to this. He was an American, big but not tall. Five seven and one ninety. He was thirty-six years old and for almost a quarter of a century he had been a drifter. His hair was whitish gold and his eyes were bottle green. His skin was oak. He wasn't a happy man; he was a bit too tough.

"Don't waste bullets," Tiggs said. He was an

Englishman. His philosophy was that life was very short and a man had to do as he damn' well pleases, provided he didn't cause grief to nice people. Tiggs was a year shy of forty and looked younger. He was tall and thin and dry. His eyes were colorless. He seemed very tired.

With Tiggs and Kelney there were seventeen honest Arabians. And in a semicircle behind the sand dune thirty yards away there were thirty-odd dishonest Arabians. There was nothing to do but crouch down behind the camels and listen to the bullets whistling.

"Let's rush them," Kelney said.

"That wouldn't be wise," Tiggs murmured. "They've got the elevation. They've got too much sand in front of them. Wait. Let them use more bullets."

"They're killing us all."

"It's bad," Tiggs admitted. "But there's nothing we can do about it right now."

"That's one man's opinion," Kelney said. His dark green eyes became black.

In shabby Arabian he shouted an order. The guides whimpered. Kelney repeated the command and the Arabians still held back. He jumped out of cover, and his pistol shoved lead. The Arabians were following. Even Tiggs joined up. They were running now, running and weaving, some of them falling as they went across the sand. The Bedouins stood up, shot downward.

Kelney saw Tiggs go down. The Englishman rolled over a few times, and then his face was to the sun and his mouth was open. Blood dribbled from his lips. Kelney didn't see the need for further study. He concluded that Tiggs was dead and that was unfortunate but then this whole business was unfortunate.

The Bedouins were coming out from behind their dune. Kelney saw his men start to run. The Bedouins were laughing and shooting them down. A bullet tore flesh from Kelney's thigh.

In another minute, the Bedouins were walking out to get him. They were grinning.

They looked mean, and their women liked to see white men die slowly, with a lot of groans and screaming. Kelney put the pistol to his head and pulled the trigger.

He had forgotten that the chamber was empty. The Bedouins had him, and he was shouting curses, squirming, kicking with his good leg.

The leader came over and told him to be quiet.

In fuming Arabic, Kelney told the leader what he could do. But then his eyes became green again and he gave the Bedouin chief a half grin.

The Bedouin was not very tall and not very wide. But his eyes and jaw line were bladelike and hard. His smile was a thread. He wore a lot of green and yellow silk, and shining belts of silvery leather. His men wore rags. Kelney, sizing it up, decided that the leader had a mixture of brains and vanity and could be talked to.

"There is precious stuff in the bags," Kelney said, pointing with his chin toward the corpses of the camels. His wrists were already behind his back and the Bedouins were drawing the hemp in tight knots.

"Why do you wish me to know that?" the Bedouin leader said.

Kelney shrugged. "It is good to know the joy of looking forward to a treasure."

"I know all about the treasure. I know all about you."

Kelney forced a laugh. He looked down to see blood fountaining from his thigh. The Bedouin reached down, arranged a somewhat capable bandage.

Then Kelney was placed on a camel and the Bedouin mob ribboned across the lake of sand.

The leader rode beside Kelney. He said, "I was in the Tarim when you brought in the last shipment. I followed you. I know that you have more spices, perfume, rugs—"

"Not quite. But I know where to get more." Kelney said it wincing.

The Bedouin smiled at the sun. "We will speak of this later."

It was all very unpleasant, the sticky heat and the smell of too many unwashed camels and the general filth of a Bedouin camp. But Kelney wasn't thinking in terms of the present. He went so far as to eat and drink from the same big dish shared by a group of Bedouins.

The leader, who had introduced himself as Sheik Nadi, was saying, "You do not mind the food?"

"Why should I?"

"It is bad food. We are very poor. Do you know why?"

Kelney shrugged.

"We are the forgotten people," Nadi said. "We are kept out of the villages. This tribe was not always nomadic by nature. They took our grazing lands away and now we are slowly starving. That is why we come out on the desert with our rifles."

"How did you get the rifles?" Kelney's tone was conversational.

"Theft," the Bedouin said. "We have been forced to make our own laws. And we will benefit. When our treasure is sufficient we will take the trade away from the stingy merchants in village bazaars. We will be the scornful rather than the scorned!"

"And why not?" Kelney gazed directly into Nadi's eyes.

Nadi breathed deeply through his nose. He folded his arms and looked past Kelney's shoulder. "You know where to get these treasures," he said. "You pay a small price, then you take the stuff to Tarim and reap a high profit."

"You have it wrong," Kelney said. "I am not my own employer. I work for Mezar, the richest merchant in Tarim. He sends me to the coast of the Red Sea. There I trade with European vessels that slip up through the Indian Ocean. I can negotiate better than the Arabian tradesmen."

He was telling the truth. He was seeing hate sparkle in Nadi's eyes.

"Mezar," the Bedouin said. "I know him well. A jackal. It is he who controls the city of Tarim. And you work for him."

"No more," Kelney said.

Nadi went into his tent, brought out water pipes. For a while the two men sat smoking quietly. Kelney made the first bid. He said, "I will get you more treasure."

"Of course." Nadi smiled. "That is why you are alive now. That is why the knives of our women remain idle."

"I will go to Tarim," Kelney said. "Mezar will send me out with another caravan."

"Am I a fool?" Nadi said. "Do I speak with fools?"

"Another caravan," Kelney said.

"And heavily armed, yes?"

Kelney nodded. "Heavily armed – with blank cartridges."

"If you would cheat Mezar, you would cheat me."

"I have more to gain by cheating Mezar."

Nadi sucked at the water pipe. He looked at Kelney and then he looked at the sand. He said, "You think wisely. Work for me and your rewards will be plentiful. But revenge can come in equal quantity if you attempt betrayal."

"I wait for your word," Kelney said.

"My word is this – you will leave Tarim with the new caravan. You will be unmolested during your journey to the sea. This time you will bring back a treasure greater than any in the past. And once again you will meet me in the desert. There will be no fighting. You will tell your men to surrender. We will take their rifles and camels."

"And my men?"

"They will die in the desert. Under the sun. Thirsting."

Kelney put down the tube of his water pipe. "Must they die?"

"They are from the city," Nadi said. "They would happily see my tribe die the slow death. We will likewise be happy to see them crawling across the desert, their tongues black."

"What about me?" Kelney said. "How can I murder my own men?"

"Speak now!" Nadi was standing. "Your life is no longer your own. The knives of my women are waiting."

Deep inside, Kelney shivered. He said, "It is agreed."

He would start out the following morning. There were no complex details. A single Bedouin would accompany him.

Alone in his tent, Kelney laughed with sound. He had never expected it would be this easy. He had given his word to Nadi, but Nadi was a bandit and a killer and you're not obliged to keep promises to the Nadis.

Kelney was awakened at dawn by an old Bedouin who informed him that his camel was ready. He was offered food and gulped it down hurriedly. Walking toward the camel, he turned to the man and said, "Sheik Nadi?"

"Gone," the old Beduoin said. "Out of the desert, waiting for another caravan. A great one, our chief."

"Yes," Kelney said. "And very clever."

"Cleverer than you think," the old man said.

After a moment the old man nodded. "You will keep your word. Because I will tell you that Nadi is a man of honor and he believes that honor means more than life itself. There have been those who have broken their word to Nadi, and they have died. I could tell you how they died but I will let you imagine it for yourself. They thought they had tricked Nadi: they thought once they were out of the desert they were free of him. But he followed them. And eventually he caught them. One by one. When Nadi decides to pursue a man, the man never gets away."

It hit Kelney with the force of a hammer. He had the ability to recognize profound truth when he heard it, and he was hearing it now.

The old man was saying, "Your fellow traveller will be the tongueless fool who waits now on his camel."

Kelney got a look at the man who would journey with him for two hundred miles across sand. It wasn't a pleasant look. The ragged Bedouin had a face that could turn a stomach. Some terrible disease had left scars, blotches and pulpy masses that distorted his features into a hideous mask. The diseased one opened his mouth to speak and his lips moved but he made gargling sounds and nothing more.

Shuddering, Kelney said, "I must travel with that?"

The old man grinned. "It is the wish of Sheik Nadi."

Kelney was climbing onto his camel. His body jerked violently as the beast rose from a placid crouch, shook itself to get blood into its legs.

The old Bedouin looked up at Kelney. "Your camel is strong," he said. "May your will have the same strength."

Kelney nodded slowly. He really meant it as he said, "Thanks for the tip."

And the two camels, bearing silent riders, went eastward, towards Tarim.

Short and fat and sloppy, Mezar wallowed in his wealth. Once he had been a whining, begging seller of spices. In a miserable, hollowed-out space, he had made his living not on routine sales, but on certain practices that at times offered themselves when a customer was careless.

Slowly Mezar had pulled himself up, and now he had wealth. He was powerful and he had many persons working for him and it was good to think about all this, particularly the efficient white men he had working for him, this Kelney, this Tiggs, with their crisp, clear way of doing business. In short time, if things kept on the way they were going, his wealth would be doubled.

A servant came in, babbled loud and fast.

"Send him in!" Mezar said.

Kelney came in. His jacket and white linen breeches were rags. His pith helmet was cracked. He limped. But it was his face that made Mezar stare. His face was pale; the eyes had deepened in green until they were almost black.

The Arabian leaped up and almost choked on a mouthful of figs.

Kelney was in there first. He waved wearily at the fat merchant, he folded his arms and gazed at the floor and said, "Bedouins."

"But the shipment—"

"I had more luck than the others," Kelney said. His nerves were a sunbroiled mass dangling from an ever-thinning thread. He wanted to hit Mezar in the face.

"The shipment!" Mezar screeched. He was leaping around the silk-curtained room. "The shipment is gone! Why did you let the Bedouins—" He coughed on the figs.

His eyes were glass. Then he saw the silent man standing in the doorway and he looked at the pulpy, scarred face and he said, "Who is that?"

"The man saved me," Kelney said, just as he had rehearsed it. "I do not know who he is. He has no tongue."

Mezar was slowing down. His eyes were retreating into the fat folds of his face. He walked past Kelney, kept walking toward the mute. As he did so, he clapped his hands, twice.

Then he stood in front of the mute, hitting his palms together lightly, smiling as he stood there waiting.

"He befriended me," Kelney said.

Two tall, half-naked Arabians entered the room. They were sweating, always groping for more energy.

Mezar pointed to the mute and said, "Take him."

Kelney saw the mute struggling in the grasp of the two big men. He pushed Mezar's elbow and said, "Leave him be. Reward him and let him go."

"He is a Bedouin," Mezar said.

Kelney was very tired. He was nearly broken in two. He said, "If any harm comes to the mute one, I will leave your employ. The Englishman is dead, and you will have no one to get the low prices. Hear me, Mezar."

"But he is a Bedouin!" Mezar insisted. "Can you understand how I hate them? Can you understand what a plague they are?"

"This one is sick and harmless," Kelney said.

"I will make sure that he will always be harmless," Mezar replied, and now his smile had enjoyment in it. Gesturing toward the writhing, gurgling Bedouin, the fat merchant addressed the tall men and said, "Take him out and cut off his ears and the tip of his nose."

Then, as Mezar changed the smile to a laugh, Kelney cursed. He sensed himself going across the room, his hands shaping a couple of fists. He landed a hard one on an Arabian's chest and the tall man lurched. The other man moved toward Kelney and at that point the mute became an eel, went sliding away. His gurgling was now an awful sort of laughter, fading quickly as he made his escape down a narrow street.

Kelney had nothing to do and no place to go and he stood there and waited until the two tall men came back. They looked at Mezar. And Mezar nodded.

Mezar had seated himself and now he studied Kelney's face. He said, "You seem to like the Bedouins."

"There are good and bad in all tribes."

"I do not understand."

"It's very necessary to understand," Kelney said. "Every nation and every tribe has its good people and it's bad. Does it take much intelligence to get that?"

Mezar rubbed a finger across a huge carbuncle amethyst that dangled from his neck. "All Bedouins are fiends," he said. "You know that, as I do. But you helped the mute one to escape. I want to know why."

Biting his lip, Kelney looked at Mezar and let out a sigh and said, "I told you why."

"I do not believe it," Mezar said. "I will tell you, Kelney, I expected that at some time you would try to trick me, but I did not suppose that you would be so foolish as to enlist the help of Bedouins. You are working with them now, is it not so?"

"Don't be a fool."

"The Englishman, too. And all the rest of the caravan. All working with the Bedouins. And you arranged it. Tell me with you own lips. Say it now!"

"All right," Kelney said. "Go to hell."

Then he squirmed and tried to get away, knowing that it was a crazy idea, knowing it would be a tough process from here on in. The violent part of it lasted about a minute. Afterward they were able to half carry him out of the room, and he felt himself going down some corridor. And then he got the feeling of metal clamps fastened around his wrists, and he was vertical and his boots and socks were being pulled away; his naked feet just about tagged the floor.

"You will be alone for a while," Mezar said. "I grant you complete darkness and silence. In an hour I will be back here with gifts of agony. It is my hope that you will tell the truth."

Footsteps were going away, a door was closing, and Kelney was calling himself the same names he had called Mezar. It occurred to him that perhaps he had deserved this sort of thing for a long, long time and now there was nothing to do but take it with philosophy.

Blank cartridges, he was thinking. That was a lovely arrangement and for that deal alone he deserved to get his head kicked in. Even though he hadn't been given the opportunity to go through with the transaction, the fact remained that he had agreed to it and he certainly would have gone through with it to soften his own mattress. And that made him a thousand varieties of louse and he was lower than any Bedouin.

He had to grin. It was so easy to feel this noble remorse, this inner cleansing, when the four surrounding walls were walls of odds. Give him a chance to get out of this and he would go back to the strategy, the fencing, the scummy bargaining that he was always engaged in when he was bargaining with what he recognized as scum.

But was Nadi scum? What about those Bedouins? Were they really scum? He gave himself a picture of them, their rags, the food they ate, the sad faces of their children. On another canvas he was seeing fat Mezar with a mouthful of figs, and gems against fleshy fingers and all the silk. He thought about the good Arabians, honest and fairly decent men crawling across sand and dying of thirst because a noble soul named Kelney had placed blank cartridges in their rifles. He heard the door again, and then footsteps.

Slanting light straightened itself out as Mezar placed a torch in a wall bracket. Mezar was alone and breathing hard.

This is going to be good, Kelney thought.

But he hadn't dreamed it would be this good, because Mezar was unfastening the clamps and saying, "I am humble."

Kelney rubbed his wrists. "Say it again."

The fat Arabian said it again.

"So what brings about the change of heart?"

"Tiggs is here."

"You can say that again, too."

"Tiggs has been brought in. He was picked up by another caravan coming this way from the coast. He was dying. They had a physician with them, a famous man from Charfa. An operation was performed in the desert, and a bullet taken from Tiggs' body. He is recovering fast. And he has told me what happened with the Bedouins. I know now that you spoke the truth."

"Thanks," Kenley said, "for nothing."

"Let us forget this unpleasant affair," Mezar said. "In a short time Tiggs will be well again. You will take out another caravan—"

"I want more payment," Kelney said.

"Of course. You are a good tradesman, Kelney, and I am happy to reward my best workers."

"I don't work for you," Kenley said. "I only deal with

you. Remember that. And here's another thing. I don't want to wait around for Tiggs to get back on his feet. I'll take out the next caravan as soon as you make out your buying schedule."

"But Tiggs knows the route better—"

"I'm in a hurry."

"Yes, but Tiggs—"

"The buying is the important thing."

Kelney was thinking of the blank cartridges, calling himself a skunk even as he called himself a nice guy for making this attempt to save Tiggs.

"You say that you do not work for me." Mezar's tone was level. "I tell you that you are wrong and that my word is the last. You will wait until Tiggs recovers and he will go with you on the next caravan."

All at once Kelney was very tired. He shrugged and said all right, he would wait for Tiggs.

It was an ordeal itself, counting the days, pacing them in ratio with Tiggs' recovery. The day when Tiggs sat up. The day when he walked around. The day when he was able to eat and drink as a normal man. Kelney watched him come back to full life and realized that it would not be long before Tiggs was back there with death. The bargain with Nadi must be kept, otherwise Nadi would come creeping. And Nadi would find him.

There came a day when the caravan set out across the desert, aiming at the string of ports on the Red Sea coast. Kelney and Tiggs walked ahead of their camels. And following were thirty Arabians, whom Kelney had supplied well with water and food and rifles and cartridges. The cartridges were blank.

"I'd like to meet the Bedouins again," Tiggs said.

"A bullet can't settle an issue."

"In a way you're right," Tiggs said. "But I've had a lot of pain. I'd like to make at least one Bedouin go through what I've been through."

Kelney glanced to the side and saw that Tiggs' lean, dry face was working slightly. Tiggs' lips were drawn like expanded rubber and his eyes aimed ahead like rifle muzzles.

The caravan reached the coast in eleven days. It had been slow going. On the trip northward, however, along the coast, Kelney made good progress. His negotiating was more clever than it had ever been. When the caravan was headed back toward Tarim, the packs were loaded with quality that would make Mezar smile.

They moved onto the desert, and the big sun was there to greet them. They watched it as it floated along with them. There was half a day of this, and hardly any talk, and then during a rest period Tiggs was lighting a cigarette and saying, "Well, we have our treasure. Now let the Bedouins try to take it away from us."

Kelney leaned his head toward the match in Tiggs fingers. "Maybe we shouldn't talk about it too much."

For a while Tiggs was quiet. Then he said, "I've been wondering about something. That mute Bedouin who guided you back to Tarim. Rather odd that any of them would do something like that, don't you think?" And when there was no reply, Tiggs went on. "They're clever as well as mean, those buzzards. You've got to be careful."

"All right," Kelney said. "What's on your mind?"

They looked at each other, and Tiggs said, "What's on yours?"

"I'm not worrying about a thing," Kelney said.

They had moved another mile or so when Tiggs suddenly darted ahead. Something was on the sand, writhing out there in front of them.

It was a dying camel, left there by another caravan. They looked it over and Tiggs said there was no use, there was no saving the beast. And then Tiggs lifted his rifle, pointed it at the camel's head.

Kelney knocked down the rifle.

"Why not?" Tiggs said. He didn't move. There was no expression in his eyes. Kelney was rolling invisible dice, telling himself that Tiggs had examined the cartridges in his rifle. Anyway, there was a quick means of finding out for sure. "All right," he said, "if you think you're being merciful, go ahead and give it a bullet."

The Englishman said, "I can't do it, Kelney. I adore these animals. You take the job."

Kelney breathed hard, trying to keep his relief from showing. He told himself everything was fine now. As he pulled the trigger he asked himself if he was actually as clever as he thought.

Ninety miles out of Maqlaf, Tiggs said, "They're about due."

"Who?"

"The Bedouins."

"Bad ones?"

"They're all bad," Tiggs said.

Injecting it with a stiff dose of sarcasm, Kelney said, "How long does it take to learn about Arabia?"

Tiggs laughed. "I've been here nine years and I'm just beginning to learn."

"Maybe you're slow to catch on," Kelney said. "Sometimes I think—"

A bullet cut in on that one. It came from a rise in the sand about seventy yards away. There was a string of bush fringing the rise, and above its meagre green there were bits of white that were Bedouin headdress.

Kelney acted electrically. His eyes made a chart of the surrounding sand. He saw that a deviation in the slope would afford a barrier against bullets. He yelled an order. His voice slicing hard. The Arabians backed up, swayed their camels behind the sand barrier. During all this there was quiet and Kelney knew what it meant. Nadi was waiting it out, waiting for rifled response. Nadi wanted to see if the American was playing him clean.

Tiggs' voice barged in. "Well, you're in charge. What do we do?"

"Just wait," Kelney said. He was flat on his belly behind the barrier, and Tiggs, at his side, was inching up to peep over the barrier.

"Stay down," Kelney said. He raised his voice to give the command in Arabic. "Stay down – hold fire!" He knew it was loud enough for Nadi to hear.

Kelney waited for the Bedouin bullets and they didn't come and he pushed his tongue over dry lips. He didn't like the quiet. He didn't like himself. He had brought these men out to die.

"You don't look well," Tiggs said.

Kelney heard that clearly but it didn't mean anything to him. He sensed that he was breaking up inside. And all at once the break came and he realized that he could not let this thing go on. He had to do something drastic and he had to do it alone. He looked at Tiggs and he looked at the Arabians and he started to crawl backward down the barrier.

"What's the object?" Tiggs said.

"I'm going roundabout," Kelney said. "I'm edging out to skirt that bush and get in behind them. I want to see just what their plans are. Don't do anything, just stay here and hold fire. I don't want a single bullet wasted."

Then without waiting for Tiggs' reply, he was following

the barrier around its shape of an arc. He became older by a few years as he worked wide of the bush, then came in behind the bush, and all the time there was just that same thick quiet, and he knew that Nadi was wondering about the cartridges. Pressed flat against the sand, he crawled another twenty yards and then he was back there behind the Bedouins. He could see Sheik Nadi, the green and gold distinct against the colorless rags of Nadi's followers.

Kelney stood up and walked forward. A few Bedouins became conscious of his approach, raised their rifles, then lowered them as Nadi shouted something. Kelney stopped and waited as Nadi came toward him. When they faced each other they were both smiling and Nadi lowered his rifle and that was when Kelney made a subtle gesture with the pistol. Nadi lost the smile.

"A trick?" Nadi said.

"No trick. I have kept the agreement. My men are holding rifles that have blank cartridges. But in this pistol are real bullets. If you cry out I'll kill you. Now walk with me and try to be patient."

They walked back and away from the Bedouin position. Nadi was smiling. "Before you kill me let me tell you that my followers will someday find you, and your death will be a terrible thing."

"Aw, knock it off," Kelney growled in his own tongue. Then, going back to Arabic, he said, "I said that I had kept our agreement, and I was not lying. All I ask now is that you spare the lives of my men. I will see that you get the entire shipment."

"You are loyal to Mezar."

"I am loyal to myself. I hate Mezar even as you do, even as my men do. Your followers and my men are brothers."

Nadi lowered his head and rubbed his chin and it was

done perfectly. The change of pace was also perfect, because Nadi was a streak as he smashed with both hands. The pistol went out of Kelney's grasp and Kelney went back with the Bedouin tearing at him. They went down together, grappling, and Kelney grinned as he thought of every other man who had tried to use this method of argument with him. And a few moments later he was upright again and he was frowning. And Nadi, who had gone sliding out of a bear hug to take the pistol, now had it pointed at Kelney's chest.

"It's too bad," Kelney said. "I was trying to be fair."

And he was telling himself that it didn't pay, there was no logic to it. If he had handled it from the evil side, if he had kept it dirty according to the original idea, he would have been in the cream.

He blinked and waited for the bullet.

And then he heard Nadi saying, "I cannot."

"You're teasing me. I'm dead already and I know it." He was trembling, he was very frightened, very agitated, because he was a man who got real taste out of life and this was a sure and final thing that would happen to him.

"I cannot kill you," Nadi said.

"I'm listening."

Nadi's smile was vague. "When you went back to Tarim, I went with you. I was the mute."

Kelney stared.

"I did not trust you," Nadi said. "I wanted to be sure. I used a clay-and-rice paste to mask my face. But I was foolish enough to stay with you when you reported to Mezar. He would have given me death, slow and with agony. And you saved me. I cannot kill you. I want to, but I cannot. I will give you back your pistol and you will return to your men. Go on to Tarim. You will not be molested. But from now on you must take a different route. I do not want us to meet again."

Butt foremost, the pistol was handed back to Kelney. And Nadir turned and started back toward the rise where his men faced the Mezar caravan, and where all the rifles were silent and waiting.

Tiggs turned when he heard Kelney coming up. He smiled with sincerity and said, "It's a surprise. I never thought you'd come back."

"You mean that?"

"Of course," Tiggs said. "I thought they'd spot you and shoot you down."

"Oh," Kelney said. "I thought you meant something else." Then he bit his lip for a few seconds. "We'll move on. They won't bother us."

They shouted orders but the entire party was watching the Bedouins who were now moving away, a string of ragged figures on bony beasts, winding into the yellow distance.

Among the Arabians there were murmurs of puzzlement. Even the camels made questioning noises. The caravan formed line and moved on. Tiggs and Kelney walked ahead, saying nothing, and it went on like that for a long chain of hollow minutes.

Finally Tiggs laughed softly. "A good thing the Bedouins went home."

Kelney stopped and faced the Englishman and said, "Whatever you've got to say, say the whole thing now."

"I made a little change in our ammunition," Tiggs said. "I took out the blanks and put in the genuine."

Kelney had a feeling he was two feet tall. "Which shows," he said, "how much you trusted me."

"Which shows how much I trust anyone before I come

to know him," Tiggs said. "I always make a private inspection of the rifles before a caravan goes out. Every once in a while a guide makes a deal with the Bedouins. The blank cartridge business is an old trick. But this is the first time I ever watched a man change his mind."

"You knew I'd change my mind?"

"Let's say I was hoping for it so strongly I made myself believe it. It's this way, Kelney — you and I work well together and I've been planning that we should break away from Mezar and start our own little trade."

"Hold it," Kelney said. "After what's happened out here, you think I can be trusted? I'm not exactly a saint."

Tiggs voice was as gentle as his smile. "Not exactly," he said, "but you've got possibilities."

It's a Wise Cadaver

It was on the desk, waiting for him. Renner cursed. He disliked this habit that the boss had of going out on a case and leaving him nothing except one of these notes with a brief – too brief – description of the deal plus a few careless directions. Renner picked up the note, scowled at it.

On that village kill – big dough involved. Believe it or not, I'm working for Calotta.

Al

And then an address – Renner swore and walked heavily out of the little office, chewing imaginary gum.

Driving downtown he worried, as usual, about himself. There was no getting away from the fact that he had been a fool to punch a certain house sergeant in the mouth. The unfortunate incident had occurred little more than a year ago and it had resulted in his being toed off the force and into the lap of Al Reid. Reid, a wise guy, had been kicked out a year or so before that and had started his own little agency. Upon hearing of Renner's trouble, he had offered to take his ex-colleague in, on the premise that two could starve to death as cheaply as one.

He brought his sour speculations back to the present.

If Calotta is mixed up with us and if Reid is working for Calotta, then the payoff has been reached.

Calotta, in legal, technical parlance, had no visible means of support – but the technicality was only in force because the police from Miami to Manhattan assiduously kept their eyes shut. Five years earlier Reid had engaged one of Calotta's boys in a gun duel and had killed him. A week later Al Reid had narrowly missed a trip to the morgue when somebody put a time bomb in his apartment – and if the two had become bosom pals and co-workers since, Renner hadn't heard about it.

However, time heals all wounds.

Renner's destination was a typical Greenwich Village tenement. A lot of kids on the street and a lot of noise and thick air. He saw a few loiterers in the doorway and muttered, "Calotta," figuring it would work as a password.

It did and he found himself taken inside, up a dark flight of steps, through a dark hallway, and into a room. Al was there, along with three frightened women, a frightened old man, a heavy-set man who looked sore and mean – and a corpse.

The corpse was stretched out on the floor and it was almost swimming in its own blood. The blood came from a big hole in the head and an axe leaning against a dirty bed told the rest of the story.

Al grinned at Renner and said, "The guy on the floor is Dominic Varella. He is a very intelligent kid of twenty who got the idea that he could get rich quick. Imagine, in times like these!"

"Then what?"

"He was not very original, even alive. He told a lot of nice people that a boat loaded down with gold is sunk off the Asbury Park beach, and he is organizing a diving expedition, and do they care to share in the box office receipts?"

"That is an old one," Renner agreed.

"Quite true," Al smiled. "But Dominic had a new angle. He went to a printer and had a fake newspaper story made up. Then he had other literature prepared, including accounts of his success as a deep-sea diver on the Pacific Coast, together with photographs. Pretty smart and thorough, don't you think?"

"It wouldn't take me over," Renner said.

"It took me," Calotta snarled.

Renner looked him over. He and Calotta were about of a size – which was big. The other was forty if he was a day, and he had a low forehead, a heavy blue beard, a broken nose and thick lips. With a face like that, Renner thought, a man couldn't stay honest.

Al said, "Yeah, what do you think of that? This Dominic actually hooked our Calotta for ten grand. Imagine that! And there were several more personages who have been taken over for even larger sums."

Renner said, "Who killed this guy?" He looked at Calotta and right away they parted friendship.

"Here's what I know," Al said. "Calotta called me down here. This is Dominic's room. He says that someone murdered Dominic and wants me to dins out who done it. He don't want the cops in on this deal because the cops are sore at him, and besides, he is sore at the cops. Is that right, Calotta?"

"Yeah," the gangster said. "I want to find out who killed Dominic, because whoever did it knows what I want to know."

"And what's that?" Renner said.

"Use your head!" Al suddenly yelled. "This Dominic has salted all the dough he took in on this swindle away somewhere and Calotta wants to know where it is. Do I have to draw you a picture?"

Renner shrugged. "Well," he said, "what do we have to work on?"

Al gestured toward the three frightened women, the frightened old man. He said, "These three girls are all tenants in this place. Our friend Dominic nicked them for a few hundred bucks apiece with his Asbury Park treasure story. The old guy is the printer who set up the phoney newspaper story."

"That all?" Renner asked. "Who found out about the printer?"

"I did," Al said, "and believe me, pal, it was a neat piece of work. No sooner does Calotta call me in on this case and shows me the newspaper clippings, than I put two and two together and get four. I visit the three printers who are situated within convenient radius of this neighborhood and one of them turns out to be this happy lad, who did the job for our friend Dominic."

"Well, that's something," Renner said, without the least glimmering idea of what he was talking about.

Al turned to Calotta. "Tell you what," he said. "We'll need a little time to work on this. We'll go back to our office and figure on it. We will have an answer for you tonight."

"Okay," Calotta said. There was a smart grin on his face. "You go back to your office and figure the job out. I'll stay here and wait for you to come back. Of course you won't go to the cops?"

"Of course I won't go to the cops," Al smiled.

He and Calotta grinned amiably at one another. Calotta's face reminded Renner of the hyenas he had seen at the Bronx Zoo.

*

In the coupe, before he kicked the car into motion, Renner said, "We'll go to the cops, of course."

"Yeah? And from there to the cemetery," Al replied. "You're a moron."

"Why?"

"Because Calotta has more than dough wrapped up in this deal. That should have been obvious even to you. And he isn't taking any chances, particularly with us. Right now he has guys following us."

Renner looked in the rear-view mirror and saw a big black convertible swing out as he pulled from the curb. He swore uncomfortably and said, "Look, Al, are you tryin' to kid me, or something?"

"How?"

"This thing all points to Calotta. What are you stalling with him for? Forget that car behind us. Go to the cops and tell them that Calotta killed a guy. That's all there is to it."

"I called you a moron," Al said. "I wasn't kidding about that."

"Have your own way," Renner said.

He drove the rest of the way in silence and parked the car a block away from the office.

Al said, "Just act natural and dumb. We're going upstairs."

They went into the office and Al shut the door and then he said, "They're out in the hall and waiting for us. They'll want to know what we're doing, so they won't start anything unless they get suspicious."

"That's nice," Renner said. "What do we do, stay here and wait until they do?"

"You stay," Al said. "In the meantime I'm taking a chance with the window. I'm going back to the village. I just pulled this gag to get Calotta's boys out of the way.

Now I'm going back there and finish the case. You sit here and talk out loud and argue with me."

"But you won't be here," Renner said.

"That's just the point," Al smiled. "I won't be here."

He walked over to the window, opened it and looked down. Then he climbed out, and Renner heard him making his way down the fire escape.

The three frightened women were still there. So was the frightened man. So was the corpse. Calotta was master of ceremonies. He had a revolver in his hand. He was telling the four frightened people to keep quiet. That was when Al came in.

Calotta looked at Al and said, "Well?"

"I got it figured out," Al said. He looked at the revolver in Calotta's hand and he said, "Play nice."

"Don't stall," Calotta said. He levelled the revolver at Al's chest.

"Put down the toy or I don't talk," Al said. He sighed and then he added, "You're not a very trusting employer, are you, Calotta? I'm telling you that I got this case all figured out and I'm ready to earn my pay check as soon as you put the revolver away."

Calotta frowned and put the revolver back in his shoulder holster. As soon as he was sure that the rod was in its leather, Al jumped. He had to do this fast and he couldn't depend on his fists, because of Calotta's size. He kneed him again in the chin. Calotta went up against the wall, but he didn't go out. He threw fists, cursing, spitting teeth and blood as Al jabbed fast. Then it was the knee again, and this time it caught Calotta on the point of the chin and knocked him cold.

While the three frightened women and the frightened old man were jabbering like peacocks in a typhoon, Al took the revolver from Calotta's shoulder holster. He waved the women out of the room. Then he brought his arm up slowly and aimed the rod at the frightened old man.

"You killed Dominic, didn't you?"

The frightened old man began to shiver. "No – no – not me. I—"

"Aw, cut it out," Al said. "You oughta be glad I saved you from Calotta. You know what he would have done to you? He would have cut off your nose, and then he would have cut out your tongue, and then he would have cut your eyes out, and maybe he'll still do it, unless—"

"All right," the frightened old man said. "I'll tell you. I killed Dominic. I made an agreement with him. I would fix up the newspaper clippings, and in return he would give me a share of the money. It was my idea to start with. He told me that he had it in his room—"

"And you believed him," Al said. "You came up here with an axe and you killed him and then while you were looking for the money Calotta knocked on the door and you got away while the getting was good. You didn't know till then Calotta was mixed up in it. You went back to your print shop and you were minding your own business at the press when I came in."

The frightened old man said, "How – can you know all this?"

"I'm a smart guy," Al said. "But it's easy when you take a good look at the axe. It's all red from Dominic's blood. But besides the red there's a lot of black on the blade and on the handle. It's printer's ink. You used the axe to crack open the lids of ink barrels. Then you were dumb enough to use the same axe to crack open Dominic's skill."

The old man said, "Dominic was no good – he betrayed an old man's trust. Calotta is a gangster – a murderer. If he goes free, he will do more harm than is left in me. Let me go."

"Sure," Al said, stepping aside. "Still, there wasn't any real reason Dominic couldn't have told about your little deal – to his father."

The old man started, looked at Al oddly with comprehending eyes, then stepped hurriedly past him.

Renner had been talking to himself for over an hour when the door opened, and Calotta was there. So was Al. And the sharp boys.

"What do you call this?" Renner said.

"It's payday," Al said.

Calotta looked sore and mean, but as he walked into the office he took out a check book. As he made out a check for a thousand dollars he said, "Any other guy I'd bump off, Reid. But I've always appreciated brains, and that's why I'm taking this the right way. I made a bargain with you and I'm keeping it. I told you to find out who killed Dominic. And I told you to keep the cops strictly out of this."

"And the only way I could keep the cops out of it was to knock you cold before you got nasty with the gun," Al said.

"That's right, Reid," Calotta said. He handed Al the check. "You found out who killed Dominic, and you kept the cops out of it, and I'm paying you off. But now, Reid, I'm going back there and I'm getting hold of the old guy!"

He went out and the sharp boys followed him.

Fifteen seconds after the door closed, Renner said, "I don't get it."

"It's what you call a fair bargain," Al said. "And now it's closed. But it's a shame that Calotta don't know about the old guy. He jumped out that sixth story window just before Calotta came to."

Renner shrugged. "You can give me the details later," he said. "Right now we better hurry and cash this check. I don't trust them crooks."

The Time of Your Kill

As I turned into Black Bear road the wind whipped the arclight, making my shadow leggy and dancing and uncatchable in the night. It was raining white bubbles. The damp air smelled salty. It bit the inside of my skull and it talked to me. It said, *Tonight you can't miss.* I cinched my trenchcoat and threw a playful punch at the storm trying to hold me back. And it wasn't just the gun under my arm that made me feel good.

"Well," my old man used to say, "some people are born for pleasure and some are born for work. You were born for work, Matt."

You call this work, Pop? When Ernie Tarlton walks out of that big red house with his briefcase – you call that work?

The white bubbles turned Black Bear road into a changing carpet of dandelions gone to seed. With each gust they lost their fragile heads and were reseeded instantly with new dandelions immediately old. Even in daylight this wasn't familiar grounds to a kid brought up in Rambletown. But all that afternoon I'd cased it, walking the handsome, curving streets around the big red house, then tramping what passed for alleys behind Black Bear road. Alleys! You could have eaten off them. Funny, I'd never heard the old man speak bitterly of the people who lived on Black Bear road.

"Work," he'd say, "and you'll be living there yourself."

What work did Ernie Tarlton do to get here? Riddle me that, Pop . . .

A couple surly birds started a Dutch concert when I ducked through the gap in the hedge. It looked like a mile and five eighths of slow track across the black, squishy lawn to the clump of blue firs that bordered the main walk. I seemed to take a half day, flat, to cover the distance. When I hunkered down in the dark among the firs even my teeth were sweating, like that day at the Beeler Brothers.

The house was three floors high with broad white-framed windows set deep in the red brick. Warm yellow light gleamed from some of the windows. In all Rambletown there wasn't a building like it, except the telephone exchange . . .

You had it all wrong, Pop. Ernie Tarlton got to Black Bear road without work. Even if he's only here on a two-months sublease.

My pants legs lay cold and wet against my ankles. Funny how the house reminded me of the old man. He'd done a father's best without help of a woman. He'd quit the ring the night I was born, not because she'd died but because he'd decided his son wouldn't have a club fighter for an old man. Though he was a neat man he let his hair grow long on his neck, to hide the ancient, cobwebby crisscross of scars from glove laces hammered on him by pasties long since dead. For some time after he'd joined the cops he'd had trouble at inspection about his neck shave.

Rain sifted through the firs and I could have used a cigarette. Pop didn't favour smoking; he was a chewing man. I remembered a day I was maybe thirteen and we were sitting on the stoop, about the time I started hanging around Dorfmeyer's pool hall. The old man spoke casually.

"Lend me a chew of Nigger Hair, Matt."

I quit breathing. And then I saw he was telling me he knew, and giving me a pass.

"I'm out too," I said. "I'll run down to Dorfmeyer's for a couple of packages."

"Get one," the old man said. "Bad habit."

Ernie Tarlton had bad habits, too, Pop. And he's very good at his bad habits. You know that. Though I'm not pleading that.

I looked at my watch. Ernie Tarlton had a drawing room on the Rover, pulling out at eleven-thirty. Figure he'd allow himself an hour for the cab ride to the station. That left me fifteen minutes more under the firs.

The old man had never ridden a train like the Rover. Once we'd taken a trip to Salt Lake City, though. Fifteen hundred miles on a day coach. The guys in the rackets called the old man Sixty Per Cent Sutton; they thought he was slugnutty from his ring days. Imagine a cop having to ride in a day coach! That part of it really burned me up. Maybe he wasn't the smartest cop in the world. Maybe he never did get higher than riding the wagon or guarding payrolls. But he wasn't punchy; Paddy Sutton was never sixty per cent at anything. It was just that his complete honesty was mistaken for stupidity by guys who can't understand honesty.

One hot evening on the stoop in Rambletown the talk had got around to money. I said, *"You can't get rich just by living right."*

"No," the old man agreed, *"you've got to work, too. At that, if you live right you don't especially want to get rich."*

Work again, you see? Always work, work.

A cab stopped at the curb and the driver ran up the walk. His yellow slicker swished past just inches from my hiding hole. He came back carrying two grips and climbed into his hack to wait. Then a man came out on the porch of the red house. He carried a briefcase.

That's when things caught up with me. Just a trembling, at first. A wobble in my wrists, a helpless twitch in my neck. I could hardly draw my thirty-eight. I could hardly pull the flashlight from my trenchcoat pocket. *Ernie Tarlton's coming down that walk with his briefcase stuffed. And my shakes won't stop.*

Tarlton's finally coming . . . I remembered the day he drifted into Dorfmeyer's, about as lovely as a gibbon ape but smart and shifty. I remembered the day he first mentioned Beeler Brothers to me. Payrolls are soft, Matt, he'd said. Give it a try. Easy street. I remembered the day under the El tracks that he showed me the two chamois masks.

Ernie Tarlton's coming down that walk . . . We walked out of the alley wearing our masks and the cop turned around and I dropped my gun. Of all the cops in town! Then Ernie fired and Pop slammed against the brick wall of Beeler Brothers, and Ernie Tarlton legged it down the alley with the satchel. I remember throwing my chamois mask over the fence and lifting Pop off the dirty alley; the confusion in the hospital, the hasty questions – then me fading across the lawn.

Tarlton's coming . . . The cops hadn't found him. Matt Sutton had found him. Sixteen, sometimes eighteen hours a day, 'round and 'round; every bus station, railroad, airline, every hotel desk in town. 'Round and 'round for two weeks, never letting the desk clerks know why I asked. Just coaxing them to watch for an ugly guy who didn't stride as far with his left foot as he did with his right. Until one clerk recognized him. Sixteen hours a day for two weeks and all the time on the dodge myself . . .

I wasn't born for work, Pop. That wasn't work. You call that work?

Tarlton's coming and I've got the shakes. Do I flub it now after all that . . . not work, Pop! Through the rain I saw him plodding toward me with his fraggy gait. A man born for pleasure limping through the night to meet a man born for work.

I stood up and put the flashlight on him.

In the spear of light Ernie Tarlton blinked and hugged his briefcase with both arms.

"What is this?" he whispered.

"This?" I said. "This is a pleasure."

His gibbon's face tattled on him. "Matt? Matt?"

He turned and ran back up the walk, toward the red house. I steadied the thirty-eight. The wobble in my wrists, the twitch in my neck were gone. A bullet in his head, and I could be leaving town on the Rover with a fat briefcase. Or—

I put the slug in his hip. Tarlton lurched and went down in the rain.

Moving up the walk, I could picture the old man, waiting. Turning his head on the pillow to look at me, the soft gray hair on his neck hiding the old crisscross scars of glove laces.

The old man would say, *"You'll get five to ten for that Beeler Brothers hold-up, Matt."*

"It'll be a pleasure, now," I'd tell him.

"No," he'd say. *"It'll be work."*

Never Too Old to Burn

I was an old man, but I died hard. It isn't easy to die. Not even in your own bed. It's a hell of a lot harder, writhing soundlessly in a fiery mist, seeing it coming and trying to yell until the heat gets to you for good. After that you can't yell, but you still fight it, wriggling like a beetle, long after you don't know any more.

It wasn't easy to die that way. But I did, and laughed all the time. I was still laughing long after the thing that had been I was hanging there still and shrivelled, with only the smoke to show what had been a man.

I guess I had better explain. That still, smoking thing down there wasn't really me. But I was the only man in the world who didn't think so. It was really old Andy Graffner. But on the police record it was going to be me, Paddy Sloan. And that was fine. Because Andy Graffner needed to die. Needed it like I, Paddy Sloan, needed to live. And boy, that was going to be just fine. Because I had a lot of living coming to me, a lot of hell to forget . . .

Andy and me, we don't count. We're just a couple of old gaffers you guys see and forget. We don't wash our necks too often and we can't see so good and we shuffle when we walk, because the iron spatters once in a while and when you're old you can't get out of the way like the young fellows. But when you're that old and you can't get another job, you just keep on doing the same old thing every day, and the hell with bum legs. You still eat, and that is enough.

Like I said, you probably never even noticed Andy and me, unless one of us was later, getting down there to pull the hook to open that furnace door, or if there was too much sludge left in the vats after we scoured them, or if I had a hangover and didn't come in on time and your precious production schedule was held up half an hour or something. Then you'd be down there with you fat, roast-beef faces and your damned charts and scream how we better get the lead out of our pants or we'd be out on the sidewalk looking for a job.

You'd do that maybe once in a year. But Andy and me, we didn't mind that. Because we were old and a little thick in the head and very, very smart too in our own way. Smart enough to know that you knew that you couldn't get a young fellow to do that kind of work, not even for five times the handful of dough you paid us. Because a young fellow can't take the furnace work. You got to have an old gaffer with leather for skin and no hope. So we stayed on, long after you got a better job or got fired or died from too much good whiskey. Andy and me, we couldn't afford to get drunk much. So we stayed on, and were forgotten, like part of the furniture.

We didn't exist, to you guys. Even when you had a factory party, you forgot all about asking us. Or maybe you didn't, at that.

One year, after Andy and me had been there only a little time, you had a party up on the main floor and we went up.

I guess you won't forget that day. Andy, he was always a little shy about being around with people. He didn't want to go but I told him, "You old coot, you can stand a little fun. We'll go up there with the big shots and have a drink. Ain't no harm in that, is there?"

This Andy was a queer one, all right. His pale little eyes blinked and he shook his head.

"I don't want no people around," he said nervously. "People, they get you in trouble."

Anyway, I grabbed his arm and made him go up with me.

I guess you still remember that day. We came in the door. We could hear all the noise from outside. They had a radio on and drinks on the table and a lot of pretty girls from the front office, dancing with the foundry men just like they didn't have old working shirts on and smoke smudges on their faces. They were democratic, all right. But when they saw us they weren't so democratic at all. One of them, the one in the bosses' office, made a face and said, "Really! There ought to be a law against some things!"

A big forge worker said, "What the hell! It's Christmas. Come on up and have a drink, boys." But you could see from their faces that they thought we were pretty ripe.

What the hell. You can't work in those sludge pits and smell like a rose. Andy and me, we were pretty smart. We didn't spend our money washing them pants and shirts. They were full of holes, where the iron splattered, and I guess they would stand up by themselves. We had a couple of drinks and stood around awhile, but nobody paid any attention to us and finally we went down in the pit again. I don't think anybody minded when we left.

After that, when you had a party, we didn't get asked. It was all right with me. Andy, he got so deaf about that time that he wasn't good for anything. The guy was always a queer one. Never speaking to anybody, slinking around with a scared look on his face, cringing whenever he came out of that damned dark hole into the sun as if he was going to be sick or something.

Okay, we were two forgotten old men. We lived alike, we dressed alike. After a time, I guess, we even looked alike, because the sludge pits get you if you stay there long enough. Just two dirty old walking zeros who did your sludge pits and went home at night and out of your lives.

You get the picture?

After a time the boss didn't pay no attention to us any more. You know how it is. You get a couple of dogs and you train 'em to pick up sticks, say, when you drop 'em. At first you watch 'em close and maybe punish 'em when they forget. But after a while, when they never fail you, when you haven't even got the excuse to hit 'em any more, you think of more important things, like maybe more dogs to train, and the first ones fade back into the shadows of your mind.

"Oh yeah, Paddy and Andy," you'd maybe say, when the payroll survey came up, once a year. "Damned old dirty nobodies. If I had any gumption, I'd get rid of 'em and get a coupla kids. Yeah. But – they get that sludge out and that's what counts. They don't get much dough and after all a guy doesn't have to live with 'em, or anything. Yeah. Now, that new office setup . . ."

Yeah. That's about what you'd say. So we stayed on. Month after month, forever.

I guess the first time I notice how completely forgotten we were was that time I went up for our pay.

That brassy-haired girl was at the window. One of the ones that was dancing with a big forge man at the Christmas party. Andy and me, we even kept away from the forge men, which shows how far out of the world we were. Those guys are all right. Big yellow fellows with money in their pockets and a good word for everyone. At first I kind of like to hang around them. But Andy cured me of even that. He was always saying, "People. They can get you in trouble. You stay down in the pit with me and we can get along fine. No trouble."

Like I said, I went up for my pay that day. I was feeling kind of low, a little bitter about the world. It wasn't so long after that party, maybe a year. I was still a little hurt and mad. After all, I was only sixty-five. Young enough to like to be around young people, have some fun. That Andy, he was sixty-eight if he was a day.

This brassy-haired babe at the window, she wasn't bad to look at, if you liked that kind. Plenty of curves, and a low-necked dress, and eyes that didn't miss anything in trousers. Plenty of trouble for some poor guy who wasn't smart.

I went up to the pay window, and this babe, she was giving the eye to some kid down the other end of the office. I had to wait until she looked around to me. It must have been quite a change, at that.

I had a couple of days' beard, and the dirt and the sweat was about even on me. It gets to a hundred twenty down in the pit. This babe was a good-natured slob, but I could see a kind of veil come over her eyes. And then, quick, as though she were ashamed of herself, she grinned at me, like I was an old pal or something.

I'd better explain that Andy, he'd got so funny lately that I'd been getting the pay for both of us. He wouldn't even come up in the main office for his dough. That's how scared he was of people.

This girl said, "Let's see now. Don't tell me. You boys are so much alike, a girl just can't separate you nohow. There's Paddy something and Andy Gaffer, or is it

Graffner? Yes, that's it. Oh, I know now" – she pulled out the two pay envelopes, with a silly grin on her face.

"You're Andy. Andy Graffner. Right?"

Well, I was a little sore, like I said. Pushed around, forgotten. I'd told the dumb skirt a hundred times and she still didn't know or care. Couldn't even get my name straight.

I said, very carefully, "Yeah, sister. Graffner. Andy Graffner. That's me. I'll be seein' you."

I wondered why I said that. It wasn't for months later that I knew. By that time I was "Andy" to the whole office.

That Andy, he got harder and harder to live with in the next year. I guess I had always hated him, come to think of it. It wasn't him. It was the dirty, hard things we had to do, the smoke and steam that hurt you all day, never seeing decent people, living in hell and going home just long enough to sleep it off for another day.

We didn't even speak now. Andy, he looked like he was even afraid of me. I was sitting up in our room one night, thinking it over. I had an envelope in my hand. It was the only thing I had in the world. It was an insurance policy for ten thousand dollars. I don't know why I'd kept on paying for that, long after I had given up everything else in my life.

I don't know why. Or I didn't, until I saw that little note in the envelope.

It was the same notes that always was there. I'd got so used to seeing it, I'd forgotten to read it for years. But this time, for no reason, I did.

". . . Within the thirty-one day grace period, your policy will lapse. Changes of beneficiary may be made on the attached form . . ."

I looked at dirty old Andy on his bed. The guy hadn't even washed or taken his clothes off. His mouth was open and he looked like he was ten years older. The dirty, scared old man, I was thinking. He was fading out fast. Two years more on that job would finish him off and he'd just disappear, like a dirty old leaf, blown away, and nobody would even know or care.

I could feel my heart starting to pound. That was it, I was thinking. Nobody would care, not even me, who lived with him.

Some guys were the mousy kind, I was thinking. Some guys had to be the Andies. Scared of their shadow, never daring to take the big chance. Some—

My hand was steady as a rock, holding the pen. Sure, I owed Andy Graffner something. A chance to get away from his fears, forever.

I filled in the form on the policy blank. Andrew J. Graffner. Beneficiary on a ten-thousand-dollar policy on the life of one Patrick Sloan.

It looked awful good. That night, I slept without dreaming.

It was like shooting fish in a barrel. I had to wait a couple of months for the acknowledgment to come back from the insurance company. I was going to wait longer, but I couldn't.

It was in July. Andy always knocked the sludge off the vat hooks himself. It was kind of a scary job. You had to go up a ladder onto a narrow platform, high over the ovens, with a sledge hammer. Lean over with one hand, pull that hook over and chip off the metal that had splashed from the vats.

I was lying on the platform, waiting. I'd been in there for an hour. It was plenty hot up there. The furnaces were building up pressure.

That Andy, he was a funny old man. He came up the

ladder, grumbling and growling at the climb. Making faces. All alone with himself, at that dirty job. He didn't even see. He leaned way over, testing the purchase, and there was that first hook, hanging like a Christmas present right over his neck.

The point fitted right through the reinforced braces of his overalls, right between his skinny shoulder blades.

I said, "So long, Andy. It's been a long time." It didn't take hardly any push at all.

His mouth hung open. As the hook took him away, he made a little choked noise, like cold water was falling on him. After that, I guess, he didn't feel cold at all.

I went out the back way. Not a soul could have seen me.

An hour later, when I came back, the brassy-haired girl was at the gate. Her face was gray and scared-looking. One of the bosses was beside her, and he didn't look so good either.

The boss said, "Graffner, you can't work that job no more. I – uh—"

He looked like he was going to be sick. That girl, she had more guts, or maybe she hadn't been inside that pit room. She said, "I— Andy, your friend Paddy has had an accident. You – you better come up to the main office. I – can't stay down here any longer!"

That was all right with me.

I was sitting on the porch when they came.

It had been a good month. They'd given me a small pension. Not enough to live on, but enough to take me away from the pits for the rest of my life. It was a funny thing. I had to get used to the daylight all over again. And my new clothes didn't feel right. But I was going to get used to all them things.

There was quite a crowd. Three men and a girl. It seemed like a lot of fuss over the money. I began to feel kind of funny, watching them come up the walk. That brassy-haired dame was with them.

A big guy in a blue suit said, "There's a little trouble about this claim, Mister. Maybe you can straighten us out."

I could feel the sick rage swell up in me. Trouble. If they thought they could—

I said, "Sure, I'll straighten you out. I'm due ten grand. I want it. I seen the policy. Let's get it over with."

The man in the blue suit said, "Yeah. Let's get it over with, like you say." He pulled a check out of his pocket, and let me see it. It wasn't much, just a sheet of paper. Just ten thousand bucks.

The man in blue said, "Andrew J. Graffner. That's your name? You'll swear to it, under penalty of the law?"

They were all looking at me. My breath was coming a little faster, but I made myself calm. I even grinned. I said to the girl, "Sister, you tell 'em. It sounds silly to me."

The brassy-haired babe said, "Why, this is plain silly. Of course it's Andy Graffner. Haven't I been making out his pay checks for ten years?"

I said, "Yeah. Like she said. Let's see the money, gents. I got a trip to make."

A man on the other side of me said, "Sure, Andy. You got a trip. A long one. It's been a long time."

I stared at them. It didn't make sense.

The big guy in the blue suit said, "Andy Graffner. Three murders and two hundred grand stashed away. And you didn't even change your name, and got away with it for thirty years. Let's go, boy."

They tell me I was yelling but I didn't know it. Yelling

while they went through the room Andy and I had. And there, under Andy's old trunk, was the bank notes. Crummy and big and beautiful. But he was too scared to spend 'em. Lived in hell and died in fear, because of 'em.

I said, "This is all a mistake, gents. I can—"

I stopped. I couldn't. I was Andy Graffner. I'd seen to that.

I rode along with them. I could see a long corridor, with the death chair waiting at the end. I could feel my head being shaved and the straps pulling me down, down to the end and the final blackness.

I watched myself die, all the hell-marked days that remained to me. And – this time I didn't laugh.

Man Without a Tongue

CHAPTER ONE
The Doll That Moved

Sleep all the while – Humbel style! cajoled the sign in the furniture window.

Beneath the sign were two twin beds. In them, as though doggedly obedient to the slogan, lay a wax dummy man and woman. Stiffly at rest, artfully displayed. Sleeping all the while – forever.

Outside, it was cold. So cold that here and there among the crowd spewed from the subways a man would sink his neck into a turned-up collar and gaze enviously in at the sleepers, so warm and still. But the wax husband slept woodenly on, with the blankets slipped bravely from his twisted neck, so that the curve of his wax shoulders showed. It was lifelike, intimate. Humbel's would sell a lot of beds today, with such a window show to follow up their full page Sunday ad.

On the second bed the wax lady, with feminine perversity, had buried her head in the sheets. Only her startlingly realistic hair could be seen, spread in charming disarray upon the silk pillow. So they lay there, while envious shoppers looked and went about their business and forgot them, and the sun turned the walks into coffee-hued slush and it was noon.

At noon the woman sleeper moved. It was not the first time. For hours, she had been moving, with stealthy, cunning genuflections of her covered body, but no one had noticed.

Instead, her painted mate, with his shoulder so staunchly bared, his too nice face, had stolen the show.

But now, for the first time, her movements were visible. Stiffly, as became a store window automaton, she elevated her upper body slightly from the hips, so that the sheets slid slowly across her forehead: her hair began to trail along the pillow as her head lifted.

Then it was seen by some that her hair was gray. Strange, they thought, that this handsome young wax man should take to wife a creature with sooty, gray hair!

Until after two the gray lady moved; furtively, as though she were pushing against the drag of the blankets which held her to her bargain sale bed. The silly, baby blue binding on the side of the blanket began to strain and quiver where it was jammed against the tucked-in sheets. A thin edge came free, snaked jerkily loose. The gray lady was held no longer against her will.

Only a few late bargain hunters were looking at that precise moment, but those few stopped, nudged one another. What would these merchants do next! See – the lady is even sitting up in bed. You'd almost believe it, it was that real!

A blowsy old slattern tittered vacantly, pressed her nose against the cold glass. And stiffly, as if her dummy soul had been curious to see who thus profaned her rest, the gray lady sat up to meet her.

As she arose her hair fell suddenly down across her eyes. It was unlovely, spare: it cut a sorry figure beside the gloss of the wax man beside her. It was not the kind of hair poets sing about. Not the kind to sell twin beds. No: not the kind of hair for a wax dummy.

"I – Gawd, I nearly – thought—"

The gray lady sat up straight, so that her face came out of the shadows. And the watchers gasped at the grayness of it, on lips too dark, too bruised for a store window doll. Suddenly the mouth gaped horribly and the afternoon sun hit coldly into the orifice of her throat.

And the slattern screamed harshly and pushed her elbows into those who blocked her way, and ran tipsily down the sidewalk, still screaming.

Still the gray lady sat in her bargain bed, simpering stiffly with smeared, set lips, while they hurriedly pulled the curtains over the furniture window and ran to phone the police.

The gray, murdered lady, without a tongue. The gray, murdered lady somebody had put in the twin bed in Humbel's window, where she had lain until, with the stiffening of rigor mortis, she had sat up to gape sightlessly out at the street.

That was item one. Item two came six days later, as Detective Sergeant Ricco Pasquale Maguire stared glumly at the top of his scarred desk. On the desk was a tabloid. Its inch-high lead screamed blackly across the page:

NO CLUES TO WAX DOLL MURDER!

Sergeant Maguire cursed roundly in a surprisingly cultivated voice and stared at the fly-specked ceiling.

A fist like a small, underdone ham rested on one knee; after a minute the fist started to wave. Maguire swivelled around, faced its owner.

"Bellamy," he said, "there's no need to . . . kill ourselves. Or get excited. Or get sore, like you are now. This is a case we'll probably never break."

"Why, you—"

Captain Pat Bellamy was fat; his jowls hung loose under the frame of a fighting jaw. He hit the desk and the ink bottle jumped. He said hoarsely, "We got to, and you damn well know it."

Ricco Maguire riffled the sheaf of papers headed: Homicide – Humbel's.

"I know," he said. "They're on your back. From that commissioner on down. Humbel's put him in office. Now he has to deliver for them, and when he can't he's . . . like a bound up alligator." He hurled the ink bottle out of rage. "Did it never occur to you," he said, "that the old girl was the second victim of this fellow – and that the first one didn't even make a headline on an inside page?"

"To hell with the first!" screamed Bellamy, and Maguire put the ink in the drawer. "This one means my job!"

"It's all alike you are," Maguire grimaced. "You and the commissioner and the papers. This poor lady down in the morgue as a symbol to all of you. A symbol to the power and the balance sheet of Humbel's. You're hot as hell and yelling about her fate – because she died in Humbel's window and like to spoiled their sale. The first victim wasn't so lucky. They fished him out of the East River nice and quiet, and no dames to faint when they carted him off to a slab. A nice looking lad, too."

"A damned floater, you talk about." Bellamy's face was red.

"A nice, clean-looking fellow he was," said Ricco Maguire, "all lost and dead on a slab, and him holding in his hand the note that may cleave a path to the devil who sent him there. D'you look over that music, Captain?"

Pat Bellamy spat wide of the cuspidor. "Phah." He fished in his pocket. "I know. Two pieces of music. One of them in the pocket of the stiff they fished out of the river, the other one held in the fist of the lady in Humbel's window." He threw two stained fragments of sheet music on the desk and scowled at them. "My daughter stuck 'em together and played 'em to me on the piano. They sound like hell and it's a hell of a clue to give a man before they throw him out on his fanny. Me, the best damn—"

Ricco Maguire took the paper from his superior and tore it neatly in half. "Sure it must have sounded like Chinese," he said grinning, "with the front on the back like you pasted it. Listen!"

He put his feet on the desk, gazed soulfully at his toes, and sang:

"Tum, tum, didee di, ta tum, ti di di de e-e, di—"

"Rick," wheezed Captain Bellamy, "I'm not a patient man, and—"

Maguire waved him to silence.

"That," he said, "is a death threat. And all we know of the murder of the floater in the river. And here, sir, is its supplement, the message the poor lady hugged to her when she lay murdered in a store window bed." Ignoring the chief's apoplectic squirming, he cleared his throat mightily and intoned:

"Ta, ta, de dah-h-h, de dah de dah-h-h, de dum."

There was a knock at the door and a patrolman poked his head in.

"A man's outside, Maguire. Wants to see you personal."

"Make him wait," Bellamy yelled. The door shut hastily. When the latch clicked Bellamy wailed, "I hand

him a case and ask for action. And everybody gives me
hell and you give me music! Jumping be glory!" Bellamy
wiped his mouth with the back of a hairy hand.

Ricco stopped smiling. "Take it easy, Captain. You're
tired and bedevilled and up a tree. So'm I. Because the
day – God forbid – they send you pounding a beat, that
day I'll turn in my badge." He looked fixedly out the window. After a time he said, "I guess you know I don't want
that to happen – yet."

Bellamy sat down massively. He said, quietly, "Sorry,
Rick. Allus right, you are. Only you, a millionaire, can
walk out of here and tell them to go to hell."

"No," said Ricco Maguire, "not until a certain job is
finished."

Bellamy said hastily, "You mean your mother?" And,
"Sorry. I don't mean all I say, Rick. Only" – he spread his
hands – "I got two years to go for a pension, and the girl
to think of. Helen's a big girl now, Rick. Big enough to
gallivant around with a guy I wouldn't spit on, an'
workin' on crazy heathen jobs – oh, well, give me the
story. I'll listen quiet. Honest."

"This thing the papers call the wax doll murder," Ricco
said, "is crazy. It breaks all the rules. Because we know
everything. We know the killer was one Ray Salvo. We
know he was a night watchman at the store."

"And the old dead 'un was a scrub lady there," moaned
Bellamy, beginning to wave his arms again. Ricco looked
at him and he subsided.

"Last Saturday night," said Ricco Maguire, "this Salvo
killed and mutilated the woman on the steps of the toy
department. He concealed the body in Humbel's best sale
bed. He punched the time clock every hour along his
round. He waved goodbye to the man at the time gate at
seven in the morning and went out. Leaving a corpse.

Good old rigor mortis made her sit up and raise hell with the commissioner."

"My head," said Bellamy tentatively. "It don't feel so good, sittin' quiet like this."

"He went out," said Ricco, "leaving nothing. Only a name and a locker number. And the fact that he's old and average size. No one down there can describe him, not even his voice. Nothing."

Bellamy muttered, "I guess maybe I'll trot along an' let you work on—"

"The man called Ray Salvo," said Ricco Maguire, "was one crazy smart Tillicum. So smart he sent taunting notes to his victims, musical notes they couldn't read."

"Yeah," growled Pat Bellamy ominously, "it's my head that can't stand the talking and doing nothing. I got to move my fists to—"

"So we've got to be crazy smart, too," said Ricco Maguire inexorably, "and here's a start: the musical notes came from a suite of chamber music called 'Songs Without Words', and the title of this particular song is 'Consolation.'"

"Get 'im," grated Captain Bellamy. "Find 'im for me, Rick. Give me an hour alone with him – an hour of reasonable grilling, as you might say. But" – he bounced up to the thus-and-so and by-whose-ancestors rhythm of good unprintable words – "I'll be a" – he added to them – "before I'll sit and listen to a blasted music lesson."

"'Consolation,'" murmured Ricco to the slamming door. "'Songs Without Words.' I wonder . . ."

CHAPTER TWO
A Lump of Dead Fish

A moment later the visitor entered.

A middle-aged man who bore his leanness erectly. His face was austere, alert, the face of a retired soldier or a professional man. Just now it was moist and a little whitish.

He shut the door, surveyed Ricco Maguire. What he saw seemed to reassure him.

"I'm in a bit of a mess," he said. "So I came to you. That man Bellamy — I heard about you from him."

Ricco sighed. "Why didn't you see Bellamy yourself, sir?"

The visitor made sundry clucking noises, leaned forward. "Because." He whispered, with the air of a man imparting a secret, "I detest Captain Bellamy. I may add, sir, I have good and personal reasons for doing so. Captain Bellamy is a fat pig and no gentleman. A pig, even, would treat me better than Cap—"

Ricco said, "Oh." He was thinking: the damned, fighting slob. Doing three men's work, blustering, crazy-brave when the danger came, and too pig-headed, stubborn to do the hard thing — keep peace with the people. Making enemies, antagonizing the gray lean men of the world, the men who hired and fired. They wouldn't fire Bellamy — he left too many scars on the rats the gray men feared — but when there was a vacancy in the department it was easy to pass over a man who had insulted them, keep them on the battle front.

Ricco said, "Let's have the grief. Begin at the beginning. For instance, who are you?"

The thin man smiled wanly. "Bleakney — ah, Doctor Bleakney's my name."

"Some months ago," Bleakney continued, "I found a newspaper clipping in my mail. Sort of a crazy thing. About the discovery of a corpse in the river. I recognized the name of a man who used to be an intern at Bellevue when I was there.

"I reported it here. We doctors get funny notes sometimes." The thin man frowned. "Bellamy told me to forget it. Said hundreds of crank notes are mailed every day. We – he got rather abusive. I left.

"A week ago I got another clipping. This time about a woman's death. Quite a widely discussed case, I understand. They called it the wax doll murder." He leaned forward solemnly. "There was more, this time, in the envelope. With the clipping—"

Ricco said, "I know. This time there was a piece of music."

Dr Bleakney gulped. "My word!" he said faintly.

"Your death note," said Ricco Maguire. In his black eyes a lambent flame had kindled. He said, "And that was a week ago?" For six days he and Bellamy had combed Manhattan for a single thread of information, anything to stall off a hostile press and save Bellamy his shield.

"Precisely," Bleakney said primly, "and except for one thing I'd never have bothered you. Only—"

He handed Maguire a piece of music.

Ricco fitted it mechanically to the torn edge of the paper the wax lady had clutched in death. It fitted, note against note, stave against stave. He grunted, pulled the desk lamp closer, saw the writing in the corner. A date, scrawled in ink the color of fresh-spilled blood. December 10. His eyes sought the date on the tabloid on his desk.

"That," said Dr Bleakney, "is why I had to come back

here. Today is the tenth of December. I – I haven't been sleeping well lately." And quite suddenly his austerity and pomp fell like a cast off mask, and left a pale, troubled man.

"I'm scared," he said simply.

"You should be," said Ricco Maguire.

"Don't misunderstand me." The doctor stiffened, not without a certain dignity. "I'm no hero. But I'm getting along. I wish that murdering devil knew how little I dreaded death, as such. Death's an old story, Sergeant, to a doctor. Only," he pulled at his moustache, "there's a girl. A young girl I'm fool enough to be very fond of. I'm not anxious for the curtain call yet."

Ricco stood up. "Doc, you were crazy to stall around on a thing like this, even if you did get a bum steer the first time you saw us. In a way, without meaning to, you've put us in a bad hole. Now, the man mentioned in the first clipping turned out to be someone you once knew. That wasn't just a coincidence, if I know anything. Chances are, this wax doll lady, being tied up with you too, must be someone you can recognize and identify."

"I have an appendectomy at ten," protested the doctor.

"Nearly an hour. Five minutes will tell us a lot right now. Hop into that coat. It's heading for the morgue we are, fast."

Ten minutes later they stood beside a cold slab. On the slab lay something covered by a sheet.

Without any hesitation the surgeon pulled down the cloth, gazed on the ravaged features of the gray lady. Quite suddenly he hit his forehead with his clenched fist.

"My God, Peters," he said dully to the gray lady. And, turning to the sergeant, "I begin to get the picture, sir. I

– I haven't seen Peters for fifteen years, but I murdered her last Sunday night!"

Ricco Pasquale Maguire was an ordinary shamus. In appearance he was an old man. But if you got close enough to him to see past the gray hair and the ravaged look of his eyes you would be looking at the face of a man of thirty. Ricco Maguire was, in fact, thirty. But his hair had turned gray in a single night – the night that they paged him at a Plaza dinner dance to gaze for the last time on the face of his murdered mother.

Terry Maguire, his father, had been wealthy, and full of the joy of living as only an Irishman can be. And as ready to fight for the love of fighting or to settle a round of drinks.

Then, one night, Terry met Rosa DeLisa. He met her on the ebb of a roistering brawl which began in the Waldorf and ended in a dirty side street just off Chinatown. When he saw her he went strangely and completely sober, and as soon as the City Hall opened in the morning they were married.

Ricco Pasquale Maguire had been the only child of that union. A curious looking child, with a square Irish chin and fair features, topped off by the blackest eyes north of Sicily.

Ever since Ricco could remember, his mother had carried her East Side birthplace in her thoughts. Had kept, with her joy of new wealth, a fervour to use much of it to help old and poorer friends. Which was why she made weekly charitable visits to the narrow, dark streets of her youth. And which was most certainly why, one day, a cold-eyed young punk had crept from under the arch of Brooklyn Bridge to wait for her in an alley off the

Bowery and take her purse and beat her to death in the taking.

Ricco Maguire remained the same man, externally. But from that day he took upon himself a holy mission. Just what it was he probably couldn't define. Even after he, a millionaire in his own right, had taken police examinations and on his merits had reached the homicide squad in four years.

Ricco Maguire had the Celtic frame to carry him through the fighting and the Machiavellian guile to find the way to it. Ricco Maguire ate lunch with the commissioner on odd Mondays. Ricco Maguire got along with Pat Bellamy, who said he was a natural. Ricco Maguire could trace his ancestry, by virtue of one murder and two scandals, to a second Borgia dynasty. Ricco Maguire paid his dues as a member of the Order of Hibernians, and had gone to school in Milan.

So, being what he was, Ricco Maguire had neither handcuffed Doctor Bleakney nor called the psychopathic ward when that distraught man had shouted that he had murdered the wax doll lady. Instead he had set his square jaw and let his black eyes narrow slightly. He said, "You'll make that operation in time, Doc. But I want some information first."

"Peters," said Dr Bleakney, again seated in Maguire's office, "was a nurse at Bellevue. A damned good one. She was that rare kind that would work extra hours and wear herself to a frazzle and not tell anyone about it. It was back in nineteen seventeen, as I recall—"

Ricco Maguire said, "About this wax doll murder now—"

But the doctor waved a hand peremptorily.

"One day back in seventeen, I was in charge of the

emergency ward. The flu was on us like a scourge and we had been working like dogs. Peters, as usual, the most. She, I later discovered, was running a temperature herself and should have been in bed. But she wouldn't quit.

"A stretcher case came in. It was a young fellow, about thirty, who'd been in an auto crash. Not serious, but his head had been snapped forward by the collision and he had jolted his chin against the wheel. The blow had caused him to bite his tongue nearly off."

Ricco Maguire hummed softly.

"It wasn't as bad as it sounds. I could stitch the thing back on, since it was hanging by a thin shred of tissue. The patient was fully conscious, of course. And he was crying. I was a little sharp, gave him hell for being such a baby.

"His sister was with him. She was carrying on, yelling – you know how these damned Latins are. Er, yes, quite. Anyhow, after a time she got a grip on herself and explained what the grief was all about. Her brother, the injured man, was a wonderful singer, she said. San Carlo, Covent Garden – he'd been through the mill. He was angling for a Metropolitan contract.

"He thought, you see, he was losing his tongue, that he'd never be able to sing again. That's why he was crying. He was saying goodbye to music, his life."

Ricco Maguire, who had known music with the Italian soul of him, nodded gravely. "Songs without words," he murmured to the ink bottle.

"I laughed at him, told him we'd have him back on the stage in a month, shot a hypo to calm him, and told Peters to prepare him for the operation. Then I went into my office to get aseptic, leaving him alone with a new intern and a girl, Peters, who was herself a walking hospital case.

"When I came out to operate, something seemed wrong, something I couldn't place. I made the preliminary sutures, took off the clamps, picked up the tongue to join it to the oral muscle. It wasn't the right colour. Awful, dead looking. Then I looked at Peters, and I saw what she had done, and I knew.

"Living tissue, you see, can be made aseptic by certain things. It can be made sterile by others. And in her addled state Peters had somehow laved the wound, saturated it with the wrong stuff. The tongue of my crying friend was a tongue no longer. Just a hunk of sterile, dead flesh. It wouldn't have done any more good to sew it back than a piece of raw liver.

"I went sort of crazy for a minute. I caught myself up, but not before the patient – who was fully conscious, mind you – had heard me yell at Peters, and had heard what I said. There was only one thing to do, I put him under anaesthesia, pressed his eyes closed so I didn't have to look at them, and did the only thing left. I cut off the tongue which a tired, sick nurse had robbed of the thing that made it live.

"Hell broke when I made my report to the chief of staff. I was fair, but you can't excuse a thing like that. Anyway, Peters was fired. Disgraced. Done for.

"I never saw Peters again until I found her under that sheet. On a slab."

Dr Bleakney blew his nose loudly. He took some time doing it.

Ricco Maguire said, "You've helped us no end, Doc. When our murdering friend comes for his third trophy, he's due for hell on a raft. Captain Bellamy'll—"

"Not Bellamy!" the doctor fairly bleated; the ends of his chin quivered. "I – there's reasons. Personal reasons. I can't allow you, sir—"

"Sorry," Ricco Maguire soothed, "this isn't any time for nice social distinctions. When there's this kind of work, sir, they don't send out contact boys and the glad-hand artists. They send Bellamy."

Bleakney put on his gloves. He looked as though he wanted to be sick. As though he hadn't heard anything. He scribbled hurriedly on a card, handed it to Ricco.

"When – if I get killed," he said, "please go to this address and ask for – Doc Bleakney's fiancée. I'd like – a gentleman to break the news to her. Not – not a pig."

Ricco looked at the card, laughed, and sent two of the boys to escort the doctor to the hospital, telling them that Bellamy would arrive later to take charge.

But after Dr Bleakney had departed, Ricco Maguire breathed, "Mama mia!" and scowled at the dirty wall. A poor, mad, homicidal friend. A singer with a mute voice in him, a throat with imprisoned glory rotting within, a man who, when he curses his fate, hears only horrible, inarticulate squawks come from the botched mess three people made of his mouth. Yes, Ricco Maguire could understand how such a man could go mad, go looking for the thing he called "Consolation."

He dialled Captain Bellamy. "We have a hot lead," he murmured into the phone, "on the wax doll murder at Humbel's. Now don't shout, Chief, it's a lulu. Because all we have to do to solve the crime is to find, in a city of eight million, a man of forty-five. A man without a tongue!"

CHAPTER THREE
An Echo From Hell

Item three was the perspicacity of Patrolman Gannon, while on desk duty. At three-fifteen Patrolman Gannon poked his head into Maguire's office.

"Sarge," he said, "I thought I heard a drunk sounding off."

The man at the desk looked up. His eyes were black puddles of fatigue. "Curious," said Ricco Maguire. "Come in. Any news from Bellamy?"

"He's swearing like hell because you're sitting here, but he's got Bleakney's place covered like a blanket," Gannon said. "I'd hate to be the wax doll killer when Pat Bellamy gets his mitts on him."

"A fine, fighting copper he is," said Ricco, absently.

"The big, dented fists on him," enthused Gannon. "Say, that damned croaking, like a wake. I thought I'd better check up—"

"That noise," said Ricco Maguire, "was me. It's singing I've been for five hours."

"Yes, Sarge." Gannon lost his aplomb and his colour. " 'Course in that case—"

"Fine, grand music it is," said Ricco soberly. "No tune to be murdered by, but two people were. It's called 'Consolation.' I'll render it now to you." Unsmiling, he hummed the themes found on the first two victims.

"Maybe," said Gannon helpfully, "you got a cold."

"You see," said Ricco Maguire, "those musical phrases are all we know about two murders. They are threats to kill. Threats which ended with a man and a woman dead in the morgue. Now, Gannon, you're a bright lad with a fine future. I want you to tell me what's wrong with this passage, the third threat, which is due to be consummated before midnight tonight." He sang it.

"I think," opined Gannon sagely, "you're flat and hoarse, like."

Ricco Maguire looked unhappy. "My old man could hear the banshee wail," he said, "but maybe I'm just a nut. That ending doesn't sound like another wax doll murder to me."

"It sounds like hell, anyway," Gannon assured him. "Forget it, Sarge. Bellamy's waiting for you. He says Bleakney smells bad."

"It's far grander, more passionate music than the rest," Ricco said. "It's the sun after the moon has been shining. Remember, the man who sent those notes knows his music. And in those notes he says what he's going to do."

"Bellamy'll get him," said Gannon, confidently.

Ricco stood up. "Don't you see?" he cried. "This is the climax of the poor, daft fellow's revenge! His final masterpiece. And Bleakney said to me, 'I'm old, I'm not afraid to die.' What good's it going to do the wax doll man, where's the passion and the fire of that piece of music, bumping off an old, tired man – who isn't afraid of death?"

"I saw a movie like that once," said Gannon brightly.

"You," said Ricco, "annoy me."

"This movie," said Gannon raptly, "had a guy going to kill the heroine's old man. But then he said no. I'll make him suffer through the ages. That was the caption. So instead of killing the old coot, he went chasing after the girl."

Ricco Maguire looked up. The weariness sloughed from his eyes. "Suffer through the ages," he said. "Suffer a million deaths, remembering how his loved one died. Yes, that's the kind of music—"

He smiled. "Some day, Gannon," he said, "you'll be a fine copper like Bellamy." He took out the card Dr Bleakney had given him. It said:

The Mott Mission, 27 Mott St.

"I'm going downtown," he said, "to find a girl. Going to save, maybe, a girl's life."

"Sarge," Gannon said, "Bellamy's kind of touchy about—"

"What do you think Bellamy would do if he should hear, maybe, that this wax doll killer was alone with his victim?" Ricco Maguire said. "Cornered, maybe holding the victim as hostage?"

"Hell or taxes wouldn't stop Bellamy," paeaned Gannon. "The grand fighter he is. He'd be first in the door, and the squad behind him. And when he came out there'd be blood on his fists and the wax doll killer draggin' after."

"And the victim, now?" said Ricco Maguire.

"The victim?" Gannon grunted, "Hell! Bellamy'd have the killer!"

"A good cop you'll be, like Bellamy," said Ricco Maguire. "Reminds me of a general in the war. He could wipe out a German trench, could that general, but for one thing. There was a handful of doughboys there, fighting hand to hand with those Germans. So he blasted the whole lot to hell."

"That's the way Bellamy works," chanted Gannon.

"A medal he got, and he saved the day," said Ricco Maguire. "But they sent him home to Plattsburg, so he wouldn't get shot in the back. Some people don't like to see their own kind killed.

"If I'm right, Gannon, a girl may be in that kind of fix.

Bleakney's sweetheart, she is. I don't even know her name. But she's on our side. Like the handful of doughboys. I'm going to do this alone."

"Bellamy hates Bleakney," Gannon said, "I wonder why."

"Listen," said Ricco, "I'm going hunting for that girl. If I find her and if she's in danger, I'll call you, tell you where I am. I want you to skip regulations, Gannon, I don't want Bellamy to know."

"Huh?" said the bewildered Gannon.

"Not for thirty minutes after my first call," said Maguire. "But if I don't call you again in thirty minutes, get Bellamy and the squad. Let the big slug crash through then, and to hell with the torpedoes. Because," he added quietly, "if I don't call you that second time, I'm going to need Bellamy – bad!"

The Mott Mission was hot and it stank.

At the door an old man set aside a dog-eared book and smiled toothlessly.

"You Mr Mendelssohn?" the ancient croaked.

Ricco shook his head and made for the fat, perspiring woman who seemed to be in charge.

"Where can I reach Dr Bleakney's fiancée?" he inquired.

The woman squinted up, pushed back her hair.

"I wish I knew," she said resignedly. "She's the only one who can keep these flop artists in order."

Ricco felt his temples begin to throb.

"She's gone?"

The woman looked at him quizzically. "You have a date? She left here half an hour ago. An old man was taken sick upstairs, and she said she was going to help him home. She ought to be back by—"

She gave a little cry of alarm when Ricco grabbed her arm. Silently, he showed her his shield.

The woman looked surprised. "Why – why, I do hope there's nothing wrong?"

"Who was he – this old man? Where does he live?"

The custodian looked relieved. "I knew it couldn't be her you was after. She's kind of tops around here. No, I never saw the old man before. Just another bum. She was teaching him sign language. He was deaf and dumb, I guess."

Ricco swore softly. So he had guessed right, five hours too late! The man without a tongue had been there, in this dingy room. And now the wax doll killer was gone – gone through Ricco's fingers to the most pitiful triumph of all.

Someone tugged at his coat. It was the studious oldster. When Ricco whirled around he sighed disappointedly.

"Excuse it," he wheezed. "I didn't recognize you from the back. I thought you must be Mr Mendelssohn."

Undoubtedly the girl was dead by now.

Ricco whistled between his teeth. It was not music, that which he whistled, and the notes of it made his blood freeze. It was a girl's dreadful requiem – the last passionate bars of a song called 'Consolation.'

He went to the door, had it half open when the thought came. Or was it the banshee wail? His dash to the desk at the corner made the goggle-eyed custodian duck in alarm.

"Say," cried Ricco Maguire. "For sure, I am Mr Mendelssohn!"

It was insane, but so was the creature Ricco trailed. Insane enough to strew his path on previous killings with taunting, musical clues. This might be another –

why not? The theme song of his revenge, the piece called 'Consolation,' had been written by Felix Mendelssohn.

"I'm your man," said Ricco Maguire. "Why?"

The toothless one eyed him with marked disfavour. "Mendelssohn, hah! With a nose like that?"

Ricco shoved the shield under the old man's chin, and he looked very unhappy.

"Why," gritted Ricco Maguire, "are you looking for a man named Mendelssohn? Quick!"

The ancient sighed, relieved. "Oh. When the girl – we boys call her our girl – when she went out with some old fellow, she said to him, 'If you want to leave word for anyone, Ike here is the man to leave it with.'

"The man with her made some waves with his hands. He was a dummy. Such faces he made at her. Then she turned to me and said, 'He tells me the only one who will ever want to see him is Mr Mendelssohn, but he guesses he's going to be too late, as usual.' She gave me a quarter and said, 'The poor man. If his friend comes, tell him he's sick.' Then she put him in a taxi."

Ricco looked down the dirty street hopelessly. He said tightly, "Know where they went?"

Toothless raised mangy brows. "Naw. How'd I know?"

Then, as Ricco started for the car:

"But your pal, I can tell you about him. He lives on the corner of Barrow and Hudson, over my boy's delicatessen."

The motor roared into sudden life.

"She calls us her kids," shouted the ancient. "She's goin' to buy me 'The Count of Monte Cristo'."

"I hope so," said Ricco Maguire. But he was a block away by that time.

*

The bell button gave suddenly when he pressed, standing at the door of the apartment above the delicatessen. The bell made no sound within. He tried the lock, and the latch clicked under his hand. He stepped over the threshold.

Inside, silence pressed like a vast blanket of doom. And from its depths, a stirring, the sense that in the black was breathing and the pad of groping steps. Steps that come on steadily, searching.

The butt of the Police Positive was cold to his fingers. He froze, felt the wall, pressed the strap of his shoulder holster. He began to wonder whether Bellamy's ways were not, after all, better. To go in there might be throwing live flesh after dead. Still Gannon, at the station, would give Ricco a half hour. If the girl was inside, alive, alone with the wax doll killer, Bellamy's siren-screaming charge would seal her death warrant. Bellamy wouldn't risk losing the wax doll killer, not to save Doc Bleakney's girl.

The steps came down from above, hesitated by the door, moved closer. They came so close that Ricco pulled the gun close to his side lest it touch the thing he could not see. But the steps came on. Something brushed by him; he felt the swish of it. And as he set himself to leap it moved into the thin beam of light that came through the door.

"I'm so terribly sorry," said the sick-eyed girl. "I — please throw your gun on the floor."

Ricco Maguire sucked in his breath, bemused. For the girl, apparently, had no arms. Only writhing hands, which sprang, flipper-fashion, from her rounded shoulders. It was, he told himself, the damnable darkness. And after the first long stare the girl was looking, not at him, but at the moving fingers near her shoulder.

"You will," repeated the girl, in a dead, flat voice, "throw your gun on the floor. You will remove the second gun from your shoulder holster. You will kick it across the carpet. You will" – still staring at the hands, never at him, the girl's face blanched – "you will do this at once or my brains will splatter your fine clothes."

Then Ricco saw the two little eyes that peered beadily over the girl's shoulder. And the white of her half-inclined head, watching the brown flipper-hand at her right shoulder. In that showed the glint of a gun, pressed to her temple.

Ricco dropped the guns as directed. "You're Doc Bleakney's girl, I judge," he said. "Tell that Zombie to step out from behind you. He ought to feel safe enough now, with your own hands tied behind your back."

The girl nodded bitterly. "You and I are going to catch hell, Ricco Maguire," she said. "There's no chance for us. I know, I'm Pat Bellamy's daughter."

Something like a chuckle came from behind the girl. The hands gyrated, half covering her face. She stammered, a little breathlessly:

"He says, 'Salute!' He didn't think the police had any-one who could read his message. He congratulates you. He found pleasure in the little game. But he's bored by it now. He says you can go or stay, unarmed. But – but if you go, when the door closes behind you – I'll die. That's what he says."

Ricco could see ankles, skinny as sticks, braced behind Helen Bellamy's silk legs.

The hands moved jerkily, Helen caught her breath.

"He says, if you stay for the – the finale – I will live, and live, and live . . . Oh, I don't know what he means . . . He's saying it over and over with his fingers and shaking from laughter. I—"

The hands move peremptorily, gun shinning as it spun with the dumb message. She stepped fearfully backward, into the deeper gloom.

Ricco drew a deep breath. Never, he thought, could a man be made more ridiculous. For Bellamy's kid to be watching him, Ricco Pasquale Maguire, helpless, like a schoolboy. Sapristi, but if he could—

As Helen stepped out of his vision her eyes widened, left the hands. If the kid got crazy, made a break, with that devil—

"You're dad's on the way," he called to her. And to the shadow behind, "I can't – seem to find you."

It was the glint of the gun he sought. That and the white of the girl's face. If the gun were away from Helen's head he'd jump. The only way. Ricco could imagine the torture threatened by that "live, and live and live."

He stepped into the dark. The white was ahead. And the gun was low, no longer near the girl. Ricco felt his back muscles creep. He said, "Are you there?" walking up carelessly. "I can't find you in the dark but I'll be along, soon as I—"

He dove, hands outstretched and taloned for the gun.

Even as he left his feet, Helen screamed. In that second, Ricco knew. The white was not Helen's face. The scream had been far to the side. And the gun – there was no gun! He sensed it as the shadow he sprang for left its feet as he leaped, as it came hurtling to meet his dive. Knew it as glass cracked and smashed against his head, and he fell stunned beneath the shattered wall mirror. Not until then did he see the real gun. It was waving crazily above him. He gave a sick lurch at it, heard, from a vast distance, his own voice yelling. Then there was nothing but the shock of steel against his head, and then – nothing at all.

He opened his eyes into tomb-like darkness, peopled with little rustlings and the sound of shuffling steps. As, by degrees, his faculties returned, he perceived that he was seated, bound hand and foot to a chair.

Only a half hour he had until Pat Bellamy would pound at the door, make the noise that would fire a gun against his daughter's head.

"Damn you," yelled Ricco Maguire, "where's Helen Bellamy?"

There was a silence for a moment. Then, from some distance there was the sound of chuckling, long-drawn paroxysms. No man, he felt, had ever laughed like that, yet the chuckling came from a man's throat. The back of Ricco's neck bristled.

The steps had paused at his cry. He heard the snap of a switch, and the light came on. And Ricco Maguire saw her.

She was writhing, helpless in a chair not an arm's length away. Tight-lashed cords held her down. Over her entire visage, adhesive tape had been wound. Holes had been cut in the tape; through them he could see her eyes roll sidewise. There was, doubtless, a slit through which she could breathe, for her chest rose and fell and strained against the rope.

But it was not these things that made Ricco Maguire's flesh creep. It was the fact that in that swathed, mummy-like face there was no mouth, no lips – yet from it a human tongue hung. On either side of it, like malformed jawbones, steel clamps savagely pinched and held the tongue, so that it could not be withdrawn into the slit in the tape through which it protruded.

It looked like a creature without a face, an obscene freak of nature sculptured by one to whom horror was a thing to laugh at.

CHAPTER FOUR
The Beast That Needed Blood

The eyes, Ricco saw, were straining around to his, scared, questioning.

He said, "Steady, Helen." The eyes widened and clouded with moisture.

Ricco Maguire looked for a clock. If Bellamy broke in now he'd sign his daughter's death warrant.

How much of that half hour still remained?

He saw that they were in a shabby, ill-tended room. Evidently a combined eating and sleeping place. A gas range, flaked with rust, stood behind the girl, and a couch, wadded with bedraggled bedding, lay against the wall. They were alone.

Then he heard the voice. From the adjacent room it came. Throaty, sonorous, half intelligible – like the voice of an actor heard from the lobby of a playhouse, when the meaning of the words is incomprehensible, and only the sound of the phrases is heard. This was like that; yet in some macabre way it was not.

This voice was loud. And the other room was close by. There was no reason why Ricco could not have understood that voice – the phrases being in English – if it had been speaking human words!

At first the voice spoke alone. Nothing answered except the sound of Helen's muffled breathing. As the voice reached a higher pitch, impatient, cajoling, little scurrying sounds answered it, and the sound of frantic animal twitterings. Then the voice laughed and Ricco, jerking his head sharply, saw the shadow that darkened across the threshold.

The wax doll murderer blinked owlishly in at them,

one bony hand half raised, the other bearing a wire basket – heavy, from the way the weight of it slanted his body sidewise. He was fifty – or eighty; he should have been screamingly funny – but he wasn't.

Dripping wet, he might tilt a hundred pounds. His head would have been a skull, if skin were not over the bone. His neck disappeared under the jut of his jaw until it seemed there could be no room for a throat. And billowing loosely around him, flopping before and behind, hung a faded opera costume. It was the motley of Pagliacci! Pagliacci, the clown!

He set the cage on the stove and inspected his two prisoners, little eyes darting suspiciously over their bonds. Then, clucking with satisfaction, he stood arms akimbo, in front of Ricco's chair, and spoke.

There weren't any words. Ricco shrugged impotently. A madman, talking to a damn blind fool.

The murderer in a clown's costume wagged his head. Hopped to a chair, repeated a query slowly, a dozen times. No malice here, only an infinite hunger to be understood.

"Oo owe usich?" it sounded like.

Ricco listened, closed his eyes to shut out the face. It was hard to think, staring at it. The singsong voice repeated it, interminably.

Out of the rhythm, which was language and yet was not, the speech patterns came clearer and clearer to Ricco. It was only the vowel sounds he heard. The hard consonants were lacking in that strange speech. He listened, supplied consonants in his mind.

"Oh, sure, I know music," said Ricco Maguire. "If you'll take off these damned cords, I'll—"

The creature chirped in satisfaction, darted back into the other room and emerged dragging a massive phonograph. Leaned solicitously over it, making minute adjustments. Selected a twelve-inch record, primed an adjuster, evidently a repeating mechanism, and plugged in a cord which took the place of the ordinary hand winder.

Helen Bellamy's head had fallen forward. Outward life seemed to have left her but when Ricco called sharply to her he saw her eyes follow him, numbly. There was good stuff in that girl. But good blood can flow as freely as bad, under the touch of steel.

The wax doll killer fumbled beneath his robes, drew out something that glinted metallically in the gloom. A pair of scissors.

"Listen," Ricco said quietly, "in ten minutes this room will be full of coppers. Understand – they're speeding for this house now. For every deviltry you do that girl they'll do it to you three times over. I'm offering you a chance to live, man. Those boys of mine are going to make you wish you were dead."

Ricco could translate readily now. The garbled jargon the killer costumed as a clown was shouting back at him!

"I died many years ago." The tongue-less clown continued his preparations.

On the wire basket was a lock; this he unfastened. As he did so, the frantic twittering, which had died down, broke out afresh. And the lid of the basket jerked up and down, and shook to the scurrying of little, rasping feet.

Dispassionately he fastened a piece of twine to the handle of the basket, fingers gingerly wary of the unseen contents. Then, holding he rest of the twine in his hand he sidled away from it, playing out the cord, until he had reached Helen Bellamy's side.

Ricco could see the girl flinch, saw her brace stiffly against the chair, her swathed face held proudly posed, waiting. But her eyes, dry and feverish, couldn't mask her panic.

Impotent, Ricco watched.

The creature moved between Ricco and the girl. Ricco heard a snip of the scissors and a choked scream. And when the creature stepped back again, Ricco saw that a little drop of blood hung on the end of the girl's protruding tongue.

Blood! It seemed to charge the room with some elixir. From the basket came a craving, twittering sound as old as the first mammal – who ate lest he himself might die.

The vowelish voice said:

"Three there were. Now only one. You know what they did to me?"

Ricco nodded. "But this girl was not to blame. The others – yes. This girl – surely you won't make her suffer for what they—"

"Yes." The creature preened himself complacently.

He went to the phonograph, started the record. "After the aria," he said, "you'll see I kept my promise. About her living and living. I'll die – after I pull the string and take a little powder. The little beasts in the basket are so hungry, you see. But never fear, they can't kill her. All they can eat is her little pink tongue. Like the one her lover stole from me."

Then Ricco understood. He screamed incoherent things in two languages at the man without a tongue. The madman postured, beat his thin breast and protested, justified himself, and into the clamour slid the music of a world-famous orchestra.

He gave one great cry:

"Silence! The Maestro – it is his cue!"

And shattering the horror came the aria for "Pagliacci."

"Laugh, poor clown, while your heart is breaking . . ."

There weren't any words. A mad gentleman, telling of the ghastly surgical blunder that had taken away his hope, his future.

There were not any words, yet he sustained the tremendous, mighty climax of the music rising on the point of his toes, finished with the dying chord. Postured in a vague, blurred bow, stumbled, clutched at his throat – and fell dead across the stove.

But in his death the wax doll killer's pledge of life to his victims was horribly and unwittingly violated. As he staggered his arms had jerked the cord; the netting over the basket came free. And from it eyes gleamed and tiny clawed feet scurried across the floor.

This much the mad clown had promised.

But besides, the man without a tongue, in falling, had caught a sleeve on the stove. Not much, but enough to turn a gas jet full around. The cloying, deadly sweetness of gas came to Ricco's nostrils.

"Helen," implored Ricco, "for the love of God, girl, don't faint!"

At his shout she stirred.

"I'm coming over there, but it'll take awhile," he encouraged. "Breathe easy, and keep your head moving!"

It was then he saw the thing that squeaked and crawled upon her lap.

It was a rat. A rat so emaciated he hardly knew what it was, it was a living skeleton, so enfeebled that it crept uncertainly on tottering gray sticks of legs. It looked like some gaunt, plucked bird. Yet there was some life in it; with its fellows it groped towards the sent of the life-fluid its empty veins craved, the blood that dripped from the wounded tongue. So near . . .

If Bellamy didn't come soon. Bellamy had to come—

Ricco scraped the chair forward, his head spinning. The gray skeletons scurried, a-twitter, before him. On the floor beneath the girl they fought for the drops that had come from her lacerated tongue. And above it, on her dress, a trail of it led to the swathed face with the protruding tongue. After a minute three of them were squeaking and fighting on the trail.

His chair was next to hers. How long it had taken, he could not know. Consciousness was ebbing and returning in dark, circling mists. He struggled through a black wave, gasped:

"I'm going to fall across your chair. Hold your head over me! And fight it off now, or—"

He wrenched himself forward, and to the side, felt the chair teeter and carry him down.

Thank God he had judged the distance! His chair, holding him immovable, was aslant over Helen's lap.

The blood dripped slowly from the nip the scissors had made in Helen's tongue. It fell on his arm. She was sluggish; he yelled savagely before she comprehended what he was saying. Then, at last, she moved her head; he could feel the warm drops on his bound wrists. Only a minute he dared stay.

Short as it was, that minute was going to be too long. Leaden, sleepy numbness pressed down on back and shoulders. He could not move the chair. A little it gave, no more.

"Can – you – tip it—"

He could feel Helen's body stiffen against his head. Helping him. Two half-conscious automatons straining against a weight a child could topple. And then he fell.

On the floor the gas was not as overpowering. He was conscious of a light rasping weight on his hand; something slid away, piping shrilly. A foot from him, tiny eyes, wary, predatory, wavered between two trails – and passed out of his vision.

The bolder, more active fellows had clung to Helen's garments. The weaklings, worsted in the fight, and too far gone to jump upward, were on the floor. Could they scent the blood on his wrists? Life for all of them depended on it.

Helen's head was moving, but jerkily, more slowly. One, the largest of the rats, had reached her shoulder. Beneath her, holding still, Ricco felt the first nibble at his wrists. And with it came the mental flash that the girl's head, stricken eyes glassy, had fallen forward . . .

Ricco lost the count of time. Nothing remained but the black waves and the faint pinprick of claws that kicked and fought and ran over his bound hands.

He flung himself athwart the chair, getting all the traction of his back and legs against the lever of the wood. Strained until his own blood ran with the girl's over his lacerated wrists. And – after he couldn't feel it – saw his arms break free.

Bellamy saw them a block away, and his bellow dwarfed the siren, the two heads that propped grotesquely out of a smashed window. Ricco Maguire and the swathed mummy face, tongue sticking out at the crowd that gaped below.

"Them two'll pull through," hazarded the intern as the stretchers got shoved in the ambulance. "Kind of sacrilegious, that damned music playing in there where that guy died."

It wailed above him, long after Ricco Maguire and Helen Bellamy were revived at the hospital. Music which seemed to search for a tongue to frame the words: poor Pagliacci.

The Blue Sweetheart

Thick sticky heat came gushing from the Indian Ocean, closed in on Ceylon, and it seemed to Clayton that he was the sole target. He sat at the bar of a joint called Kroner's on the Colombo waterfront, and tried vainly to cool himself with gin and ice. It was Saturday night and the place was mobbed, and most of them needed baths. Clayton told himself if he didn't get out soon, he'd suffocate. But he knew he couldn't walk out. If he walked out, he'd be killed.

It was a weird paradox. A man who feared violent death would never come near Kroner's, let alone sit at the bar with his back to the tables. The place was a hangout for agents who dealt in violence, a magnet for thugs and muggers and professional murderers. They'd tackle any job for money or its equivalent in opium, and because they had nothing to lose they were afraid of nothing. Except one element. The element was Kroner.

And Kroner was Clayton's friend, the only friend he had. That was why he felt safe here. Two days ago he'd managed to sneak in from the interior of Ceylon, had told Kroner about the blue treasure, the huge sapphire he'd found in the earth. Kroner had smiled and said he already knew about it. This kind of news traveled fast in Colombo.

Kroner hadn't asked to see the sapphire. He wasn't

interested in sapphires. He placed a premium on friendship, he always said, and his prime concern was the welfare of his friends. Built short and wide and completely bald, the fifty-year-old Dutchman was a quiet-spoken man whose sentimental nature was a soft veneer. Under it, there were rock-hard muscles and the ferocity of a water-buffalo.

He'd given Clayton a room upstairs, and promised to make arrangements for passage on the next available boat out of Colombo. Until that was accomplished, he emphasized, Clayton must stay here and not worry and not do anything foolish.

Clayton wondered if he could handle the latter item. In the course of his life he'd made countless impulsive moves, some of them absurdly foolish. Now, at twenty-nine, his appetite for danger was tempered with a grim hunger to stay alive.

He was a medium-sized man, built like a fast welterweight, the build nicely balanced for power and agility. A long time back he'd boxed professionally, and his face showed it. But despite the marks, it was a face that women liked to look at. They didn't seem to mind the broken nose and the scar tissue above the eyes. And Alma used to put her lips against the scars, and when she did it, she purred. He was remembering the sound of it, the way she purred. His mouth hardened with bitter memory.

He leaned across the bar and told Kroner to sell him another drink. As Kroner poured the gin, a hand came down on Clayton's shoulder. It came down like a feather, settling gently. Clayton turned slowly on the bar stool and saw the shiny smiling face of the Englishman.

The Englishman's name was Dodsley and he was a greasy whiskered derelict of some forty-odd years. He was a crumpled slob who took opium but managed to control it enough so that he was coherent at intervals. Now his face showed his thoughts were in order and Clayton knew what was coming. Dodsley's profession was displayed in his glowing eyes. He was an agent for anyone who wished to obtain gems, whether it meant purchase, swindle or downright theft.

The Englishman went on smiling. It seemed he was carefully choosing his first words. He waited another moment, then said, "They say it's a very big stone. They tell me it's almost two hundred carats."

Clayton didn't say anything.

"May I see it?"

"No," Clayton said.

"I can't make an offer unless I see it."

"It isn't for sale," Clayton said. He turned to face the bar and focus on the gin.

He heard the Englishman breathing behind him, and then the voice saying, "You found the stone near Anuradhapura, at the Colonial mines. My client is part-owner of the mines. I think you know who my client is, and I'm sure you understand his business methods—"

"That's enough," Clayton cut in. Again he was facing the Englishman. "The stone is my property. I didn't find it in the mine area. I picked it up in the hills at least three miles away from their land holdings."

Dodsley shrugged. "There were witnesses."

"Of course there were witnesses. They flocked around like hungry hyenas. But they went away when I showed them the gun. It's a neat little gun. I always have it with me and I always keep it loaded."

"The gun is not important," Dodsley said. "This is a legal matter. They said you were working at the mines—"

Clayton was grinning and shaking his head. "I quit the mines two weeks before I found the stone. Got checking-out papers to prove it." The grin faded as he went on, "Just tell your client about the gun. Tell him I'm always ready to use it."

The Englishman looked up at the ceiling and sighed. It was a mixture of sad prophecy and ruthless pronouncement. It caused Clayton to stiffen, and he was thinking of Dodsley's client.

He was thinking of a man named Rudy Hagen. It was Hagen who'd booted him out of Colombo more than a year ago. And it was Hagen who'd taken Alma from him. The memory of it seared his brain.

Now it came back, cutting hard and deep. He was in Hagen's private office again in the warehouse on the waterfront. He was broken and bleeding at Hagen's feet. And Alma was in Hagen's arms, looking down at him as though he were mud. As they dragged him to the door to throw him out, he heard the laughter. He didn't feel the rough hands of Hagen's men. He felt only the ripping pain of hearing the laughter. It was like acid, and it came burning into him from Alma's lips.

He could hear it again in his brain. He quivered with rage. He was telling himself to leap off the stool and run out of here and race along the docks to Hagen's place, and let it happen any way it was going to happen. Just then he heard the soft whistle.

He moved his head and saw the warning gesture. It was Kroner's finger going from side to side. And Kroner's eyes were saying, "Don't do it, be sensible."

Clayton took a deep breath. He turned to Dodsley. His voice was calm and level. "Tell Hagen to leave me alone and I'll leave him alone. I'm willing to forget what he did to me. All he did was take some little stones and a woman. As far as I'm concerned, *everything* he took was junk."

He shoved Dodsley and the Englishman bumped into a table where a bearded Hindu gave him another shove. It became a succession of shoves that sent Dodsley all the way to the door. Kroner was there at the door, waiting for him, smacking the back of his head to make the exit emphatic. Clayton tossed off the remainder of the gin and went up to his room.

The knocking was a parade of glimmering blue spheres bouncing in blackness. He opened his eyes and the spheres were gone but the blackness stayed there. Then he heard the knuckles rapping against the door.

The gun was under the mattress and he reached for it, found it, released the safety catch and quickly hauled himself out of bed.

Outside the room a voice said, "It's me, Kroner."

He switched on the light and opened the door. Kroner saw the gun in his hand and nodded approvingly.

Clayton yawned. "What time is it?"

"Past three. She's downstairs."

He stared at the Dutchman. He said, "Send her up." He said it automatically, without thinking.

Kroner sighed. He didn't say anything. He waited there in the doorway. His eyes told Clayton it would be a serious mistake to let her enter this room.

Clayton's mouth hardened. He could feel the challenge of her presence on the floor below. He spoke louder. "You heard what I said. Send her up."

"Now?"

"Right now."

"Don't you want time to shave? Look at you. You aren't even dressed."

"The hell with that. She'll see me the way I am."

Kroner sighed again, backed out of the room, and closed the door. Clayton lit a cigarette and stood staring at himself in the wall mirror. His hair was a black storm on his head and he had a two-day growth on his face and all he wore was a pair of shorts. But then, still focusing on the mirror, he wasn't seeing his unkempt appearance. He was seeing something beyond the mirror. Again his brain made the tortuous journey along the paths of bitter memory.

It was three years ago and he was meeting her for the first time. They had a few drinks and then she told him to let it ride and forget about her. She said it was just a matter of cold cash and he didn't have it and that put him out of the picture.

But he knew she wasn't a professional, and he begged her to explain. So then she told him about it, the husband who'd been killed in the Okinawa campaign, a series of hard knocks, one or two crackups and finally the decision to put money ahead of anything else.

And even though her eyes were saying it wasn't money now, he made up his mind to get the money. Then came two years of trying to get it, digging for sapphire in the hills, coming back with empty hands. But his arms were never empty. Alma was always there to meet him. They never talked about money.

Then, a year ago, he'd come back from the hills with some stones of fairly decent size. It wasn't a fortune, but it meant enough money so he could ask her to marry him. On the night of his arrival in Colombo, she wasn't in the bus depot to meet him. He waited an hour, two hours and she didn't show. He called her apartment and she wasn't there and his eyes had hardened as he thought of Rudy Hagen.

Hagen had always been in the picture, flitting in and out of it like the shadow of a vulture. And now Hagen was saving him the trouble of walking to the waterfront and moving in for a showdown.

A Rolls Royce arrived at the depot and a few men got out and told him he was wanted in Hagen's office and they'd be glad to drive him there. He took one look at their faces and realized that the news of his sapphires had preceded him to Colombo. He took another look and knew there was no use. He shrugged and climbed into the Rolls Royce.

Hagen made it brief and blunt. The gems were Hagen's property. The stones had been found on land holdings of which Hagen was part owner. Clayton wasn't listening. He was looking at Alma. She had her hand on Hagen's shoulder, and Hagen's arm was around her waist.

When he lunged at Hagen, it had nothing to do with the sapphires. And later, when he was tossed out of the office, a sack of bleeding meat, he didn't hear the clinking sound of the stones in Hagen's hand. All he heard was a woman's laughter, a disdainful laugh that told him he'd been played for a sucker.

Now, a year later, he stood before the mirror and saw his lips moving and heard himself saying, "God damn her."

But when the door opened, his body seemed to melt and the fire came into his eyes. It was the fire that always leaped up at the sight of her.

She was dazzling. She had the kind of face that couldn't be captured with camera or paint-brush. Only the living flesh could show the perfection of eyes and nose and lips. Her hair was platinum, and her skin had the softness of camellia petals. The slender elegance of her body was sheathed in pale green satin, cut low in front to display the cleavage of her breasts. She had exquisite breasts. Everything about her was perfect, her shoulders and her belly and her hips and her thighs.

He was making an effort to steady himself. He tried not to look at her. He said, "You here on business?"

"Strictly."

"If that's a business outfit you're wearing, I got a few dollars ain't busy."

She didn't even flinch. She was like a clever boxer neatly slipping a right-hand smash to the jaw. "I'll do the buying," she said very softly. She helped herself to one of his cigarettes, lit it and took a long drag and let it go way down. As it came up and out of her lips, she was smiling at him. "May I see the stone?"

"No." Then he looked at her. "I didn't show it to Dodsley and I won't show it to you. And tell Hagen to stop sending representatives. If he wants to know what it looks like, I'll let him see it. But he'll have to phone for an appointment."

She was quiet for some moments. When she spoke, her voice was calm and level. "Let's leave Hagen out of this. The only buyer I'm representing is myself."

"You?" He was caught off balance. But then his eyes narrowed and he said, "Where's your money?"

She was carrying a small kidskin handbag. Her fingers tapped the side of it. "In here," she murmured. "I think it's enough for a down payment."

Then she opened the bag and took out a roll of bills. They were thousand-dollar bills and as she leafed through the roll, he counted twenty of them.

His eyes remained narrow and he said, "The full price is three hundred thousand."

She smiled dimly. "Rather expensive." Then the smile

went away and she said, "I'll have the balance here tomorrow."

The roll of bills was extended toward him but he made no move to take it. He was watching her eyes. Finally he shook his head slowly and said, "No sale."

"Why not?"

He laughed at her. "You think I'm stupid or something? You give me the twenty, I give you the stone, and then you hand it over to Hagen. That's as far as it would go." The laugh became sour and jagged. "Tell Hagen to think of a better scheme."

"This isn't a scheme, and Hagen knows nothing about it." She took a deep breath. "I'll show you Hagen's scheme. Here's the method he wants me to use."

She reached into the handbag and took out a small automatic revolver.

Clayton tensed himself.

But the gun wasn't pointed at him. She held it loosely, did nothing more than display it, then let it fall into the handbag. She inserted the roll of bills in the bag, closed the bag and tossed it onto the bed. In almost the same gesture she pointed toward the window, indicating that Clayton should take a look outside.

He hurried across the room and peered through the blinds. Outside a man was waiting in the street below. He saw the greasy face and sloppy white suit of Dodsley.

He turned and looked at her.

Her voice was low. "It would have been so easy," she said. "The gun would have forced you to give me the stone. But Hagen's plan went further than that. He wanted me to shoot you dead, then go to the window and throw the stone to Dodsley. I'd be waiting here when the police arrived. My dress would be torn and I'd tell them

I did it only to protect myself. And of course I'd know nothing about a sapphire."

Clayton was quiet for some moments. Finally, he said, "An old idea, but a good one. And I'm sure it would have worked. Why didn't you use it?"

Her eyes tried to penetrate the stoniness of his face. "Can't you answer that?"

"There's more than one answer. You're a shrewd operator."

"At times," she admitted. "At other times I'm a woman."

She was moving toward him. His brain reeled with the thought *I want her, I want her.* And then the ice-cold thought, *I don't trust her.* And finally the snarling decision, *Damn her, I can play this just as cheap as she can.*

The platinum hair came nearer. He stood there waiting, watching the parted lips, watching her tongue moisten them. He felt the mild caress of her breath against his face, and suddenly he found her in his arms, and her lips crushed against his mouth. His hands followed the smooth curve of her back, and he breathed deeply of her hair, drugged with the nearness of her. He didn't see the clock that said *Now* and the bed that said *Here.* He was aware only of her closed eyes, the swell of her breasts against his chest, the warmness of her. He was swept outward and away from the boundaries of reality and yet somehow he knew this wasn't a dream, it was something he had waited for and hungered for and it was happening . . .

The warmth left him too soon. He felt the steely grin forming on his lips again. He watched her adjust her skirt, smoothing it over her hips, watched the long flash of thigh as she got to her feet.

"Before you go downstairs, you better fix your mouth," he said. "You need new lipstick."

It wasn't the words. It was the look on his face. She stared at him incredulously. "Is . . . is that all you can say? After . . . after . . . haven't I proved . . .?" She stopped, choking on the words.

Clayton said, "You've proved you're a filthy tramp. Now get out."

"Clayton—" She sobbed it.

He had turned away. "Go on, get the hell out of here."

He was facing a wall. He heard her moving toward the door, and the door opening and closing. Minutes passed, and he stood there gazing vacantly at the wall. Gradually he began to think about taking a bath. He felt dirty and he told himself he really needed a bath.

Showered and shaved and wearing clean linen and a freshly pressed suit, he stood at the bar and watched Kroner tilting the bottle. Kroner poured with a seemingly clumsy motion but the gin came up to the edge of the glass and stopped right there. Clayton reached for the glass, lifted it, spilled some of the gin, and shot the rest down his throat. He extended the empty glass and mumbled, "Another."

"You can't hold another."

"I said give me another."

Kroner poured it. They were alone in the place except for two drunken natives who had fallen asleep and were stretched out on the floor like a couple of dead men. A dirty-faced clock above the bar indicated twenty minutes past four. The small window behind the bar showed that it was still dark outside.

"Almost morning," Kroner commented. He watched Clayton. "You want me to help you upstairs?"

"I'm not going upstairs." Clayton emptied the glass. He looked at the Dutchman. "How much have I had?"

"Plenty," Kroner said. "It's a wonder your legs can hold you up."

"Let me buy you one."

"My dear Clayton, you know I never touch liquor."

"You mean liquor never touches you. Nothing ever touches you."

Kroner looked hurt. "Friendship touches me. It means more than jewels to me. I'm thinking only of your welfare and I beg you to take my advice. Go up to your room and stay there. And tomorrow, if I can manage it, you'll be on a boat."

Clayton wasn't listening. He was reaching toward the wide pocket of his jacket and feeling the bulk of the revolver. His fingers went up along the short barrel, onto the chamber and past the trigger-guard and finally grasped the thick butt. Then he let go of the revolver and took his hand from the pocket. He looked to see if his hand was shaking. He saw that his fingers were steady. He said, "The eyes always tell the truth." And then, slowly and softly, "I'm going out for a walk. I want to take a look at something."

He moved away from the bar, heading toward the door leading to the street. When he arrived at the door, Kroner was there to block his path. The Dutchman was a wide thick wall of beef, the arms spread out, the fat face glimmering with sweat.

"My friend—" Kroner pleaded.

Clayton smiled wearily. "You're in my way."

"My very dear friend," Kroner said. "Please try to be logical. If you walk out of here, you'll be playing into Hagen's hands. His men are posted all along the waterfront, waiting for you—"

Clayton went on smiling, his eyes aiming past the Dutchman and focused on the door.

"Please," Kroner said thickly. "The important thing is to stay alive."

Then they were looking at each other and Clayton was saying, "I don't have time to write out a will. But if I don't come back, the sapphire belongs to you. You'll find it in a cardboard box stuffed in the head-side of the mattress."

He took a step toward the door. Kroner did not budge. Kroner said, "I'm very sorry, but I cannot allow you to leave."

Clayton shrugged. And he sighed. Then rather gently he pushed at Kroner's chest with his left hand, chopped short and hard with his right and caught the Dutchman on the jaw. Kroner sagged and went to the floor, stretched out prone and motionless.

Clayton opened the door and walked out. He was met with a flood of very hot and syrupy air coming in from the Indian Ocean.

Lights blinked against the oily black surface of the Colombo harbor. On the waterfront it was quiet except for the steady lapping of little waves coming in to caress the docks. Clayton moved close to the piers, his head working like something in a socket, his eyes studying the darkness that seemed to revolve around him.

Then he was in a narrow alley between a splintered pier and the thick concrete walls of a British cotton warehouse. He came out of the alley and started a turn that would take him toward Hagen's private office. There was a light in the window, and the light seemed to beckon and he hurried forward. He'd taken only a few footsteps when he heard the sound behind him.

He pivoted and stared and saw them. Two of them.

They were coming in fast, and as they came closer he saw the mashed noses and thick lips of dock ruffians who made their living with their muscles and their twisted brains. One of them had a knife and the other carried a short club. Clayton took the gun out of his pocket, released the safety catch and aimed the gun and then decided to try it without bullets. The bullets would make too much noise. It would bring Hagen and his men out of the office, and that would ruin it. He told himself he hadn't come here to fight or kill, but just to learn something, to prove something to himself.

The thugs hadn't seen the gun, they were concentrating on their own target. As they lunged, Clayton side-stepped and brought the gunbutt crashing against the skull of the man nearest him. The man went down like a toppled statue. The other man let out a curse and forgot Hagen's orders not to use the knife for killing, and slashed the blade toward Clayton's throat. Clayton stepped back, wielding the gun so that the butt hit the man's wrist. There was the cracking sound of splintered bone. The man opened his mouth to yell, and Clayton rushed in and used the gun like a hammer on the man's mouth. The man went to his knees, spitting blood and teeth and choking on more blood. Clayton gave him a rap on the temple that knocked him flat and put him to sleep.

The sign above the lit window read *Rudolph Hagen Co., Ltd.* Under the printed words there was a painted symbol of a jeweler's eye-piece, framed in the curving lines of elephant-tusks. This meant that Rudy Hagen was a dealer in gems and ivory and any kind of treasure he could get his hands on. Hagen had extremely large hands and Clayton was looking at them now.

He was crouched at the wall and looking through the

window and focusing on Hagen's hands resting on a teakwood table. The thick fingers were stretched, showing the two rings, a large cat's eye and a larger opal. Clayton studied the hands for some moments, and then his gaze went up to the face.

Hagen had brutish good looks, the heavy features well-shaped and balanced, the light brown hair thick and neatly brushed. He was a tall stoutish man in his early forties, in splendid physical condition except for the red complexion that told of too much drinking. He was drinking now. He was taking sips from a high-ball glass as he smiled at Alma. She sat facing him and seemed to be looking past him. The drink in front of her was untouched.

The window was open at the bottom but Clayton didn't hear any sound coming from the room. It was an extremely ornate room. A Kerman rug covered the entire floor, and the walls were decorated with silk-screen paintings. On the far side of the room, placed there like a weapon pointing at the world, was Hagen's strongvault, a block of polished black iron with a silver combination-dial and handle. Clayton thought of the countless men who'd been cheated and robbed and sometimes slaughtered to feed the maw of the strongvault. His eyes were dull with hate and for a moment he wanted to leap through the window and use the gun.

He pulled brakes on the impulse, and as he did it, he heard Hagen saying, "What's the matter with your drink?"

"Nothing," Alma said. "I just don't feel like drinking."

"That's unusual," Hagen remarked. He took a long gulp from the high-ball glass.

Then they were quiet again but Clayton saw the way Hagen was smiling at her and the way she tried to keep her eyes off Hagen's face. Some moments passed, and then Dodsley entered the room. The Englishman placed a fresh drink on the table in front of Hagen, and in that instant the two of them traded a glance. Clayton saw that and then he switched his stare to Alma. She had stiffened just a little. As Dodsley walked out of the room, Hagen went on smiling at her. She took a very deep breath, as though her lungs were straining for air.

Hagen stood up and began pacing the floor between the teakwood table and the strongvault. He walked very slowly, his head lowered contemplatively, like a man rehearsing a speech. He stopped at the table, folded his arms and looked down at Alma and now he wasn't smiling.

He gestured toward the high-ball glass she hadn't touched. "Drink it," he said. "You're always better company after a few drinks."

She didn't look at him. She stared straight ahead. "I told you I'm not drinking."

"It's a pity to waste the whiskey," he murmured. "Thirty-year-old Scotch. Besides, it's bad luck to fill a glass and then not even taste it." His mouth tightened. "Take one sip. Just one."

"No." She looked at him. "And stop coaxing me."

"I'm not coaxing you, my dear. I'm telling you." Hagen took hold of the high-ball glass and lifted it toward her lips. She drew her head back and pushed the glass aside and some of the contents spilled on the table.

Outside the window, Clayton watched. His hands had a tight grip on the lower edge of the window-frame.

He saw the angry flush on Hagen's face. He saw Alma getting up and he heard her saying, "It's very late, and I need sleep. I'm going back to my apartment."

She started past Hagen, but he grabbed her wrist and

held her there and said, "I didn't tell you to go. You'll wait until I tell you."

"Let go, Rudy." She made a move to pull away.

Hagen smiled at her and put more pressure on her wrist.

"Let go." She said it very quietly. "Let go, damn you."

"That's more like it," Hagen said, and he released her wrist. "At least, when you're angry, I can talk to you."

Alma went back to the table and stood looking down at the high-ball glass. Almost half of the whiskey had been spilled but the remainder was a liquid magnet that pulled her hand toward the glass. She took hold of the glass as though it contained some bitter medicine that wasn't easy to take. And then, with one long convulsive gulp, she drained the glass.

"Want another?" Hagen asked.

She shook her head. She was staring down at the polished surface of the teakwood table. The glimmering wood was like a mirror and she was seeing herself in it and hating what she saw.

She had her back turned to Hagen and he came toward her and put his hand on her shoulders. She squirmed away. Hagen's face darkened again and he muttered, "What's wrong with you?"

"I want to be left alone. I told you I was tired."

"Look at me." Hagen's tone was a mixture of seething anger and frantic pleading.

She still kept her back to him.

"You can't even look at me." Hagen spoke through his teeth. His lips trembled. Then, with an effort, he controlled himself and said more calmly, "I'm trying to reason with you, Alma. I'm hoping you'll change your attitude and let me talk to you."

"All right," she said. "I'm listening."

But Hagen, standing behind her, couldn't see what Clayton saw. She had her eyes closed and her throat muscles contracted and she was trying to steady herself.

Then she turned slowly to face Hagen and he was quiet for some moments and finally he said, "I don't like the way things are going between us. Day after day it's like a stalemate. It's as if we're sitting playing chess. It's just a game, and I'm tired of it."

"What do you want, Rudy?"

"You. All of you."

"That wasn't in the contract."

"The hell with the contract." He said it loudly. "I've loved you ever since we first met."

"What do you know about love?" she asked.

"I'm flesh and blood," he shouted. "I need something more than a pretty toy to play with. I need real affection. And warmth. And happiness."

She was looking at the heavy safe in the corner. "There's your happiness."

"Is that a complaint?" He stabbed it at her. "You're a fine one to complain. You can't even play it straight with the man who pays your bills."

She stood rigid, not saying anything.

Hagen's voice was a blade going in deeper. "You think I'm blind or something? You think I believed one word of what you told me about Clayton? You said he took the gun out of your hand. I say you're a rotten liar."

She started to turn away. Hagen grabbed her arms and held her and forced her to look at him.

"Liar," Hagen said. "You've been giving me a lie from the very beginning. You've been cheating me and playing me for a fool. And every time I held you in my arms and you closed your eyes, you were seeing another man. You were seeing Clayton."

She was trying to twist away. Hagen tightened his grip on her arms.

"Now you'll tell me the truth," he shouted. "You'll admit it's been Clayton all along. Let me hear you say it. You'll say it if I have to choke it from your mouth—"

His hands went up to her throat. She let out a strangled cry. Hagen went on squeezing as she sagged to her knees. His teeth showed in a crazy grimace and he didn't know or care that he was forcing the life from her body.

And then the window went all the way up and Clayton leaped into the room. As he rushed at Hagen, his thoughts had nothing to do with strategy or tactics or remembering the gun in his pocket. He lunged like a wild animal and Hagen heard him coming, looked up and gaped at him and let go of Alma. She fell to the floor, gasping for breath. Hagen instinctively raised the big hands and clenched them and braced himself to meet the attack.

Clayton came in like a maddened bull. He threw both fists at Hagen's face, stepped back as Hagen ducked low and tried to hold, then used his right hand like a cleaver and sliced a line of red running harsh and wide and wet above Hagen's left eye.

Hagen groaned and made another attempt to hold on, and Clayton stepped to the side, speared the eye again, threw an uppercut that exploded on Hagen's chin. The big man went crashing into the teakwood table, sailing over it as it toppled to the floor. Clayton circled the table and moved in for the finish.

But Hagen had something left and got up fast and grabbed him as he lunged. Hagen held his arms, lifted him, and butted him in the stomach. Then he was hurled to the floor and kicked hard in the ribs. He tried to rise and Hagen kicked him again. He made a grab for Hagen's ankle, found it and yanked with all his might and Hagen went down. He threw himself at Hagen and landed on top. He hauled off to collect all the power in his arm for the final smash. But he didn't have time to send it in.

A door opened and four men came rushing into the room. As they closed in on Clayton, he remembered the gun in his pocket, reached for it, then realized it was a little late in the evening for the gun. The men had him flat on his face with one arm pulled high up between his shoulder blades. A heavy shoe crashed against his jaw and as he fell into a red-streaked fog he wryly told himself it was Hagen's night.

The fog didn't last long. Within a few minutes he was able to get his eyes in focus, and from the floor he obtained a clear view of what was taking place in the room. He saw Hagen seated at the table and dabbing a handkerchief against the bloodied brow. Dodsley was applying a strip of gauze-and-adhesive to the side of Hagen's mouth. The other four men were sitting around with cigarettes and glasses and waiting for further orders. Alma stood rigidly against the wall, staring at the teakwood table. The gun was on the table. Hagen's hand moved idly toward it and picked it up and gestured with it.

The gesture told Clayton to get up from the floor and sit at the table. He got up, and the gun pointed at his chest.

Hagen said, "I think maybe I'll do it."

"If you do," he said, "you'll have to travel."

Hagen smiled. "I don't think so. I'm a respected man in this community. As far as the police are concerned, I'm the owner of a legitimate enterprise. I have the privilege of shooting any thief who tries to ransack my office."

Clayton copied the big man's smile. "Why would I want to do that? I'm a rich man in my own right. Everybody knows about the stone. They know how big it is and how much it's worth."

Hagen frowned thoughtfully. "True," he murmured. "Quite true." Then he was smiling again. "Let's talk about that. Let's talk sapphire."

"No deal."

"It's got to be a deal," Hagen said. "Name your price." And then he glanced at Alma and said, "It doesn't have to be money. Besides, you're in no position to bargain."

Clayton looked at her. He saw the stiffening of her body. He said to her, "Are you willing?"

She didn't reply. Her face was expressionless.

Every fibre of him strained toward her, and he spoke thickly, saying, "It's you in exchange for the sapphire."

Hagen was laughing softly. "Let the lady make up her own mind. After all, it's her decision."

She parted her lips to make the reply. Clayton felt the pounding of his heart and he couldn't breathe as he waited to hear the sound of her voice. He saw the glow in her eyes and he almost leaped up, knowing that now he could take her in his arms and have what he wanted more than anything. But all at once the glow went out of her eyes, and she wasn't even looking at him. His veins froze as he saw her moving toward Hagen.

She stood beside Hagen and there was a thin smile on her lips as she put her hand on the big man's shoulder. Her fingers played with the expensive fabric of his suit. "It's a nice suit," she murmured. "It's silk, isn't it?" She aimed the smile at Clayton. "I like silk. I like the feel of it. I wouldn't settle for anything less."

"Smart girl," Hagen murmured. He took her hand and kissed her fingers. She fondled him, slowly curving her body to sit in his lap.

Clayton lowered his head and felt the pain lacing through him. On the level of sanity he called himself a moon-maddened idiot, craving something that was worthless. And yet he was torn with yearning, and the core of the wound was a horrible sense of futility and loss.

And all that remained was a shred of consoling thought as he remembered the sapphire. It lifted him just a little to know that Hagen would never get the stone.

He heard the sound of a door, and then a voice. It was the voice of Kroner. He blinked a few times and told himself he was hearing things, he was letting himself go crazy. He looked up and his widened eyes saw the Dutchman.

He stared at the cardboard box in Kroner's fat hands. He saw Kroner moving toward the table, placing the box on the table and grinning at Hagen and saying, "Open it. You'll see the biggest and the finest."

Hagen's face was wet with perspiration as he opened the box. His fingers went in like hungry fangs, and came out clutching the huge chunk of dull blue stone. He let out a gasp and for a moment it almost seemed he wanted to cram the gem into his mouth and make it a part of his insides.

"Look at this thing," Hagen cried. "Just look at it." He held it up to the light. He spoke to it, saying, "Oh, you sweetheart. You great big blue sweetheart."

"Like it?" Kroner murmured.

"It's my baby," Hagen exulted.

"Good," Kroner said. "Now let's talk business."

Clayton glared at the Dutchman. "You talk as if it's your stone."

"It is." Kroner was grinning. "Didn't you will it to me? I knew you wouldn't come out of here alive."

Then it was hate coming from Clayton's eyes as he shouted, "You double-crossing bastard."

"Please," Kroner murmured. "I beg you, do not misunderstand my intentions."

Clayton studied the Dutchman's face. And suddenly he realized the truth of it, the absolute truth, that Kroner's purpose was founded on pure honor and integrity. He knew that Kroner had come here in a desperate effort to save him from death. The Dutchman was gambling on Hagen's mad craving for the big blue stone, and hoping that a financial transaction would settle the matter and prevent a killing.

Kroner was looking at Hagen and saying, "Make me an offer."

Hagen didn't seem to hear. He was fully occupied with feasting his eyes on the stone. He seemed to have forgotten the gun in his other hand. And he paid no attention to Alma, who still sat in his lap, her arm around his shoulder and her fingers caressing the side of his face. He seemed to feel nothing, see nothing, know nothing but the big blue gem that glittered in his palm.

"It's flawless," Hagen said ecstatically. "I don't need an eye-piece to tell me that. It's flawless and it's absolutely priceless. There isn't another like it in the world." There was fever in his eyes and mania in his voice as he cried, "Now I own the biggest and the best."

"You don't own it yet," Kroner said quietly. "I'm still waiting to hear your offer."

"My offer?" Hagen blinked a few times. He seemed to be coming out of a blue mist, a vapor that drifted up from the sapphire. His eyes narrowed, a hard smile curved his lips, and he said, "You're a fool, Kroner. Can't you see the stone in my hand? You've delivered the merchandise and now it's mine."

Kroner's face stiffened. "You imply that I'm not to be paid?"

Hagen laughed lightly. "You'll be paid," he said. "I'll even give you a pen to sign the receipt. It's a special kind of pen. It writes under water."

The Dutchman winced. He gazed helplessly at Clayton. Then he shook his head sadly and said, "It was too much to hope for. But at least I can tell myself that I tried."

"You tried hard." Clayton's throat was thick with feeling. "You're a real friend."

"I'm an imbecile," the Dutchman said. "I made the mistake of thinking that Mr Hagen was a human being. My stupidity in that matter cannot be measured." He shrugged and then he smiled dimly at Clayton, and his eyes said, *Let's see if we can take it without flinching.*

Clayton returned the smile. An instant later he saw Hagen making a gesture that told his four men to get busy. He saw them reaching into their pockets and taking out the knives. In his mind he could see the process that would soon take place, the quick and efficient slaughtering, the blades slicing his flesh and Kroner's flesh. And after that, the weights attached to the ankles and the two corpses hurled into the harbor where the water was forty or seventy or ninety feet deep, anyway deep enough to hide all traces of a wet burial.

Without words he was saying good-bye to Kroner. And then, for some unaccountable reason, he decided on a silent farewell to Alma. He looked at her and he saw her sitting there in Hagen's lap.

His lips curled just a little to show his defiance and contempt. But then he saw the look in her eyes, the look that told him to keep his gaze focused on her face, to wait for a signal. He couldn't be wrong this time.

A moment later she gave him the signal. It was a wink. In almost the same moment she made a grab for the gun in Hagen's hand. Clayton lunged across the table, seeing the gun pointed to the ceiling as Alma twisted Hagen's wrist.

In a fraction of a second, Hagen's finger pulled the trigger, and the bullet went straight up, and Clayton grabbed for the gun but couldn't get it because Hagen freed his wrist from Alma's grasp and the motion caused the gun to fall out of his hand and off the table. The four men were lunging with their knives and Clayton dived to the floor, and made another grab for the gun.

But now Dodsley was there to kick the gun aside. Dodsley reached down to pick up the gun and received a hammer blow in the stomach from Kroner's fist. Then Kroner made a try for the gun and Hagen came leaping in to give the Dutchman a shoulder in the ribs that sent him to his knees.

Hagen kept on going, getting closer to the gun, getting very close and then reaching the gun, grabbing it, aiming it at Clayton's face. Clayton's arm went out like a piston, his hand closed on the barrel, jerked it up as Hagen yanked on the trigger. Another bullet went into the ceiling. A third bullet went into a wall.

They were still grappling for the gun when a fourth bullet plowed into the floor. Then Clayton had the gun and the fifth bullet went into Hagen's heart.

Clayton showed the gun to Dodsley and the four men.

They didn't need to be told to drop their knives. Kroner was standing motionless and taking deep breaths.

And Alma was at the phone, calling the police.

It was an hour later and the police had departed with a corpse and five handcuffed men. Kroner went along with them to tell the full story. Clayton stood on the pier and watched the police-car moving away.

The first grey ribbons of dawn were sliding across the sky as he turned slowly and moved toward the woman who had her back to him and was looking out at the dark water which was reflected in his eyes.

As he came up to her, she faced him, and he saw the sadness in her eyes.

She made no attempt to hide her feelings. She just stood there silently.

He said quietly, "It's a complicated game, isn't it?"

She nodded slowly. "We make it complicated," she managed to say in a quiet tone.

"Sometimes we're forced to," he said. "For example, a certain woman I know. She sat on the lap of a man she hated. And all she was thinking about was the gun in his hand. A gun that could get me."

She nodded again. And then she was trying to control her emotions, trying to speak calmly and objectively, as she said,

"A year ago I stood with my arm around Hagen and I laughed at you. If I hadn't laughed, if I'd let him know what I really felt, he would have killed you. Tonight it was the same routine. I was doing the only thing I could to keep you alive."

He was quiet for some moments. Then he said, "A few hours ago we were in my room. Why didn't you tell me then? What stopped you from telling me?"

"I didn't think it would get across. The only time it gets across is when it's all there, and there's nothing else, no doubts and no contradictions." Her eyes were clear and steady.

"You're right about that," he murmured. "I wouldn't have believed you. I was too angry, too bitter, too much of a damn fool."

"No," she said. "You were right in thinking that I came to get the sapphire. The gun, of course, was Hagen's plan. My plan was my money, every cent I have, twenty thousand dollars. But it wasn't quite enough."

Clayton smiled dimly. "That was just the down payment. You said you could bring the balance."

She copied the smile. "The strongvault in Hagen's office. I know the combination."

She said slowly, "I meant it when I promised to bring the rest of the money."

"And you'd have kept your promise. And then Hagen would have found out. Chances are, he'd have killed you. Did you figure that one out?"

She didn't reply. But he already knew the answer.

He said, "You were willing to die for me."

Her head was lowered and she said, "You make it sound very noble." Then she looked up. "Remember, I'm just a blonde tramp with a weakness for rich men."

He reached into his pocket and took out the sapphire. "Look at this." He was grinning. "It'll bring a lot of money."

"Yes, I know. She was drifting into his arms, ignoring the gleam of the big blue gem. "And please don't show me the money. All I want is the man."

Professional
Man

At five past five, the elevator operated by Freddy Lamb came to a stop on the street floor. Freddy smiled courteously to the departing passengers. As he said good-night to the office-weary faces of secretaries and book-keepers and executives, his voice was soothing and cool-sweet, almost like a caress for the women and a pat on the shoulder for the men. People were very fond of Freddy. He was always so pleasant, so polite and quietly cheerful. Of the five elevator-men in the Chambers Trust Building, Freddy Lamb was the favorite.

His appearance blended with his voice and manner. He was neat and clean and his hair was nicely trimmed. He had light brown hair parted on the side and brushed flat across his head. His eyes were the same color, focused level when he addressed you, but never too intent, never probing. He looked at you as though he liked and trusted you, no matter who you were. When you looked at him you felt mildly stimulated. He seemed much younger than his thirty-three years. There were no lines on his face, no sign of worry or sluggishness or dissipation. The trait that made him an ideal elevator-man was the fact that he never asked questions and never talked about himself.

At twenty past five, Freddy got the go-home sign from the starter, changed places with the night man, and walked down the corridor to the locker room. Taking off the uniform and putting on his street clothes, he yawned a few times. And while he was sitting on the bench and tying his shoelaces, he closed his eyes for a long moment, as though trying to catch a quick nap. His fingers fell away from the shoelaces and his shoulders drooped and he was in that position when the starter came in.

"Tired?" the starter asked.

"Just a little." Freddy looked up.

"Long day," the starter said. He was always saying that. As though each day was longer than any other.

Freddy finished with the shoelaces. He stood up and said, "You got the dollar-fifty?"

"What dollar-fifty?"

"The loan," Freddy said. He smiled off-handedly. "From last week. You ran short and needed dinner money. Remember?"

The starter's face was blank for a moment. Then he snapped his finger and nodded emphatically. "You're absolutely right," he declared. "I'm glad you reminded me."

He handed Freddy a dollar bill and two quarters. Freddy thanked him and said good-night and walked out. The starter stood there, lighting a cigarette and nodding to himself and thinking, *Nice guy, he waited a week before he asked me, and then he asked me so nice, he's really a nice guy.*

At precisely eight-ten, Freddy Lamb climbed out of the bathtub on the third floor of the uptown rooming house in which he lived. In his room, he opened a dresser drawer, took out silk underwear, silk socks, and a silk handkerchief. When he was fully dressed, he wore a pale grey roll-collar shirt that had cost fourteen dollars, a grey silk gabardine suit costing ninety-seven fifty, and dark grey suede shoes that had set him back twenty-three ninety-five. He broke open a fresh pack of cigarettes and slipped them into a wafer-thin sterling silver case, and then he changed wrist watches. The one he had been wearing was of mediocre quality and had a steel case. The one he wore now was fourteen karat white-gold. But both kept perfect time. He was very particular about the watches he bought. He wouldn't wear a watch that didn't keep absolutely perfect time.

The white-gold watch showed eight-twenty when Freddy walked out of the rooming house. He walked down Sixteenth to Ontario, then over to Broad and caught a cab. He gave the driver an address downtown. The cab's headlights merged with the flooded glare of southbound traffic. Freddy leaned back and lit a cigarette.

"Nice weather," the driver commented.

"Yes, it certainly is," Freddy said.

"I like it this time of year," the driver said, "it ain't too hot and it ain't too cold. It's just right." He glanced at the rear-view mirror and saw that his passenger was putting on a pair of dark glasses. He said, "You in show business?"

"No," Freddy said.

"What's the glasses for?"

Freddy didn't say anything.

"What's the glasses for?" the driver asked.

"The headlights hurt my eyes," Freddy said. He said it somewhat slowly, his tone indicating that he was rather tired and didn't feel like talking.

The driver shrugged and remained quiet for the rest of the ride. He brought the cab to a stop at the corner of Eleventh and Locust. The fare was a dollar twenty.

Freddy gave him two dollars and told him to keep the change. As the cab drove away, Freddy walked west on Locust to Twelfth, walked south on Twelfth, then turned west again, moving through a narrow alley. There were no lights in the alley except for a rectangle of green neon far down toward the other end. The rectangle was a glowing frame for the neon wording, *Billy's Hut*. It was also a beckoning finger for that special type of citizen who was never happy unless he was being taken over in a clip joint. They'd soon be flocking through the front entrance on Locust Street. But Freddy Lamb, moving toward the back entrance, had it checked in his mind that the place was empty now. The dial of his wrist watch showed eight-fifty-seven, and he knew it was too early for customers. He also knew that Billy Donofrio was sound asleep on a sofa in the back room, used as a private office. He knew it because he'd been watching Donofrio for more than two weeks and he was well acquainted with Donofrio's nightly habits.

When Freddy was fifteen yards away from *Billy's Hut*, he reached into his inner jacket pocket and took out a pair of white cotton gloves. When he was five yards away, he came to a stop and stood motionless, listening. There was the sound of a record-player from some upstairs flat on the other side of the alley. From another upstairs flat there was the noise of lesbian voices saying, "You did," and "I didn't," and "You did, you did—"

He listened for other sounds and there were none. He let the tip of his tongue come out just a little to moisten the centre of his lower lip. Then he took a few forward steps that brought him to a section of brick wall where the bricks were loose. He counted up from the bottom, the light from the green neon showing him the fourth brick, the fifth, the sixth and the seventh. The eighth brick was the one he wanted. He got a grip on its edges jutting away from the wall, pulled at it very slowly and carefully. Then he held it in one hand and his other hand reached into the empty space and made contact with the bone handle of a switchblade. It was a six-inch blade and he'd planted it there two nights ago.

He put the brick back in place and walked to the back door of *Billy's Hut*. Bending to the side to see through the window, he caught sight of Billy Donofrio on the sofa. Billy was flat on his back, one short leg dangling over the side of the sofa, one arm also dangling with fat fingers holding the stub of an unlit cigar. Billy was very short and very fat, and in his sleep he breathed as though it were a great effort. Billy was almost completely bald and what hair he had was more white than black. Billy was fifty-three years old and would never get to be fifty-four.

Freddy Lamb used a skeleton key to open the back door. He did it without sound. And then, without sound, he moved toward the sofa, his eyes focused on the crease of flesh between Billy's third chin and Billy's shirt collar. His arm went up and came down and the blade went into the crease, went in deep to cut the jugular vein, moved left, moved right, to widen the cut so that it was almost from ear to ear. Billy opened his eyes and tried to open his mouth but that was as far as he could take it. He tried to breathe and he couldn't breathe. He heard the voice of Freddy Lamb saying very softly, almost gently, "Good night, Billy." Then he heard Freddy's footsteps moving toward the door, and the door opening, and the footsteps walking out.

Billy didn't hear the door as it closed. By that time he was far away from hearing anything.

*

On Freddy's wrist, the hands of the white-gold watch pointed to nine twenty-six. He stood on the sidewalk near the entrance of a nightclub called "Yellow Cat." The place was located in a low-rent area of South Philadelphia, and the neighbouring structures were mostly tenements and garages and vacant lots heaped with rubbish. The club's exterior complied with the general trend; it was dingy and there was no paint on the wooden walls. But inside it was a different proposition. It was glittering and lavish, the drinks were expensive, and the floorshow featured a first-rate orchestra and singers and dancers. It also featured a unique type of strip-tease entertainment, a quintet of young females who took off their clothes while they sat at your table. For a reasonable bonus they'd let you keep the brassiere or garter or what-not for a souvenir.

The white-gold watch showed nine twenty-eight. Freddy decided to wait another two minutes. His appointment with the owner of "Yellow Cat" had been arranged for nine-thirty. He knew that Herman Charn was waiting anxiously for his arrival, but his personal theory of punctuality stipulated split-second precision, and since they'd made it for nine-thirty he'd see Herman at nine-thirty, not a moment earlier or later.

A taxi pulled up and a blonde stepped out. She paid the driver and walked toward Freddy and he said,

"Hello, Pearl."

Pearl smiled at him. "Kiss me hello."

"Not here," he said.

"Later?"

He nodded. He looked her up and down. She was five-five and weighed one-ten and Nature had given her a body that caused men's eyes to bulge. Freddy's eyes didn't bulge, although he told himself she was something

to see. He always enjoyed looking at her. He wondered if
he still enjoyed the nights with her. He'd been sharing
the nights with her for the past several months and it
had reached the point where he wasn't seeing any other
women and maybe he was missing out on something. For
just a moment he gazed past Pearl, telling himself that
she needed him more than he needed her, and knowing
it wouldn't be easy to get off the hook.

Well, there wasn't any hurry. He hadn't seen anything
else around that interested him. But he wished Pearl
would let up on the clinging routine. Maybe he'd really go
for her if she wasn't so hungry for him all the time.

Pearl stepped closer to him. The hunger showed in her
eyes. She said, "Know what I did today? I took a walk in
the park."

"You did?"

"Yeah," she said. "I went to Fairmount Park and took a
long walk. All by myself."

"That's nice," he said. He wondered what she was
getting at.

She said, "Let's do it together sometimes. Let's go for a
walk in the park. It's something we ain't never done. All
we do is drink and listen to jazz and find all sorts of ways
to knock ourselves out."

He gave her a closer look. This was a former call-girl
who'd done a stretch for prostitution, a longer stretch for
selling cocaine, and had finally decided she'd done
enough time and she might as well go legitimate. She'd
learned the art of stripping off her clothes before an
audience, and now at twenty-six she was earning a
hundred-and-a-half a week. It was clean money, as far as
the law was concerned, but maybe in her mind it wasn't
clean enough. Maybe she was getting funny ideas, like
this walk-in-the-park-routine. Maybe she'd soon be

thinking in terms of a cottage for two and a little lawn in the front and shopping for a baby carriage.

He wondered what she'd look like, wearing an apron and standing at a sink and washing dishes.

For some reason the thought disturbed him. He couldn't understand why it should disturb him. He heard her saying, "Can we do it, Freddy? Let's do it on Sunday. We'll go to Fairmount Park."

"We'll talk about it," he cut in quickly. He glanced at his wrist watch. "See you after the show."

He hurried through the club entrance, went past the hat-check counter, past the tables and across the dance-floor and toward a door marked "Private." There was a button adjoining the door and he pressed the button one short, two longs, another short and then there was a buzzing sound. He opened the door and walked into the office. It was a large room and the color motif was yellow-and-gray. The walls and ceiling were gray and the thick carpet was pale yellow. The furniture was bright yellow. There was a short skinny man standing near the desk and his face was gray. Seated at the desk was a large man whose face was a mixture of yellow and gray.

Freddy closed the door behind him. He walked toward the desk. He nodded to the short skinny man and then he looked at the large man and said, "Hello, Herman."

Herman glanced at a clock on the desk. He said, "You're right on time."

"He's always on time," said the short skinny man.

Herman looked at Freddy Lamb and said, "You do it?"

Before Freddy could answer, the short skinny man said, "Sure he did it."

"Shut up, Ziggy," Herman said. He had a soft, sort of gooey voice, as though he spoke with a lot of marsh-mallow in his mouth. He wore a suit of very soft fabric, thick and fleecy, and his thick hands pressed softly on the desktop. On the little finger of his left hand he wore a large star emerald that radiated a soft green light. Everything about him was soft, except for his eyes. His eyes were iron.

"You do it?" he repeated softly.

Freddy nodded.

"Any trouble?" Herman asked.

"He never has trouble," Ziggy said.

Herman looked at Ziggy. "I told you to shut up." Then, very softly, "Come here, Ziggy."

Ziggy hesitated. He had a ferret face that always looked sort of worried and now it looked very worried.

"Come here," Herman purred.

Ziggy approached the large man. Ziggy was blinking and swallowing hard. Herman reached out and slowly took hold of Ziggy's hand. Herman's thick fingers closed tightly on Ziggy's bony fingers, gave a yank. Ziggy moaned.

"When I tell you to shut up," Herman said, "you'll shut up." He smiled softly and paternally at Ziggy. "Right?"

"Right," Ziggy said. Then he moaned again. His fingers were free now and he looked down at them as an animal gazes sadly at its own crushed paws. He said, "They're all busted."

"They're not all busted," Herman said. "They're damaged just enough to let you know your place. That's one thing you must never forget. Every man who works for me has to know his place." He was still smiling at Ziggy. "Right?"

"Right," Ziggy moaned.

Then Herman looked at Freddy Lamb and said, "Right?"

Freddy didn't say anything. He was looking at Ziggy's

fingers. Then his gaze climbed to Ziggy's face. The lips quivered, as though Ziggy was trying to hold back sobs. Freddy remembered the time when nothing could hurt Ziggy, when Ziggy and himself were their own bosses and did their engineering on the waterfront. There were a lot of people on the waterfront who were willing to pay good money to have other people placed on stretchers or in caskets. In those days the rates had been fifteen dollars for a broken jaw, thirty for a fractured pelvis, and a hundred for the complete job. Ziggy handled the black-jack work and the bullet work and Freddy took care of such special functions as switchblade slicing, lye-in-the-eyes, and various powders and pills slipped into a glass of beer or wine or a cup of coffee. There were orders for all sorts of jobs in those days.

Fifteen months ago, he was thinking. And times had sure changed. The independent operator was swallowed up by the big combines. It was especially true in this line of business, which followed the theory that competition, no matter how small, was not good for the overall picture. So the moment had come when he and Ziggy had been approached with an offer, and they knew they had to accept, there wasn't any choice, if they didn't accept they'd be erased. They didn't need to be told about that. They just knew. As much as they hated to do it, they had to do it. The proposition was handed to them on a Wednesday afternoon and that same night they went to work for Herman Charn.

He heard Herman saying, "I'm talking to you, Freddy."

"I hear you," he said.

"You sure?" Herman asked softly. "You sure you hear me?"

Freddy looked at Herman. He said quietly, "I'm on your payroll. I do what you tell me to do. I've done every job exactly the way you wanted it done. Can I do any more than that?"

"Yes," Herman said. His tone was matter-of-fact. He glanced at Ziggy and said, "From here on it's a private discussion. Me and Freddy. Take a walk."

Ziggy's mouth opened just a little. He didn't seem to understand the command. He'd always been included in all the business conferences, and now the look in his eyes was a mixture of puzzlement and injury.

Herman smiled at Ziggy. He pointed to the door. Ziggy bit hard on his lip and moved toward the door and opened it and walked out of the room.

For some moments it was quiet in the room and Freddy had a feeling it was too quiet. He sensed that Herman Charn was aiming something at him, something that had nothing to do with the ordinary run of business.

There was the creaking sound of leather as Herman leaned back in the desk-chair. He folded his big soft fingers across his big soft belly and said, "Sit down, Freddy. Sit down and make yourself comfortable."

Freddy pulled a chair toward the desk. He sat down. He looked at the face of Herman and for just a moment the face became a wall that moved toward him. He winced, his insides quivered. It was a strange sensation, he'd never had it before and he couldn't understand it. But then the moment was gone and he sat there relaxed, his features expressionless, as he waited for Herman to speak.

Herman said, "Want a drink?"

Freddy shook his head.

"Smoke?" Herman lifted the lid of an enamelled cigarette-box.

"I got my own," Freddy murmured. He reached into his pocket and took out the flat silver case.

"Smoke one of mine," Herman said. He paused to signify it wasn't a suggestion, it was an order. And then, as though Freddy was a guest rather than an employee, "These smokes are special-made. Come from Egypt. Cost a dime apiece."

Freddy took one. Herman flicked a table-lighter, applied the flame to Freddy's cigarette, lit one for himself, took a slow, soft drag, and let the smoke come out of his nose. Herman waited until all of the smoke was out and then said, "You didn't like what I did to Ziggy."

It was a flat statement that didn't ask for an answer. Freddy sipped at the cigarette, not looking at Herman.

"You didn't like it," Herman persisted softly. "You never like it when I let Ziggy know who's boss."

Freddy shrugged. "That's between you and Ziggy."

"No," Herman said. And he spoke very slowly, with a pause between each word. "It isn't that way at all, I don't do it for Ziggy's benefit. He already knows who's top man around here."

Freddy didn't say anything. But he almost winced. And again his insides quivered.

Herman leaned forward. "Do you know who the top man is?"

"You," Freddy said.

Herman smiled. "Thanks, Freddy. Thanks for saying it." Then the smile vanished and Herman's eyes were hammerheads. "But I'm not sure you mean it."

Freddy took another sip from the Egyptian cigarette. It was strongly flavoured tobacco but somehow he wasn't getting any taste from it.

Herman kept leaning forward. "I gotta be sure, Freddy," he said. "You been working for me more than a year. And just like you said, you do all the jobs exactly the way I want them done. You plan them perfect, it's always clean and neat from start to finish. I don't mind saying you're one of the best. I don't think I've ever seen a cooler head. You're as cool as they come, an icicle on wheels."

"That's plenty cool," Freddy murmured.

"It sure is," Herman said. He let the pause drift in again. Then, his lips scarcely moving, "Maybe it's too cool."

Freddy looked at the hammerhead eyes. He wondered what showed in his own eyes. He wondered what thoughts were burning under the cool surface of his own brain.

He heard Herman saying, "I've done a lot of thinking about you. A lot more than you'd ever imagine. You're a puzzler, and one thing I always like to do is play stud poker with a puzzler."

Freddy smiled dimly. "Want to play stud poker?"

"We're playing it now. Without cards." Herman gazed down at the desk-top. His right hand was on the desk-top and he flicked his wrist as though he was turning over the hole-card. His voice was very soft as he said, "I want you to break it up with Pearl."

Freddy heard himself saying, "All right, Herman."

It was as though Freddy hadn't spoken. Herman said, "I'm waiting, Freddy."

"Waiting for what?" He told the dim smile to stay on his lips. It stayed there. He murmured, "You tell me to give her up and I say all right. What more do you want me to say."

"I want you to ask me why. Don't you want to know why?"

Freddy didn't reply. He still wore the dim smile and he was gazing past Herman's head.

"Come on, Freddy. I'm waiting to see your hole-card."

Freddy remained quiet.

"All right," Herman said. "I'll keep on showing you mine. I go for Pearl. I went for her the first time I laid eyes on her. That same night I took her home with me and she stayed over. She did what I wanted her to do but it didn't mean a thing to her, it was just like turning a trick. I thought it wouldn't bother me, once I have them in bed I can put them out of my mind. But this thing with Pearl, it's different. I've had her on my mind and it gets worse all the time and now it's gotten to the point where I have to do something about it. First thing I gotta do is clear the road."

"It's cleared," Freddy said. "I'll tell her tonight I'm not seeing her anymore."

"Just like that?" And Herman snapped his fingers.

"Yes," Freddy said. His fingers made the same sound. "Just like that."

Herman leaned back in the soft leather chair. He looked at the face of Freddy Lamb as though he was trying to solve a cryptogram. Finally he shook his head slowly, and then he gave a heavy sigh and he said, "All right, Freddy. That's all for now."

Freddy stood up. He started toward the door. Half-way across the room he stopped and turned and said, "You promised me a bonus for the Donofrio job."

"This is Monday," Herman said. "I hand out the pay on Friday."

"You said I'd be paid right off."

"Did I?" Herman smiled softly.

"Yes," Freddy said. "You said the deal on Donofrio was something special and the customer was paying fifteen hundred. You told me there was five hundred in it for me and I'd get the bonus the same night I did the job."

Herman opened a desk-drawer and took out a thick roll of bills.

"Can I have it in tens and twenties?" Freddy asked.

Herman lifted his eyebrows. "Why the small change?"

"I'm an elevator man," Freddy said. "The bank would wonder what I was doing with fifties."

"You're right," Herman said. He counted off the five hundred in tens and twenties, and handed the money to Freddy. He leaned back in the chair and watched Freddy folding the bills and pocketing them and walking out of the room. When the door was closed Herman said aloud to himself, "Don't try to figure him out, he's all ice and no soul, strictly a professional."

The white-gold watch showed eleven thirty-five. Freddy sat at a table watching the floor show and drinking from a tall glass of gin and ginger ale. The Yellow Cat was crowded now and Freddy wore the dark glasses and his table was in a darkly shadowed section of the room. He sat there with Ziggy and some other men who worked for Herman. There was Dino, who did his jobs at long range and always used a rifle. There was Shikey, six foot six and weighing three hundred pounds, an expert at bone cracking, gouging, and the removing of teeth. There was Riley, another bone-cracker and strangling specialist.

A tall pretty boy stood in front of the orchestra, clutching the mike as though it was the only support he had in the world. He sang with an ache in his voice, begging someone to "—please understand." The audience liked it and he sang it again. Then two coloured lap-dancers came out and worked themselves into a sweat and were gasping for breath as they finished the act. The M.C. walked on and motioned the orchestra to quiet down and grinned at ringside faces as he said, "Ready for dessert?"

"Yeah," a man shouted from ringside. "Let's have the dessert."

"All right," the M.C. said. He cupped his hands to his mouth and called off-stage, "Bring it out, we're all starved for that sweetmeat."

The orchestra went into medium tempo, the lights changed from glaring yellow to a soft violet. And then they came out, seven girls wearing horn-rimmed glasses and ultra-conservative costumes. They walked primly, and all together they resembled the stiff-necked females in a cartoon lampooning the W.C.T.U. It got a big laugh from the audience, and there was some appreciative applause. The young ladies formed a line and slowly waved black parasols as they sang, "—Father, oh father, come home with me now." But then it became, "—Daddy, oh daddy, come home with me now." And as they empha-sized the daddy angle, they broke up the line and dis-carded the parasols and took off their ankle-length dark-blue coats. Then, their fingers loosening the buttons of dark-blue dresses, they moved separately toward the ringside tables. The patrons in the back stood up to get a better look and in the balcony the lenses of seven lamps were focused on seven young women getting undressed.

Dino, who had a footwear fetish, said loudly, "I'll pay forty for a high-heeled shoe."

One of the girls took off her shoe and flung it toward Freddy's table. Shikey caught it and handed it to Dino. A waiter came over and Dino handed him four tens and he took the money to the girl. Riley looked puzzledly at Dino and said, "Whatcha gonna do with a high-heeled shoe?" And Shikey said, "He boils 'em and eats 'em." But Ziggy had another theory. "He bangs the heel against his head," Ziggy said. "That's the way he gets his kicks." Dino sat there gazing lovingly at the shoe in his hand while his other hand caressed the kidskin surface. Then gradually his eyes closed and he murmured, "This is nice, this is so nice."

Riley was watching Dino and saying, "I don't get it."

Ziggy shrugged philosophically. "Some things," he said, "just can't be understood."

"You're so right." It was Freddy talking. He didn't know his lips were making sound. He was looking across the tables at Pearl. She sat with some ringsiders and already she'd taken off considerable clothing, she was half-naked. On her face there was a detached look and her hands moved mechanically as she unbuttoned the buttons and unzipped the zippers. There were three men sitting with her and their eyes feasted on her, they had their mouths open in a sort of mingled fascination and worship. At nearby tables the other strippers were performing but they weren't getting undivided attention. Most of the men were watching Pearl. One of them offered a hundred dollars for her stocking. She took off the stocking and let it dangle from her fingers. In a semi-whisper she asked if there were any higher bids. Freddy told himself that she wasn't happy doing what she was doing. Again he could hear her plaintive voice as she asked him to take her for a walk in the park. Suddenly he knew that he'd like that very much. He wanted to see the sun shining on her hair, instead of the night-club lights. He heard himself saying aloud, "Five hundred."

He didn't shout it, but at the ringside tables they all heard it, and for a moment there was stunned silence. At his own table the silence was very thick. He could feel the pressure of it, and the moment seemed to have substance, something on the order of iron wheels going around and around, making no sound and getting nowhere.

Some things just can't be understood, he thought. He was taking the tens and twenties from his jacket pocket. The five hundred seemed to prove the truth of Ziggy's vague philosophy. Freddy got up from his chair and moved toward an empty table behind some potted ferns adjacent to the orchestra stand. He sat down and placed green money on a yellow tablecloth. He wasn't looking at Pearl as she approached the table. From ringside an awed voice was saying, "For one silk stocking she gets half a grand—"

She seated herself at the table. He shoved the money toward her. He said, "There's your cash. Let's have the stocking."

"This a gag?" she asked quietly. Her eyes were somewhat sullen. There was some laughter from the table where Ziggy and some of the others were seated; they now had the notion it was some sort of joke.

Freddy said, "Take off the stocking."

She looked at the pile of tens and twenties. She said, "Whatcha want the stocking for?"

"Souvenir," he said.

It was the tone of his voice that did it. Her face paled. She started to shake her head very slowly, as though she couldn't believe him.

"Yes," he said, with just the trace of a sigh. "It's all over, Pearl. It's the end of the line."

She went on shaking her head. She couldn't talk.

He said, "I'll hang the stocking in my bedroom."

She was biting her lip, "It's a long time till Christmas."

"For some people it's never Christmas."

"Freddy—" She leaned toward him. "What's it all about? Why're you doing this?"

He shrugged. He didn't say anything.

Her eyes were getting wet. "You won't even give me a reason?"

All he gave her was a cool smile. Then his head was turned and he saw the faces at Ziggy's table and then he focussed on the face of the large man who stood behind the table. He saw the iron in the eyes of Herman Charn. He told himself he was doing what Herman had told him to do. And just then he felt the quiver in his insides. It was mostly in the spine as though his spine was gradually turning to jelly.

He spoke to himself without sound. He said, *No, it isn't that, it can't be that.*

Pearl was saying, "All right, Freddy, if that's the way it is."

He nodded very slowly.

Pearl bent over and took the stocking off her leg. She placed the stocking on the table. She picked up the five hundred, counted it off to make sure it was all there.

Then she stood up and said, "No charge, mister. I'd rather keep the memories."

She put the tens and twenties on the tablecloth and walked away. Freddy glanced off to the side and saw a soft smile on the face of Herman Charn.

The floor-show was ended and Freddy was still sitting there at the table. There was a bottle of bourbon in front of him. It had been there for less than twenty minutes and already it was half-empty. There was also a pitcher of ice-water and the pitcher was full. He didn't need a chaser because he couldn't taste the whiskey. He was drinking the whiskey from the water-glass.

A voice said, "Freddy—"

And then a hand tugged at his arm. He looked up and saw Ziggy sitting beside him.

He smiled at Ziggy. He motioned toward the bottle and shot-glass and said, "Have a drink."

Ziggy shrugged. "I might as well while I got the chance. At the rate you're going, that bottle'll soon be empty."

"It's very good bourbon," Freddy said.

"Yeah?" Ziggy was pouring a glass for himself. He swished the liquor into his mouth. Then, looking closely at Freddy, "You don't care whether it's good or not. You'd be gulping it if it was shoe-polish."

Freddy was staring at the tablecloth. "Let's go somewhere and drink some shoe-polish."

Ziggy tugged again at Freddy's arm. He said, "Come out of it."

"Come out of what?"

"The clouds," Ziggy said. "You're in the clouds."

"It's nice in the clouds." Freddy said. "I'm up here having a dandy time. I'm floating."

"Floating? You're drowning." Ziggy pulled urgently at his arm, to get his hand away from a water-glass filled with whiskey. "You're not a drinker, Freddy. What do you want to do, drink yourself into a hospital?"

Freddy grinned. He aimed the grin at nothing in particular. For some moments he sat there motionless. Then he reached into his jacket pocket and took out the silk stocking. He showed it to Ziggy and said, "Look what I got."

"Yeah," Ziggy said. "I seen her give it to you. What's the score on that routine?"

"No score," Freddy said. He went on grinning. "It's a funny way to end a game. Nothing on the scoreboard. Nothing at all."

Ziggy frowned. "You trying to tell me something?"

Freddy looked at the whiskey in the water-glass. He said, "I packed her in."

"No," Ziggy said. His tone was incredulous. "Not Pearl. Not that pigeon. That ain't no ordinary merchandise. You wouldn't walk out on Pearl unless you had a very special reason."

"It was special, all right."

"Tell me about it, Freddy." There was something plaintive in Ziggy's voice, a certain feeling for Freddy that he couldn't put into words. The closest he could get to it was: "After all, I'm on your side, ain't I?"

"No," Freddy said. The grin was slowly fading. "You're on Herman's side." He gazed past Ziggy's head. "We're all on Herman's side."

"Herman? What's he got to do with it?"

"Everything," Freddy said. "Herman's the boss, remember?" He looked at the swollen fingers of Ziggy's right hand. "Herman wants something done, it's got to be done. He gave me orders to break with Pearl. He's the employer and I'm the hired man, so I did what I had to do. I carried out his orders."

Ziggy was quiet for some moments. Then, very quietly, "Well, it figures he wants her for himself. But it don't seem right. It just ain't fair."

"Don't make me laugh," Freddy said. "Who the hell are we to say what's fair?"

"We're human, aren't we?"

"No," Freddy said. He gazed past Ziggy's head. "I don't know what we are. But I know one thing, we're not human. We can't afford to be human, not in this line of business."

Ziggy didn't get it. It was just a little too deep for him. All he could say was, "You getting funny ideas?"

"I'm not reaching for them, they're just coming to me."

"Take another drink," Ziggy said.

"I'd rather have the laughs." Freddy showed the grin again. "It's really comical, you know? Especially this thing with Pearl. I was thinking of calling it quits anyway. You know how it is with me, Ziggy. I never like to be tied down to one skirt. But tonight Pearl said something that spun me around. We were talking outside the club and she brought it in out of left field. She asked me to take her for a walk in the park."

Ziggy blinked a few times. "What?"

"A walk in the park," Freddy said.

"What for?" Ziggy wanted to know. "She gettin' square all of a sudden? She wanna go around picking flowers?"

"I don't know," Freddy said. "All she said was, it's very nice in Fairmount Park. She asked me to take her there and we'd be together in the park, just taking a walk."

Ziggy pointed to the glass. "You better take that drink."

Freddy reached for the glass. But someone else's hand was there first. He saw the thick soft fingers, the soft green glow of the star-emerald. As the glass of whiskey was shoved out of his reach, he looked up and saw the soft smile on the face of Herman Charn.

"Too much liquor is bad for the kidneys," Herman said. He bent down lower to peer at Freddy's eyes. "You look knocked-out, Freddy. There's a soft couch in the office. Go in there and lie down for awhile."

Freddy got up from the chair. He was somewhat unsteady on his feet. Herman took his arm and helped him make it down the aisle past the tables to the door of the office. He could feel the pressure of Herman's hand on his arm. It was very soft pressure but somehow it felt like a clamp of iron biting into his flesh.

Herman opened the office-door and guided him toward the couch. He fell onto the couch, sent an idiotic grin toward the ceiling, then closed his eyes and went to sleep.

He slept until four-forty in the morning. The sound that woke him up was a scream.

At first it was all blurred, there was too much whiskey-fog in his brain, he had no idea where he was or what was happening. He pushed his knuckles against his eyes. Then, sitting up, he focused on the faces in the room. He saw Shikey and Riley and they had girls sitting in their laps. They were on the other couch at the opposite side of the room. He saw Dino standing near the couch with his arm around the waist of a slim brunette. Then he glanced toward the door and he saw Ziggy. That made seven faces for him to look at. He told himself to keep looking at them. If he concentrated on that, maybe he wouldn't hear the screaming.

But he heard it. The scream was an animal sound and yet he recognized the voice. It came from near the desk and he turned his head very slowly, telling himself he didn't want to look but knowing he had to look.

He saw Pearl kneeling on the floor. Herman stood behind her. With one hand he was twisting her arm up high between her shoulder blades. His other hand was on her head and he was pulling her hair so that her face was drawn back, her throat stretched.

Herman spoke very softly. "You make me very unhappy, Pearl. I don't like to be unhappy."

Then Herman gave her arm another upward twist and pulled tighter on her hair and she screamed again.

The girl in Shikey's lap gave Pearl a scornful look and said, "You're a damn fool."

"In spades." It came from the stripper who nestled

against Riley. "All he wants her to do is kiss him like she means it."

Freddy told himself to get up and walk out of the room. He lifted himself from the couch and took a few steps toward the door and heard Herman saying, "Not yet, Freddy. I'll tell you when to go."

He went back to the couch and sat down.

Herman said, "Be sensible, Pearl. Why can't you be sensible?"

Pearl opened her mouth to scream again. But no sound came out. There was too much pain and it was choking her.

The brunette who stood with Dino was saying, "It's a waste of time, Herman, she can't give you what she hasn't got. She just don't have it for you, Herman."

"She'll have it for him," Dino said. "Before he's finished, he'll have her crawling on her belly."

Herman looked at Dino. "No," he said. "She won't do that. I wouldn't let her do that." He cast a downward glance at Pearl. His lips shaped a soft smile. There was something tender in the smile and in his voice. "Pearl, tell me something, why don't you want me?"

He gave her a chance to reply, his fingers slackening the grip on her wrist and her hair. She groaned a few times and then she said, "You got my body, Herman. You can have my body anytime you want it."

"That isn't enough," Herman said. "I want you all the way, a hundred percent. It's got to be like that, Pearl. You're in me so deep it just can't take any other route. It's got to be you and me from here on in, you gotta need me just as much as I need you."

"But Herman—" She gave a dry sob. "I can't lie to you. I just don't feel that way."

"You're gonna feel that way," Herman said.

"No." Pearl sobbed again. "No. No."

"Why not?" He was pulling her hair again, twisting her arm. But it seemed he was suffering more than Pearl. The pain racked his pleading voice. "Why can't you feel something for me?"

Her reply was made without sound. She managed to turn her head just a little, toward the couch. And everyone in the room saw her looking at Freddy.

Herman's face became very pale. His features tightened and twisted and it seemed he was about to burst into tears. He stared up at the ceiling.

Herman shivered. His body shook spasmodically, as though he stood on a vibrating platform. Then all at once the tormented look faded from his eyes, the iron came into his eyes, and the soft smile came onto his lips. He released Pearl, turned away from her, went to the desk and opened the cigarette-box. It was very quiet in the room while Herman stood there lighting the cigarette. He took a slow, easy drag and then he said quietly, "All right, Pearl, you can go home now."

She started to get up from the floor. The brunette came over and helped her up.

"I'll call a cab for you," Herman said. He reached for the telephone and put in the call. As he lowered the phone, he was looking at Pearl and saying, "You want to go home alone?"

Pearl didn't say anything. Her head was lowered and she was leaning against the shoulder of the brunette.

Herman said, "You want Freddy to take you home?"

Pearl raised her head just a little and looked at the face of Freddy Lamb.

Herman laughed softly. "All right," he said. "Freddy'll take you home."

Freddy winced. He sat there staring at the carpet.

Herman told the brunette to fix a drink for Pearl. He said, "Take her to the bar and give her anything she wants." He motioned to the other girls and they got up from the laps of Shikey and Riley. Then all the girls walked out of the room. Herman was quiet for some moments, taking slow drags at the cigarette and looking at the door. Then gradually his head turned and he looked at Freddy. He said, "You're slated, Freddy."

Freddy went on staring at the carpet.

"You're gonna bump her," Herman said.

Freddy closed his eyes.

"Take her somewhere and bump her and bury her," Herman said.

Shikey and Riley looked at each other. Dino had his mouth open and he was staring at Herman. Standing next to the door, Ziggy had his eyes glued to Freddy's face.

"She goes," Herman said. And then, speaking aloud to himself, "She goes because she gives me grief." He hit his hand against his chest. "She hits me here, where I live. Hits me too hard. Hurts me. I don't appreciate getting hurt. Especially here." Again his hand thumped his chest. He said, "You'll do it, Freddy. You'll see to it that I get rid of the hurt."

"Let me do it," Ziggy said. Herman shook his head. He pointed a finger at Freddy. His finger jabbed empty air, and he said, "Freddy does it. Freddy."

Ziggy opened his mouth, tried to close it, couldn't close it, and blurted, "Why take it out on him?"

"That's a stupid question," Herman said mildly. "I'm not taking it out on anybody. I'm giving the job to Freddy because I know he's dependable. I can always depend on Freddy."

Ziggy made a final frantic try. "Please, Herman," he said. "Please don't make him do it."

Herman didn't bother to reply. All he did was give Ziggy a slow appraising look up and down. It was like a soundless warning to Ziggy, letting him know he was walking on thin ice and the ice would crack if he opened his mouth again.

Then Herman turned to Freddy and said, "Where's your blade?"

"Stashed," Freddy said. He was still staring at the carpet.

Herman opened a desk-drawer. He took out a black-handled switch-blade. "Use this," he said, coming toward the couch. He handed the knife to Freddy. "Give it a try," he said.

Freddy pressed the button. The blade flicked out. It glimmered blue-white. He pushed the blade into the handle and tried the button again. He went on trying the button and watching the flash of the blade. It was quiet in the room as the blade went in and out, in and out. Then from the street there was the sound of a horn. Herman said, "That's the taxi." Freddy nodded and got up from the sofa and walked out of the room. As he moved toward the girls who stood at the cocktail bar, he could feel the weight of the knife in the inner pocket of his jacket. He was looking at Pearl and saying, "Come on, let's go," and as he said it, the blade seemed to come out of the knife and slice into his own flesh.

The taxi was cruising north on Sixteenth Street. On Freddy's wrist the white-gold watch said five-twenty. He was watching the parade of unlit windows along the dark street. Pearl was saying something but he didn't hear her. She spoke just a bit louder and he turned and looked at her. He smiled and murmured, "Sorry, I wasn't listening."

"Can't you sit closer?"

He moved closer to her. A mixture of moonlight and streetlamp glow came pouring into the back seat of the taxi and illuminated her face. He saw something in her eyes that caused him to blink several times.

She noticed the way he was blinking and said, "What's the matter?"

He didn't answer. He tried to stop blinking and he couldn't stop.

"Hangover?" Pearl asked.

"No," he said. "I feel alright now, I feel fine."

For some moments she didn't say anything. She was rubbing her sore arm. She tried to stretch it, winced and gasped with pain, and said, "Oh Jesus, it hurts. It really hurts. Maybe it's broken."

"Let me feel it," he said. He put his hand on her arm. He ran his fingers down from above her elbow to her wrist. "It isn't broken," he murmured. "Just a little swollen, that's all. Sprained some ligaments."

She smiled at him. "The hurt goes away when you touch it."

He tried not to look at her, but something fastened his eyes to her face. He kept his hand on her arm. He heard himself saying, "I feel sorry for Herman. If he could see you now, I mean if you'd look at him like you're looking at me—"

"Freddy," she said. "Freddy." Then she leaned toward him. She rested her head on his shoulder.

Then somehow everything was quiet and still and he didn't hear the noise of the taxi's engine, he didn't feel the bumps as the wheels hit the ruts in the cobblestoned surface of Sixteenth Street. But suddenly there was a deep rut and the taxi gave a lurch. He looked up and heard the driver cursing the city engineers. "Goddamit," the driver said. "They got a deal with the tire companies."

Freddy stared past the driver's head, his eyes aimed through the windshield to see the wide intersection where Sixteenth Street met the Parkway. The Parkway was a six-laned drive slanting to the left of the downtown area, going away from the concrete of Philadelphia skyscrapers and pointing toward the green of Fairmount Park.

"Turn left," Freddy said.

They were approaching the intersection, and the driver gave a backward glance. "Left?" the driver asked. "That takes us outta the way. You gave me an address on Seventeenth near Lehigh. We gotta hit it from Sixteenth—"

"I know," Freddy said quietly. "But turn left anyway."

The driver shrugged. "You're the captain." He beat the yellow of a traffic light and the taxi made a left turn onto the Parkway.

Pearl said, "What's this, Freddy? Where're we going?"

"In the park." He wasn't looking at her. "We're gonna do what you said we should do. We're gonna take a walk in the park."

"For real?" Her eyes were lit up. She shook her head, as though she could scarcely believe what he'd just said.

"We'll take a nice walk," he murmured. "Just the two of us. The way you wanted it."

"Oh," she breathed. "Oh, Freddy—"

The driver shrugged again. The taxi went past the big monuments and fountains of Logan Circle, past the Rodin Museum and the Art Museum and onto River Drive. For a mile or so they stayed on the highway, bordering the moonlit water of the river, and then without being told the driver made a turn off the highway, made a series of turns that took them deep into the park. They came to a section where there were no lights, no movement, no sound except the autumn wind drifting through the trees and bushes and tall grass and flowers.

"Stop here," Freddy said.

The taxi came to a stop. They got out and he paid the driver. The driver gave him a queer look and said, "You sure picked a lonely spot."

Freddy looked at the cabman. He didn't say anything.

The driver said, "You're at least three miles off the highway. It's gonna be a problem getting a ride home."

"Is it your problem?" Freddy asked gently.

"Well, no—"

"Then don't worry about it," Freddy said. He smiled amiably. The driver threw a glance at the blonde, smiled, and told himself that the man might have the right idea, after all. With an item like that, any man would want complete privacy. He thought of the bony, buck-toothed woman who waited for him at home, crinkled his face in a distasteful grimace, put the car in gear and drove away.

"Ain't it nice?" Pearl said. "Ain't it wonderful?"

They were walking through a glade where the moonlight showed the autumn colours of fallen leaves. The night air was fragrant with the blended aromas of wild flowers. He had his arm around her shoulder and was leading her toward a narrow lane slopping downward through the trees.

She laughed lightly, happily. "It's like as if you know the place. As if you've been here before."

"No," he said. "I've never been here before."

There was the tinkling sound of a nearby brook. A bird chirped in the bushes. Another bird sang a tender reply.

"Listen," Pearl murmured. "Listen to them."

He listened to the singing of the birds. Now he was guiding Pearl down along the slope and seeing the way it levelled at the bottom and then went up again on all sides. It was a tiny valley down there with the brook running along the edge. He told himself it would happen when they reached the bottom.

He heard Pearl saying, "Wouldn't it be nice if we could stay here?"

He looked at her. "Stay here?"

"Yes," she said. "If we could live here for the rest of our lives. Just be here, away from everything—"

"We'd get lonesome."

"No we wouldn't," she said. "We'd always have company. I'd have you and you'd have me."

They were nearing the bottom of the slope. It was sort of steep now and they had to move slowly. All at once she stumbled and pitched forward and he caught her before she could fall on her face. He steadied her, smiled at her and said, "Okay?"

She nodded. She stood very close to him and gazed into his eyes and said, "You wouldn't let me fall, would you?"

The smile faded. He stared past her. "Not if I could help it."

"I know," she said. "You don't have to tell me."

He went on staring past her. "Tell you what?"

"The situation." She spoke softly, almost in a whisper. "I got it figured, Freddy. It's so easy to figure."

He wanted to close his eyes, he didn't know why he wanted to close his eyes.

He heard her saying, "I know why you packed me in tonight. Orders from Herman."

"That's right." He said it automatically, as though the mention of the name was the shifting of a gear.

"And another thing," she said. "I know why you brought me here." There was a pause, and then, very softly, "Herman."

He nodded.

She started to cry. It was quiet weeping and contained no fear, no hysteria. It was the weeping of farewell. She was crying because she was sad. Then, very slowly, she took the few remaining steps going down to the bottom of the slope. He stood there and watched her as she faced about to look up at him.

He walked down to where she stood, smiling at her and trying to pretend his hand was not on the switchblade in his pocket. He tried to make himself believe he wasn't going to do it, but he knew that wasn't true. He'd been slated for this job. The combine had him listed as a top-rated operator, one of the best in the business. He'd expended a lot of effort to attain that reputation, to be known as the grade-A expert who'd never muffed an assignment.

He begged himself to stop. He couldn't stop. The knife was open in his hand and his arm flashed out and sideways with the blade sliding in neatly and precisely, cutting the flesh of her throat. She went down very slowly, tried to cough, made a few gurgling sounds, and then rolled over on her back and died looking up at him.

For a long time he stared at her face. There was no expression on her features now. At first he didn't feel anything, and then he realized she was dead, and he had killed her.

He tried to tell himself there was nothing else he could have done, but even though that was true it didn't do any good. He took his glance away from her face and looked down at the white-gold watch to check the hour and the minute, automatically. But somehow the dial was blurred, as though the hands were spinning like tiny propellers. He had the weird feeling that the watch was showing Time traveling backward, so that he found himself checking it in terms of years and decades. He went all the way back to the day when he was eleven years old and they took him to reform school.

In reform school he was taught a lot of things. The thing he learned best was the way to use a knife. The knife became his profession. But somewhere along the line he caught onto the idea of holding a daytime job to cover his night-time activities. He worked in stockrooms and he did some window-cleaning and drove a truck for a fruit-dealer. And finally he became an elevator operator and that was the job he liked best. He'd never realized why he liked it so much but he realized now. He knew that the elevator was nothing more than a moving cell, that the only place for him was a cell. The passengers were just a lot of friendly visitors walking in and out, saying "Good morning, Freddy," and "Good night, Freddy," and they were such nice people. Just the thought of them brought a tender smile to his lips.

Then he realized he was smiling down at her. He sensed a faint glow coming from somewhere, lighting her face. For an instant he had no idea what it was. Then he realized it came from the sky. It was the first signal of approaching sunrise.

The white-gold watch showed five fifty-three. Freddy Lamb told himself to get moving. For some reason he couldn't move. He was looking down at the dead girl. His hand was still clenched about the switchblade, and as he tried to relax it he almost dropped the knife. He looked down at it.

The combine was a cell, too, he told himself. The combine was an elevator from which he could never escape.

It was going steadily downwards and there were no stops until the end. There was no way to get out.

Herman had made him kill the girl. Herman would make him do other things. And there was no getting away from that. If he killed Herman there would be someone else.

The elevator was carrying Freddy steadily downward. Already, he had left Pearl somewhere far above him. He realized it all at once, and an unreasonable terror filled him.

Freddy looked at the white-gold watch again. A minute had passed and he knew suddenly that he was slated to do a job on someone in exactly three minutes now. The minutes passed and he stood there alone.

At precisely five fifty-seven he said goodbye to his profession and plunged the blade into his heart.

Black Pudding

They had spotted him on Race Street between Ninth and Tenth. It was Chinatown in the tenderloin of Philadelphia and he stood gazing into the window of the Wong Ho restaurant and wishing he had the cash to buy himself some egg-foo-yung. The menu in the window priced egg-foo-yung at eighty cents an order and he had exactly thirty-one cents in his pocket. He shrugged and started to turn away from the window and just then he heard them coming.

It was their footsteps that told him who they were. There was the squeaky sound of Oscar's brand-new shoes. And the clumping noise of Coley's heavy feet. It was nine years since he'd heard their footsteps but he remembered that Oscar had a weakness for new shoes and Coley always walked heavy.

He faced them. They were smiling at him, their features somewhat greenish under the green neon glow that drifted through after-midnight blackness. He saw the weasel eyes and buzzard nose of little Oscar. He transferred his gaze to the thick lips and puffed-out cheeks of tall, obese Coley.

"Hello, Ken." It was Oscar's purring voice, Oscar's lips scarcely moving.

"Hello," he said to both of them. He blinked a few times. Now the shock was coming. He could feel the waves of shock surging toward him.

"We have been looking for you," Coley said. He flipped

his thick thumb over his shoulder to indicate the black Olds 88 parked across the street. "We've driven that car clear across the country."

Ken blinked again. The shock had hit him and now it was past and he was blinking from worry. He knew why they'd been looking for him and he was very worried.

He said quietly, "How'd you know I was in Philly?"

"Grapevine," Oscar said. "It's strictly coast-to-coast. It starts in San Quentin and we get tipped-off in Los Angeles. It's a letter telling the Boss you been paroled. That's three weeks ago. Then we get the letters from Denver and Omaha and a wire from Chicago. And then a phone call from Detroit. We wait to see how far east you'll travel. Finally we get the call from Philly, and the man tells us you're on the bum around Skid Row."

Ken shrugged. He tried to sound casual as he said, "Three thousand miles is a long trip. You must have been anxious to see me."

Oscar nodded. "Very anxious."

He sort of floated closer to Ken. And Coley also moved in. It was slow and quiet and it didn't seem like menace but they were crowding him and finally they had him backed up against the restaurant window.

He said to himself, *They've got you, they've found you and they've got you and you're finished.*

He shrugged again. "You can't do it here."

"Can't we?" Oscar purred.

"It's a crowded street," Ken said. He turned his head to look at the lazy tenderloin citizens on both sides of the street. He saw the bums and the beggars, the winos and the gin heads, the yellow faces of middle-aged opium smokers and the grey faces of two-bit scufflers and hustlers.

"Don't look at them," Oscar said. "They can't help you. Even if they could, they wouldn't."

Ken's smile was sad and resigned.

"You're so right," he said. His shoulders drooped and his head went down and he saw Oscar reaching into a jacket pocket and taking out the silver-handled tool that had a button on it to release a five-inch blade. He knew there would be no further talk, only action, and it would happen within the next split second.

In that tiny fraction of time, some gears clanged to shift from low to high in Ken's brain. His senses and reflexes, dulled from nine years in prison, were suddenly keen and acutely technical and there was no emotion on his face as he moved. He moved very fast, his arms crossing to shape an X, the left hand flat and rigid and banging against Oscar's wrist, the right hand a fist that caught Coley in the mouth. It sent the two of them staggering backward and gave him the space he wanted and he darted through the gap, sprinting east on Race Street toward Ninth.

As he turned the corner to head north on Ninth, he glanced backward and saw them getting into the Olds. He took a deep breath and continued running up Ninth. He ran straight ahead for approximately fifteen yards and then turned again to make a dash down a narrow alley. In the middle of the alley he hopped a fence, ran across a backyard, hopped another fence, then a few more backyards with more fencehopping, and then the opened window of a tenement cellar. He lunged at the window, went in head-first, groped for a handhold but couldn't find any, and then plunged through eight feet of blackness onto a pile of empty boxes and tin cans. He landed on his side, his thigh taking most of the impact, so that it didn't hurt too much. He rolled over and hit the floor and lay there flat on his belly. From a few feet away a pair of green eyes stared at him and he stared back, and then he grinned as though to say, *Don't be afraid, pussy, stay here and keep me company, it's a tough life and an evil world and us alley cats got to stick together*.

But the cat wasn't trusting a living soul. It let out a soft meow and scampered away. Ken sighed and his grin faded and he felt the pressure of the blackness and the quiet and the loneliness. His mind reached slowly for the road going backward nine years . . .

It was Los Angeles, and they were a small outfit operating from a first-floor apartment near Figueroa and Jefferson. Their business was armed robbery and their work-area included Beverly Hills and Bel-Air and the wealthy residential districts of Pasadena. They concentrated on expensive jewellery and wouldn't touch any job that offered less than a ten-grand haul.

There were five of them, Ken and Oscar and Coley and Ken's wife and the Boss. The name of the Boss was Riker and he was very kind to Ken until the face and body of Ken's wife became a need and then a craving and finally an obsession. It showed in Riker's eyes whenever he looked at her. She was a platinum blonde dancer, a former burlesque dancer named Hilda. She'd been married to Ken for seven months when Riker reached the point where he couldn't stand it any longer and during a job in Bel-Air he banged Ken's skull with the butt end of a revolver. When the police arrived, Ken was unconscious on the floor and later in the hospital they asked him questions but he wouldn't answer. In the courtroom he sat with his head bandaged and they asked him more questions and he wouldn't answer. They gave him five-to-twenty and during his first month in San Quentin he learned from his lawyer that Hilda had obtained a Reno divorce and was married to Riker. He went more or less insane and couldn't be handled and they put him in solitary.

Later they had him in the infirmary, chained to the bed, and they tried some psychology. They told him he'd regain his emotional health if he'd talk and name some names. He laughed at them. Whenever they coaxed him to talk, he laughed in their faces and presently they'd shrug and walk away. His first few years in Quentin were spent either in solitary or the infirmary, or under special guard. Then, gradually, he quieted down. He became very quiet and in the laundry-room he worked very hard and was extremely co-operative. During the fifth year he was up for parole and they asked him about the Bel-Air job and he replied quite reasonably that he couldn't remember, he was afraid to remember, he wanted to forget all about it and arrange a new life for himself. They told him he'd talk or he'd do the limit. He said he was sorry but he couldn't give them the information they wanted. He explained that he was trying to get straight with himself and be clean inside and he wouldn't feel clean if he earned his freedom that way. So then it was nine years and they were convinced he'd finally paid his debt to the people of California. They gave him a suit of clothes and a ten-dollar bill and told him he was a free man.

In a Sacramento hash-house he worked as a dish-washer just long enough to earn the bus-fare for a trip across the country. He was thinking in terms of the town where he'd made a wrong start in Philadelphia and the thing to do was go back there and start again and make it right this time, really legitimate. The parole board okayed the job he'd been promised. That was a healthy thought and it made the bus-trip very enjoyable. But the nicest thing about the bus was its fast engine that took him away from California, far away from certain faces he didn't want to see.

Yet now, as he rested on the floor of the tenement cellar, he could see the faces again. The faces were worried and frightened and he saw them in his brain and heard their trembling voices. He heard Riker saying, "They've released him from Quentin. We'll have to do something."

And Hilda saying, "What can we do?" And Riker replying, "We'll get him before he gets us."

He sat up, colliding with an empty tin can that rolled across the floor and made a clatter. For some moments there was quiet and then he heard a shuffling sound and a voice saying, "Who's there?"

It was a female voice, sort of a cracked whisper. It had a touch of asthma in it, some alcohol, and something else that had no connection with health or happiness.

Ken didn't say anything. He hoped she'd go away. Maybe she'd figure it was a rat that had knocked over the tin can and she wouldn't bother to investigate.

But he heard the shuffling footsteps approaching through the blackness. He focused directly ahead and saw the silhouette coming toward him. She was on the slender side, neatly constructed. It was a very interesting silhouette. Her height was approximately five-five and he estimated her weight in the neighborhood of one-ten. He sat up straighter. She was very anxious to get a look at his face.

She came close and there was the scratchy sound of a match against a matchbook. The match flared and he saw her face. She had medium-brown eyes that matched the color of her hair, and her nose and lips were nicely sculptured, somewhat delicate but blending prettily with the shape of her head.

He told himself she was a very pretty girl. But just then he saw the scar.

It was a wide jagged scar that started high on her forehead and crawled down the side of her face and ended less than an inch above her upper lip. The color of it was a livid purple with lateral streaks of pink and white. It was a terrible scar, really hideous.

She saw that he was wincing, but it didn't seem to bother her. The lit match stayed lit and she was sizing him up. She saw a man of medium height and weight, about thirty-six years old, with yellow hair that needed cutting, a face that needed shaving, and sad lonely grey eyes that needed someone's smile.

She tried to smile for him. But only one side of her mouth could manage it. On the other side the scar was like a hook that pulled at her flesh and caused a grimace that was more anguish than physical pain. He told himself it was a damn shame. Such a pretty girl. And so young. She couldn't be more than twenty-five. Well, some people had all the luck. All the rotten luck.

The match was burned halfway down when she reached into the pocket of a tattered dress and took out a candle. She went through the process of lighting the candle and melting the base of it. The softened wax adhered to the cement floor of the cellar and she sat down facing him and said quietly, "All right, let's have it. What's the pitch?"

He pointed backward to the opened window to indicate the November night. He said, "It's chilly out there. I came in to get warm."

She leaned forward just a little to peer at his eyes. Then, shaking her head slowly, she murmured, "No sale."

He shrugged. He didn't say anything.

"Come on," she urged gently. "Let's try again."

"All right." He grinned at her. And then it came out easily. "I'm hiding."

"From the Law?"

"No," he said. "From trouble."

He started to tell her about it. He couldn't understand why he was telling her. It didn't make sense that he should be spilling the story to someone he'd just met in a dark cellar, someone out of nowhere. But she was company and he needed company. He went on telling her.

It took more than an hour. He was providing all the details of events stretched across nine years. The candle-light showed her sitting there, not moving, her eyes riveted to his face as he spoke in low tones. Sometimes there were pauses, some of them long, some very long, but she never interrupted, she waited patiently while he groped for the words to make the meaning clear.

Finally, he said, "It's a cinch they won't stop, they'll get me sooner or later."

"If they find you," she said.

"They'll find me."

"Not here."

He stared at the flickering candle.

"They'll spend money to get information. There's more than one big mouth in this neighborhood. And the biggest mouths of all belong to the landlords."

"There's no landlord here," she told him. "There's no tenants except me and you. Only mice and rats and roaches. It's a condemned house and City Hall calls it a firetrap and from the first floor up the windows are boarded. You can't get up because there's no stairs. One of these days the City'll tear down this dump but I'll worry about that when it happens."

He looked at her. "You live here in the cellar?"

She nodded. "It's a good place to play solitaire."

He smiled and murmured, "Some people like to be alone."

"I don't like it," she said. Then, with a shrug, she pointed to the scar on her face. "What man would live with me?"

He stopped smiling. He didn't say anything.

She said, "It's a long drop when you're tossed out of a third-storey window. Most folks are lucky and they land on their feet or their fanny. I came down head first, cracked my collar-bone and got a fractured skull, and split my face wide open."

He took a closer look at the livid scar. For some moments he was quiet and then he frowned thoughtfully and said, "Maybe it won't be there for long. It's not as deep as I thought it was. If you had it treated—"

"No," she said. "The hell with it."

"You wouldn't need much cash," he urged quietly. "You could go to a clinic. They're doing fancy tricks with plastic surgery these days."

"Yeah, I know." Her voice was toneless. She wasn't looking at him. "The point is, I want the scar to stay there. It keeps me away from men. I've had too many problems with men and now, whenever they see my face, they turn their heads the other way. And that's fine with me. That's just how I want it."

He frowned again. This time it was a deeper frown and it wasn't just thoughtful. He said, "Who threw you out of the window?"

"My husband." She laughed without sound. "My wonderful husband."

"Where is he now."

"In the cemetery," she said. She shrugged again, and

her tone was matter-of-fact. "It happened while I was in the hospital. I think he got to the point where he couldn't stand to live with himself. Or maybe he just did it for kicks, I don't know. Anyway, he got hold of a meat-cleaver and chopped his own throat. When they found him, damn near didn't have a head."

"Well, that's one way of ending a marriage."

Again she uttered the soundless laugh. "It was a fine marriage while it lasted. I was drunk most of the time. I had to get drunk to take what he dished out. He had some weird notion about wedding vows."

"He went with other women?"

"No," she said. "He made me go with other men."

For some moments it was quiet.

And then she went on, "We lived here in this neighbor-hood. It's a perfect neighborhood for that sort of deal. He had me out on the street looking for customers and bringing the money home to him, and when I came in with excuses instead of cash he'd throw me on the floor and kick me. I'd beg him to stop and he'd laugh and go on kicking me. Some nights I have bad dreams and he's kicking me. So then I need sweet dreams, and that's when I reach for the pipe."

"The pipe?"

"Opium," she said. She said it with fondness and affec-tion. "Opium." There was tenderness in her eyes. "That's my new husband."

He nodded understandingly.

She said, "I get it from a Chinaman on Ninth Street. He's a user himself and he's more than eighty years old and still in there pitching, so I guess with O it's like any-thing else, it's all a matter of how you use it." Her voice dropped off just a little and her eyes were dull and sort of dismal as she added, "I wish I didn't need so much of it. It takes most of my weekly salary."

"What kind of work you do?"

"I scrub floors," she said. "In night-clubs and dance-halls. All day long I scrub the floors to make them clean and shiny for the night-time customers. Some nights I sit here and think of the pretty girls dancing on them polished floors. The pretty girls with flowers in their hair and no scars on their faces—" She broke it off abruptly, her hand making a brushing gesture as though to disparage the self-pity. She stood up and said, "I gotta go out to do some shopping. You wanna wait here till I come back?"

Without waiting for his answer, she moved across the cellar toward a battered door leading up to the backyard. As she opened the door, she turned and looked at him. "Make yourself comfortable," she said. "There's a mattress in the next room. It ain't the Ritz Carlton exactly, but it's better than nothing."

He was asking himself whether he should stay there.

He heard her saying, "Incidentally, my name is Tillie."

She stood there waiting.

"Kenneth," he said. "Kenneth Rockland."

But that wasn't what she was waiting for. Several moments passed, and then somehow he knew what she wanted him to say.

He said, "I'll be here when you come back."

"Good." The candlelight showed her crooked grin, a grimace on the scarred face. But what he saw was a gentle smile. It seemed to drift toward him like a soothing caress. And then he heard her saying, "Maybe I'll come back with some news. You told me it was two men. There's a chance I can check on them if you'll tell me what they look like."

He shook his head. "You better stay out of it. You might get hurt."

"Nothing can hurt me," she said.

She pointed her finger at the wreckage of her face. Her tone was almost pleading as she said, "Come on, tell me what they look like."

He shrugged. He gave a brief description of Oscar and Coley. And the Olds 88.

"Check," Tillie said. "I don't have 20-20 but I'll keep them open and see what's happening."

She turned and walked out and the door closed. Ken lifted himself from the floor and picked up the candle. He walked across the cement floor and the candle showed him a small space off to one side, a former coal-bin arranged with a mattress against the wall, a splintered chair and a splintered bureau and a table stacked with books. There was a candle holder on the table and he set the candle on it and then he had a look at the books.

It was an odd mixture of literature. There were books dealing with idyllic romance, strictly from fluttering hearts and soft moonlight and violins. And there were books that probed much deeper, explaining the scientific side of sex, with drawings and photos to show what it was all about. There was one book in particular that looked as though she'd been concentrating on it. The pages were considerably thumbed and she'd used a pencil to underline certain paragraphs. The title was, "The Sex Problem of the Single Women."

He shook his head slowly. He thought, *It's a damn shame* . . .

And then, for some unaccountable reason, he thought of Hilda. She flowed into his mind with a rustling of silk that sheathed the exquisite contours of her slender torso and legs. Her platinum blonde hair was glimmering and her long-lashed green eyes were beckoning to say, Come on, take my hand and we'll go down Memory Lane.

He shut his eyes tightly. He wondered why he was thinking about her. A long time ago he'd managed to get her out of his mind and he couldn't understand what brought her back again. He begged himself to get rid of the thought, but now it was more than a thought, it was the white-hot memory of tasting that mouth and possessing that elegant body. Without sound he said, *Goddamn her*.

And suddenly he realized why he was thinking of Hilda. It was like a curtain lifted to reveal the hidden channels of his brain. He was comparing Hilda's physical perfection with the scarred face of Tillie. His eyes were open and he gazed down at the mattress on the floor and for a moment he saw Hilda naked on the mattress. She smiled teasingly and then she shook her head and said, *Nothing doing*. So then she vanished and in the next moment it was Tillie on the mattress but somehow he didn't feel bitter or disappointed; he had the feeling that the perfection was all on Tillie's side.

He took off his shoes and lowered himself to the mattress. He yawned a few times and then fell asleep.

A voice said, "Kenneth—"

He was instantly awake. He looked up and saw Tillie. He smiled at her and said, "What time is it?"

"Half-past five." She had a paper bag in her hand and she was taking things out of the bag and putting them on the table. There was some dried fish and a package of tea leaves and some cold fried noodles. She reached deeper into the bag and took out a bottle containing colorless liquid.

"Rice wine," she said. She set the bottle on the table.

Then again she reached into the bag and her hand came out holding a cardboard box.

"Opium?" he murmured.

She nodded. "I got some cigarettes, too." She took a pack of Luckies from her pocket, opened the pack and extended it to him.

He sat up and put a cigarette in his mouth and used the candle to light it. He said, "You going to smoke the opium?"

"No, I'll smoke what you're smoking."

He put another cigarette in his mouth and lit it and handed it to her.

She took a few drags and then she said quietly, "I didn't want to wake you up, but I thought you'd want to hear the news."

He blinked a few times. "What news?"

"I saw them," she said.

He blinked again "Where?"

"On Tenth Street." She took more smoke into her mouth and let it come out of her nose. "It was a couple of hours ago, after I come out of the Chinaman's."

He sat up straighter. "You been watching them for two hours?"

"Watching them? I been with them. They took me for a ride."

He stared at her. His mouth was open but no sound came out.

Tillie grinned. "They didn't know I was in the car."

He took a deep breath. "How'd you manage it?"

She shrugged. "It was easy. I saw them sitting in the car and then they got out and I followed them. They were taking a stroll around the block and peeping into alleys and finally I heard the little one saying they might as well powder and come back tomorrow. The big one said they should keep on searching the neighborhood. They got into an argument and I had a feeling the little one would win. So I walked back to the car. The door was open and I climbed in the back and got flat on the floor. About five minutes later they're up front and the car starts and we're riding."

His eyes were narrow. "Where?"

"Downtown," she said. "It wasn't much of a ride. It only took a few minutes. They parked in front of a house on Spruce near Eleventh. I watched them go in. Then I got out of the car—"

"And walked back here?"

"Not right away," she said. "First I cased the house."

Silly Tillie, he thought. *If they'd seen her they'd have dragged her in and killed her.*

She said, "It's one of them little old fashioned houses. There's a vacant lot on one side and on the other side there's an alley. I went down the alley and came up on the back porch and peeped through the window. They were in the kitchen, the four of them."

He made no sound, but his lips shaped the word. "Four?" And then, with sound, "Who were the other two?"

"A man and a woman."

He stiffened. He tried to get from the mattress and couldn't move. His eyes aimed past Tillie as he said tightly, "Describe them."

"The man was about five-ten and sort of beefy. I figure about two hundred. He looked about forty or so. Had a suntan and wore expensive clothes. Brown wavy hair and brown eyes and—"

"That's Riker," he murmured.

He managed to lift himself from the mattress. His voice was a whisper as he said, "Now let's have the woman."

"She was something," Tillie said. "She was really something."

"Blonde?" And with both hands he made a gesture begging Tillie to speed the reply.

"Platinum blonde," Tillie said. "With the kind of face that makes men sweat in the wintertime. That kind of a face, and a shape that goes along with it. She was wearing—"

"Pearls," he said. "She always had a weakness for pearls."

Tillie didn't say anything.

He moved past Tillie. He stood facing the dark wall of the cellar and seeing the yellow-black of candlelight and shadow on the cracked plaster. "Hilda," he said, "Hilda."

It was quiet for some moments. He told himself it was wintertime and he wondered if he was sweating.

Then very slowly he turned and looked at Tillie. She was sitting on the edge of the mattress and drinking from the bottle of rice-wine. She took it in short, measured gulps, taking it slowly to get the full effect of it. When the bottle was half empty she raised her head and grinned at him and said, "Have some?"

He nodded. She handed him the bottle and he drank. The Chinese wine was mostly fire and it burned all the way going down and when it hit his belly it was electric-hot. But the climate it sent to his brain was cool and mild and mildness showed in his eyes. His voice was quiet and relaxed as he said, "I thought Oscar and Coley made the trip alone. I didn't figure that Riker and Hilda would come with them. But now it adds. I can see the way it adds."

"It's a long ride from Los Angeles," Tillie said.

"They didn't mind. They enjoyed the ride."

"The scenery?"

"No," he said. "They weren't looking at the scenery. They were thinking of the setup here in Philly. With Oscar putting the blade in me and then the funeral and Riker seeing me in the coffin and telling himself his worries were over."

"And Hilda?"

"The same," he said. "She's been worried just as much as Riker. Maybe more."

Tillie nodded slowly. "From the story you told me, she's got more reason to worry."

He laughed lightly. He liked the sound of it and went on with it. He said through the easy laughter, "They really don't need to worry. They're making it a big thing and it's nothing at all. I forgot all about them a long time ago. But they couldn't forget about me."

Tillie had her head inclined and she seemed to be studying the sound of his laughter. Some moments passed and then she said quietly, "You don't like black pudding?"

He didn't get the drift of that. He stopped laughing and his eyes were asking what she meant.

"There's an old saying," she said. "Revenge is black pudding."

He laughed again.

"Don't pull away from it," Tillie said. "Just listen to it. Let it hit you and sink in. Revenge is black pudding."

He went on laughing, shaking his head and saying, "I'm not in the market."

"You sure?"

"Positive," he said. Then, with a grin, "Only pudding I like is vanilla."

"The black tastes better," Tillie said. "I've had some, and I know. I had it when they told me what he did to himself with the meat-cleaver."

He winced slightly. He saw Tillie getting up from the mattress and moving toward him. He heard her saying, "That black pudding has a wonderful flavor. You ought to try a spoonful."

"No," he said. "No, Tillie."

She came close. She spoke very slowly and there was a slight hissing in her voice. "They put you in prison for nine years. They cheated you and robbed you and tortured you."

"That's all past," he said. "That's from yesterday."

"It's from now." She stood very close to him. "They're itching to hit you again and see you dead. They won't stop until you're dead. That puts a poison label on them. And there's only one way to deal with poison. Get rid of it."

"No," he said, "I'll let it stay the way it is."

"You can't," Tillie said. "It's a choice you have to make. Either you'll drink bitter poison or you'll taste that sweet black pudding."

He grinned again. "There's a third choice."

"Like what?"

"This." And he pointed to the bottle of rice-wine. "I like the taste of this. Let's stay with it until it's empty."

"That won't solve the problem," Tillie said.

"The hell with the problem." His grin was very wide and he didn't realize that it was forced.

"You fool," Tillie said.

He had the bottle raised and he was taking a drink.

"You poor fool," she said. Then she shrugged and turned away from him and lowered herself to the mattress.

The forced grin stayed on his face as he went on drinking. Now he was drinking slowly because the rice-wine dulled the action in his brain and he had difficulty lifting the bottle to his mouth. Gradually he became aware of a change taking place in the air of the cellar; it was thicker, sort of smoky. His eyes tried to focus and there was too much wine in him and he couldn't see straight. But then the smoke came up in front of his eyes and into his eyes. He looked down and saw the white clay pipe in Tillie's hand. She was sitting on the mattress with her legs crossed, Buddha-like, puffing at the opium, taking it in very slowly, the smoke coming out past the corners of her lips.

The grin faded from his face. And somehow the alcohol-mist was drifting away from his brain. He thought, *She smokes it because she's been kicked around*. But there was no pity in his eyes, just the level look of clear thinking. He said to himself, *There's only two kinds of people in this world, the ones who get kicked around and the ones who do the kicking*.

He lowered the bottle to the table. He turned and took a few steps going away and then heard Tillie saying, "Moving out?"

"No," he said. "Just taking a walk."

"Where?"

"Spruce Street," he said.

"Good," she said. "I'll go with you."

He shook his head. He faced her and saw that she'd put the pipe aside. She was getting up from the mattress. He went on shaking his head and saying, "It can't be played that way. I gotta do this alone."

She moved toward him. "Maybe it's good-bye."

"If it is," he said, "there's only one way to say it."

His eyes told her to come closer. He put his arms around her and held her with a tenderness and a feeling of not wanting to let he go. He kissed her. He knew she felt the meaning of the kiss, she was returning it and as her breath went into him it was sweet and pure and somehow like nectar.

Then, very gently, she pulled away from him. She said, "Go now. It's dark outside. It'll be another hour before the sun comes up."

He grinned. It was a soft grin that wasn't forced. "This job won't take more than an hour," he said. "Whichever way it goes, it'll be a matter of minutes. Either I'll get them or they'll get me."

He turned away and walked across the cellar toward the splintered door. Tillie stood there watching him as he opened the door and went out.

It was less than three minutes later and they had him. He was walking south on Ninth, between Race Street and Arch, and the black Olds 88 was cruising on Arch and he didn't see them but they saw him, with Oscar grinning at Coley and saying, "There's our boy."

Oscar drove the car past the intersection and parked it on the north side of Arch about twenty feet away from the corner. They got out and walked toward the corner and stayed close to the brick wall of the corner building. They listened to the approaching footsteps and grinned at each other and a few moments later he arrived on the corner and they grabbed him.

He felt Coley's thick arm wrapped tight around his throat, pulling his head back. He saw the glimmer of the five-inch blade in Oscar's hand. He told himself to think fast and he thought very fast and managed to say, "You'll be the losers. I made a connection."

He smiled at Oscar. Then he waited for Coley to loosen the arm-hold on his throat. Coley loosened it, then lowered it to his chest, using both arms to clamp him and prevent him from moving.

He made no attempt to move. He went on smiling at Oscar, and saying, "An important connection. It's important enough to louse you up."

"Prove it," Oscar said.

"You're traced." He narrowed the smile just a little. "If anything happens to me, they know where to get you."

"He's faking," Coley said. Then urgently, "Go on, Oscar, give him the knife."

"Not yet," Oscar murmured. He was studying Ken's eyes and his own eyes were somewhat worried. He said to Ken, "Who did the tracing?"

"I'll tell that to Riker."

Oscar laughed without sound. "Riker's in Los Angeles."

"No he isn't," Ken said. "He's here in Philly."

Oscar stopped laughing. The worry deepened in his eyes. He stared past Ken, focusing on Coley.

"He's here with Hilda," Ken said.

"It's just a guess," Coley said. "It's gotta be a guess." He tightened his bear-hug on Ken. "Do it, Oscar. Don't let him stall you. Put the knife in him."

Oscar looked at Ken and said, "You making this a quiz game?"

Ken shrugged again. "It's more like stud poker."

"Maybe," Oscar admitted. "But you're not the dealer."

Ken shrugged again. He didn't say anything.

Oscar said, "You're not the dealer and all you can do is hope for the right card."

"I got it already," Ken said. "It fills an inside straight."

Oscar bit the edge of his lip. "All right, I'll take a look." He had the knife aiming at Ken's chest, and then he lowered it and moved in closer and the tip of the blade was touching Ken's belly. "Let's see your hole-card, sonny. All you gotta do is name the street and the house."

"Spruce Street," Ken said. "Near Eleventh."

Oscar's face became pale. Again he was staring at Coley.

Ken said, "It's an old house, detached. On one side there's a vacant lot and on the other side there's an alley."

It was quiet for some moments and then Oscar was talking aloud to himself, saying, "He knows, he really knows."

"What's the move?" Coley asked. He sounded unhappy.

"We gotta think," Oscar said. "This makes it compli-cated and we gotta think it through very careful."

Coley muttered a four-letter word. He said, "We ain't getting paid to do our own thinking. Riker gave orders to find him and bump him."

"We can't bump him now," Oscar said. "Not under these conditions. The way it stacks up, it's Riker's play. We'll have to take him to Riker."

"Riker won't like that," Coley said.

Oscar didn't reply. Again he was biting his lip and it went on that way for some moments and then he made a gesture toward the parked car. He told Coley to take the wheel and said he'd sit in the back with Rockland. As he opened the rear door he had the blade touching Ken's side, gently urging Ken to get in first. Coley was up front behind the wheel and then Oscar and Ken occupied the rear seat and the knife in Oscar's hand was aimed at Ken's abdomen.

The engine started and the Olds 88 moved east on Arch and went past Eighth and turned south on Seventh. There was no talk in the car as they passed Market and Chestnut and Walnut. They had a red light on Locust but Coley ignored it and went through at forty-five.

"Slow down," Oscar said.

Coley was hunched low over the wheel and the speedometer went up to fifty and Oscar yelled, "For Christ's sake, slow down. You wanna be stopped by a red car?"

"There's one now," Ken said, and he pointed toward the side window that showed only the front of a grocery store. But Oscar thought it might really be a side-street with a police car approaching, and the thought was in his brain for a tiny fraction of a second. In that segment of time he turned his head to have a look. Ken's hand moved automatically to grab Oscar's wrist and twist hard. The knife fell away from Oscar's fingers and Ken's other hand caught it. Oscar let out a screech and Ken put the knife in Oscar's throat and had it in there deep just under the ear, pulled it out and put it in again. The car was skidding to a stop as Ken stabbed Oscar a third time to finish him. Coley was screaming curses and trying to hurl himself sideways and backward toward the rear seat and Ken showed him the knife and it didn't stop him. Ken ducked as Coley came vaulting over the top of the front seat, the knife slashing sideways to rip from navel to kidney, then across again to the other kidney, then up to the ribs to hit the bone with Coley gurgling and trying to sob, doubled over with his knees on the floor and his chin on the edge of the back seat, his arms flung over the sprawled corpse of Oscar.

"I'm dying," Coley gurgled. "I'm—" That was his final sound. His eyes opened very wide and his head snapped sideways and he was through for this night and all nights.

Ken opened the rear door and got out. He had the knife

in his pocket as he walked with medium-fast stride going south on Seventh to Spruce. Then he turned west on Spruce and walked just a bit faster. Every now and then he glanced backward to see if there were any red cars but all he saw was the empty street and some alley cats mooching around under the street lamps.

In the blackness above the rooftops the bright yellow face of the City Hall clock showed ten minutes past six. He estimated the sky would be dark for another half-hour. It wasn't much time, but it was time enough for what he intended to do. He told himself he wouldn't enjoy the action, and yet somehow his mouth was watering, almost like anticipating a tasty dish. Something on the order of pudding, and the color of it was black.

He quickened his pace just a little, crossed Eighth Street and Ninth, and walked faster as he passed Tenth. There were no lit windows on Spruce Street but as he neared Eleventh the moonlight blended with the glow of a street lamp and showed him the vacant lot. He gazed across the empty space to the wall of the old-fashioned house.

Then he was on the vacant lot and moving slowly and quietly toward the rear of the house. He worked his way to the sagging steps of the back porch, saw a light in the kitchen window, climbed two steps and three and four and then he was on the porch peering through the window and seeing Hilda.

She was alone in the kitchen, sitting at a white-topped table and smoking a cigarette. There was a cup and saucer on the table, the saucer littered with coffee-stained cigarette butts. As he watched, she got up from the table and went to the stove to lift a percolator off the fire and pour another cup of coffee.

She moved with a slow weaving of her shoulders and a

flow of her hips that was more drifting than walking. He thought, *She still has it, that certain way of moving around, using that body like a long-stemmed lily in a quiet breeze. That's what got you the first time you laid eyes on her. The way she moves. And one time very long ago you said to her, "To set me on fire, all you have to do is walk across a room." You couldn't believe you were actually married to that hothouse-prize, that platinum blonde hair like melted eighteen-carat, that face, she still has it, that body, she still has it. It's been nine years, and she still has it.*

She was wearing bottle-green velvet that set off the pale green of her eyes. The dress was cut low, went in tight around her very narrow waist and staying tight going all the way down past her knees. She featured pearls around her throat and in her ears and on her wrists. He thought, *You gave her pearls for her birthday and Christmas and you wanted to give her more for the first wedding anniversary. But they don't sell pearls in San Quentin. All they sell is plans for getting out. Like lessons in how to crawl through a pipe, or how to conceal certain tools, or how to disguise the voice. The lessons never paid off, but maybe now's the time to use what you learned. Let's try Coley's voice.*

His knuckles rapped the kitchen door, and his mouth opened to let out Coley's thick, low pitched voice saying, "It's me and Oscar."

He stood there counting off the seconds. It was four seconds and then the door opened. It opened wide and Hilda's mouth opened wider. Then she had her hand to her mouth and she was stepping backward.

"Hello, Hilda." He came into the kitchen and closed the door behind him.

She took another backward step. She shook her head and spoke through the trembling fingers that pressed against her lips. "It isn't—"

"Yes," he said. "It is."

Her hand fell away from her mouth. The moment was too much for her and it seemed she was going to collapse. But somehow she managed to stay on her feet. Then her eyes were shut tightly and she went on shaking her head.

"Look at me," he said. "Take a good look."

She opened her eyes. She looked him up and down and up again. Then, very slowly, she summoned air into her lungs and he knew she was going to let out a scream. His hand moved fast to his coat pocket and he took out Oscar's knife and said quietly, "No noise, Hilda."

She stared at the knife. The air went out of her without a sound. Her arms were limp at her sides. She spoke in a half-whisper, talking to herself. "I don't believe it. Just can't believe it—"

"Why not?" His tone was mild. "It figures, doesn't it? You came to Philly to look for me. And here I am."

For some moments she stayed limp. Then, gradually, her shoulders straightened. She seemed to be getting a grip on herself. Her eyes narrowed just a little, as she went on looking at the silver-handled switchblade in his hand. She said, "That's Oscar's knife—?"

He nodded.

"Where is Oscar?" she asked. "Where's Coley?"

"They're dead." He pressed the button on the handle and the blade flicked out. It glimmered red with Oscar's blood and Coley's blood. He said, "It's a damn shame. They wouldn't be dead if they'd let me alone."

Hilda didn't say anything. She gave a little shrug, as though to indicate there was nothing she could say. He told himself it didn't make sense to wait any longer and the thing to do was put the knife in her heart. He wondered if the knife was sharp enough to cut through ice.

He took a forward step, then stopped. He wondered what was holding him back. Maybe he was waiting for her to break, to fall on her knees and beg for mercy.

But she didn't kneel and she didn't plead. Her voice was matter-of-fact as she said, "I'm wondering if we can make a deal."

It caught him off balance. He frowned slightly. "What kind of deal?"

"Fair trade," she said. "You'll give me a break and I'll give you Riker."

He changed the frown to a dim smile. "I've got him anyway. It's a cinch he's upstairs sound asleep."

"That's fifty percent right," she said. "He's a very light sleeper. Especially lately, since he heard you were out of Quentin."

He widened the smile. "In Quentin I learned to walk on tip-toe. There won't be any noise."

"There's always noise when you break down a door."

The frown came back. "You playing it shrewd?"

"I'm playing it straight," she said. "He keeps the door locked. Another thing he keeps is a .38 under his pillow."

He slanted his head just a little. "You expect me to buy that?"

"You don't have to buy it. I'm giving it to you."

He began to see what she was getting at. He said, "All right, thanks for the freebee. Now tell me what you're selling."

"A key," she said. "The key to his room. He has one and I have one. I'll sell you mine at bargain rates. All I want is your promise."

He didn't say anything.

She shrugged and said, "It's a gamble on both sides. I'll take the chance that you'll keep your word and let me stay alive. You'll be betting even-money that I'm telling the truth."

He smiled again. He saw she was looking past him, at the kitchen door. He said, "So the deal is, you give me the key to his room and I let you walk out that door."

"That's it." She was gazing hungrily at the door. Her lips scarcely moved as she murmured, "Fair enough?"

"No," he said. "It needs a tighter contract."

Her face was expressionless. She held her breath.

He let her hold it for awhile, and then he said, "Let's do it so there's no gamble. You get the key and I'll follow you upstairs. I'll be right in back of you when you walk into the room. I'll have the blade touching your spine."

She blinked a few times.

"Well?" he said.

She reached into a flap of the bottle-green velvet and took out a door key. Then she turned slowly and started out of the kitchen. He moved in close behind her and followed the platinum blonde hair and elegant torso going through the small dining-room and the parlor and toward the dimly-lit stairway. He came up at her side as they climbed the stairs, the knife-blade scarcely an inch away from the shimmering velvet that covered her ribs.

They reached the top of the stairs and she pointed to the door of the front bedroom. He let the blade touch the velvet and his voice was a whisper saying, "Slow and quiet. Very quiet."

Then again he moved behind her. They walked slowly toward the bedroom door. The blade kissed the velvet and it told her to use the key with a minimum of sound. She put the key in the lock and there was no sound as she turned the key. There was only a slight clicking sound as the lock opened. Then no sound while she opened the door.

They entered the room and he saw Riker in the bed. He saw the brown wavy hair and there was some grey in it along the temples. In the suntanned face there were wrinkles and lines of dissipation and other lines that told of too much worry. Riker's eyes were shut tightly and it was the kind of slumber that rests the limbs and not the brain.

Ken thought, He's aged a lot in nine years; it used to be mostly muscle and now it's mostly fat.

Riker was curled up, his knees close to his paunch. He had his shoes off but otherwise he was fully dressed. He wore a silk shirt and a hand-painted necktie, his jacket was dark grey cashmere and his slacks were pale grey high-grade flannel. He had on a pair of argyle socks that must have set him back at least twenty dollars. On the wrist of his left hand there was a platinum watch to match the large star-emerald he wore on his little finger. On the third finger of his left hand he had a three-carat diamond. Ken was looking at the expensive jewellery and thinking, *He travels first-class, he really rides the gravy train.*

It was a bitter thought and it bit deeper into Ken's brain. He said to himself, *Nine years ago this man of distinction pistol-whipped your skull and left you for dead. You've had nine years in Quentin and he's had the sunshine, the peaches-and-cream, the thousands of nights with the extra-lovely Mrs Riker while you slept alone in a cell—*

He looked at the extra-lovely Mrs Riker. She stood motionless at the side of the bed and he stood beside her with the switchblade aiming at her velvet-sheathed flesh. She was looking at the blade and waiting for him to aim it at Riker, to put it in the sleeping man and send it in deep.

But that wasn't the play. He smiled dimly to let her know he had something else in mind.

Riker's left hand dangled over the side of the bed and his right hand rested on the pillow. Ken kept the knife aimed at Hilda as he reached toward the pillow and then under the pillow. His fingers touched metal. It was the barrel of a revolver and he got a two-finger hold on it and eased it out from under the pillow. The butt came into his palm and his middle finger went through the trigger-guard and nestled against the back of the guard, not touching the trigger.

He closed the switchblade and put it in his pocket. He stepped back and away from the bed. "Now you can wake up your husband."

She was staring at the muzzle of the .38. It wasn't aiming at anything in particular.

"Wake him up," Ken murmured. "I want him to see his gun in my hand. I want him to know how I got it."

Hilda gasped and it became a sob and then a wail and it was a hook of sound that awakened Riker. At first he was looking at Hilda. Then he saw Ken and he sat up very slowly, as though he was something made of stone and ropes were pulling him up. His eyes were riveted to Ken's face and he hadn't yet noticed the .38. His hand crept down along the side of the pillow and then under the pillow.

There was no noise in the room as Riker's hand groped for the gun. Some moments passed and then there was sweat on Riker's forehead and under his lip and he went on searching for the gun and suddenly he seemed to realize it wasn't there. He focused on the weapon in

Ken's hand and his body began to quiver. His lips scarcely moved as he said, "The gun – the gun—"

"It's yours," Ken said. "Mind if I borrow it?"

Riker went on staring at the revolver. Then very slowly his head turned and he was staring at Hilda.

"You," he said. "You gave it to him."

"Not exactly," Ken said. "All she did was tell me where it was."

Riker shut his eyes very tightly, as thought he was tied to a rack and it was pulling him apart.

Hilda's face was expressionless. She was looking at Ken and saying, "You promised to let me walk out—"

"I'm not stopping you," he said. Then, with a shrug and a dim smile, "I'm not stopping anyone from doing what they want to do." And he slipped the gun into his pocket.

Hilda started for the door. Riker was up from the bed and lunging at her, grabbing her wrist and hurling her across the room. Then Riker lunged again and his hands reached for her throat as she tried to get up from the floor. Hilda began to make gurgling sounds but the noise was drowned in the torrent of insane screaming that came from Riker's lips. Riker choked her until she died. When Riker realized she was dead his screaming became louder and he went on choking her.

Ken stood there, watching it happen. He saw the corpse flapping like a rag-doll in the clutching hands of the screaming madman. He thought, *Well, they wanted each other, and now they got each other*.

He walked out of the room and down the hall and down the stairs. As he went out of the house he could still hear the screaming. On Spruce, walking toward Eleventh, he glanced back and saw a crowd gathering outside the house and then he heard the sound of approaching sirens. He waited there and saw the police-cars stopping in front of the house, the policemen rushing in with guns. Some moments later he heard the shots and he knew that the screaming man was trying to make a getaway. There was more shooting and suddenly there was no sound at all. He knew they'd be carrying two corpses out of the house.

He turned away from what was happening back there, walked along the curb toward the sewer-hole on the corner, took Riker's gun from his pocket and threw it into the sewer. In the instant that he did it there was a warm sweet taste in his mouth. He smiled, knowing what it was. Again he could hear Tillie saying, "Revenge is black pudding."

Tillie, he thought. And the smile stayed on his face as he walked north on Eleventh. He was remembering the feeling he'd had when he'd kissed her. It was the feeling of wanting to take her out of the dark cellar, away from the loneliness and the opium. To carry her upward toward the world where they had such things as clinics, with plastic specialists who repaired scarred faces.

The feeling hit him again and he was anxious to be with Tillie and he walked faster.

The Plunge

Seven out of ten are slobs, he was thinking. There was no malice or disdain in the thought. It was more a mixture of pity and regret. And that made it somewhat sickening, for he was referring specifically to the other men who wore badges, his fellow-policemen. More specifically still, he was thinking of the nine plainclothesmen attached to the Vice Squad. Only yesterday they'd been caught with their palms out, hauled in before the Commissioner, and called all sorts of names before they were suspended.

But, of course, the suspensions were temporary. They'd soon be back on the job, their palms extended again, accepting the shakedown money with the languid smile that seemed to say, *It's all a part of the game.*

He'd never believed in that cynical axiom, had never let it touch him during his seventeen years on the city payroll. From rookie to Police Sergeant and on up to Detective Lieutenant he'd stayed away from the bribe, rakeoff and conniving and doing favors for certain individuals who required official protection to remain in business.

Of course, at times he'd made mistakes, but they were always clean mistakes. He'd been trying too hard or he was weary from nights without sleep. It was honest blundering and it put no shadows on his record. In City Hall he was listed Grade-A and they had him slated for promotion.

His name was Roy Childers and he was thirty-eight

years old. He stood five-feet-ten and weighed a rock-hard one-ninety. It was really rock-hard because he was a firm believer in physical culture and wholesome living. He kept away from too much starches and sweets, smoked only after meals, had a beer now and then, but nothing more than that, and the only woman he ever slept with was his wife.

They'd been married eleven years and they had four children. In a few months Louise would be having the fifth. Maybe five was too many, considering his salary and the price of food these days. But, of course, they'd get along. They'd always managed to get along. He had a fine wife and a nicely arranged way of living and there was never anything serious to worry about.

That is, aside from his job. On the job he worried plenty. It was purely technical worriment because he took the job very seriously and when things didn't go the way he expected, he'd lose sleep and it would hurt his digestion. When he'd been with the Vice Squad, it hadn't happened so frequently. But a year ago he'd become fed up with the Vice Squad, with all the shenanigans and departmental throatcutting and, of course, the never-ending shakedown activity he saw all around him.

He'd requested a transfer to Homicide, and within a few months his dark brown hair showed grey streaks, pouches began to form under his eyes, the unsolved cases put creases at the corners of his mouth. But mostly it was the fact that Homicide also had its slobs and manipulators, its badge-wearing bandits who'd go in for any kind of deal if the price was right.

On more than one occasion he'd been close to grabbing a wanted man when someone tipped off someone who tipped off someone else, with the fugitive sliding away or building an alibi that caused the District Attorney to shrug and say, "What's the use? We've got no case."

So that now, after eleven months of working with Homicide, there was a lot of grey in Childers' hair, and his mouth was set tighter, showing the strain of work that demanded too much effort and paid too little dividends.

He was sitting at his desk in Homicide, which was on the ninth floor of City Hall. His desk was near the window and the view it gave him from that angle was the slum area extending from Twelfth and Patton Avenue to the river. Along the riverfront the warehouses looked very big in contrast to the two-storey rat-traps and fire-traps where people lived or tried to live or didn't care whether they lived or not.

But he wasn't focusing on the slum-dwellings that breeded filth and degeneracy and violence. His eyes sought out the warehouses, and narrowed in concentration as they came to rest on the curved-roof structure labeled "No. 4" where not so very long ago there'd been a $15,000 payroll robbery, with one night-watchman killed and another permanently blinded from a pistol-whipping.

He'd been assigned to the case three weeks ago, after coming to the Captain and saying it looked like a Dice Nolan job. For one thing, he'd said, Dice Nolan was a specialist at payroll robbery, going in for warehouses along the riverfront and using a boat for the getaway. Nolan had used that method several times before they'd caught up with him some ten years ago.

They gave him ten-to-twenty, and according to the record he'd been let out on parole this year – in the middle of March. Now it was the middle of April and that just about gave him time enough to get a mob together and plan a campaign and make a grab for loot.

Another angle was the pistol-whipping. Dice Nolan had a reputation for that sort of thing, always going for the eyes for some weird reason planted deep in his criminal brain. Childers had said to the Captain, "What makes me sure it's Nolan, I've checked with the parole officers and they tell me he hasn't reported in for the past ten days. He's on a strict probation and he's supposed to show them his face every three days."

The Captain had frowned. "You figure he's still in town?"

"I'm betting on it," Childers had said. "I know the way he operates. He wouldn't be satisfied with a fifteen-grand haul. He'll stick around for a while and then go for another warehouse. He knows every inch of that neighborhood."

"How come you're wise to him?"

"It goes back a good many years," Childers had said. "We were raised on the same street."

The Captain was quiet for some moments. And then, without looking at Childers, he'd said, "All right, go out and find him."

So he'd gone out to look for Nolan and the search took him along Patton Avenue going toward the river, past the rows of tenements where now they were strangers who'd been his childhood playmates, past the gutters where he'd sailed the matchbox-boats, unmindful of the slime and filth because it was the only world he'd known in that far-off time of carefree days.

Days of not knowing what poisonous roots were in the squalor of the neighborhood. Until the time when ignorance was ended and he saw them going bad, one by one, Georgie Mancuso and Hal Berkowski and Freddie Antonucci and Bill Weiss and Dice Nolan.

He'd pulled away from it with a teeth-clenched frenzy, like someone struggling out of a messy pit. He'd promised himself that he'd never breathe that rotten air again, never come near that dismal area where the roaches thrived and a switchblade nestled in almost every pocket. He'd gone away from it, telling himself the exit was permanent, feeling clean. And that was the important thing, to be clean, always to be clean.

He'd been acutely conscious of his own cleanliness as he'd questioned the men in the taprooms and poolrooms along Patton. They looked at him with hostile eyes but were careful to keep the hostility from their voices when they told him, "I don't know" and "I don't know" and "I don't know."

And some of them went so far as to state they were unacquainted with anyone named Dice Nolan. They'd never even heard of such a person. Of course he knew their lying and evasive answers were founded more on their fear of Nolan than on their instinctive dislike of the Police Department.

It told him his theory was correct. Nolan had engineered the payroll heist, and certainly Nolan was still in town.

But that was as far as he'd got with it. There were no further leads, and nothing that could come to a lead. Night after night he'd come home with a tired face to hear his wife saying, "Anything new?" And he'd try to give her a smile as he shook his head.

But it was getting more and more difficult to smile. He knew if he didn't come in with something soon, the Captain would take him off the case. He hated the thought of being taken off the case, he was so very sure about his man, so acutely sure the man was hiding somewhere near. Very near—

The ringing phone sliced into his thoughts. He lifted it from the hook and said hello and the switchboard girl downstairs said to hold on for just a moment. Then a man's voice said, "This Childers?"

Instantly he had a feeling it was something. He could almost smell it. He said, "Yes," and waited, and heard the man saying, "I'm gonna make it fast before you trace the call. Is that all right with you?"

He didn't say anything. For a moment he felt awfully weary, thinking: It's just some crank who wants to call me some dirty names—

But then the man was saying, "It's gonna be good if you wanna use it. I got some personal reasons for not liking Dice Nolan. Thing is, I can get you to his girl friend."

Childers reached automatically for a pencil and a pad. The man gave him a name and an address; and the pencil moved very rapidly. Then the call hung up, and Childers leaped from the desk, ran out of the office and down the hall to the elevator.

It was a seventeen-story apartment house on the edge of Lakeside Park. He went up to the ninth floor and down the corridor to room 907. It was early afternoon and he doubted she'd be there. But his finger was positive and persistent on the doorbell-button.

The door opened and he saw a woman in her middle-twenties, and his first thought was, a bum steer. This can't be Dice Nolan's girl.

He was certain she couldn't be connected with Nolan because there was nothing in her make-up that indicated moll or floosie or hard-mouthed slut. She wore very little paint and her hair-do was on the quiet side. There was no jewelry except for a wrist-watch. Her blouse was pale grey, the skirt a darker shade, and he noticed that her shoes didn't have high heels. Again he thought, *Sure, it's a bum steer*. But anyway, he said, "Are you Wilma Burnett?"

She nodded.

"Police," he said, turning his lapel to show her the badge.

She blinked a few times, but that was all. Then she stepped aside to let him enter the apartment. As he walked in, the quiet neatness of the place was impressed upon him. It was simply furnished. The color motif was subdued, and there wasn't the slightest sign of fast or loose living.

He frowned slightly, then got rid of it and put the official tone in his voice as he said, "All right, Miss Burnett. Let's have it."

She blinked again. "Let's have what?"

"Information," he said. "Where is he?"

"Who?" She spoke quietly; her expression was calm and polite. "Who are you talking about?"

"Dice." He said it softly.

It seemed she didn't get that. She said, "I don't know anyone by that name."

"Dice Nolan," he said.

For a moment she said nothing. Then, very quietly, "I know a Philip Nolan, if that's who you mean."

"Yes, that's him." And he thought, *Let's see if we can rattle her*. His voice became a jabbing blade. "I figured you'd know him. He pays your rent here, doesn't he?"

It didn't do a thing. There was no anger, not even annoyance. All she did was shake her head.

He told himself it wasn't going the way he wanted it to go. The thing to do was to hit her with something that would throw her off balance, and while he groped for an idea he heard her saying, "Won't you sit down?"

"No thanks," he said automatically. He folded his arms, looked at her directly and spoke a trifle louder. "You're doing very nicely, Miss Burnett. But it isn't good, it just can't work."

"I don't know what you mean."

"Yes you do." And he put the hard smile of law-enforcement on his lips. "You know exactly what I mean. You know he's wanted for robbery and murder and you're trying to cover for him."

That'll do it, he thought. *That'll sure enough break the ice.* But it didn't work that way, it didn't come anywhere near that. For a few moments she just stood there looking at him. Then she turned slowly and walked across the room. She settled herself in a chair near the window, folded her hands in her lap, and waited for his next remark. Her calm silence seemed to say, *You're getting nowhere fast.*

He said to himself, *Easy now, don't push it too hard.* Yet his voice was somehow gruff and impatient, more demand than query. "Where can I find him? Where?"

"I don't know."

"Not much you don't." He took a step toward her, his mouth tightening. "Come on, now. Let's quit playing checkers. Where's he hiding out?"

"Hiding?" Her eyebrows went up just a little. "I didn't know he was hiding."

"You're a liar."

She gazed past him. She said, "Tell me something. Is this the only way you can gather information? I mean, does your job require that you go around insulting people?"

He winced. He knew she had him there, and if this was

really checkers, she'd scored a triple-jump. But then he thought, *It's only the beginning of the game, we can get her to talk if we take our time and play it careful—*

Again he smiled at her. This time it was an easy pleasant smile, and his voice was soft. "I'm sorry, Miss Burnett. I shouldn't have said that. I apologize."

"That's quite all right, Mister—" She hesitated.

"Childers," he said. "Lieutenant Childers – Homicide." He pulled a chair toward hers, sat down and went on smiling at her. "It'll help both of us if you tell me the truth. I'm looking for a crook and a killer, and you're looking to stay out of prison."

"Prison?" Her eyebrows went up again. "But I haven't done anything—"

"I want to be sure about that. I'm hoping you can prove you're not an accessory."

"Meaning what?"

"Meaning if you're helping him to hide, you're an accessory after the fact. That's a very serious charge and I've known cases when they've been sent up for any-where from three to five years."

She didn't say anything.

He leaned forward slightly and said, "Of course you understand that anything you say can be held against you."

"I'm not worried about that, Lieutenant. I haven't broken any laws."

"Well, let's check on it, just to be sure." His smile remained pleasant, his voice soft and almost friendly. "Tell me about yourself."

She told him she was a free-lance commercial artist. She said her age was twenty-seven and for the past several years she'd been a widow. Her husband and two children had died in an auto accident. There was no emotion in her voice as she talked about it, but he saw something in her eyes that told him this was genuine and she'd been through plenty of hell. He thought, *She's really been hit hard.*

Then all at once it occurred to him that she was something out of the ordinary. It wasn't connected with her looks, although her looks summed up as extremely attractive. It was more on the order of a feeling she radiated, a feeling that came from deep inside and hit him going in deep, causing him to frown because he had no idea what it was and it made him uncomfortable.

He heard himself saying, "I owe you another apology. That crack I made about Nolan paying the rent. I guess that wasn't a nice thing to say."

"No, it wasn't." She said it forgivingly. "But I know you didn't mean to be personal. You were only trying to find out—"

"I'm still trying," he reminded her. His manner became official again. "I want to know all about you and Nolan."

For a long moment she was quiet. Then, her voice level and calm, "I can't tell you where he is, Lieutenant. I really don't know."

"When'd you last see him?"

"A few nights ago."

"Where, exactly?"

"Here," she said. "He came here and we had dinner."

He leaned back in the chair. "You cooked dinner for him?"

"It wasn't the first time," she said matter-of-factly.

He pondered on the next question. He wasn't looking at her as he asked, "What is it with you and Nolan? How long have you known him?"

"About a month." And then, before he could toss

another question, she volunteered, "We met in a cocktail lounge. I was alone, and I think I ought to explain about that. I don't usually go out alone. But that night I felt the need for company, and although I drink very little I really needed a lift. I'd been going with someone who disappointed me, one of those awfully nice gentlemen who leads you on until you happen to find out he's married—"

"Rough deal." He looked at her sympathetically.

She shrugged. "Well, anyway, I must have looked very lonesome and unhappy. I don't know how we got to talking, but one word led to another and I didn't know where it was leading. But to be quite truthful about it, I really didn't care. He told me he'd just been released from prison and it had no effect on me except that somehow I appreciated the blunt way he put it. Then he asked me for my phone number and I gave it to him. Since then we've been seeing each other steadily. And if you're curious as to whether I sleep with him—"

"I didn't ask you about that."

"I'll tell you anyway, Lieutenant." There was a certain quiet defiance in her voice, and it showed in her eyes along with all the pain and suffering that had been too much to take, that had led to the breaking-point where a woman grabs at almost anything that comes along.

She said, "Yes, I sleep with him. I sleep with the ex-convict you're looking for. I know what he is and I don't care. And if that makes me a criminal, you might as well put the handcuffs on me and take me in."

Childers stood up. He turned away from her and said, "You shouldn't have said all those things. It wasn't necessary."

She didn't reply. He waited for her to say something, but there was no sound in the room, and after some moments he moved toward the door. As he opened it, he glanced at her. She sat there bent far forward with her head in her hands. He murmured, "Goodbye, Miss Burnett," and walked out.

His wife and four children were looking at him and he could feel the pressure of their eyes. Their plates were empty and on his plate the pot roast and vegetables hadn't been touched. He gazed down at the food and wondered why he couldn't eat it. There was an empty feeling inside him but it wasn't the emptiness of needing a meal. It was something else, something unaccountable. The more he tried to understand it, the more it puzzled him.

"What's wrong with you?" his wife asked. It was the fifth or sixth time she'd asked it since he'd come home that evening. He couldn't remember what answers he'd given her.

Now he looked at her and said wearily, "I'm just not hungry, that's all."

The children began chattering, and the youngest, five-year-old Dotty, said, "Maybe Daddy ate some candy bars. Whenever I eat too much candy bars, I can't eat my supper."

"Grown-ups don't eat candy bars." It was Billy, aged nine. And Ralph, who was seven, said, "Grown-ups can do anything they want to."

No they can't, Childers said without sound. *They sure as hell can't.*

Then he asked himself what he meant by that. The answer came in close, danced away, went off very far away and he knew there was no use trying to reach for it.

He heard six-year-old Agnes saying, "Mommie, what's the matter with Daddy?"

"You ask him, honey," his wife said. "He won't tell me."

"What's there to tell?" Childers said loudly, the irritation grinding through his voice.

"Don't shout, Roy. You don't have to shout."

"Then lay off me. You've said enough."

"Is that the way to talk in front of the children?"

His voice lowered. "I'm sorry, Louise." He tried to smile at her. But his mouth felt stiff and he couldn't manage the smile. He said lamely, "I've had a bad day. It's taken a lot out of me—"

"That's why you need a good meal," she said. And then, getting up and coming towards him, "Tell you what. I'll warm up your plate and—"

"No." He shook his head emphatically. "I don't feel like eating and that's all there is to it."

"I wonder," she murmured.

He looked at her. "You wonder what?"

"Nothing," she said. "Let's skip it—"

"No we won't." He heard the suspicion in his voice, couldn't understand why it was there, then felt it more strongly as he said, "You started to say something and you're gonna finish it."

She didn't say anything. Her head was inclined and she was regarding him with puzzlement.

"Come on, spill it," he demanded. He rose from the table, facing her. "Tell me what's on your mind."

"Well, all I wanted to say was—"

"Come on, come on, don't stall."

"Say, who're you yelling at?" Louise shot back at him. She put her hands on her somewhat wide hips. "You're not talking to some tramp they've dragged in for questioning. I'm your wife and this is your home. The least you can do is show some respect."

"Mommie and Daddy are fighting," little Agnes said.

"And maybe it's about time," Louise said. She kept her hands on her hips. "I knew we had a show-down coming. Well, all right then. You told me to say what's on my mind and I'll say it. I want you to drop this Nolan case."

He stared at her. "What's that you said?"

"You heard me. I don't have to repeat it. I know your work is important, but your health comes first."

She pointed to the untouched food on his plate. "I had a feeling it would come to that. I've seen you walking in at night looking as if you were ready to drop. I knew it would reach the point where you wouldn't be able to eat. First thing you know, you'll have an ulcer."

He felt a thickness in his throat, a wave of tenderness and affection came over him, and he reminded himself he was a very fortunate man. This woman he had was the genuine article, an absolute treasure. His health and happiness and welfare were her primary concern. In her eyes he was the only man in the world, and after more than a decade of marriage, the knowledge of her feeling for him was something priceless.

He looked at her plump figure that was now over-plump with pregnancy, look at her disordered hair that seldom enjoyed the luxury of a beauty parlor because she was too busy taking care of four children. Than he looked at her hands, reddened and coarse from washing dishes and doing the laundry and scrubbing the floors. He said to himself, *She's the best, she's the finest*. And he wanted very much to put his arms around her.

But somehow he couldn't. He didn't know why, but he couldn't. He stood there paralyzed with the realization that she was waiting for his embrace and he could not respond.

All at once he felt a frantic need to get out of the house. He groped for an excuse, and without looking at her, he said, "I told the Captain I'd see him tonight. I'm going down to the Hall."

He turned quickly and walked toward the front door.

But his meeting was not with the Captain, his destination was not City Hall. He walked a couple of blocks, climbed into a taxi, and said to the driver, "Lakeside Apartments."

"Right you are," the driver said.

Am I? he asked without sound. *Am I right?* And there was no use trying to answer the question, his brain couldn't handle it. Yet somehow he knew that from a purely technical standpoint this move was the logical move, and he was making it according to the book. It amounted to a stake-out, going there to watch and wait for Dice Nolan. The thing to do, of course, was plant himself across the street from the apartment-house and keep an eye on the front-entrance.

Twenty minutes later he stood in the darkness under a thickly leafed tree diagonally opposite the Lakeside Apartments. A car was parking across the street and instinctively he reached inside his jacket to check his shoulder-holster. But there was nothing there to check. He'd forgotten to put on his holster and the .38 it carried.

You've never done that before, he thought. And then, with a slight quiver that went down from his chest to his stomach and up to his chest again, *What's the matter here? What the hell is happening to you?*

Across the street someone was getting out of the car. But it wasn't Nolan, it was just a tiny middle-aged woman with a tiny dog in her arms. She walked inside the apartment-house and the car moved away.

Childers leaned against the tree. For a moment he wished the tree-trunk were a pillow and he could sink into it and fall asleep. It had nothing to do with weariness. It was simply and acutely the need to get away from everything, especially himself. The thought brought a blast of anger, aimed at his own eyes, his own mind, and in that moment he fought to think only in terms of his badge and the job he had to do.

He glanced at his wristwatch. The hands pointed to seven forty-five. Assuming that Nolan would be coming to see her tonight, assuming further she'd be cooking dinner for Nolan, the chances were that Nolan hadn't yet arrived. In Nolan's line of business, dinnertime was anywhere from eight-thirty to midnight. So it figured he had time to hurry back home and get his gun and come back here and—

His brain couldn't take it past that. Before he fully realized what he was doing, he'd crossed the street and entered the apartment-house.

In the elevator, going up to the ninth floor, he wasn't thinking of Nolan at all. Somewhat absently, he straightened his tie and smoothed the hair along his temples. There was a small mirror in the elevator but he didn't look into it. He knew that if he looked at himself in the mirror, he'd see something that he didn't want to see.

The elevator was going up very fast, going up and up, and there was something paradoxical and creepy about that. Because it wasn't the way going up should seem or feel at all. It was more like falling.

*

He pressed the doorbell-button. A few moments passed and then the door of 907 opened and she stood there smiling at him. He wasn't surprised to see the smile. He had a feeling she'd been expecting him. It wasn't based on anything in particular. It was just a feeling that this was happening the way it had to happen, there was no getting away from it.

"Hello, Wilma," he said.

She went on smiling at him. She didn't say anything. But her hand came up in a beckoning gesture that told him to enter the apartment. In the instant before he stepped through the doorway, he noticed she was wearing a small apron. And then, as she closed the door behind him, he caught the smell of cooking.

"Excuse me a moment," she said, walking past him and into the kitchen. "I have something on the stove—"

He sat down on the sofa. He looked down at the carpet. It was a solid-color broadloom, a subdued shade of grey-green. But as he listened to her moving around in the kitchen, as he visualized her hands preparing a meal for Dice Nolan, the color he saw was an intense green, a furious green that seemed to blaze before his eyes.

Before he could hold himself back, he'd lifted himself from the sofa and walked into the kitchen. His voice was tight as he said, "When is he due here?"

She was pouring seasoning into a pot on the stove. "I'm not expecting him tonight."

He moved toward the stove. He looked into the pot and saw it was lamb stew and there was only enough for one person.

Again she was smiling at him. "You don't put much trust in me, do you, Lieutenant?"

"It isn't that," he said. "It's just—" He didn't know how

to finish it. Then, without thinking, without trying to think, "I wish you'd call me Roy."

Her smile faded. She gave him a level look that almost seemed to have substance, hitting him in the face and going into him, drilling in deep. For a very long moment the only sound in the kitchen was the stew simmering in the pot.

And then, her voice down low near a whisper, she said, "Is that the way it is?"

He nodded slowly. His eyes were solemn.

"Are you sure?" she murmured. "I mean—"

"I know what you mean," he interrupted. "You mean it can't be happening this fast. You want to tell me it's impossible, we hardly know each other—"

"Not only that," she said, her eyes aiming down to the thin band of gold on his finger. "You're a married man."

"Yes," he said bluntly. "I'm married and I have four children and my wife will soon have another."

She looked past him. She seemed to be speaking aloud to herself as she murmured, "I think we'd better talk about something else—"

"No." He came near shouting it. "We'll talk about this. Can't you see the way it is? We're got to talk about this."

She shook her head. "We can't. We just can't, that's all. We'd better not start—"

"We've started already. It was started as soon as we met each other."

His voice became thick as he went on, "Listen to me, Wilma. I tried to fight it the same as you're fighting it now. But it's no use. It's a thing you can't fight. It's like a sickness and there's no cure. You know that as well as I do. If I thought for a minute it hasn't hit you the same as me, I wouldn't be saying this. But I know it's hit you. I can see it in your eyes."

She tried to shake her head again. She was biting her lip. "If only—" She couldn't get it out. "If only—"

"No, Wilma." He spoke slowly and distinctly. "We won't have any *ifs* or *buts*. A thing like this happens once in a lifetime. It's more important than anything else. It's—"

He hadn't heard the sound of the key turning in the lock. He hadn't heard the door opening, the footsteps coming toward the kitchen. But now he saw her staring eyes focused on something behind his back. He turned very slowly and the first thing he saw was the gun.

Then he was looking at the face of Dice Nolan.

Nolan said very softly, "Keep talking." His lips scarcely moved as he said it, and there was nothing at all in his eyes.

The prison pallor seemed to harmonize with the granite hardness of his features. Except for a deep scar that twisted its way from one eyebrow to the other, he was a good-looking man with the accent on strength and virility. He was only five-nine and weighed around one-sixty, but somehow he looked very big standing there. *Maybe it's the gun*, Childers thought in that first long moment. *Maybe that's what makes him look so big*.

But it wasn't the gun. Nolan held it loosely and didn't seem to attach much importance to it. Now he was looking at Wilma and his voice remained soft and relaxed as he said, "You fooled me, girl. You really fooled me."

"Maybe I fooled myself," she said.

"Could be," Nolan murmured. He shifted his gaze to Childers. "Hey, you, I told you to keep talking."

"I guess you heard enough," Childers said. "Saying more would make no sense."

Nolan grinned with only one side of his mouth. "Yeah, I guess so." Then suddenly the grin became a frown and he said, "You look sorta familiar. Don't I know you from someplace?"

"From Third and Patton," Childers said. "From playing cops and bums when we were kids."

"And playing it for real when we grew up," Nolan murmured, his eyes sparked with recognition. "You put the pinch on me so many times I lost count. I guess ten years in stir does something to the memory. But now I remember you, Childers. I damn well oughta remember you."

"You're a bad boy, Dice. You were always a bad boy."

"And you?" Dice grinned again, his eyes flicking from Childers to Wilma and back to Childers. "You're the goodie-goodie – the Boy Scout who always plays it clean and straight."

Suddenly he chuckled. "Goddam, I'm getting a kick out of this. What're you gonna do when your wife finds out?"

Childers didn't reply. He wasn't thinking of his wife, nor of Wilma, nor of anything except the fact that he was a Detective Lieutenant attached to Homicide and he'd finally found the man he'd been looking for.

"Well? What about it?" Dice went on chuckling. "Tell me, Childers. How you gonna crawl outta this mess?"

"Don't let it worry you," Childers murmured. "You better worry about your own troubles."

The chuckling stopped. Nolan's eyes narrowed. The words seemed to drip from his lips. "Like what?"

"Like skipping parole. Like carrying a deadly weapon."

Nolan didn't say anything. He stood there waiting to hear more.

Childers let him wait, stretching the quiet as though it was made of rubber. And then, letting it out very slowly, very quietly, "Another thing you did, Dice. You pulled a job on the waterfront three weeks ago. You heisted warehouse number four and got away with fifteen thousand dollars. You murdered a night-watchman and the other one is permanently blinded. And that does it for you, bad boy. That puts you where you belong. In the chair."

"You—" Nolan choked on it. "You can't pin that rap on me. I didn't do it."

Childers smiled patiently. "Don't get excited, Dice. It won't help you to get excited."

"Now listen—" The sweat broke out on Nolan's face. "I swear to you, I didn't do it. Whoever engineered that deal, they fixed it so the Law would figure it was me. When I read about it in the papers, I knew what the score was. I knew that sooner or later you'd be looking for me—"

"It sounds weak, Dice. It's gonna sound weaker in the courtroom."

Nolan's features twisted and he snarled, "You don't hafta tell me how weak it sounds. I racked my brains, trying to find an alibi. But all I got was zero. I knew if I was taken in for grilling, I wouldn't have a chance. That's why I skipped parole. That's why I'm carrying a rod. I ain't gonna let them burn me for something I didn't do."

Childers frowned slightly. For an instant he was almost ready to believe Nolan's statement. There was something feverishly convincing in the ex-con's voice and manner. But then, as he studied Nolan's face, he saw that Nolan's eyes were aimed at Wilma, and he thought, *It's not me he's talking to, it's her. He's trying to sell her a bill of goods. He wants her to think he's clean, so when he walks out of here she'll be going along with him.*

And then he heard himself saying through clenched teeth, "She won't buy it, Nolan. She knows you're a crook and a killer and no matter how many lies you tell, you can't make her think otherwise."

Nolan's eyes remained focused on Wilma. His face was expressionless as he said, "You hear what the man says?"

She didn't reply. Childers looked at her and saw she was gazing at the wall behind Nolan's head.

"I'm telling you I'm innocent," Nolan said to her. "Do you believe me?"

She took a deep breath, and before she could say anything Childers grabbed her wrist and said, "Please – don't fall for his line, don't let him play you for a sucker. You walk out of here with him and you're ruined."

Her head turned slowly, her eyes were like blades cutting into Childers' eyes. She said, "Let go of my wrist, you're hurting me."

Childers winced as though she'd hit him in the face. He released his burning grip on her wrist. As his hand fell away, he was seized with a terrible fear that had no connection with Dice Nolan's presence or the gun in Nolan's hand. It was the fear of seeing her walking out of that room with Nolan and never coming back.

His brain was staggered with the thought, and again he had the feeling of falling, of plunging downward through immeasurable space that took him away from the badge he wore, the desk he occupied at Homicide in City Hall, his job and his home and his family. *Oh God*, he said without sound, and as the plunge became swifter he made a frantic try to get a hold on himself, to stop the descent, to face this issue and see it for what it was.

He'd fallen victim to a sudden blind infatuation, a maddened craving for this woman whom he'd never seen before today. And that didn't make sense, it wasn't normal behavior. It was a kind of lunacy and what he had to do here and now was—

But he couldn't do anything except stand there and stare at her, his eyes begging her not to leave him.

And just then he heard Dice Nolan saying, "You coming with me, Wilma?"

"Yes," she said. She walked across the kitchen and stood at Nolan's side.

Nolan had the gun aiming at Childers' chest. "Let's do this nice and careful," Nolan said. "Keep your hands down, copper. Turn around very slowly and lemme see the back of your head."

"Don't hurt him," Wilma said. "Please don't hurt him."

"This won't hurt much," Nolan told her. "He'll just have a headache tomorrow, that's all."

"Please, Philip—"

"I gotta do it this way," Nolan said. "I gotta put him to sleep so we'll have a chance to clear out of here."

"You might hit him too hard." Her voice quivered. "I'm afraid you might kill him—"

"No, that won't happen," Nolan assured her. "I'm an expert at this sort of thing. He won't sleep for more than ten minutes. That'll give us just enough time."

Childers had turned slowly so that now he stood with his back to them. He heard Nolan coming toward him and his nerves stiffened as he visualized the butt of the revolver crashing down on his skull. But in that same instant of anticipating the blow he told himself that Nolan would be holding the barrel instead of the butt, Nolan's finger would be away from the trigger.

In the next instant, as Nolan came up close behind him, he ducked going sideways, then pivoted hard and saw the gun-butt flashing down and hitting empty air. He saw the dismay on Nolan's face, and then, grinning at Nolan, he delivered a smashing right to the belly, a left hook to the side of the head, another right that came in short and caught Nolan on the jaw. Nolan sagged to the floor and the gun fell out of his hand.

As Childers leaned over to reach for the gun, Nolan grunted and lunged with what remaining strength he had. His shoulder made contact with Childers' ribs, and as they rolled over, Nolan's hands made a grab for Childers' throat. Childers raised his arm, hooked it, and bashed his elbow against Nolan's mouth. Nolan fell back, going flat and sort of sliding across the kitchen floor.

Childers came to his knees, and went crawling very fast, headed toward the gun. He picked it up and put his finger through the trigger-guard. As his finger came against the trigger with the weapon aiming at Nolan's chest, a voice inside him said, *Don't – don't*—. But another voice broke through and told him, *You want that woman and he's in the way, you gotta get rid of him.*

Yet even as he agreed with the second voice, even as the rage and jealousy blotted out all normal thinking, he was trying not to pull the trigger. So that even when he did finally pull it, when he heard the shot and saw Nolan instantly dead with a bullet through the heart, he thought dazedly, *I didn't really mean to do that.*

He lifted himself to his feet. He stood there, looking down at the corpse on the floor.

Then he heard Wilma saying, "Why did you kill him?"

He wanted to look at her. But somehow he couldn't. He forced the words through his lips. "You saw what happened. He was putting up a fight. I couldn't take any chances."

"I don't believe that," she said. And then, her voice dull, "It's too bad you didn't understand."

He stared at her. "Understand what?"

"When I agreed to go away with him – I was only pretending. It was the only way I could keep him from shooting you."

He felt a surge of elation. "You – you really mean that?"

"Yes," she said. "But it doesn't matter now." Her eyes were sad for a moment, and then the bitterness crept in as she pointed toward the parlor and said, "You'd better make a phone call, Lieutenant. Tell them you've found your man and you've saved the State the expense of a trial."

He moved mechanically, going past her and into the parlor. He picked up the phone and got the P.D. operator and said, "Get me Homicide – this is Childers."

The next voice on the wire was the Captain's, and before Childers could start talking, he heard the Captain saying, "I'm glad you called in, Roy. You can stop looking for Dice Nolan. We got something here that proves he's clean."

"Yeah?" Childers said. He wondered if it was his own voice, for it seemed to come from outside of himself.

"We got the man who did it," the Captain said. "Picked him up about an hour ago. We found him with the payroll money and the gun he used on those night-watchmen. He's already signed a confession."

Childers closed his eyes. He didn't say anything.

The Captain went on, "I phoned you at your home and your wife said you were on your way down here. Say, how come it's taking you so long?"

"I got sidetracked," Childers said. He spoke slowly. "I'm at the Lakeside Apartments, Captain. You better send some men up here. It's Apartment nine-o-seven."

"A murder?"

"You guessed it," Childers said. "It's a case of cold-blooded murder."

He hung up. In the corridor outside there was the sound of footsteps and voices and someone was shouting,

"Is everything all right in there?" Another one called, "Was that a shot we heard?"

Wilma was standing near the door leading to the corridor and he said to her, "Go out and tell them it was nothing. Tell them to go away. And keep the door closed. I don't want anyone barging in here."

She went out into the corridor, closing the door behind her. Childers walked quickly to the door and turned the lock. Then he crossed to the nearest window and opened it wide. He climbed out and stood on the ledge and looked down at the street nine floors below.

I'm sorry, he said to Louise and the children, *I'm terribly sorry*. And then, to the Captain, *You'll find the gun on the kitchen table. His fingerprints and my fingerprints and I'm sure you'll believe her when she tells you how it happened, how someone who's tried so hard to be clean can slip and fall and get himself all dirty.*

But as he stepped off the ledge and plunged through empty darkness, he began to feel clean again.

BIOGRAPHY

1917	David Loeb Goodis born 2 March in Logan, Philadelphia
1922	Herbert Goodis, David's brother born
1938	David graduates from Temple University, Philadelphia with a degree in journalism
1939	Publication of first novel *Retreat from Oblivion*
1939–42	Publication of many short stories for pulp magazines. David lives and works in New York on radio serials: scripts for "House of Mystery", "Superman" and "Hap Harrigan of the Airwaves"
1942	First foray into screenwriting in Los Angeles for Universal Pictures. Only leads to unpublished screenplay treatments: "Destination Unknown" and "Vicious Circle"
1943	David marries Elaine Astor in California
1946	David is divorced from Elaine. Publication of *Dark Passage* to popular and critical success. Book is purchased for movie adaptation by Warner Bros who also sign David to lucrative screenwriting contract. For next three years he divides his work time between novels and screenplays and lives between Los Angeles and Philadelphia
1947	Release of Vincent Sherman's *The Unfaithful*, the only film for which David gets a screenplay credit during his time in Hollywood. Release of Delmer Daves's film version of *Dark Passage* starring Humphrey Bogart and Lauren Bacall. Publication of *Behold This Woman* and *Nightfall*
1948	Work on unproduced screenplays: "Up Till Now",

"The Persian Cat", "Within These Gates", "Somewhere In the City" "Of Missing Persons", etc

1950 David's contract with Warner Bros ends and he returns permanently to family home in Philadelphia where he supports his parents and helps to look after his schizophrenic brother. Publication of *Missing Persons*

1951 Publication of *Cassidy's Girl*

1952 Publication of *Street of the Lost* and *Of Tender Sin*

1953 Publication of *The Burglar* and *The Moon in the Gutter*

1954 Publication of *The Blonde on the Street Corner*, *Black Friday* and *Street of No Return*

1955 David's visit to Jamaica provides research for novel published as *The Wounded and the Slain*

1956 Publication of *Fire of the Flesh* and *Down There*

1957 Release of *The Burglar* – his own film adaptation of his novel, shot on location in Philadelphia, directed by Paul Wendkos

1960 Publication of *Night Squad*

1962 David attends New York premiere of Francois Truffaut's *Shoot the Pianist*, the acclaimed French film adaptation of *Down There*

1963 Broadcast of "An Out for Oscar" (episode of *The Alfred Hitchcock Hour* based on a short story by David). Also commencement of lawsuit against ABC Televison for allegedly plagiarising *Dark Passage* as basis for *The Fugitive* TV show. David's father dies

1966 David's mother dies. David is briefly institutionalised in a psychiatric hospital but whilst he recovers, his physical health worsens

1967 David Goodis dies on 17 January and is buried in the family plot in the Jewish cemetery of Roosevelt Memorial Park in Philadelphia. Posthumous publication of *Somebody's Done For* (aka *The Raving Beauty*)

1971 Death of Herbert Goodis

BIBLIOGRAPHY

NOVELS

Retreat from Oblivion, NY: Dutton, 1939
Dark Passage, NY: Messner, 1946
Nightfall, NY: Messner, 1947
Behold This Woman, NY: Appleton, 1947
Of Missing Persons, NY: Morrow, 1950
Cassidy's Girl, Greenwich, CT: Fawcett, October 1951
Of Tender Sin, Greenwich, CT: Fawcett, March 1952
The Burglar, NY: Lion, February 1953
Street of the Lost, Greenwich, CT: Fawcett, September 1953
The Moon in the Gutter, Greenwich, CT: Fawcett, November 1953
The Blonde on the Street Corner, NY: Lion, January 1954
Black Friday, NY: Lion, September 1954
Street of No Return, Greenwich, CT: Fawcett, September 1954
The Wounded and the Slain, Greenwich, CT: Fawcett, November 1955
Down There, Greenwich, CT: Fawcett, November 1956
Fire in the Flesh, Greenwich, CT: Fawcett, August 1957
Night Squad, Greenwich, CT: Fawcett, February 1961

Published Posthumously:
Somebody's Done For, NY: Banner, October 1967

SHORT STORIES

Editorial Note
For bibliophiles and historians, the fact that David Goodis produced so much short story material, not just published under

his own name but, as he himself admitted, using no less than seven pseudonyms, is a considerable headache, especially since only a tiny percentage of the stories have ever been republished. Added to which, there is little or no documentation, such as royalty statements or contracts, to help identify and source the material. Consequently, even getting hold of a decent selection of Goodis's work in this field is an act of significant research and detection. This has meant that, hitherto, there has been no accurate bibliography assembled and, until this book, no English language collection has ever been attempted. So, in compiling this collection, first we had to find some of the material, put it into context and then decide what the priority was in reprinting it.

In the end, through the support of friends, colleagues and private collectors, I managed to get some kind of representative selection of his short story work. Then, I opted for a very simple selection method. David Goodis wrote lots of fiction but he is noted and celebrated for his work in the crime genre. Therefore, whilst it would have been interesting and enjoyable to include some samples of his work in other genres, it did not seem appropriate or relevant, especially as they are stylistically so different from his main writing output. So, in focusing on the crime stories, I have restricted myself to listing all of David Goodis's other work in what, I believe, is the largest bibliography compiled of him to date.

Having made this decision, I had to then look at the question of pseudonyms. Goodis said he wrote under seven names, including his own. I believe we have managed to identify three of the *noms de plume* pretty conclusively, i.e. David Crewe, Lance Kermit and Logan Claybourne. I also think that he could have written under the moniker of Ray P Shotwell.

There is no example of a Ray P Shotwell story in this collection because, first of all, we haven't been able to source a publishable crime story written under this moniker. There is also the problem of what magazine publishers call "house names". The magazine would invent a name, own it and the copyright pertaining to it and then commission various writers to write stories that would be published under that pseudonym. That meant that magazines could develop a particular identity for a name without having to rely on one single person's output. From the writers' point of view, it meant that authors who were perhaps known for other kinds of different and, ostensibly, more respectable kinds of fiction, could earn a few bucks anonymously. Of all of the Goodis pseudonyms, it seems that Shotwell is definitely a house name, so it is difficult, nay impossible, to establish what is and isn't David Goodis. Nevertheless, for the sake of completeness, I have included what bibliographical information is available on Ray P Shotwell's short story pulp writing.

With the other names included in this collection, the nature of the prose style and the type of stories that they are have led me to conclude that David Goodis provides the connective tissue that links all of them. Moreover, the publishing history of these pseudonyms (Goodis said that he often used multiple identities in single issues of magazines and these names crop up again and again, next to Goodis's own) suggests that Goodis developed multiple personalities to disguise his own hand. Indeed, three of the stories in this collection, penned by apparently different names, are drawn from the same magazine. Last but not least, there is also one example of the same detective character, Sergeant Rico Maguire, appearing in stories by both David Crewe and Lance Kermit, which creates the possibility that these are various identities of David Goodis.

As far as the bibliography itself goes, I have tried to be as comprehensive as possible and certainly the stories listed under David Goodis's name represent the most exhaustive list compiled to date. The information has, by common convention, been listed in alphabetical order from the story's title, rather than publication date, for ease of understanding. I would also wish to stress that this bibliography is based substantially on the work of writer and researcher, Mike Ashley, cross-referenced against the research of David Schmid and Kingsley Canham, and augmented by my own research findings.

Stories Credited to David Goodis

Ace of Spads, *Fighting Aces*, July 1944

Achtung—Stormaviks!, *Wings*, Spring 1947

All Bolixed Up, *Detective Yarns 2*, April 1941

Beyond Courage, *Battle Birds*, July 1943

Black Pudding, *Manhunt*, December 1953

The Blood of an Englishman, *Fighting Aces*, September 1943

The Blood of Warriors, *Captain Combat*, August 1940

Blood on the Eastern Front, *Battle Birds*, December 1941

Blood in the West, *Daredevil Aces*, March 1942

The Blue Sweetheart, *Manhunt*, April 1953

Boches for Breakfast, *Dare-Devil Aces*, July 1946

The Bomber from Brooklyn, *Fighting Aces*, March 1944

Bombs for the Rising Sun, *Battle Birds*, June 1942

Bullets for the Brave, *Battle Birds*, February 1940

Bullets for Nazis, *Captain Combat*, June 1940

Bullets Mean Business, *Thrilling Western, Vol XXV11 No. 3*, September 1941

Caravan to Tarim, *Collier's Weekly*, October 1946

The Ceiling of Hell, *Fighting Aces*, November 1940

The Cloud Wizard, *Sky Raiders*, February 1943

The Cop on the Corner, *Popular Detective 33*, September 1947

Courage is Silent, *Sky Raiders*, December 1942

Dark Passage, Serialised in *Saturday Evening Post*, 20 July – 7 September 1946

D-Day for Hell's Angels, *Wings*, Spring 1945

Death Flies the Coffins of Hitler, *Battle Birds*, November 1940

Death Flies Tonight, *Fighting Aces*, November 1943

Death Over Dover, *Fighting Aces*, March 1941

Death Rides My Cockpit!, *Battle Birds*, May 1941

Death Rides My Wings!, *Fighting Aces*, September 1942

Death to the Swastika, *Fighting Aces*, July 1942

Death Waits Below, *Battle Birds*, August 1941

Death's Behind that Door, *Double-Action Detective*, February 1940

Descendant of the Witch, *Mystery Novels and Short Stories*, November 1940

Destination Death, *Battle Birds*, March 1941

Diamond Dictator, *Sports Winners*, July 1941

Doom for the Hawks of Nippon, *Battle Birds*, April 1942

Dusk is for Dying, *Fighting Aces*, January 1944

East of Chunking, *Air War*, Spring 1944

Fiats over Albania, *Air War*, March 1942

The Fiftieth Mission, *Battle Birds*, May 1944

Fight and Be Damned, *Fighting Aces*, May 1941

A Fighter Needs Wings, *Fighting Aces*, March 1942

Fresh Blood for the Damned, *Sinister Stories*, May 1940

Furlough in Hell, *Fighting Aces*, January 1942

Grandstand Ace, *Dare-Devil Aces*, December 1943

The Grudge Runner, *Super Sports*, October 1941

Guns of the Sea Raiders, *Battle Birds*, November 1943

Hawk of the Sudan, *Wings*, Summer 1941

The High-Hat Squadron from Hell, *Battle Birds*, September 1940

High, Wide and Hellbound, *Fighting Aces*, September 1941

Hot Lead for Heinkels, *Air War I*, Winter 1941

It's a Wise Cadaver, *New Detective Magazine*, July 1946

The Jaguar, *Thrilling Adventures,* December 1942

Jive Bomber, *Battle Birds*, September 1943

Key to the Crooked Cross, *Wings*, Winter 1943

Kid Brother, *RAF Aces*, Fall 1942

Kill or Be Killed, *Sky Fighters*, May 1941

Kill Ride for Two (as Dave Goodis), *True Gangster Stories*, June 1942

Killer Ace, *The Lone Eagle*, February 1941

A Knife in Your Back (as Dave Goodis), *True Gangster Stories*, August 1942

The Last Dogfight, *Dare-Devil Aces*, February 1946

The Last Patrol, *Fighting Aces*, May 1943

Last Patrol of the Brave, *Fighting Aces*, May 1940

Laurels for the Brave, *Wings*, April 1943

Marauders Never Retreat, *Dare-Devil Aces*, March 1946

Mistress of the White Slave King, *Gangland Detective Stories*, November 1939

The Navy Always Knows, *Wings*, Winter 1946

Nightfall, *Two Complete Detective Books*, January 1949

No More Brains, *G-Men Detective*, September 1940

On the Black Dahlia Case (non-fiction), *Los Angeles Herald Express*, 6 February 1947

The One-Way Kid Flies West, *Fighting Aces*, November 1941

Only the Brave Return, *Fighting Aces*, March 1943

Peril Ahead, *Army-Navy Flying Stories*, Spring 1944

Periscope off Panama, *Wings*, Fall 1945

A Photo and A Voice, *G-Men Detective*, January 1947

The Plunge, *Mike Shayne Mystery Magazine*, October 1958

Pranksters, *Sky Fighters*, January 1942

Professional Man, *Manhunt*, October 1953

The Professor's Last Dogfight, *Battle Birds*, December 1942

Raiders Come Back Alone, *Fighting Aces*, November 1942

Raiders Fight Alone, *Dare-Devil Aces*, November 1946

Raiders of the Dawn Patrol, *Fighting Aces*, January 1943

Red Wings for the Doomed, *Battle Birds*, January 1941

The Secret Sky, *Wings*, Winter 1944

Sky Coffins for Nazis, *Battle Birds*, May 1940

Sky Corpses for Dictators, *Fighting Aces*, July 1940

Sky-Meat for the Nazis, *Fighting Aces*, September 1940

A Smile and A Nod, *Crack Detective 3*, September 1942

Spitfire Falcon, *Wings*, Spring 1941

Spitfire Serenade, *RAF Aces*, March 1942

Squadron of the Lost, *Fighting Aces*, July 1943

The Sweet Taste, *Manhunt*, January 1965

Things to Worry About, *Detective Fiction Weekly*, 20 July 1940

Three Aces from Hell, *Battle Birds*, July 1940

Three Guesses, *Hooded Detective 3*, January 1942

Token of Glory, *Air War*, Spring 1941

Traitor's Trail, *Wings*, Spring 1946

Tramp Champ, *Popular Sports magazine*, Winter 1941

Twilight Raid, *Battle Birds*, May 1943

Vengeance Patrol, *Fighting Aces*, July 1941

Vickers Pay-Off, *Battle Birds*, August 1942

War Birds Die Hardest, *Fighting Aces*, January 1941

The Warhawks are Coming, *Dare-Devil Aces*, May 1946

Warhawks of the Don, *Wings*, February 1943

Wings Against the World, *Battle Birds*, October 1941

Wings of the Cobra, *Fighting Aces*, May 1944
Wings of the Death Patrol, *Battle Birds*, February 1941
Wings of the Free, *Battle Birds*, March 1944
Wings Over Kiska, *Battle Birds*, January 1944
The Yanks are Coming, *Fighting Aces*, May 1942
Zero Flight, *Wings*, Winter 1942

Stories under alias Logan (C.) Claybourne

Armchair Ace, *Battle Birds*, January 1944
Blood for the Hawks of Hitler, *Fighting Aces*, November 1940
Bon Voyage – with Bullets, *Big-Book Detective Magazine*, August 1942
Come to my Dying, *10 Story Mystery Magazine,* October 1942
The Death Dealer, *Fighting Aces*, May 1942
Drink, Fly, and Die!, *Battle Birds*, January 1941
Eagle-Hearted, *Dare-Devil Aces*, May 1946
A Favor for the General, *Battle Birds*, March 1944
Furlough for the Dead, *Fighting Aces*, March 1942
Gangway to Hell, *Battle Birds*, November 1940
Get Me an Ace, *Battle Birds*, December 1941
Glory for the Doomed, *Fighting Aces*, January 1941
Heroes Won't Stay Down, *Fighting Aces*, July 1944
Kid Wings, *Battle Birds*, May 1940
King of the Mighty, *Sports Novel Magazine*, November 1947
One Life, One Bullet, *Fighting Aces*, March 1941
Red Wings for Vengeance, *Fighting Aces*, May 1941
Satan Flies West, *Captain Combat*, June 1940
Say It with Bullets, *Battle Birds*, February 1942
Skies of Valor, *Fighting Aces*, November 1943
Sky Wagons for the Damned, *Battle Birds*, July 1940
Traitors Fear the Sky, *Fighting Aces*, September 1943
Vickers Talk, *Battle Birds*, November 1943
The Way of a Warrior, *Battle Birds*, March 1941
Who's Got the Guts, *Fighting Aces*, July 1940
Wings of the Legion, *Fighting Aces*, May 1942
Wings of the Lost, *Battle Birds*, June 1942

Stories under alias Davie Crewe

Aces Die Hard, *Battle Birds*, November 1943

Bitter Medicine, *New Detective Magazine*, May 1946

Bombs Over Burma, *Dare-Devil Aces*, July 1941

Broken Ivory, *Detective Fiction Weekly*, 2 March 1935

Bury Me Not, *Fifteen Detective Stories*, February 1954

Call of the Blue, *Fighting Aces*, January 1944

Call of the Brave, *Fighting Aces*, November 1943

Congo Flight, *Fighting Aces*, May 1942

The Dead Laugh Last, *10 Story Mystery Magazine*, October 1942

The Death Cast, *New Detective Magazine*, November 1945

Death – Special Delivery, *Battle Birds*, July 1943

Death Flies Tonight, *Dare-Devil Aces*, February 1944

Death on Demand, *Fifteen Detective Stories*, April 1954

Death on the Marshes, *New Detective Magazine*, September 1942

Death Rides My Wing, *Fighting Aces*, March 1943

Death Waits Here, *Dime Western Magazine*, July 1954

An Eagle Needs Wings, *Dare-Devil Aces*, April 1944

Evidence to Order, *New Detective Magazine*, March 1942

The Failure, *New Detective Magazine*, January 1944

Fangs of the Sky Wolf, *Dare-Devil Aces*, June 1944

Five Grand for Buddy, *Big-Book Detective Magazine*, February 1942

Flight from Yesterday, *Dare-Devil Aces*, July 1946

Fly it Sailor!, *Dare-Devil Aces*, May 1942

Fokker Finis, *Fighting Aces*, September 1943

Greenland Patrol, *Fighting Aces*, July 1944

Guilt Powder, *Black Mask*, November 1947

High Dive to Hell, *Battle Birds*, June 1942

Hot Wire, *Detective Tales*, December 1951

The House that Death Built, *New Detective Magazine*, May 1945

I.O.U. – One Murder, *Big-Book Detective Magazine*, August 1942

Iran Assignment, *Fighting Aces*, March 1944

Kill and Run, *New Detective Magazine*, January 1943

The Lair of the Doomed, *Fighting Aces*, May 1943

Lightning Wings, *Dare-Devil Aces*, August 1943

Lucky Stiff, *Big-Book Detective Magazine*, December 1942

A Man Couldn't Breathe, *Detective Fiction Weekly*, 6 April 1935

The Man Who Died Too Often, *New Detective Magazine*, November 1944

The Man Who Wasn't There, *New Detective Magazine*, July 1942

Man Without a Tongue, *New Detective Magazine*, October 1951

Murder – His Mark, *Story Mystery Magazine*, December 1942

Murder, Murder – Go Away, *Fifteen Detective Stories*, June 1954

My Brother Death, *Fighting Aces*, July 1943

A Night's Lodging, *New Detective Magazine*, October 1952

No Kind of Sheriff, *Fifteen Western Tales*, June 1947

No Man's War, *Fifteen Western Tales*, August 1955

One Ticket to Hell, *Big-Book Detective Magazine*, October 1942

The Phantom Plowman, *Big-Book Detective Magazine*, June 1942

Price of Tomorrow, *Story Mystery Magazine*, June 1942

The Riddle House, *Story Mystery Magazine*, February 1943

Ring Twice for Death, *New Detective Magazine*, November 1942

Sealed, *New Detective Magazine*, January 1945

The Shape of Murder, *Detective Fiction Weekly*, 13 October 1934

Shoot Straight and Live Long!, *Fifteen Western Tales*, November 1944

Six-Gun Breed, *Western Story Roundup*, April 1951

A Star for Robbers' Town, *10 Story Western*, September 1954

Suicide Squadron, *Fighting Aces*, November 1942

The Testing of Half-Pint Logan, *Western Story Roundup*, February 1951

This One will Kill You, *New Detective Magazine*, March 1946

The Thunderbolts are Coming, *Battle Birds*, May 1944

The Time of Your Kill, *New Detective Magazine*, November 1948

Trigger Time, *10 Story Western*, June 1954

The Way of the Hell-Divers, *Battle Birds*, January 1944

Yesterday I Lived, *New Detective Magazine*, April 1951

Stories under alias Lance Kermit

The Ace of Fear, *Dare-Devil Aces*, April 1944

Aces Can't Go Home, *Fighting Aces*, January 1942

And Some Die Young, *Dare-Devil Aces*, May 1941

Asking Price – Murder, *New Detective Magazine*, January 1950

Avengers Never Retreat!, *Fighting Aces*, March 1944

Blood in the West, *Dare-Devil Aces*, July 1941

Blood on the Twilight, *Battle Birds*, November 1940

Bombers Away, *Battle Birds*, March 1944

The Bombers are Coming, *Fighting Aces*, July 1942

The Case of the Laughing Queen, *10 Story Mystery Magazine*,
  October 1942

Code of the Doomed, *Fighting Aces*, July 1941

Contact for Doom, *Fighting Aces*, September 1940

Contact for Glory, *Fighting Aces*, November 1940

Convoy Patrol, *Battle Birds*, March 1941

Crossroads of Hell, *Fighting Aces*, May 1941

The Dawn is for Dying, *Adventure*, April 1959

The Death Raider, *Fighting Aces*, September 1943

Death Rides the Night Patrol, *Fighting Aces*, March 1941

Death will not Wait, *Fighting Aces*, November 1941

Decoy for Death, *New Detective Magazine*, September 1942

Devil-Dog Wings, *Fighting Aces*, July 1944

The Devil's Last Battalion, *Captain Combat*, August 1940

Doom to the Black Cross, *Fighting Aces*, September 1942

Eight Guns and a Prayer, *Battle Birds*, May 1941

Fangs of the Winged Cobra, *Dare-Devil Aces*, December 1943

Flames over China, *Battle Birds*, November 1943

Fokkers over Chateau-Thierry, *Fighting Aces*, September 1941

The General Goes to War, *Fighting Aces*, May 1940

Glory Trail, *Battle Birds*, January 1944

Gold Miner's Court, *10-Story Western*, June 1954

Guns Over Suez, *Fighting Aces*, July 1943

Heir to Six-Gun Hate, *Fifteen Western Tales*, February 1947

The Kid from No Man's Land *(lead novel)*, *Fighting Aces*, March
  1942

Killer's Way, *Dare-Devil Aces*, March 1946

Lightnings – Watch Out!, *Dare-Devil Aces*, January 1946

Mademoiselle Mustang, *Dare-Devil Aces*, May 1946
The Man from Hell's Valley, *Fifteen Western Tales*, November 1944
Murder While You Sleep, *New Detective Magazine*, July 1942
Never Too Old to Burn, *New Detective Magazine*, January 1949
No Better Way to Die, *Fighting Aces*, July 1940
No Man's Wings, *Battle Birds*, December 1941
Peril's Payoff, *New Detective Magazine*, March 1947
Range War at Red Rock, *Fifteen Western Tales*, June 1947
Red Skies for Victory, *Dare-Devil Aces*, June 1944
Salute to the Brave, *Battle Birds*, October 1941
Sky Guns for a Killer, *Battle Birds*, July 1940
So I Killed Him, *Big-Book Detective Magazine*, August 1942
Spads Over Hunland, *Fighting Aces*, May 1944
They Shall Not Pass, *Battle Birds*, April 1942
Traitor Wings, *Battle Birds*, May 1944
Vickers for Vultures, *Battle Birds*, September 1940
Vickers Fury, *Fighting Aces*, May 1943
Warbirds Never Die, *Dare-Devil Aces*, September 1946
Wings of the Damned, *Dare-Devil Aces*, February 1944
Wings Over the Ukraine, *Fighting Aces*, November 1942
Wings Over Timor, *Fighting Aces*, January 1944

Stories under alias Ray P. Shotwell

Aces Die Hard, *Dare Devil Aces,* November 1946
Beautiful but Dead, *Big-Book Detective Magazine,* December 1942
Bitter are the Brave, *Battle Birds,* January 1941
Bring 'em Down Dead, *Battle Birds,* September 1943
Busy Body, *New Detective Magazine,* January 1949
Dawn Attack, *Battle Birds,* April 1942
Dawn Flight, *Dare-Devil Aces,* March 1942
Dead-End Ace, *Dare-Devil Aces,* January 1946
Death Demands His Cut, *Big-Book Detective Magazine,* February 1942
Death Patrol, *Dare-Devil Aces,* January 1942
Death and the Dawn are Mine, *Battle Birds,* March 1943
Dig My Grave Deep, *Big Book Detective Magazine,* April 1942

Dusk is for Dying, *Battle Birds*, November 1943

Encore for Death, *Big-Book Detective Magazine,* October 1942

Field of Honor, *Battle Birds,* May 1943

Get Up There and Fight!, *Battle Birds,* February 1942

Happy Joe's Chocolate Bar, *10-Story Mystery Magazine,* June 1942

The House that Death Built, *Big-Book Detective Magazine,* June 1942

I Fly with the Death Patrol, *Battle Birds,* June 1942

I Hate Cops!, *New Detective Magazine,* August 1941

Jungle Raider, *Battle Birds,* June 1943

The Killer in Huntsman's Clothes, *10-Story Mystery Magazine,* December 1941

Lair of the Lobos, *Battle Birds,* March 1941

The Last Ride, *New Detective Magazine,* November 1945

Little Miss Murder, *New Detective Magazine,* May 1942

Long Odds on Death, *New Detective Magazine,* November 1941

My Flag will Fly Again, *Dare-Devil Aces,* March 1943

P-40 Guy, *Dare-Devil Aces,* May 1943

Seahawks from Hell, *Dare-Devil Aces*, May 1942

Slug Shy, *Battle Birds,* May 1941

Swan Song, *10-Story Mystery Magazine,* February 1942

Take-off to Doom, *Battle Birds,* October 1941

Thunder Over Aden, *Battle-Birds,* August 1941

Token for Tokyo, *Battle Birds,* August 1942

The Valiant Never Die, *Dare-Devil Aces,* April 1944

Vengeance Guns, *Battle Birds,* January 1944

Vickers Victory, *Battle Birds,* March 1944

Wolf! Wolf!, *Big-Book Detective Magazine,* August 1942